A Circular Argument

Emerald Studies in Culture, Criminal Justice and the Arts

Edited by

Yvonne Jewkes
University of Bath, UK

Travis Linnemann
Kansas State University, USA

Sarah Moore
University of Bath, UK

This series aims to take criminological inquiry in new and imaginative directions, by publishing books that represent all forms of criminal justice from an 'arts' or 'cultural' perspective, and that have something new to tell us about space, place and sensory experience as they relate to forms of justice. Building on emergent interest in the 'cultural', 'autoethnographic', 'emotional', 'visual', 'narrative' and 'sensory' in Criminology, books in the series will introduce readers to imaginative forms of inspiration that deepen our conceptual understanding of the lived experience of punishment and of the process of researching within the criminal justice system, as well as discussing the more well-rehearsed problems of cultural representations of justice.

Specifically, this series provides a platform for original research that explores the myriad ways in which architecture, design, aesthetics, hauntology, atmospheres, fine art, graffiti, visual broadcast media and many other 'cultural' perspectives are utilized as ways of seeing and understanding the enduring persistence of, and fascination with, the formal institutions of criminal justice and punishment.

Praise for *A Circular Argument*

Martin Cathcart Fródén's new book will surely accelerate criminology's slow awakening to the potency and importance of imagination and creativity in rethinking crime and punishment. It deserves to be widely read and discussed by anyone and everyone who cares about the pursuit of justice.

–Fergus McNeill, Professor of Criminology and Social Work, Associate Director, SCCJR

Encompassing memoir, creative writing, criminology, and architecture, this unusual book is in two halves. One is a critical, multidisciplinary, autobiographical exploration of carceral space and place, time, absence and visibility, masculinities and vulnerabilities, movement and stasis, circularity and linearity. The other is a novella that explores in fiction the very same themes. The result is one of the most imaginative, ambitious, compelling, clever, and funny books I have read. It is quite simply stunning.

–Yvonne Jewkes, Professor of Criminology, University of Bath

Inspiring, bold and highly readable, *A Circular Argument* is a breath of fresh air in academic publishing. Employing practice as research to disrupt some of the hierarchies it examines, it offers a forward-thinking and transdisciplinary approach to spatial hierarchies with particular reference to carceral systems. Some of its most serious propositions are embedded in its gripping and entertaining narrative, proving that ideas are more effectively shared when rigour and humour go hand in hand. More of this, please – it's what we need to refresh our ways of working.

–Dr Zoë Strachan, Reader in Creative Writing, University of Glasgow

A Circular Argument:
A Creative Exploration of
Power and Space

BY

MARTIN CATHCART FRÖDÉN

Malmö University, Sweden

United Kingdom – North America – Japan – India – Malaysia – China

Emerald Publishing Limited
Howard House, Wagon Lane, Bingley BD16 1WA, UK

First edition 2021

Reprints and permissions service
Contact: permissions@emeraldinsight.com

British Library Cataloguing in Publication Data
A catalogue record for this book is available from the British Library

ISBN: 978-1-80071-385-7 (Print)
ISBN: 978-1-80071-382-6 (Online)
ISBN: 978-1-80071-384-0 (Epub)

INVESTOR IN PEOPLE

Table of Contents

Acknowledgments[*]

I wish to thank Dr Zoë Strachan, Prof Johnny Rodger, and Prof Fergus McNeill for their patience, insights, and constant encouragement, as well as the SGSAH, the SCCJR in general, and the prison visiting reading group in particular. Furthermore, I wish to thank the Glasgow University Creative Writing Department for an amazing few years, as well as my colleagues at 73 Great George Street for being patient with me through the various processes this work has involved. I would like to thank criminal justice arts organization Vox Liminis, Dr David Hopes of The National Trust for Scotland, Jude Barber of Collective Architecture, and the Gillian Purvis Trust, for opportunities offered and coffees supplied.

Last but not least, I want to thank my three young children, Mika, Alma, and Elias, and my wife Lucy for their ability to ensure a work/life balance and their unwavering support over the last many moons. Tack så mycket för allt!

[*] This work was supported by the Arts and Humanities Research council. Grant number AH/L503915.

Acknowledgement

Introduction

Spanning creative writing, criminology, and architecture, this work examines some of the ways power and hierarchies can be explored and exploited in space. It is a practice-led study in two parts: one primarily creative nonfiction (A Circular Argument) and the other in the form of a novel (The Out). The main focus of the nonfiction piece is the obsession with the circular as an architectural gesture and as a concept combining containment and transparency, from the ideal planned city of the Middle Ages, via Bentham's panopticon, to the all-seeing eye of modern digital society. The creative piece explores how the complications and surprises of human interaction are bound to color and change the supposedly watertight systems of social control we design as a society – how prison architecture or national road networks might be undermined, or how the power dynamics of the class system might be temporarily suspended in a heightened situation. Forgiveness, desistance, and redemption also play a part in the narrative, for both the "guilty" and "innocent" parties. Both elements of the work also examine how time moves differently inside from outside of the prison walls, and the limited success of trying to build away social problems.

Methodologically speaking, the work follows certain key features of practice-led research, where the creative outcome constitutes the research in and of itself, rather than existing as a conduit for preexisting research conclusions. The practice-led approach prioritizes the making process, in dialogue with a theoretical framework, although this may not always be visible in the finished work. Again there are hierarchies at play here, in an epistemological sense, in how knowledge is created, viewed, accessed, and consumed. In this sense, the work takes a deliberately outward-looking approach in terms of intended readership, aiming to sit alongside works of fiction as comfortably as academic texts.

On several levels, the work inhabits gray areas and liminal spaces – between the three academic disciplines across which it is situated, between fiction and nonfiction, and between multiple social and spatial hierarchies. This liminality has come to be reflected within the work through exploring nonplaces, in an explicit sense in the nonfiction work, and implicitly in the creative work – from the limbo of the motorway service station, to the carceral dead space exploited by the prison architect and his escapee. It is also interesting to note that both "nonplace" and "nonfiction" are defined by what they are not, rather than what they are. In researching and writing this book I found that the "thing" and its Janus-like twin the "nonthing" often held an inherent friction which ultimately proved to be creatively generative.

I have tried to keep the writing centered on the concrete and rebars of the various sites I've described. I've tried to conduct interviews with silent corridors. Mumbled monologues while walking down pathways, the line painter's ruler-straight line separating me from the prisoners. I've come back on trains, furiously writing in a little notebook, which I couldn't bring into the prisons. Transcribing an inner, half-remembered harangue of silent questions and slippery answers. It might have looked like I was doing one thing in the prison but I was doing something else – patching together an erratic, fictional ethnography, with a building as the main character.

The Parts and the Whole

This is a work in two parts. One part is a nonfiction piece called *A Circular Argument* and the other is a creative piece called *The Out*. In terms of word count, workload, reading, and research, the split has been roughly 70/30 – fiction/ nonfiction. I have strived to make the sometimes perceived divide quite porous. The parts are not separate, but not entirely connected either.

Prison is arguably an in-between space/place, where waiting and being processed is a large part of the structure and daily life. In the creative part of the work, the preordained escape is made possible only by connecting strips of dead space. The nonfiction component of the work purposefully teeters on the brink of a few modes or styles of writing.

Presented sequentially like this it might seem that one part has sway over the other but the reality is that neither component was written before the other. They came into being alongside each other. A contributing factor to this was a tripartite arrangement of mentors situated in Creative Writing, Architecture, and Criminology, which for me has been very fruitful and continuously surprising.

The fictional part shouldn't have to prove itself to be clever, but nevertheless in this case it is informed by critical readings, research trips, and fieldwork, mostly through monthly visits to HMP Shotts, but also drawing from my previous experience of working as a tutor in prisons. The nonfiction shouldn't have to be entertaining or in essence have wide appeal, but I have tried to make it a clean, informed read. Hopefully I have made sure that the cross-pollination between the two parts is evident and of use, both in terms of form and in content.

The Whole and the Parts

The work as a whole looks at prisons, and at civic spaces and to some extent the private spaces that exist within those spheres. In the creative part this is exemplified in the road network, the car, the cell. In the nonfiction part perhaps more abstractly so, in spaces and uses, focusing on the circular. Often from a higher point of view – both physically and socially, often looking at city planning and how the cell fits into the larger narrative of society. What unites the two parts of the work is the exploration of space and place, with a grounding in psycho-geography and the fictional space we all inhabit. It's an investigation of the idea of home and away, and of the transient – both in time and in space, which is a thought I came across early in the research. Dr Sarah Armstrong's ideas on the prison as a corridor, rather than a holding pen, quoted in *A Circular Argument*, struck a chord with me.

Throughout the writing of both parts I was also influenced by this quote by Jane Jacobs: "The architects, planners – and businessmen – are seized with dreams of order, and they have become fascinated with scale models and bird's-eye views. This is a vicarious way to deal with reality, and it is, unhappily, symptomatic of a design philosophy now dominant: buildings come first, for the goal is to remake the city to fit an abstract concept of what, logically, it should be" (Jacobs, 1957).

In both parts I wanted to see how the notion of "We make spaces and spaces make us" would fit in a carceral context, where someone imprisoned has very little control over how the space they are in is constructed, down to the placement of the bed, the desk lamp, and what can go on the walls. Put in contrast with the complex construction work that lies behind a prison – a highly complicated task, where safety, visibility, politics, rehabilitation, risk, classification, gender, not to mention light, electricity, water, and utilities, and a limited access to the internet, need to be considered in a way that is completely different from how a "normal" building is constructed.

Maybe I too was "seized with dreams of order." On a small scale (should main character Cecil be 5′ 9½″, or taller?) and on a large scale (Canberra, Baghdad, Brøndby Garden City, and the temporary city of Burning Man were all built to be circular – how can I decipher that?).

The prison is a complicated idea and a complicated building. For any person of any height it has to function like a whole city. Education, hygiene, health care, social interaction, and intimacy have to be catered for. When not, it may be part of the punishment, in ways that, if you live outside the walls, might seem, and often are, incredibly perplexing, slow, and often dehumanizing. The prison complex is very complex. I hope I have captured some of that friction in the following pages.

On Writing

Practice as Research is a lovely beast to wrangle. If nothing else, this work has taught me to wear my research lightly, and at the same time to be rigorous in my imaginings. My fictional and nonfictional output have for obvious reasons bled into one another, as they should.

This relationship between fact and fiction has meant that I have had the pleasure of translating concepts and complicated ideas into character, conflict, voice, point of view, tense, and dialogue. That I have been allowed to think about narrative structures as well as real concrete structures. I've busied myself with transforming people like one of the prisoners I have talked with, and places like the circular town of Palmanova, into imagined landscapes, townscapes, weather, and into written emotions, which lie somewhere between the real, the unreal, and the hyperreal. This porous approach has allowed me to use the structural elements of fiction to represent critical thinking, and architectural critique. To reuse bricks and marble from one kind of structure to make anew, and like all builders past and present, reimagine an edifice – in this case, a book.

I am going to miss working on this.

Part 1
A Circular Argument

A Circular Argument, 1–57
Copyright © 2021 Martin Cathcart Frödén
Published under exclusive licence by Emerald Publishing Limited
doi:10.1108/978-1-80071-382-620211021

Norrköpingsanstalten – 58°35′22.7″N 16°10′14.4″E

At the Gates

The first time I walked into a prison I was a child. I was dressed in a long white sark, which touched the steps as I ascended the worn marble incline leading to the chapel. I was wearing a conical white hat, and my mother had cut out and glued three golden stars onto it, the ornaments diminishing in size the further up the hat they went. In my left hand I was holding a stick, not unlike the ones used for propping up plants too weak to stay upright themselves. A star, the same size, shape and colour as the biggest one on the cap, was pinned to the top of the stick. Swedish winters are long and dark, and to an extent so are the traditions celebrated. Usually a mix of Viking feasts and the imported ceremonies of the latecomer Christ, in this case the feast of Saint Lucia.[1,2] Outside, the flurry of snow was temporarily brightening up life, but the crystals couldn't reach inside. With a voice devoid of puberty or irony, I sang to the prisoners in the maximum security prison. Wishing them a Happy Christmas and the Season's Blessing. I doubt they had a happy time or many blessings, but I hope the diversion was welcome.

Every second Tuesday, my mother would play unihoc with a group of long-term prisoners. The rules of the game were held in much higher regard than the laws which existed outside the triple, unscalable walls. Possibly because there was no referee. These rules made sense, as they were everyone's responsibility and not handed down from any kind of authority. In this self-governed game there was not an inch of leeway. My mum was very good at this form of indoor hockey, and I think it was partly her love of team sports, and partly the political act of playing as the only woman, keeping up with people younger, angrier and fitter than her, that kept her packing her sports bag and setting out for the prison every two weeks.

Once her knees started to balloon from excess synovial fluid accumulation, she turned her love of the game into a chat over a cup of dense Nordic coffee. She became a visitor, not to a family member, but to a series of strangers, to whom she would lend her ear, dark bob and soft socialist dogma for two hours.

A couple of years later, I returned to this prison, armed with my own music, this time in the summer. We were asked to set up our equipment outside, at the centre of a gravel football pitch, in the middle of the prison exercise yard, surrounded by walls and interested/bored eyes. It turned out to be a very weird gig, and if it was weird for me, playing guitar, and able to move freely, it must have been very strange for Oskar, who was playing drums. He had two or three burly men standing right behind him, watching his every move, beat aficionados I think. As there was no back to the stage, it was a performance experimental in form if not in

---

[1] When Lucia refused to burn sacrifice to the emperor's image, Paschasius, Governor of Syracuse, sentenced her to be defiled in a brothel. The Christian tradition states that when the guards came to take her away, they could not move her even when they hitched her to a team of oxen. Bundles of wood were then heaped about her and set on fire, but would not burn. Finally, she met her death by the sword. (http://www.romeacrosseurope.com)

[2] Lucia's is celebrated on 13 December. On that day, a girl dresses in a white dress and a red sash, the symbol of martyrdom, and wears a crown of candles, while the boys are usually dressed as saint Stefanos.

content, our audience surrounding us. It seems the intrigue of the circular, whether for the watcher or the watched, never goes away. Maybe it has always been here?

Jeremy Bentham (1748–1832), jurist, philosopher and social reformer among other things, came up with an idea for an 'Inspection House'. A panopticon, a circular building with cells arranged around the outer wall and a central watchtower, was, he felt, the best way to solve the riddle of supervision and self-supervision. As the light came into the building from the back of the cell, inmates were never able to really see the watcher, but the central inspector remained an omnipresent and unsettling presence in every cell at any given moment, a ghostly presence of power and a constant reminder of the risks of rule-breaking.

A prison called Millbank Penitentiary, based on these all-seeing principles, employing hexagons, pentagons and a central chapel, was eventually constructed in London where the Tate Modern[3] now resides. Charles Dickens, a great observer of the time and social reformer in his own right, describes the site and the surrounding area in his novel *David Copperfield*:

> There were neither wharves nor houses on the melancholy waste of road near the great blank Prison. A sluggish ditch deposited its mud at the prison walls. Coarse grass and rank weeds straggled over all the marshy land in the vicinity. In one part, carcases of houses, inauspiciously begun and never finished, rotted away. In another, the ground was cumbered with rusty iron monsters of steam-boilers, wheels, cranks, pipes, furnaces, paddles, anchors, diving-bells, windmill-sails, and I know not what strange objects, [...]. (Dickens, 2001)

The type of building Bentham helped give birth to has been built and used in many other countries too, in a few different styles and permutations, stemming from the same idea. Centralised control and self-regulation, in the fear that you might at any times be viewed by a hidden observer, seems like concept that prison architects were (are?) happy to use. The panoptic idea has germinated and spread to many parts of the world, and there are examples of buildings in Cuba, Italy, Portugal, the Netherlands, Australia, Sweden, America, South Africa and countless other places where a few people could look on, and thus dominate, many.

This kind of surveillance, the all-seeing eye enabled by bricks and mortar, is hopefully what this particular work will look at in some ways, maybe putting the spotlight on the obscured figure in the central tower for a change.

In Bentham's words, he hoped that the building would mean 'Morals reformed – health preserved – industry invigorated – instruction diffused – public burthens lightened – Economy seated, as it were, upon a rock – the Gordian knot of the Poor-Laws not cut, but untied – all by a simple idea in Architecture' (Bentham, 1791).

---

[3](https://www.tate.org.uk/visit/tate-britain/tate-britain-there-was-dreaded-millbank-prison)

I am sure it's not quite as straightforward as that, but this 'simple' idea in architecture has endured. It was here long before Bentham and Foucault. It will be here long after Facebook and the other digital village campfires we stare across, gazing at each other through the smoke of ones and zeros are all but memories.

Around 1791, architect Willey Reveley received £10 for helping Bentham with sketches of a Panopticon prison. Seen from above, the T-shaped cells of Reveley's blueprint for a panoptical prison all face inwards. In the middle of the circle is an eye. All-seeing perhaps, but surely even the eye of the state must sometimes blink? Framing this eye is a triangle, and on its sides the words, Mercy, Justice, VIGILANCE (artist's capitalisation). Reveley also wanted to straighten the Thames but parliament rejected all four of his proposals. Like the Thames scheme and the Panopticon prison, his designs for a public bath complex at Bath and an infirmary at Canterbury were never completed. This is who we base a lot of our 'design ideas' on.[4]

Minkowski space.[5]

[4](http://transcribe-bentham.ucl.ac.uk/td/JB/118/174/001)

[5]Minkowski, Hermann, from address *Space and Time*, delivered at the 80th Assembly of German Natural Scientists and Physicians (21 September 1908).

HMP Low Moss – 55°55′24.4″N 4°11′48.0″W

Just Do(n't Do) It

Coming to prison for the first time as an adult was different. This time I was in HMP Low Moss.[6] Not only was I in a foreign country, where my presence was preceded by all kinds of checks that bore little meaning to me, but the language, culture, subcultures, class system, implications and undercurrents were in some part known, in some part unknown and in some part ignored. I came straight from a stag do where I had spent two nights sleeping, almost spooning another man, in a cold kata tent. I was hungover, but not in a Bukowski way, or glamorously like Marlon Brando. I was just tired, and dirty, and I had definitely had enough of spending time with men, talking about manly things in manly ways.

I had injured a ligament at the stag do and couldn't properly bend my knee. I stank of Tiger Balm and had nervously put my stash of ibuprofen in a glove box before entering the prison car park. This was not a soldier's injury, nor was I a hero fresh off the football pitch. I was just unable to walk properly or sit down. I felt physically inferior because I knew I couldn't even run if I had to. I felt like the prison was a place where people sized you up, both in terms of actual shoulder measurements and your position on the imaginary X–Y axes of first impressions, faster than anywhere else, where a visitor would quickly be placed on a grid ranging from friend to foe via a complicated set of values. I came away not liking the place. I came away having asked the manager of the education unit if there were any jobs going. In the car, I retrieved the hidden blister pack and the personal freedom, that is silence and space.

Within the confines of the prison walls and the system, the posturing, gesturing and stylised behaviour is off the scale. As a foreigner, as a free man, as white/average height/build/looks, etc., I am happy to sidestep that. And biology has helped me in that sense. The body I inhabit raises no questions really, and in prison, I have always made an effort to keep it so, which includes choice of clothes and trainers – especially trainers, which is the only part of my attire that I have ever had a comment on (Asics Sonoma 3, if you were wondering).

This complicated sense of fashion and pride, class and money, displayed on your feet, is complex and multifaceted, and largely beyond my grasp, despite being above-average interested in trainers. This particular aspect of prison life is also illuminated in David Barton, Mary Hamilton and Roz Ivanic's *Situated Literacies*:

---

[6]"Low Moss opened in March 2012. This prison's design capacity is 784 and it manages male offenders on remand, short term offenders (serving less than 4 years), long term offenders (serving 4 years or more), life sentence offenders and extended sentence offenders (Order of Life Long Restriction) primarily from the North Strathclyde Community Justice Authority area. The facilities include a link centre where offenders are able to deal with matters relating to employment, housing, social work, through care addiction services, etc. as well as facilities to help offenders address their re-offending and support them to re-integrate back into the community on their release'. (http://www.sps.gov.uk/Corporate/Prisons/LowMoss/HMP-Low-Moss.aspx)

> At the time of the incident, credibility in the outside world was no longer to be achieved wearing Adidas trainers. This change of cultural marker explained why my informant was so adamant that his Prison shoes be customised to Nikes in order to bring him into the borderland Discourse of his community as a street-wise non-Prisonised individual. (Wilson, 2000)

And here 'informant' means 'person who takes part in a study', rather than 'snitch/grass/insider'. This illuminates another complicated detail of doing research in prisons. Worth noting too that in the example above, the shoes were neither Adidas nor Nikes to begin with. They were regulation plimsolls with tape, or marker pen applied, to make them look like 'outside' trainers. This is not unlike the myriad ways to 'corrupt' the correct use of a school tie, one of the few ways to rebel when uniformed, while under the wings of primary and secondary education.

I can see how this being in the world, and being not in this world, trying to fit in and follow trends, but being denied the apparent free will of the marketplace, easily breaks or makes men and women inside. Especially if the environment tells you that your gender role and position on the sliding scale of hierarchies is tied to what you wear, when in prison uniform there are not many ways to display oneself, barring tattoos and shoes and body size.

*

The next time I set foot in the same prison I was an employee of Motherwell College and contracted by the Scottish Prison Service to deliver classes adhering to the Curriculum for Excellence. During my day of preparatory training, I was told not to trust anyone, not to take anything from, or give anything to, anyone. I was told not to give anything away about myself either. 'If you live in a house, tell them you live in a flat. If you drive, tell them you catch the bus. If you live in Glasgow, tell them you live in Edinburgh, in town, just somewhere in town, don't go into specifics'. This advice, bordering on a set of rules, was quite difficult to take in when the rest of my life has very little risk in it. If this wasn't weird enough, after a quick lunch in the staff canteen, amongst wide men in uniform, we were taught how to fight our way out of a room. With karate chops and loud screams. I was paired up with a weedy film director called Henry, and we were given a full protective Judo kit to awkwardly step into. For about an hour, we semi-politely pretended that the other person was trying to keep us in the room, to be used as a hostage. With splayed fingers, like the instructor told us to use, as part of the Spontaneous Protection Enabling Accelerated Response (SPEAR) technique,[7] we spent the afternoon grunting, both equally convinced that this would be the very last approach we would take if things turned sour in the classroom.

---

[7]The SPEAR system (originally an acronym for Spontaneous Protection Enabling Accelerated Response) is a close quarter protection system which uses a person's reflex action in threatening situations as a basis for defence. Developed by Tony Blauer.

I sometimes see Film Henry (if that's even his real name?), and to this day, I feel we have something of a bond, though whether it's one based on violence or our ineptitude for violence I'm not sure. Either way, I passed the Personal Protection Training, admittedly not with flying colours, but there is a tick somewhere in a database telling employers I'm lethal, and that cheers me up no end. Especially in the light of the language used in the manual, and the aesthetics employed in the training video, and the assumptions they carry, as they are a far cry from the world I move in, which is mostly populated by books and my children. Tony Blauer, SPEAR founder, says:

> Back in the day, castles created the illusion of safety. Over time, this eroded our survival instincts and skills. The walls are long gone. Domestication has made us complacent, dulled awareness and stymied physicality. Political correctness has diluted our voice and assertiveness. Now, during a violent encounter, most people wait, hoping & praying the cavalry will rush in. They do... eventually. People need to realize that they are the 'first-responder' in their violent encounter.[8]

It might be easy to look at the Personal Protection Training as a joke. The image of the self-aggrandising male hero in full combat gear showing me how to battle my way out of a chokehold is almost absurd. Reflecting on the experience, I think that's the way I decided to deal with the threat of violence. If I can be glib about it, then it might not happen, is one approach. Playing with my mind is the notion that if the authorities tell me I need this, there must be a reason. Compare: car seat belts, lifeboats on ferries, and, 'In the unlikely event of a water landing, please assume the brace position. Your seat cushion can be used as a flotation device'.

This training is the very first encounter you have with the prison system. The language used is of 'Baddies' who are trying to kill/restrain 'Goodies'. It comes as a shock, possibly on purpose, as teaching staff are sometimes seen as lily-livered. This polarisation sets the tone in a fairly unhelpful way. I'm not against Personal Protection Training, but the blow could be cushioned by a cup of tea and a chat with 'normal' prisoners, to ease the tension for all parties. I'm sure it's unhelpful for the prisoners too to have a tutor who is initially on edge, expecting violence to erupt any second, from any angle. In many ways, the prison teacher experience is presented backwards. With this training as a framing device, you start with the worst case scenario and have to work backwards to reach humanity and connections with the students, which makes it difficult for everyone.

One insight into researching (physical) violence can be found in 'Allegiance and Ambivalence' by Alison Liebling and Betsy Stanko:

> Those who choose to research violence will always be walking on shaky (i.e. socially and politically constructed) ground. Some of us know we are studying violence, even when the topic chosen is something more mundane (Incentives and Earned Privileges for prisoners).

---

[8](https://blauerspear.com/choosesafety/)

> Researching violence means we choose to (or become obliged to) explore the dangerousness of violent groups or settings. Sometimes this means we put ourselves at risk. Concern for personal safety may impact upon the manner in which data are collected. It may also affect ethical and analytical objectivity. While there may be many reading this issue who have not faced the raw emotions emanating from these dilemmas, we think there are many more who have. Few of us share how we resolve or understand them. (Liebling & Stanko, 2001)

Prison shouldn't be about violence, but the training tells me it is. Prison shouldn't be about fear or loneliness, but some of these side effects are desired, and some are accidental. Some are part of the architecture, and some are part of the sustained myth of what prison is and how a prisoner should behave. Some affect staff, where guards jokingly talk about 'doing life', if they've worked in one prison for a long time, and some don't. I get to go home to my family and friends at the end of the day. Once I have been in the right place for the right amount of time that is. As I weave through the turnstiles, soon outside, I salute Minkowski.

I have decided that the best organising principles to apply to this work are Time (mainly chronological) and Space (mainly physical). Time is a major consideration when incarcerated, as evident in the expression 'doing time'. 'How much time has been spent,' 'how much time is left', is constantly present on a prisoner's mind. Day-to-day activities are tightly organised with precise starting times and ending times, in a way that is sometimes foreign to many of us, but which echoes Foucault's ideas about disciplinary institutions and controllable spaces, such as the school, the factory, the barrack and the university too. Time is plastic in these institutions. Good behaviour might buy you back time, deducted from your sentence. A 4* article might propel you faster, buying you future time climbing upwards. No one escapes Robert Owen's Silent Monitor(-ing).[9]

As a wider society, we have agreed that 'time' is the factor by which we punish, not pain as such. Here you won't be lashed or lose a hand for your crimes. We keep people in a particular space for a particular time, to make them pay for what they've done.

---

[9]"Robert Owen [1771–1858] [of New Lanark Mills] was strongly opposed to the use of corporal punishment, so in order to keep discipline at the New Lanark Mills, he devised his own unique system. The "silent monitors" were hung next to each worker in the mills, with each side displaying a different colour. "Bad" behaviour was represented by the colour black; "indifferent" was represented by blue; "good" by yellow; and "excellent" by white. The superintendent was responsible for turning the monitors every day, according to how well or badly the worker had behaved. A daily note was then made of the conduct of the workers in the "books of character" which were provided for each department in the mills'. (https://www.peoplescollection.wales/items/10456)

We spend our lives between Time and Space, both inescapable entities, each in our own way forging alloys and breaking the relationships set by ourselves and by others. Continuously interpreting the methods by which we have decided to encode the sun's route across the heavens, meanwhile trying to make sense of the places we find our bodies in. This relationship is made even more clear in a prison, and it is one I want to investigate further.

'Some societies appear to invest much more in the physical patterning of space than others, while others have clear global, even geocentric forms; and some societies built a good deal of social significance into spatial form by, for example, linking particular clans to particular locations, while others have recognisable spatial forms, but lack any obvious investment of social significance' (Hillier & Hanson, 1984, p. 5).[10]

Coins are almost always circular. But do they have to be? Why is democracy often depicted as, or at least housed in, circular buildings or chambers? Is our instinct to sit around the campfire so strong that even on the highest levels of decision-making we want to project the image of the circle? Does commerce + community (fire) = society?

---

[10]Dade-Robertson, M. (2011). *The architecture of information: Architecture, interaction design and the patterning of digital information.* London: Routledge, quoting Hillier, B., & Hanson, J. (1984). *The social logic of space.* Cambridge University Press.

Talking about buildings, 'The Beehive' is the Executive Wing of the New Zealand Parliament Buildings. 'The Beehive's circular footprint is generally considered an elegant and distinctive design feature. However it is also quite impractical, as many of its rooms are wedge-shaped, curved or asymmetrical. An extension has been built out the front to allow for a new security entrance. A new, bomb-proof mail delivery room has already been built at the rear of the building. Scottish architect Sir Basil Spence provided the original conceptual design of the Beehive in 1964'.[11]

---

[11]Rodgers, K. (2011). The contentious Beehive, *Building Today Magazine*. Retrieved from https://www.buildingtoday.co.nz/2011/07/01/the-contentious-beehive/

HMP Greenock – 55°56′33.0″N 4°46′55.7″W

Putting the Old Green Oak on the Map

I had completed my security training and was about to start working – I thought. The time between me getting accepted for the job as a teacher in HMP Greenock, and starting it, became months rather than the usual weeks. I was about to learn how perplexing the notion of time can be when it comes up against the carceral institution, and how strange spaces, and in my case learning spaces, become when situated within a prison.

The night before I was to go to the prison, I recall looking on Google Maps for the best way to get from the train station to the prison, and having difficulties locating the destination. The only thing on the map that corresponded with the postcode looked like a nice green park. It was only after reading the 'How to get here' advice on the Scottish Prison Service's website, that I realised that this was my destination. In my mind, I had thought that Google Maps represented a real image of what was on the ground.

This apparent distortion of the bird's-eye view of the world – traditionally held by the white, privileged, Christian, god-like man, architect was strange to come up against. Compare to the way Africa was parceled out at the Berlin Conference 1884–85, as ruler-straight lines, or arbitrary natural borders, soon dissected the continent. The extended power this worldview possesses when it hides something instantly interested me, especially as I was soon to walk up to the prison walls, experiencing what urban philosopher, Jane Jacobs calls 'The eyes on the street'.

Jacobs' *The Death and Life of Great American Cities* (1961) remains one of the most influential books in the history of American city planning. It introduces terms like 'social capital', 'mixed primary uses' and 'eyes on the street,' which became popular in urban design, sociology, and other fields. Jacobs painted a devastating picture of the entire profession of city planning, labelling it a pseudoscience. This led to angry responses from various rich and powerful men. Jacobs was criticised as a 'militant dame' and a 'housewife': an amateur who had no right to interfere with an established discipline (Sparberg Alexiou, 2006).

Interesting to note at this juncture might be the formation of *A New Chapter*, 'an independent open association [which] is expanding and galvanising support from architects across the country to work together for transparency, account-ability and a new progressive future for the Royal Incorporation of Architects in Scotland (RIAS)'.[12]

Jacobs applied her concepts to urban landscapes, taking a horizontal approach to architecture, a discipline usually dealt with vertically. Although she is primarily known as an urban theorist, I think you can draw parallels between city design and carceral design.

I think it matters greatly too that Jacobs walked and cycled a lot. As a way to explore the living city I, and all the flâneurs and flâneuses before me and beside me, have found walking a superior way to view life. In literary terms, I have found Franz Hessel, Walter Benjamin, Lauren Elkin, Rory Maclean, Dr Meri Kytö of

---

[12](https://www.judebarber.com/rias-new-chapter-and-uncovention)

Tampere University and Professor Dee Heddon of University of Glasgow, especially her Walking Library, very inspiring.

Jacobs' choice of transport meant she knew her environment horizontally. She knew the pace of a place. Not from a car, the mode of transport so much of America, and modern planning in general centres around, or from a vertical vantage point – the blueprint – but intimately and slowly. Jacobs 'argued that modernist urban planning rejects the city, because it rejects human beings living in a community characterised by layered complexity and seeming chaos (Holliss, 2015)'. Complexity and chaos are both space/time events that prison design strives to minimise. Modernist urban planning policies, according to Jacobs, had a destructive effect on communities, through the 'isolated, unnatural urban spaces' (Jacobs, 2011) they created. Her vision was of diverse urban spaces characterised by 'mixed uses, short blocks, buildings of various ages and states of repair, and density' (Jacobs, 2011).

If this is a checklist of what makes us human and happy when living in close proximity to each other, i.e. in a city or in a prison, carceral designers are continuously constructing a very difficult day-to-day life for the watched and for the watchers.

In this context, I wanted to briefly look too at the way prisons are gradually moving out of city centres. This is mostly due to an increasing (prison) population and the increasing price of land in inner cities. Prisons were traditionally built to be close to other citizens, close to the courthouse and the gallows, but more and more often they are now built in the countryside. There are also regenerative concerns at play here, as the projects and employment opportunities help boost the rural economy. In contrast, there are examples of prisons that have been kept in the city, but only after changing form, making themselves innocuous to the eyes of burghers. One example is the Metropolitan Correctional Center (MCC) in Chicago, which is housed in a skyscraper and outwardly not visibly a prison, so it functions quite differently in the urban fabric from the prisons of old. At MCC, the vertical is used as a razor wire. Due to safety concerns, for staff and prisoners in case of fire or similar, prisons in the United Kingdom are built in a horizontal fashion, taking up a lot of valuable space. Using gravity as an extra guard is both smart and sinister, and possibly something we will see more of in the future.

It is also interesting to look at the rising commercialisation of prisons and the unease the public feels about it. 'Four big jails are being built to cope with a predicted 2,000-inmate rise in the prison population by 2022. But the government is yet to decide whether to offer them to private operators such as G4S, Serco and Sodexo, which dominate the privatised prison estate, or keep them in state hands. Many would welcome the exclusion of the private sector. "The idea of the private jailer rightly makes people uneasy", said Richard Garside, director of the Centre for Crime and Justice Studies…' (Ford & Plimmer, 2018). There's money to be made from running a facility and from the inner city space that old prisons occupy.

To return to my journey to HMP Greenock and Jane Jacobs, I found the mismatch between the bird's-eye view and what was on the ground, between map and reality, quite disconcerting. I can understand that for safety reasons a prison's blueprint can't be handed over to members of the public, but to realise that the digital map of the world had been altered or was incomplete made me wonder where else and how often this happens. I presumed military bases, and maybe power stations, but what else? Schools, hospitals, Number 10? My house? Or maybe looking over my shoulder, thinking **Big Brother** was sitting in a central watchtower, had made me overly suspicious?

Those privileged enough to be allowed to see the world from great heights and to plan, change, build and oversee hold great power. Not for nothing did the Church control mapmaking for a long time, trying to combine dogmas and geography. Venetian power and wealth was helped by Galileo's improved spyglass, his telescope, which enabled the user to see further than the naked eye and in essence predict the future. The image of a military nation looking at approaching armies, mapping foreign coastlines, as well as a mercantile nation looking for approaching ships, weather systems, surveying arable land, combined with increasingly accurate maps captures some of the correlation between the powerful gaze (assisted by technology) which coupled with altitude (whether that's the top of St Mark's Campanile or a satellite) often results in power.

Now, as I am writing this, more information is available than a few years ago, and when I now revisit the site that had looked like 'a nice green park', there's a fairly full image of the prison there, which for the purposes of this text is somewhat annoying. Nonetheless, the discrepancy between reality and commercial digital cartography, where areas are blurred out or left in low resolution, is widely documented. According to the Federation of American Scientists:

> Google Earth occasionally does this at the request of governments that want to keep prying eyes away from some of their more sensitive military or political sites. France, for example, has asked Google to obscure all imagery of its prisons after a French gangster successfully conducted a Hollywood-inspired jailbreak [...].[13]

In the end, I made it to HMP Greenock. Walking up from the train station, I was experiencing 'the eyes on the street'. I was full of ideas about how to make my students engage with Orhan Pamuk and Maria Barbal. Once inside, I was quickly introduced to staff and asked if I knew anything about computers. My class had been cancelled, but there was an IT class, beginners Excel and could I please run that? And did I by any chance play an instrument, enjoy music, or actually just possess a pair of ears? If so, could I run the guitar class back to back with the computer one?

After a two-hour lunch break, when I couldn't leave the building, let alone open a window, or indeed go anywhere beyond the 50 m², the educational unit was made up of, I was wondering if my English class would ever happen. Instead, I accompanied one of my colleagues down to the multifaith room, which doubles up as a cooking class facility, one wall lined with ovens. HMP Greenock is a mixed prison, but the male and female populations are kept segregated, and the afternoon's class was all female, apart from me. Carefully counting scissors and circular needles, we set up the afternoon knitting class.

I couldn't contribute any expertise to the circle of knitters, but I think again I was more of a welcome distraction than anything else. Just as when

---

[13](https://fas.org/blogs/security/2018/12/widespread-blurring-of-satellite-images-reveals-secret-facilities/)

I 'entertained the troops' as a child, only this time I was paid, even though I was much less qualified for the task at hand. The women found it hilarious that I, a man, was knitting, and they found my crocheting attempts ridiculous. Especially as I was trying to talk about masculine fishermen of yore and, I don't know, the Gordian Knot. And I was maybe realising that solving the knots in our social fabric, the knit and the purl of people on the inside and people on the outside was difficult. That crime and punishment was a complicated tangle to unravel, at least by an idea in architecture.

> [...]'in the Anatolian interior at Gordium, the old capital of the Phrygian kings, there occurred the famous episode of the "cutting of the Gordian Knot". The old prophecy was that whoever unloosed the knot or fastening of an ancient chariot would rule Asia. Alexander [the Great] cut it instead [... and] solved the problem by abolishing it.[14]

Once the class was over, I gathered and triple-counted the sharp implements and locked them into a toolbox adorned with a padlock. This was the first time I was entrusted to turn a key, but it wouldn't be the last. And every time would be just as nerve-wracking. The click of the padlock marked the end of my first working day. The weeks proceeded just as unpredictably.

Greenock is both a 'top end' prison and a local one.[15] This means that inmates who are at the end of a sometimes very long sentence come to Greenock, which will be their last prison before reintegration into society. These men and women might have seen a few different prisons on their journey through the system. They are, in general, oddly hardened, disappointed and easy to deal with. They have little to prove and a lot to lose. They have a release date, and unless their fear of the outside world overrides their wish for freedom, they won't do anything to risk leaving Greenock for another prison, instead of going home. At least, that was the case in my limited experience.

At the other end of the spectrum are people who have been sentenced to a shorter stay. They will mostly be sent to whatever prison is closest their home postcode, to make it easy for relatives to visit, and maybe to make the already unfamiliar experience a little less alien for those new to prison life. This mix means that the same person who punched a bouncer in the local pub will sit next to someone at the end of their 22-year sentence. There is also an automatic age difference where if you've been in even for 'just' 10 years for a serious crime,

---

[14](www.britannica.com/place/ancient-Greece/The-4th-century#ref298258g)

[15]'Greenock's range of offenders is one of the most diverse in the SPS. We manage adult male and female offenders for those with short term sentences, long term sentences and on remand. We also manage long term males in our national Top End facility, Chrisswell House. Accommodation comprises of three main residential areas: Ailsa Hall has 133 cells and accommodates a male, predominantly local, population including remand and short term convicted offenders. Darroch Hall accommodates a mix of short term female convicted and untried female offenders. It has 54 single cells and one safe cell. Chrisswell House accommodates long term males who are low supervision. There are 64 single cells over two floors'. (www.sps.gov.uk/Corporate/Prisons/Greenock/HMP-Greenock.aspx)

you will be at least in your late twenties, and might have matured as a person. If Greenock is your first prison for your first crime, you might well be a lot younger and more impressionable, possibly keen to show the others who you are and your potential. The pressure of entering prison is unimaginable to me. And once in, it seems to be a difficult circle to break. Especially, young offenders (YOs) are often thought of as coming in and out of prison, as if they were stuck in a set of revolving doors. The implications of this in a progressively privatised society are worth considering.

> Returning Customers Generate Growth. A new survey from SumAll shows that 25% to 40% of the total revenues of the most stable businesses in the SumAll network come from returning customers. Focusing on repeat customers can also help your business through tough economic times.[16]

Some days, I would teach a class with a mixture of men. To my left a man with pretty serious dyslexia, *dvslexia, dsslaxya, dslaixiya,* which I was trained to deal with, but obviously did my best to help. Next to him, a man who was doing his last module of Philosophy through the Owen University and who would ask me if I could help conjugate Latin verbs, *durare, duravi, duratus.*

Next to him, an obviously depressed man, also highlighted by the fact that his trousers kept bothering him. There are no belts inside, due to the risk of strangulation, self, or other, but most people wear tracksuit bottoms, or at least jeans that fit in a way, so you don't need a belt. This man only wanted to do sheet after sheet of Word Search, but could never seem to find all the words. But at least he might have acquired some difficult-to-use knowledge.

Shark species:
Angelshark (*Squatina squatina*)
    Basking shark (*Cetorhinus maximus*)
        Blue shark (*Prionace glauca*)
            Common smooth-hound (*Mustelus mustelus*)
                Nursehound (*Scyliorhinus stellaris*)
                    Porbeagle (*Lamna nasus*)
                        Small-spotted catshark (*Scyliorhinus canicula*)
                            Spiny dogfish (*Squalus acanthias*)

Next to him, a man who had no inclination to do any work, but was happily asking me questions like, 'Why did the second world war start? Why did it end? Can I go to the toilet? What will happen to the pound as a currency if we vote for independence? Who do you rate more, Zlatan or Larsson?'

All this at the same time, plus another couple of voices and constant requests to photocopy, which took place in a different room. Because I was from the outside, I was expected to know not just my thing but everything. Not just how to teach but also to possess the knowledge of an oracle. It was a bit like a high-pressure University Challenge with lots of Jeremy Paxmans.

---

[16](https://dynamicweb.com/company/blog/returning-customers-generate-growth)

I was in HMP Greenock around the time of the Scottish Independence referendum in 2014, and as the prisoners were not allowed to vote, they were voting vicariously through me. There were some fascinating, enlightening conversations due in part to the referendum, and to the fact that the prisoners were being denied democracy, solely based on a sentencing date. I found this quite jarring. Especially for a decision that would affect the whole country and one that would have effects on them once they were out, regardless of how long their sentences were.

> The European Court of Human Rights has repeatedly ruled that banning most prisoners from voting is a breach of their human rights. Although the UK has promised to abide by the Court's decisions, nobody can force Parliament to change the law on prisoner votes. The stalemate looks likely to continue for some time, but no compensation has ever been paid to a prisoner denied the vote. The European Court of Human Rights has now ruled on four occasions that the UK is violating prisoners' rights by banning almost all of them from voting. The UK has not yet changed the law in response to these judgments, which go back over a decade.[17]

How can you ask a person to reintegrate quickly, stop using the revolving doors, if one of the basic rights of society, the freedom to vote, is being denied? How can you ask a person to trust that society wants what's best for them, when society doesn't want to hear their voice? What is the purpose of prison? Manifold and simple at the same time, it seems.

After a short period of working in HMP Greenock, I felt myself normalising the abnormal, slowly taking on gestures and ways of expressing myself, as if this Greenock language was another acquired one. A language I could pick up and learn the same way I have learned English as a second language, being Swedish by birth and upbringing.

In the beginning when the prisoners asked me 'What's happening?' I tried to explain; later, I would just say 'What's happening?' back to them. More and less would be happening in my life than theirs, but that wasn't the question. It was just a greeting phrase. As was the 'Where you fae?' To which the answer could be 'Sweden', 'Glasgow', 'the West End', and then the Personal Protection Training would kick in and if pressed I would say 'Braemar Street', which is not where I live. Which was fine until we got talking about football and trying to avoid the Rangers/Celtic divide I said my home team was Partick Thistle. They quickly, and correctly, guessed that I lived around Maryhill. This admission of sorts didn't bother me, but I could see that on some level, this information was retained. Soon they knew I cycled in, and one guy kept trying to sell me a bike. He would happily arrange for me to meet one of his pals up by the lockups, the ones behind the train station.

I believe people were often just trying to be helpful. As I would be to someone, a stranger in a new place, offering local information, bus schedules, the best takeout, a handy shortcut to the Old Bank Bar in 'downtown' Greenock – that's

---

[17](fullfact.org/law/votes-prisoners-politics-versus-human-rights-law/)

all part of normal human interaction. It's the way we make acquaintances, who might later become friends and close friends.

What affected me the most was the constant shift between social modes. Walking five meters/five seconds, from one place to another, I would go through various levels of what architects call 'public', 'semi-public', 'semi-private' and 'private space'. These terms show the relationship between physical walls and mental states in our lives. It is interesting and chilling to compare this to a prison where private and semi-private spaces don't exist. There might be what looks like an approximation of the two terms, but embedded in the genetics of the building, as part of the punishment and as part of the control, is a force making sure that the private is a privilege removed.

I used one set of parameters on the sliding Public → Private scale in the classroom, a different one out in the hall where there was a guard, but the door behind me into the classroom was still open, and then a third, and maybe the one closest to the social mode that is the most natural to me, at least with new colleagues, in the little teacher's room. In there, hidden from direct view, I was sometimes completely alone and, thus, completely myself.

During the classes I would copy worksheets, hand out stationery – deducting from a mental tally of who was using erasers and borrowing pens, as well as double-checking previously completed The Scottish Qualifications Authority (SQA) levels and a hundred other things, probably above my pay grade. For example, depending on behaviour on completed SQAs and to some degree the length of sentence served, a prisoner could move up on the scale of wages to "enhanced wages." I was never quite sure how this system worked, but it involved a hidden folder, finding the right name/prison number in a choppy sea of paperwork while the classroom was left rudderless, signing the form, finding someone to countersign it and keeping half an ear on the corridor/classroom. These tasks were performed over and over, hour after hour, in and out of social modes, in and out of direct view, possible view, obscured view (to the toilet where there was no possibility of being viewed, but which I couldn't use during class even though it was only three steps away). This movement was easily the most draining aspect of the working day, but I think this was one of the reasons I felt attracted to the idea of looking at how relations shift in space and how power is governed by bricks and mortar.

In the schematics of a revolving door it is apparent how little space they take up, and how, despite the more inviting design of a circle, not a hard border, an I/O, they keep the inside elements and the outside elements separated by a continuous pocket of air, more separate than a traditional door.

It is also a lot easier to get stuck in the not-so-merry go round of a door which ensures that 'Every square foot of the floorplan is now productive, energised and revenue driven. Ca-ching!', in the words of Boon Edam's Vice President of Marketing.[18]

Which fairly seamlessly brings us back in history to the schematics of the 'Squirrel Cage', A rotary Prison, which needed only two guards. The whole prison was operated by a hand crank and could rotate, with gears beneath the building, enabling one (or no), cell at a time to be turned to a solitary portal. A number of these were built in America in early twentieth century. A revolving twist on the static Panoptical revolving door. Most of them quickly failed and had to be welded into a static position.[19]

The (Same Old) New

Culture shock, Ostalgie[20] and http://

There is no internet inside a prison. At least not officially, but who knows how many 4G phones are circulating inside – and why it's so hard to block the signal. Maybe there's an element of choice from the authorities not to crack down too hard, in an effort to keep people happy. I couldn't say. This lack of technology, and what for most of us constitutes normality, makes for a strange journey back in time for the staff when working, and a terribly big leap forward for the people who leave prison after a longer sentence. For those who maybe went inside before the use of the internet exploded, which in itself seems like an alien, sepia-tinted world to us reading this today. This also means that the tasks performed and qualifications gained in the computer lab are sometimes of questionable value, mostly due to the quick expiry date of technical knowledge, however basic. What I saw inside that seemed useful was the mock Driver and Vehicle Licensing Agency (DVLA) driver's licence theory tests, and to some extent, the European Computer Driving Licence.

I can't imagine the shock of coming out through the gates and that's *only* taking into account the jarring difference in technology then and now. Almost whenever 'then' was. Leaving an environment operating in technological terms as if it was 1991 to enter the complete ubiquity of Wi-Fi and the smartphone must be confusing. To go from an era of landlines and Ceefax to eBay snipers

---

[18](https://blog.boonedam.us/what-else-is-your-entrance-letting-into-yourbuilding)

[19]United States Patent and Trademark Office, Patent #: US000244358.http://pdfpiw.uspto.gov. https://patentimages.storage.googleapis.com/c1/c1/0f/1e318bdf69c212/US244358.pdf.

[20]Portmanteau of the German words 'Nostalgie' (nostalgia) and 'Ost' (east). (https://www.dw.com/en/ostalgie/a-16196893)

and Twitter bots in three steps must hurt. It is possibly similar to the shock of the new when the Berlin Wall came down and East met West in full technicolour.

It is almost ironic that inside the walls, where there should be less chaos compared to the, in comparison, kaleidoscopic freedom of the outside world, there are many more factors playing into the disruption of the sense of linear achievements upsetting time. Some of these are internal, some of these are external and accidental, and some are external and not accidental. The spheres of influences beyond control are very big. It's not easy being in charge of one's fate while inside. It is possibly in the interest of the prison services to keep it that way, which is an approach that punishes the well-meaning prisoners with the same force as it keeps the less well-meaning in check. And if not in check, then at least confused.

At Greenock, I felt hemmed in by walls and people, which meant that if nothing else, the space was performing its function. Even the relatively quiet Greenock to Glasgow afternoon train was too much for me, so I devised a longer, less direct route. I went home, to my made up address on Braemar Street, via Bishopton and the Erskine Bridge, via the Forth and Clyde Canal and mud, and rain and all the little freedoms of stopping, starting, turning, turning back on myself, that for me only cycling can provide. At the time, I was also editing my first novel *Devil Take the Hindmost*, which features cycling, in my two-hour locked-up lunch break, so putting in the miles was also research and conceptually pleasing. I can't imagine what an imprisoned person must feel like, deprived of this access to the outdoors, rainy or not, or more to the point, the lack of freedom to choose to go outside, to turn left here, right there, stop for a minute, run for 10, to be soaked to the skin.

One of the reasons I like cycling, and why I chose to use it as a form of easing the effects of a day inside the prison, is the direct relationship between time and speed that you experience on a bike. The faster you go, the further you get. The more effort, the more time saved. This was one of the things I found the prison lacking in. This relationship between time, space and effort that I use without much reflection in my outside/thinking/inner life, just didn't seem applicable inside. Not even on a physical, fundamental level anchored in the body, was this relationship between effort, time, speed, distance relevant in prison. When it's possible to be outside, most exercise yards are used for walking in circles, in the same somehow predetermined direction. Once my working day was over, I tried in my personal way, to rectify this perceived imbalance between effort and effect, by turning the pedals faster and faster.

> [...] time is the longest distance between two places. (Williams, 2009)

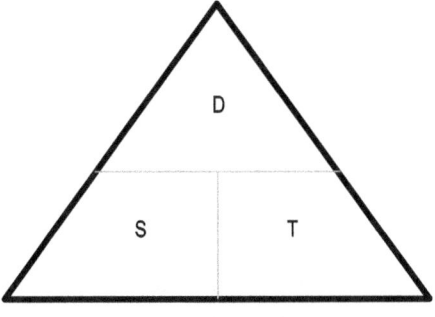

Distance = Speed x Time

Time = Distance/Speed

Speed = Distance/Time

Maybe I should have written Mercy, Justice, VIGILANCE on the sides of the triangle just there, placed an unblinking eye in the middle of it, but my skills in Word only stretch so far.

Personally, I found I needed to be outside after a working day where I had been inside 'inside'. I am not claustrophobic, nor in any other way bothered by closed spaces, but despite the fact that I was able, within reason, to come and go as I pleased and knew I would be out by the end of the day, being outside took on an almost holy aspect for me. This is also a faint echo of my Swedish upbringing where secularisation has in many ways replaced religion with a worship of nature and the outdoors.

> Does every prisoner have opportunity for at least one hour of exercise every day in the open air, weather permitting? The rules state that if the weather permits and subject to the need to maintain good order and discipline, a prisoner shall be given the opportunity to spend time in the open air at least once every day, for such period as may be 'reasonable in the circumstances'. There is a right to one hour's physical exercise a week and the aim is to allow one hour's exercise in the open air a day, if circumstances permit. Health care advice is that this period should not normally be reduced to less than half an hour a day. However, the Inspectorate (Annual Report 2011/12) found that, contrary to its expectations, many prisoners in England and Wales did not have the opportunity to spend one hour in the open air every day. (Silvestri, 2013)

England and Wales are not Scotland, but it rains there and possibly more here. There is a point to be made about the organisational structure of the prison service here too, as it is by necessity and possibly design, quite confusing. Regardless, the weather affects us all.

Toward the end of my classes, when the students were looking out of the one barred window even more than usual, I often heard them grumble about the weather. In the light of rain, some of the students would visibly be climbing the walls, even more than the usual. Others would resign themselves to wait another 24 hours for a chance to see the sky, calmly climbing their own inner walls. And, in this, they too were forced to normalise the abnormal.

Figures from the Scottish Government show that in 2014–15, three in ten offenders were reconvicted within a year, and that in the case of short custodial sentences of six months or less, a lot of which are served in prisons like HMP Greenock, almost six in ten were reconvicted within a year.[21] This cyclical relation between life inside and life outside, and the way prison quite quickly becomes part of normal life, reduced almost to a long commute, must desensitise a person quite quickly.

In HMP Greenock, there were a lot of reoffenders. Becoming institutionalised, getting used to 'two hots and a cot', whether that's to the practical side of things or to the more emotional relief of the routine and discipline that prison can provide must be a difficult net to untangle. One that I can imagine is also difficult to escape once released into the world again.

Prison is also doing a lot of the work that mental health services would be able to help with much more effectively and cost-effectively if they were not so over-stretched. The old link between prisons and asylums seems hard to break. It remains a harmful one, both personally for the prisoner not receiving the help they might require and for the allocation of funds in general, seeing that a prisoner is very expensive. According to the Howard League, 'The average annual cost per prisoner place for 2013–14 was £33,153, excluding capital charges, exceptional compensation claims and the cost of the escort contract. This is an increase of £1,227 on the previous year. A 2011 report found that it costs £126 per week to keep someone on HDC [Home Detention Curfew], compared to a notional cost of £610 per week to keep them in prison'[22]

To make sure that a person never has to end up in prison should be high on society's list of priorities. And if a person goes to prison, it should be very easy for them to never have to go back in again,[23] even from a purely economic point of view, disregarding the human factor.

In Scottish prisons, the term for a group of prisoners going somewhere, being transported, is sometimes 'the route'. Once my class was over, 'the route' left, headed, and sometimes tailed by a guard. This was done by a precise time

---

[21](www.gov.scot/publications/reconviction-rates-scotland-2014-15-offender-cohort/)
[22](http://howardleague.scot/tags/prison-costs)
[23]'An important connection exists between the concept of recidivism and the growing body of research on criminal desistance. Desistance refers to the process by which a person arrives at a permanent state of nonoffending. In effect, an offender released from prison will either recidivate or desist'. (https://www.nij.gov/topics/corrections/recidivism/pages/core-concern.aspx).

schedule, so that two 'routes' wouldn't be out in the corridors at the same time, meaning the number of 'free' prisoners would be too many, and that the percentage of prisoners to guards would exceed some kind of safety limit. In some prisons, there's also the further complication in that various groups of prisoners (women, sex offenders, vulnerable prisoners on protection or suicide watch, etc.) can't meet each other or even pass each other in corridors. In Greenock, this meant that it took the guards two hours to lead the prison population to the lunchroom and back, in what must have seemed like an endless reenactment of the same play.

Soon, and somewhat against my will, I was trusted with keys to HMP Greenock. Not to all doors, only to one or two. Maybe more. I never really knew. I never really wanted to find out. As most doors were watched by closed-circuit television (CCTV), where a request button allowed access or exit, my keys in someone else's hands would probably have been quite ineffective anyway. The key, a symbol for freedom and power, so closely related to its spouse, the lock, with the opposite symbolism, was an unpleasant reward to receive. I carried the key, clipped to a nylon tool belt, on a steel lanyard, inside a pouch. The key was concealed, so that a prisoner with photographic memory wouldn't be able to manufacture a replica from a remembered glimpse. The tool belt also held what looked like a pager with a red panic button, and I was forever moving this belt around, when standing up, when sitting down, when leaning, when going to the toilet, when photocopying, etc., to avoid accidentally pressing the button and calling guards to my location or putting the prison into lockdown. With the key in my possession, I could now leave the prison building for my two-hour lunch break, to get crisps from the corner shop or marvel at the local duck pond, but the trouble of checking out and then checking back in wasn't worth it. Coming and going was a process very similar to passing through security at an airport, with the added complication of leaving my key with the last guard in exchange for a small, easily lost chit with a number on. A bit like a coat check, but with legal implications attached. I would gladly have exchanged the freedom to come and go for the millstone around my neck of being a key holder. Right or wrong, I also felt the prisoners looked at me more closely now that I had graduated up to wearing the black belt. And so the dance of the watched and the watcher, the watched and the watchers, continued.

The Large Hydron Collider on the French-Swiss border near Geneva is the largest single machine in the world. It lies in a twenty-seven kilometre ring-shaped tunnel.

Few people get to see this machine. There are some fascinating images of it.[24] Ones that remind me of the snake that eats its own tail in Norse mythology. Underneath the quiet fields and towns lies a huge 'miðgarðsormr'. According to the myth, when this serpent releases its own tail, the end times or 'ragnarök' will begin. The LHC circle is used to smash (I'm no scientist) tiny circles or spheres, the way we tend to depict atoms, together for unexpected results.

In life and in death, the circular/spherical seems to be our best idea. A pregnant belly, an egg, an urn, a cenotaph. Maybe a macabre juxtaposition, but alongside the images of the atom and the campfire maybe it makes some sense. Holding this collection of images up against the blinding light of an in-between life, where if Bentham had had his way, we would spend a large part of a carceral life, maybe it makes even more sense.

In his sketches for a 'Cenotaph for Newton', Étienne-Louis Boullée (1728–1799) stretched what could be imagined in terms of spherical structures. Boullée made sketches for a huge monument, one that would dwarf the human simply by the scale of it.

---

[24](https://phys.org/news/2018-06-cern-major-reap-atom-smasher.html)

Boullée wanted to build a monument to the long dead Newton. A long row of trees, a huge spherical tomb 150 m high, and inside, an element of day and night where small holes in the outer shell would let through sunlight, to paint a starry sky in light, would allow visitors to worship at the marble feet of a scientist buried somewhere else.

'Minuscule clusters of visitors ascend a monumental stairway at the base of a spherical monument rising higher than the Great Pyramid of Giza. An arc of waning sunlight catches a small portion of the sphere, leaving the excavated entry portal and much of the mass in deep shadow. Bringing together the emotional affects of romanticism, the severe rationality of neoclassicism and grandeur of antiquity.'[25]

Maybe an apple tree would have been easier? A small, hard sphere hitting the scientist at the right time seems to have been the catalyst for a long train of thought.

---

[25](https://www.archdaily.com/544946/ad-classics-cenotaph-for-newton-etienne-louis-boullee)

HMP Glenochil – 56°08′29.4″N 3°48′58.2″W

O'er the Hills and Far Away

That summer I also covered a teaching position in HMP Glenochil.[26] This was a completely different kind of building for me. Newer than HMP Greenock and more spacious. Freshly painted and with a more inviting, if that's possible, entry point. The price of land per square metre is obviously much lower the further away from cities you decide to build – if you disregard enticing geographical features or possibilities for commuting that might attract buyers of land/property developers. HMP Glenochil sits at the back of an industrial park, neither here nor there. Surrounded by beautiful hills, but otherwise in a forgotten corner of the country.

One definition offered of this kind of cheaper in-between space, relating both to bits of land and unloved bits of buildings, comes from architect Rem Koolhaas' book *Junkspace*: 'If space-junk is the human debris that litters the universe, junk-space is the residue mankind leaves on the planet. The built product of modernisation is not modern architecture but Junkspace. Junkspace is what remains after modernisation has run its course or, more precisely, what coagulates while modernisation is in progress, its fallout. Modernisation had a rational program: to share the blessings of science, universally. Junkspace is its apotheosis, or meltdown. Although its individual parts are the outcome of brilliant inventions, lucidly planned by human intelligence, boosted by infinite computation, their sum spells the end of Enlightenment, its resurrection as farce, a low-grade purgatory' (Khoolhas, 2006).

Another well-known example of how this liminal space can be viewed, but relating more closely to buildings, and reacting to and against Modernity, is Marc Augé's well-known work *Non-Places*. In it, among other things, he dissects spaces of transience. Whether we think of the prison as a site of transience, as in the corridor discussed elsewhere, or a holding pen, it is still true that modern prisons are integrated in the postindustrialised landscape, into a car-dependent society where life is viewed at 55 miles an hour.

> But this turning away, this bypassing, is not without some feeling
> of remorse, as we can see from the numerous signboards inviting
> us not to ignore the splendours of the area and its traces of history.
> Paradoxically, it is at the city limits, in the cold, gloomy spaces of
> big housing schemes, industrial zones and supermarkets, that the

---

[26]'Glenochil manages adult male offenders who are short term offenders, long term offenders, life sentence offenders and extended sentence offenders (Order of Life Long Restrictions). The prison has been completely rebuilt in recent years and is a large community facing prison, giving priority to Forth Valley and Fife ("FK" and "KY" postcodes). It is one of the major sites in Scotland for managing sex offenders and those with an Order of Lifelong Restriction (OLR). Offenders are not committed to Glenochil direct from the courts but are admitted following conviction from other local prisons around Scotland. The current design capacity is 670 and we hold on average a daily population of 660'. (www.sps.gov.uk/Corporate/Prisons/Glenochil/HMP-Glenochil.aspx).

signs are placed inviting us to visit the ancient monuments; and alongside the motorways that we see more and more references to the local curiosities we ought to stop and examine, instead of just rushing past; as if alluding to former times and places were today just a manner of talking about present space. (Augé, 1992)

Prisons are often camouflaged as warehouses or bus depots, to the point where our eyes pass over these unremarkable buildings. In the light of the panoptic eye employed in the prison and elsewhere, Augé suggests some interpretations in his *Non-Places*. These modern and supermodern spaces might offer both a performance of sorts and a hiddenness. It is not surprising that the prison complex, the site for spectators and the spectacle, the site for meted-out ordeals of solitude looks a lot like a shopping mall, the archetypal non-space, the space to see and been seen in.

Fittingly, the modern exterior of HMP Glenochil is reminiscent of an airport, a ferry terminal, a (newer) school/college/university. Standing outside before my shift, squinting and mentally removing some of the safety features, I could have been anywhere in civic society. Which is a nice thought, to think that prisons are not entirely removed from the bits of society we all know so well. It is also a frightening thought, in that the powers of control and people flow might be largely the same in 'free' society as they are inside an institution. I wonder who tells me where to go.

In the case of HMP Glenochil, situated at the bottom of the Ochil Hills, nature is more evident than outside HMP Greenock, but as difficult to access. This view of the hills, possibly both comforting and an awful reminder of how distant normal life is, must seem taunting and pleasingly distracting at the same time. Given the choice I don't know if I'd pick a cell with a view of this freedom or not.

If HMP Greenock is segregated down a gender line, as well as different security classifications, HMP Glenochil has a different division to take into account. There are different strands and freedoms, depending on time served/to serve, but the most obvious separation is that of sex offenders, who all wear red tops, as opposed to the general blue of the wider prison population. For their own safety, sex offenders are kept separate from other prisoners.

One fellow researcher, Samir (not his real name), who was charting prisoners' smoking habits in light of the incoming smoking ban, told me that he had gone to one particular prison unaware of what the Scottish Prison Service (SPS) colour code for sex offenders was. By coincidence, Samir was wearing a red top. He was walking around one of the wings trying to get conversations going, but was finding it very hard to even get eye contact. The prisoners had heard 'researcher' and saw he was wearing red, and no one wanted to be seen speaking to him. Eventually, someone told Samir about his poor choice of clothes, and he took off his top to reveal a nonred t-shirt. All of a sudden, as is the norm when outsiders, who are not any kind of authority, come in, prisoners were very keen to speak to him about their smoking habits and all sorts of things.

Initially, I had no idea either about these colour codes. I taught classes of all colours, and it was only once in a 'blue' class, when the students suddenly all ran to the window overlooking the football field, populated by men in red tops, that I realised the difference. The 'blue' students were shouting about 'filthy animals' and how it was unfair that they were allowed outside. I had to ask everyone to return to their desks. It was a strange thing to do. To tell people what they could and couldn't look at, where they could direct their gaze and where they couldn't.

Thankfully I wasn't at HMP Glenochil long enough to gain their key trust, but as it was too far away from where I live (at Braemar Street in 'sous rature/ erasure') to cycle, I found myself driving longer routes home than necessary. I was recognising my old cycling behaviour, and reveling in it, as it had been helpful. Left here, right over there. Stop. Start. Follow diversion. I could go where I fancied with little thought about consequences. Again, small choices equaling big freedoms.

On Punishment:
(i)   'It must involve pain or other consequences normally considered unpleasant.
(ii)   It must be for an offence against legal rules.
(iii)   It must be of an actual or supposed offender for his offence.
(iv)   It must be intentionally administered by other humans than the offender.
(v)   It must be imposed and administered by an authority constituted by a legal system against which the offence is committed'.

Hart, H. L. A.
The Presidential Address: Prolegomenon to the Principles of Punishment.
Proceedings of the Aristotelian Society, vol. 60, 1959

Punishment seems to be defined by an action in the past, resulting in a countdown, forcing time back towards a point. A strange friction between past, present, and future. Time itself doesn't care. It's perfect. It's part of nature. It is a perfect continuous force.

'The time is out of joint – O cursèd spite (Shakespeare, 1992).

Carceral Choreography

We are all just bodies in space, trapped in time for a predetermined duration. Like celestial bodies, we spin in relation to each other, until our orbits collapse. Like the maps of dance steps laid out on the ground, flimsy sheets with footprints, most often his and hers, circling, stopping, starting. Time and place tells us where to go and at what tempo.

As a group, the prisoners I've come across have been fairly similar or looked similar at least. This 'research finding' is not to be taken too seriously. Partly because the population of the West of Scotland is quite homogeneous (at least to Swedish eyes), partly because I have had neither the scope nor the inclination to classify groups of people in that way, so, I will talk about the group of students I have dealt with. There were no traditionally feminine traits or much care taken of the body on display. Unless you count those who clearly had a lot of access to the gym, or just knew how to do hundreds of push-ups a day. From what I could see, some had lived a tough life, which is a cliché but still true. When someone is missing half their teeth and the person next to them has scars crisscrossing their face, it's difficult to think otherwise.

Here too all my students wore trainers. Some expensive, some not. And who deserves the best trainers? I don't know. Rich people, poor people, professional athletes, everyone? Is symbolic violence, mentioned below, and financial self-harm, at play here too? Some of the students wore jeans, some tracksuit bottoms, and all wore the same top, with small variations. In a sense, these were local versions of the same top, not unlike football shirts that change depending on where you are in the country.

It can be argued that the prison is a site of symbolic violence. It has whiffs and outbursts of real violence, but the 'damage' is probably wider than the physical side of things. 'In terms of consumer culture, symbolic violence might be seen to be at work through the definitional characterisation of some things (goods, tastes, lifestyles) as better than others and as accruing rightly to those who deserve them. In this context, Bourdieu's characterisation of working-class life as operating on a principle of closing off possibilities ("that's not for the likes of us") is relevant' (Lawler, 2011).

Lynsey Hanley writes at length and very well, especially in her 2007 memoir/ investigation 'Estates: An intimate history', on class, social housing, social mobility and the difficulties of escaping your physical surroundings, as well as on the (class) walls constructed in your mind (Hanley, 2007). I'm not good at judging class, not being from this country, but in my classes, there was very little small talk about quinoa and skiing in the Alps, and more on the beauty and dangers of drink and ripping copper wiring out of empty buildings and joining the French Foreign Legion on release.

Many prisoners will struggle to find regular employment once out, so putting your uniform, uniformed body to work is one approach. You can't join the regular or territorial army with a record, but the 'Légion étrangère' might take you. You can't be older than 39.5 years old, and you must 'be sure you have healthy teeth (or treated), maximum number of missing teeth between 4 and 6, depending on the value of the teeth, masticatory coefficient (to have quite healthy teeth) greater than or equal to 40%'.[27] If you tick those boxes, you might be able to be anonymised in khaki. Unless you're a woman, then you must find other venues.

In terms of gender, who goes to prison? 'About 95% of prisoners in Scotland are male. There are on average about 400 women in prison in Scotland on any given day, […]. However, many women are serving short prison sentences and about 3,000 women go through prison every year (compared to around 34,000 men)'.[28]

This has implications reaching out beyond and back across the walls. The workforce, in general, is approaching a 50/50 split between men and women. This should be viewed also in relation to an increase in 'feminized' work opportunities in care, retail, etc., and a marked decline in the traditional routes to lower waged job opportunities in industry/construction, traditionally male jobs. Especially in places like Greenock, once a thriving Clydeside community, heavily industrialized, now a blown out egg. And what there is to 'return' to once ejected from the prison.

Simply by being stuck in space and time, the prisoners have become a drain on societal resources, much more so than if they were simply out of a job, as it is very expensive to house prisoners. This is sometimes difficult to relate to, for those on the outside and those on the inside. Everything in prison feels cheap – the clothes, the food, and often the resources and furniture, yet there's a lot of money spent on prisoners. It just doesn't show in the building.

To serve in the military, to work on an oil rig, to travel with work, to do 'good work' as a missionary, etc., are all instances of (traditionally and possibly outmoded) male absence from the family/community. For better or worse, we, as a society, are used to these roles. It is much harder to 'explain' a woman's absence. The

---

[27](https://foreignlegion.info/joining/)
[28](http://www.sccjr.ac.uk/wp-content/uploads/2015/10/SCCJR-Whos-in-prison.pdf)

monastic fantasy, nurtured by the creative industries as a way to portray the prison stay, contributes to this idea.

There are few places more 'masculine' than a men's prison. It could be argued, without going too deep into gender politics, that female prisons are intrinsically male environments too, partly based on the tradition of the gender of the prison population, which remains firmly in place. Not everything is about gender, but to a large extent, the body is. The function of a prison is to trap a body in a space for an amount of time. Primarily the body is being punished, with repercussions for the mind.

One of the features that have united every single prisoner I have ever met is a hyper-awareness of the distance to, and more importantly from, one body to another body. As if the prisoners were a group of magnetic force fields, all charged with the same polarity, repelling, feeding off each other. As is possibly the case in non-prison populations too, the awareness of this space, and how it is enforced, was slightly less stringently upheld by the female prisoners. Again, trying to avoid oversimplifying, it seemed to me that the women prisoners were more comfortable with human contact than the men were, or that it was more socially accepted, which is the case of course in 'outside' society too. I should have known by then that the somewhat concave mirror of 'normal' society forcefully focussed certain elements inside the institution.

Either way I think you could fit more seasoned prisoners into an underground carriage than seasoned commuters, the difference being that in the prisoner's carriage, no one would touch anyone else. Not by accident at least. The feats of mind-bending spatial awareness displayed, acrobatic yet casual, were both interesting and somehow touching. This focus on the body is quite different from the one we employ outside the prison walls. In my daily life, I'm sure I bump into people all the time. In prison, never. No one ever came close to touching me, despite the very low chance of repercussion. This force field extending out, invisible, yet tangible, from bodies used to cells, made a real impact on me. I don't think I am on touching terms with many other people in society, but I have never measured this in the same way as I did inside. Apart from the overly firm man-to-man, free man to prisoner, handshake, which was often unexpected as it was initiated by me, and often appreciated, there was nothing. I don't know if the importance is due to a certain starvation of human touch or the lack of signs of respect shown to prisoners from members of outside society, but the handshake seemed to carry with it a much greater emotional weight than I had appreciated before.

This hyper-awareness made me wonder: What good is the body? What use is the good body? If it is not put to use for work, for meaningful exercise (to be able to better perform a task outside the gym environment), not even for sex – is it just there to provide an example of what can be done, either with tattoos or with muscle mass? Or its opposite, to show the lack of care for the own body, which carries with it a certain power too. Is the body there for display, a confidence boost, an unspoken threat? Is exercise simply used as a way to turn off the mind for a while? To sleep better? The same mechanisms can, of course, be applied to the heterotopic spaces we pay to enter and use, gyms, with their segregation, self-improvement and willing acceptance of constructive pain. For lack of space, I will refrain from talking about gyms, but in an increasingly body image centred world, this is something I would like to explore further in the future.

In prison, stripped of most ways to portray yourself (bar trainers), you are left with your body, so it's not strange that we choose to celebrate it. In portable aspects such as tattoos and haircuts and muscle mass, just as we do in most other areas of society. However, prison is a place where shoulder size matters even more. This body cult, does it relate to certain kinds of crimes? What is the body mass index (BMI) and watt/kg of your average prisoner sentenced for tax fraud compared to someone in prison for assault? (I don't actually know how you'd go about finding out, and I don't want to draw any more conclusions from this line of thinking. There's enough anthropometry in architecture already.)

What is the relationship between violence and the body? Physical violence is done by one body onto another body, so if violence is part of your personal palette, or if you find yourself in a context where a certain show of strength matters, you would want to make sure that your body was prepared for it or at least looked prepared for it, as a deterrent, resulting in a cold war on multiple fronts.

*

Soon after I began looking at the workings of the prisons, the notion of the prison as a theatre/stage production came to me. This was before I had any reason to read Erving Goffman's *The Presentation of Self in Everyday Life* (Goffman, 1990) (now canon, alongside his 'Asylums' [Goffman, 1991]). As an aside, it could be argued that prison isn't part of everyday life. Goffman writes on aspects of maintaining face, avoiding embarrassment, and navigating the front – on display and the back – the private and unmannered, of our personalities.

Theatre, and spectacle, also works as a symbol for the wider life inside walls. In a prison, much more so than in outside life, every day consists of an interlocked sequence of events, repeated with minor alterations/variations, just like in a play. One word/line/act leads to another, and without this train of thought – this practical storytelling – the overarching idea of the day and the prison's purpose ceases to be as effective. The logic of the routine stumbles quite easily, just like a play does if an actor forgets a line, or if the décor falls apart. Often, due to incidents, the prison operations cease to work as they should. This can be due to a riot in the C-Wing, a water tank that won't refill properly in the loo in the educational unit, meaning no one can come up and learn anything, or a shortage of sweetener meaning lunch is cancelled for diabetics, meaning communal lunch is cancelled for everyone. The prison play balances on a knife-edge.

To look at this in architectural terms, I want to compare prison movements to the concept of 'circulation' or 'flow'. In normal life, as in prison, people have to be in particular spaces, at particular times, and the easier they can move between these holding areas/stages, the better and safer (for example in traffic). This applies regardless of whether the stage is a train station, a nursery, a prison or a dance floor.

> [C]irculation routes are the pathways people take through and around buildings or urban places. Circulation is often thought of as the 'space between the spaces', having a connective function, but it can be much more than that. It is the concept that captures the experience of moving our bodies around a building, three-dimensionally and through time. [...] Although every space a person could access or occupy forms part of the circulation system of a building, when we talk about circulation, we typically don't try to account for where every person might go. Instead, we approximate the main routes for the majority of users. [29]

Circulation is a factor that has been considered in OOIIO Architecture's proposal for a female prison in Iceland. The plan is hard to describe. It looks organic, it looks constructed, it looks like two oversized cartoon mouse ears attached to a smaller head, which itself is attached to a sated caterpillar.

According to the architects, this proposed structure 'dismisses the dark spaces, small cells and grey concrete walls typical of a traditional prison. [...] The project started with the team asking people who live and work in the establishments what it felt like. The conclusion was that the worst thing about living in a correctional facility is the feeling that you are actually in one. Instead of containing the functions in a singular building, this breaks into several tiny and more human scaled pavilions. The program is complex, similar to a small village, with a hospital, schools, church and theatre, all working precisely at the same time'.[30]

It is a proposal that maps out workers and prisoners, colour-coded, and the paths they are allowed to take through the circular buildings. The way fluids would fill and empty out of the pear-shaped flasks in a lab is the way the inhabitants, some staying for longer than others, would move, unless they undermined the proposal by not.

We can consider circulation with regard to a city block, a university campus, a train station, or a cell (a biological one or a prison one). Circulation helps us to consider the use of that space over time, as well as how agency and self-organisation might change the flow of a space. I find this interesting in the case of a prison, which is a highly designed and prescribed environment, populated by people with low agency (within the walls and arguably outwith too).

It is difficult to think about the movement of prisoners. Compare to shoppers in a mall, children at a playpark, ships in a harbour, the docking/berthing of spacecraft

---

[29](http://portico.space/journal//architectural-concepts-circulation)
[30](www.archdaily.com/244702/female-prison-ooiio-architecture)

(utilising, in astral-lingo, 'androgynous/ungendered' or 'non-androgynous/gendered' systems). These individuals/groups/entities are more free to move in space. The admittedly limited space of consumerism, of childhood, of water, of dark matter, that of hope and possibilities, but how do you best map the circulation of a population who would rather not be where they are.

As a side note, even in space, we seem unable to escape the ghost of gendering. 'Generally cable connectors have a male component and a female component, except in the case of hermaphroditic connectors such as the IBM data connector'[31] this is true on Earth, and seemingly the same goes for space stations. So much for a new frontier.

The architecture of glossy magazines, in the spacious, white, carefully arranged sense, has little in common with the complications of housing a population that do not want to be in a space. This friction obviously puts a stress on the building and on its design, one that has bearing on agency and imagined agency too. On the imagination. A stress that leaves traces in individuals.

Taking the concept of 'flow' or one step further, into language, which after all is my home field, rather than criminology or architecture, I want to look at how this might work in communication.

hs eHa'elSl'o ys makes no sense. *She says 'Hello'*, makes more sense. Letters, words, sentences, paragraphs, numbers, sequences, etc. are all obvious ways that we use flow in language and communication. We also use storytelling tropes to make sense of the seemingly sequential progress of our lives, in time if not in circumstances at least. As French-Swiss film director, Jean-Luc Godard puts it: 'A story should have a beginning, a middle and an end, but not necessarily in that order' (Sterritt, 2008). That's more possible in fiction and film perhaps than in life where we are trapped by time passing and where it's difficult to edit backwards. Every story, however, brief or tedious, has a beginning, a middle and an end, as does every life (our meted-out time); it's just that we never know just where the middle is.

Moving through a text, as moving through a building, is the only way to spot mistakes and make improvements. This way, going over previously spent time, constructing a palimpsest, to arrive at a final version. An important part of the architectural practice is 'snagging', often with the use of a 'punch list'. The snagging is in some ways very much like the editing or proofing of a manuscript, however brief. Spelling and grammar, all the way 'up' to concept and implication, readability, as well as intended reader/user, is considered, re-considered and fixed until the work is the highest standard achievable. For a building, this means it should work, that the flow should be uninterrupted.

Reflecting on language and etymology, especially when writing, while using the program Word that will automatically start my sentences with a capital letter and strongly suggest full stops where they should be if I falter in my flow, it struck me that the word 'sentence' is quite interesting. It implies a definite start and a

---

[31](http://www.cables-solutions.com/three-types-of-cable-connectors-used-in-cablinginstallation-techniques.html)

definite end, and it has to have certain parts within it to be valid. The 'sentence' is something self-contained and perfect in form, with a clear beginning and a clear end.

*

Sentence

Noun: (grammar) A grammatically complete series of words consisting of a subject and predicate, even if one or the other is implied, and typically beginning with a capital letter and ending with a full stop.

Verb: To declare a sentence on a convicted person; to doom; to condemn to punishment.

Under the rubric of 'flow', there are many considerations. From how people move through and understand the building on a conceptual level, as in, there shouldn't have to be signs for 'Exit', you should know/feel it, to making sure there's enough hot water in the pipes, the right kind of electricity in the sockets, a pot of the correct paint sitting in a cupboard to fix the spot where the paint has flaked on the banister on level 4, and so on.

A prison is both more complicated and less complicated than a 'normal' building. It needs to fulfil all the complex human needs that we use in homes, workplaces, parks, schools, etc., for buildings that usually take up vast resources and/or space. A prison is a compressed city as well as a remote environment where you have to travel to goods/services or where goods/services have to travel to you. At the same time, a prison's function is simple. It's to keep people contained. Making sure the right bodies remain in the right spaces, and that the play plays on and remains tightly choreographed.

On the circular, the Highway Code states:
'All signs giving orders have the same shape'.
Another example of flow/circulation management.

On the imperative mood:
In this code there's a circular sign with a black car in the middle of a thick red circle.
At the top of this car, a Morris Minor or a Rover P4 possibly, there's a flame
shooting out, scattering pieces of the roof. A vehicular St. Elmo's fire, or an eternal
flame, like the one that might have flickered in Newton's cenotaph? The sign tells us
'No cars carrying explosives allowed', implying that there are roads where cars
carrying explosives are welcome.

A Walled City within the City

In 'Carceral Spatiality', Eric (no last name), prison architect, from Belgium, says: 'It is a dream project for an architect because this is a global project. To think a prison is thinking about everything. It is to think of life. A prison is a dormitory, it's a restaurant, it's a sports club, it's a hospital, it's a factory, it's a school, it's a public square' (Scheer & Lorne, 2017, p. 201). Though I'm not sure how many inmates would share this somewhat wide-eyed enthusiasm, it is still true in some sense that a prison has to meet many more needs than a normal building. Through choice and specialisation, we have made most buildings in society great for one or two functions but not great for other. Try sleeping in your office for a week. Try having a symphony orchestra in your front room. Make a meal in the gym. Try segregating a modern workplace down the established gender line used by the prison services. And the two sides can't eat lunch at the same time. The task we are asking of the prison building is almost impossible.

We are increasingly blurring the boundaries between the prison and the outside life. Not only in how many CCTV cameras we put up and how high the walls of our gated communities are.

> 'Although prisons are increasingly built away from cities, prison architects are imagining prisons *as* cities. Such an urban metaphor is perhaps unsurprising; both the prison and the city are often assumed to be relatively bounded places, prisons arguably resembling self-sufficient cities [...]' (Scheer & Lorne, 2017, pp. 201–202).

Think city limits, 'Welcome to Cherryfield, ME, The blueberry capital of the world', meaning that somewhere this capital's world-leading reach ends. Or how you can drink in the streets of Edinburgh, but you can't in Glasgow. Think demarcation of national borders and how in essence your left hand in Bolivia can do what your right hand in Peru is not allowed to. The list of geographical examples of similar absurdities is endless, but on some level, we have become obsessed with marking space. This is Denmark, this isn't. This is Khovd, this isn't. This is my parking space, this isn't.

These painted lines, whether on tarmac, on a prison blueprint or on the world map, are increasingly ubiquitous on every level, as spaces and territories are allocated and defined. At the same time, language bleeds across these boundaries, here between the urban and the carceral in architecture:

> The vocabulary of the city is also pervasive when justifying prison architecture [...] using terminology such as 'walled bungalows', 'penitentiary houses', 'vertical prisons' and 'cell apartments'. (Scheer & Lorne, 2017, p. 202)

Not only are we using metaphors for leisure and freedom and trying to apply them to carceral spaces, but we are also inviting the ordered and watched to come out and to enter our lives. Here, I could talk about willingly volunteering private information to commercial outfits like Facebook, Twitter, Alexa and whoever else really, but I will refrain from it.

In case they're reading this.

Keeping with the bricks and mortar, I know of no other building that like the prison seems to have such a clear function, to hold someone in one place. This said, several academics are starting to highlight the ever-increasing softening of the walls, often aided by technology, such as mobile phones and the internet. Prison is also a space that is made more complicated by visits.

Dominique Moran writes on prison visiting rooms as liminal spaces, 'A significant contribution of carceral geography is in advancing the understanding of the spatiality of prison visiting. Criminologists and prison sociologists recognise the liminality of visiting space'; Comfort (2003, p. 80) described a 'border region of the prison where outsiders first enter the institution and come under its gaze', theorising this space as one in which visitors became subject to 'secondary prisonization' as a collateral effect of incarceration, 'a liminal space, at the boundary between "outside" and "inside", where visitors convert from legally free people into imprisoned bodies for the duration of their stay in the facility' (p. 86). Codd (2007, p. 257) similarly described 'liminal space' in which prisoners' families 'are not entirely prisoners; however, they are within the prison establishment and thus defined as not entirely free either' (Moran, 2013b).

Seeing how the 'total institution' is becoming more and more like a Swiss cheese, both in terms of practical contact with society and family, and through technology and the forthcoming inclusion of the internet, or at least an intranet, it is still a lot less permeable than its siblings; the airport, the factory, the gym, the school, the hospital, the clinic, the army barracks and the further types of disciplinary institutions/controllable space which Foucault examines in his *Discipline and Punish*.[32]

Using the city as a metaphor for the prison is also part of our semi–self-delusion in saying that 'I am such a complex human being. I need a whole city (whether real, or ephemeral (the internet)) to meet my various needs'. I am writing this from the comfort of a city, where I can meet and never meet again, where I can potentially have every wish fulfilled and where there will always be a pocket of like-minded people whatever my field of interest is.

Architects sometimes move on to become city planners. Finding a larger canvas this way. Le Corbusier's massive project to cleanse Paris, called 'The City of Tomorrow,' and his 'Capitol Complex in Chandigarh', India's first planned city, come to mind. Also how Lúcio Costa, together with Oscar Niemeyer, started with an empty field to construct the new capital of Brazil, 'Brasília'. It is supposedly in the shape, only imaginable from above, of an aeroplane, a symbol of modern times. Brasília was designed to have a 'Monumental Axis' and a 'Thoroughfare/Residential Axis'. It is also divided into numbered blocks and sectors for specified activities, for example, the 'Hotel Sector', the 'Banking Sector' and the 'Embassy Sector'.

---

[32]Michel Foucault, Discipline and Punish: The Birth of the Prison, Allen Lane, London, 1977, Translated by Alan Sheridan. I find it interesting to note that the original French edition is called Surveiller et Punir: Naissance de la prison. Surveiller is much closer in translation to 'monitor, control, watch, guard, mind, stake', than 'discipline'.

Here, we could draw a comparison with the wings of a prison, and the total institution, and exchanging Hotel/Banking/Embassy for Vulnerable Prisoner Units/Education/Laundry. Also as Brasília is landlocked, difficult to access and clearly not the location for an 'organic' capital (traditionally determined by waterways, trade routes, sites of ceremony, etc.), it makes some sense to think of the city in this example and a prison, in general, as an isolated unit.

Deborah Che's article 'Constructing a Prison in the Forest: Conflicts over Nature, Paradise, and Identity', where she talks about rural economic development, scoring political points and to some extent colonisation, comes to mind.

> Prison expansion can be considered a geographical solution to deindustrialization and globalization. Post-industrial prison development to address declining productive industries in amenity – rich rural areas, however, can catalyze struggles over shifting rural land uses, ideals, and identities. (Che, 2005)

Is a prison, or a prison city, then the best stage for the actors within it? The space with the best flow? Is stemming the flow part of an excellent design? Is bad design good design? As in, if the function of the prison is not optimal, is that in itself optimal? I think the non-functioning aspect is part of the invisible punishment. Prisoners are not only kept in one space, one place, for a meted out time. They are also usually kept in conditions that, although far from medieval, are usually not optimal in making recovery easy, shrouded in perplexities and frustrations.

The stuff of structural dreams and mood boards seems a lot more interesting to talk about, and a lot easier to invoice for, than ensuring that reform is easily facilitated, and that basic needs are met.

*

The planned city is interesting as a concept, as the circle as a gesture of both inclusivity and protection is often employed. 'Washington Circle' appeared in planner Pierre L'Enfant's early maps of the American capital toward the end of the 1700s. Washington also took its design cues from Versailles, the seat of an absolute monarch. It is maybe a good example of a planned capital and the avenues, sight lines and ease of transport of goods for a burgeoning middle and upper class. This ease of transport also facilitates the movement of troops in and out of the capital, to protect heads of state or quell uprisings. At the beginning of his term in office, President Nicolas Sarkozy invited city planners and urban thinkers to talk about the future of Greater Paris. Architect Roland Castro put forward a proposal which would have moved the presidential palace to the outskirts of the city,[33] an egalitarian gesture that has yet to materialise.

Canberra is another planned capital, where the circular is more obvious. It is interesting to compare Walter Burley Griffin's 'Plan of Canberra as Finally Revised

---

[33](https://www.nytimes.com/2009/06/14/magazine/14paris-t.html)

and Accepted', illustrated by (early female 'starchitect') Marion Mahony Griffin's water colour visualisations, with the present-day bird's-eye view of the Australian capital. I've never been so can only talk about the maps, what it looks like from an elevated viewpoint, but a lot of the circular elements, basins and residential suburbs, as well as parks and streets that appear in the plan are still visible, often with the same use, or repurposed, or inspired by the circular foundations of the past. Collins Park, Manuka Oval, Nabin Circle Park, Woden Cemetery to name a few, as well as a long succession of crescent-shaped streets.

Keeping to the round subject, there are almost endless examples of circular cities/towns. Early Baghdad was known as the 'Round City' (Madinat al-Salam), and Circleville, Ohio, a town created in 1810, had a starting point of a circle 340m in diameter, with the courthouse in the middle. Anthropologist Claude Lévi-Strauss has written extensively on older examples of Indigenous peoples' circular villages, most famously on the Bororo villages in his *Tristes Tropiques (1955)*. Auroville, an experimental township in India, is another, with a master plan called 'Galaxy'.

Other round jewels in the round crown of architecture include Palmanova, just outside Venice, Italy. It is a small town with a central square (although the irony is apparent when the square is a circle) and circular ramparts. Walking around the town navigating is immediately made more complicated by the ingrained sense of linear blocks we are used to from newer cities. Or if not straight, then at least the complete mishmash of streets we are used to and enjoy in medieval towns. This pattern characterises urban spaces made for pedestrian traffic, so we travel slower, we are not in the path of vehicles in the same way and we don't know quite what is around the corner – the opposite feeling of the open, straight roads of Haussmann and others. Trying to find a shortcut within a concentric street plan is really confusing and also very liberating.

Moving into the visionary/unbuilt, there are several notable circular plans. For example, 'Sforzinda' the ideal city, named after Francesco Sforza, then Duke of Milan, designed by Renaissance architect Antonio di Pietro Averlino (c.1400–c.1469), 'Civitas Veri', or City of Truth, by Bartolomeo Del Bene, Thomas More's 'Utopic Island' community, as well as the central building in the painting 'The Ideal City' of Urbino, by Luciano Laurana, as well as buildings in 'The Ideal City' of Baltimore, by Fra Carnevale.

Whether it is a planned or a dreamed ideal, the circular seems to act like a magnet on the iron filings of an architect's ideas.

The Ethics of a Building

The ubiquitous 'all persons fictitious' disclaimer states: 'The story, all names, characters, and incidents portrayed in this work are fictitious. No identification with actual persons (living or deceased), places, buildings, and products is intended or should be inferred'

Is a building just a building? An empty shell we pour emotions and ideas of practical use into? Or is it more than that? Or less? While writing 'The Out', dealing with the fictitious HMP Cromlix, and with 'A Circular Argument', I have in effect been spying on a series of buildings, as if I was planning a prison break. I have been acting as if I was engaged in an anthropological project, void of humans, which is impossible, but that's part of the self-delusion needed to do the work and not to veer too far into sociology, which is not my field. There's no denying it though, the prisons I have visited are full of people and some of them are indirectly present in this work.

And taking the analogy further, is an architect a maker or an imitator? A 'carpenter' or a 'painter'? '[...] in The Republic Book 10 (Plato 1961), [...] Socrates speaks about the Form of the bed, and then the carpenter's bed as a secondary image and, thirdly, of the painter's representation of the bed as at yet another remove from reality' (Irwin, 2016).

I have been acting in the hope that the prison buildings I have looked at are in some ways perfect representations of their kind of building. Time and power represented in concrete. In the hope that I am not dealing with a vulnerable building, but a solid mass of law enforced correctly. Perhaps drawing on Plato's discussions about 'form' and the 'perfect bed', while keeping in mind that artists were banned from Plato's Perfect Republic. There would have been no Impressionists in Canberra, no sharks preserved in formaldehyde in Brasília, no Louvre in his perfect republic.

> [...] poetry – the right sort of poetry – will be a pervasive presence in the society he describes. Yes, he did banish Homer, Aeschylus, Sophocles, Euripides, Aristophanes – the greatest names of Greek literature. But not because they were poets. He banished them because they produced the wrong sort of poetry. (Burnyeat, 1998)

After a period of disuse, architect Rem Koolhaas proposed a renovation study of the Koepelgevangenis Panoptical Prison in Arnhem, the Netherlands.[34] The first thing that strikes you is that the images are beautiful. There are several visual parallels with the presentation sketches that helped Marion Mahony Griffin secure the contract for Canberra. She was an early member of the Prairie School, which would have affected her choice of palette. I don't know what school the artist who painted the Koepelgevangenis images considers themselves to be part of, but there's an abundance of light, the images almost washed out, presenting a happy and sunny quality, which I for one associate with Australia, and not so much a Dutch prison.

At the time of writing, the prison building is called FutureDome and is used for events and houses escape rooms under the moniker of 'Prison Experience', receiving good reviews on Tripadvisor. Maybe this will happen to more prisons, at least if the actual buildings are 'beautiful'. This should also be viewed against a backdrop of several prisons in the Netherlands closing, as the jail population is shrinking.[35]

---

[34](https://oma.eu/projects/koepel-panopticon-prison)
[35](https://www.theguardian.com/world/2019/dec/12/why-are-there-so-few-prisoners-in-the-netherlands)

Were you to put these images next to the digital watercolour presentation of the new Le Louvre[36] in Abu Dhabi, there are some striking resemblances. In Le Louvre, the elements of the buildings are quite scattered, the impression almost chaotic, in terms of the bird's-eye view. For shade, or continuity, or for aesthetic reasons, the architects have put a lid, the pileus of a mushroom on top of the collection of buildings. Between the 'Temppeliaukio Church' in Helsinki, Finland, Koepelgevangenis prison and the gleaming new centre for art in Abu Dhabi, there's a thread that to me speaks of the gaze, either from above or from within, onto the viewed.

As a fiction writer, I am a spy. So to assemble a series of physical, yet unconnected details, into an imaginary world is maybe the only way to go about my work to act much like an architect with free reign, in the pursuit of a folly. An unlikely real-life scenario for an architect, and if possible, probably very costly for everyone involved. I have been trying to catch the oleaginous idea of incarceration as it leaps from 1789, to Bentham, and into the isolation cell of a Supermax prison and beyond, steering away from specifics, real names, or identifiable features. All the while trying to be aware of my role as an observer, onlooker, noter – writing down, squirreling away for future use. While visiting prisons I have often been half in the world and half on the page, which coincidentally is the same formula I apply to the rest of my time.

Practice, influences and copying (intentional or otherwise) are a thorny issue. In the practice-based element of this work, I have based the rhythm of the chapters, and to some extent, the length of the chapters, on those of one of my favourite writers. In a sense that's neither here nor there for a reader and it's not obvious in any way, but it has been useful as a waymark for me. Should I even be mentioning this? Am I situating my work in a cultural context or am I xeroxing? Am I playing around, am I sketching, planning, constructing? Am I as faintly ridiculous as the G/god's-view-like architects I have been mocking above?

How does fiction work? There's the suspension of disbelief, the authorial reticence, the bird's-eye view of the author. There's chance, planning and everything in between. Sought out serendipity and pure luck. A piece of writing, a novel for example, is an edifice, an absolute with a beginning and an end. This applies both to time and space (while reading), but the time aspect also applies to its physical life cycle (even though we think of the cloud as eternal) and its cultural life cycle (few people still read Ethel Lilian Voynich's *The Gadfly*, despite its success when it was published in 1897). A piece of writing is a construction in the same way as a building is. We need an entry point, we need pointers, we need exits, and the pace is dictated by someone with full access to the complete idea, the overview.

Authorial reticence is the 'deliberate withholding of information and explanations about the disconcerting fictitious world'.[37] This withholding is what makes us want to finish a book. I think this is exactly one of the functions of the building that the SPS uses to great effect to control an unruly population. Prison is arguably so alien to most of us, and to the natural state of humans, that it is almost a 'disconcerting fictitious world'.

---

[36](http://theartnewspaper.com/interview/the-architect-of-louvre-abudhabi-reveals-his-sources-of-inspiration)

[37](http://www.academia.edu/35323229/magical_realism.pptx)

There is a lot of withholding of information, but more to the point, I think there is, from the SPS, or any prison authority, a desire for uncertainty and grey areas. There can't be too much routine or too many clear-cut rules. The same staff can't go on shift at the same time every day, the gym might not be open today, letters might be delayed and visits from family members might be cancelled. Not necessarily out of malice. This is sometimes just the gravel in the bureaucratic machine. It is also done as a safety measure in the belief that if everything is predictable, prisoners will find cracks to exploit. This results in a strange experience going in as a visitor and for the staff too. To work in a building where a certain amount of uncertainty and authorial reticence is built-in, makes for an odd, fictitious world, for everyone.

In writing (mainly fiction), we concern ourselves with 'external consistency' (= as in the real world. For example, humans can't fly) and 'internal consistency' (= any rules established should continue to function as they did previously, unless we are notified. For example, Superman can fly, unless...). Stories move in time, both in the action and in the actual reading page after page. From early on, we are trained to expect external and internal consistency from life as well as from stories. These two elements are heavily undermined in the prison.

In creative writing workshops, both within and outside the prison walls, people are often classed, or class themselves, as 'gardeners' or 'architects'. Either you start with a messy, organic patch of land, and you order it. Weeding, watering, raking your story until it makes sense to you (think Château de Villandry). Or you might start with a more blank space where fictional building blocks rise from carefully poured foundations to spiral, often beautifully, out of control (think Gaudí). This set of self-images may or may not be helpful, but to some extent it is interesting to see that the urge to create order from chaos versus creating chaos from order is how we see the making of a novel or equal project. That we, in this twin metaphor, feel compelled to control nature, with a plan and an action plan, or go about the task coolly detached, armed with measurements and the precision tools needed for the job, clutching a master plan, operating in white space, making onto the white page. In both approaches, we the makers are standing up, over-looking ground to be mastered and creatures to be compartmentalised and housed in accordance to our wishes.

I think it is interesting to note that there is a book called *Foucault for Architects*, as part of a series of books, also containing
Kant
Merleau-Ponty
Virilio
Lefebvre
Goodman
Foucault
Gadamer
Derrida
Benjamin
Bourdieu
Bhabha
Irigaray
Heidegger
Deleuze & Guattari
...for Architects.

This series exists maybe in a Word Search–like effort to capture the main philosophical sharks trawling the imagined waters of building sites past and future. There's a lot of interest for what is strictly speaking not necessary for buildings. CAD/CAM can't kill the spirit. The field of Architectural Phenomenology[38] is far from outmoded despite us now being supermodern, usually turning away from phenomena.

A large part of writing is observing in the first place. A large part of controlling is watching. To briefly turn to Foucault's description of disciplinary power in his Discipline and Punish as 'hierarchical observation, normalisation, and examination', is maybe to see parallels in writing and in prison design. Echoing the intention to create the perfect environment for a drama where the full cast can be observed, as they act out their time on top of a tabula rasa. In distilling human characters down to manageable units fulfilling predestined functions, normalising them, 'transforming the confused, useless or dangerous multitudes into ordered multiplicities', in Foucault's words (Fontana-Giusti, 2013), sitting back to examine what happens when your characters collide. This control through gaze is similar in fiction to the one used in heavily CCTV:d environs.

> *As we all know, prison is not exciting, or anything like what you see on TV.*
> *It is not Prison Break or Escape from Alcatraz, it's long periods of*
> *nothingness. Of boredom and apathy. Is there any sense of how the creators*
> *of the series have dealt with that? With the reality of incarceration?*

Question by delegate at the 2nd International Conference for Carceral Geography, in Q&A session following talk by Dr Aylwyn Walsh (Applied Theatre, University of Leeds) on 'The Breach, Fugitivity as/and resistance in Orange is the New Black'.

---

[38]A discipline centred on place, movement, supergraphics, regionalism, dwelling and building materials in their sensory aspects.

HMP Shotts – 55°49′37.7″N 3°49′36.0″W

A Stationary Train, Moving at 1079252848.8 km/h

Paul (not real name), one of the men I've chatted to in-between activities in HMP Shotts, describes his sentence, or more to the point, the strategy he has devised for coping with his sentence, as a journey. His cell is just a carriage. As anonymous as if he was on a train. If this is the case, he can't change it/the view/the speed/the other passengers/or any of the conditions really. He can't alter or better anything, so he doesn't waste emotional or physical energy trying to do so, which carries with it the positive by-product of not having to deal with the disappointment when he fails. Another side effect of this is the time he uses up, productively it can be argued, undertaking journeys inwards, busying himself with trying to come up with various kinds of stratagems to cope. Translating time into space back and forwards, over and over, into various modes of transport he is observing the glitches. As when you translate a word into another language and then translate it back to the original, only to find it has changed a little, widening your understanding of the word and of language as a whole.

The image of the train carriage is useful. When the world speeds by just outside, you can turn a lazy eye to it, skimming over time passing, making sure that the outside stays out of focus and remains of little importance. As long as linear time and distance proceed outside, you don't have to emerge out of the daze to engage. Perhaps at the beginning of the journey, it might be difficult to switch off the normal awareness of life, and towards the end of the stay in the carriage/cell, the external world (events, consequences, the weather, etc.) will come into sharper focus. Faced with the bulk of a journey, or a sentence, it is probably a good idea to locate a coping mechanism.

Sarah Armstrong talks about the prison being a corridor, rather than a holding pen (Armstrong, 2018). A place where inmates are making a (slow) transition rather than being warehoused. That's not to say that the corridors are straight. Many of the imaginary corridors are circular. They are sites where you might circulate in space, but progress in time. 'Corridors, like any other built space, communicate a social purpose and narrative' (Yanow, 1998). 'Spaces of circulation are central considerations in prison architecture. Their design and positioning are recognised as crucial to security and control' (Matthews, 2009).

'This narrative [of the sentence] enlists time to discipline docile bodies; the physical organisation of the prison into cells is essential to this' (Armstrong, 2018). 'The linearity of past, present and future dissolves into a plurality of oppressive temporal scales of numbing repetition within the day and variability over the sentence. These different examples of waiting and mobility in prison reveal temporal flows which are multiple, nested, distorted and disciplining' (Armstrong, 2018, p. 141). Anyone stuck on a stationary train, delayed, with no information, might know some of this wait. Multiply that feeling by 10+ years and we would still get nowhere near the hopelessness imparted by a long sentence. 'The cell is where the prison's purpose, and purposelessness is found', says Armstrong (2018, p. 134).

When we travel, we spend time on moving in space. The faster we can go in time, the further we can travel in space. In normal conditions, a prison is almost exclusively a place centred on the spending of time – 'doing time'. 'Space' too is an interesting concept to consider here. On the one hand, it means something definite, measured and absolute – especially in terms of living space where every square foot is accounted and paid for. On the other hand, it means the cosmos, infinite space, ever expanding, the opposite of confined space. I don't know enough about time in space, but life on Mars, where a year is 687 Earth Days, would/will be very different. That's not even addressing the fact that '[b]ecause astronauts like the ones on the International Space Station (ISS) are moving so quickly, they're also aging a bit more slowly than the rest of us. Due to a principle of physics known as time dilation, after a six-month stint on the ISS, returning astronauts are just a tiny bit younger than the rest of us'.[39] Space turns out to be as unpredictable and messy as time, and their relationship very complex.

To set out on a journey, to encounter something, to come back and tell the tale, is deeply embedded in the human psyche (Campbell, 1968). Whether that's going to the shops for milk, or to the moon for rock samples, on our return, the same method of storytelling applies. The cause and effect, the linear movement and display of events are so inextricably rooted in us that we apply the techniques of storytellers in our daily life without much reflection. Here too, we use the circular structure. We set out and return, now able to use the experience, and the knowledge gained from the tribulations.

Stories are our way to make sense of the world and to feel that we build on knowledge and progress. Myths are told in the past tense for a reason. The hero/ine returns with the treasure and takes their place at the (round) campfire to tell the story, for a reason. They impart wisdom onto those too scared to set out. Sometimes, the cautious are right, and you could argue that some 'heroes' should never have set out on their journey.

We progress automatically in time, but neither in prison nor in 'real' life do we always progress in the positive connotations of the word. Rust and entropy never sleep. To push the metaphor of the train carriage into a more modern and, thus, faster sphere, something that uses time/space better, one can look at the airport to see how it compares to the prison:

> The airport is a new and quintessentially twentieth-century building type. Composed principally of airfield, control tower, hangars, terminal(s), administration and service buildings, as well as runways and access roads, it is a totally designed and extraordinarily complex architectural space. It is also a special social environment, and the airport functions as a modern heterotopia of both freedom and control. Flight and its land-based expression of the airport, particularly the passenger terminal, are integral to modern life, and, as this dissertation discusses, played an important role in the constitution of modernity. (Eggebeen, 2007)

---

[39] (https://science.howstuffworks.com/humans-age-in-space.htm)

In an alternate reading, this becomes: The prison is a new and quintessentially nineteenth- and twentieth-century building type. Composed principally of cell-blocks, corridors, holding areas, yards, control tower, areas off-limit for prisoners, visiting area(s), perimeter walls, administration and service buildings, as well as access roads. Historically often close to mines, forts and road construction sites. It is a totally designed and extraordinarily complex architectural space. It is also a special social environment, and the prison functions as a modern heterotopia of both containment and control. Crime and its time-based expression of the prison, particularly the cell and the corridor, are integral to modern life and, thus, play an important role in the constitution of modernity.

To contrast further: 'Prisons are normally surrounded by fencing, walls, earth-works, geographical features, or other barriers to prevent escape. Multiple barriers, concertina wire, electrified fencing, secured and defensible main gates, armed guard towers, security lighting, motion sensors, dogs and roving patrols may all also be present depending on the level of security'.[40]

Which might become: Airports are normally surrounded by fencing, walls, earthworks, geographical features, or other barriers to prevent people escaping either from an aeroplane or onto an aeroplane. Multiple barriers, concertina wire, electrified fencing, secured and defensible main gates, armed guard towers, security lighting, motion sensors, dogs and roving patrols may all also be present depending on the level of security and depending on whether the country is a desired one to escape to or escape from.

The similarities between the mechanics of air travel and a prison sentence are many. The wait, the uncertainty, the fear of the future, the fact that you are quickly reduced to a number, that you are assigned either a cell or a seat – a physical place for a limited time – the same as everyone else. Whatever privileges or preferences you have in normal life might or might not be taken into account as you are assigned a temporary space in time. Aisle or corridor, chicken or beef? Upper or lower bunk, instant coffee or tea? As you travel in space and time, small choices take on great importance.

A similar way of viewing this relationship between air travel and prison time can be applied to the prison as a building and the airport as a building. Both are complex architectural constructs, with wide-stretching ideas of control and far-reaching concepts of fear and freedom surrounding them.

'Airports are gateways that differentiate. [...] Forcing people through these bottlenecks means that those in the corridors of power may exert influence over those in the corridors of movement' (Adey, 2008) which, of course, can also be said about a prison.

When you fly, or when you're in prison, you might put your trust in a pilot, a governor, or a God. You part with your belongings, on the promise by the same authority you submit to for the duration of your journey that your things will be

---

[40](http://www.newworldencyclopedia.org/entry/Prison)

returned to you, in the same shape and form as when you left them, at the end of your journey. In modern criminological and sociological language, a prison sentence is sometimes referred to as a journey (a blunt and imprecise term), and here again, the architectural image of the corridor seems to fit better than the cell – an image permeated with stasis.

I don't know anything about Paul in his cell carriage, in his assigned seat, but I know it's probably many years before he can travel anywhere. On leaving a prison, I had been visiting the same sense of guilt and relief would often wash over me. I was free. I was incredibly privileged. I was on my way home to a loving family. I was probably upholding certain class structures and by going along with the wider system probably barring others from attaining the same luxuries of food, travel, security, financial, or other, that I was enjoying. Above all, I enjoy a lot of agency, which has been entrusted to me through no merit other than my birthplace. I don't have an offshore account, nor did I go to private school, I am mostly a struggling novelist, but I often forgot and re-realised that I was closer to those almost pantomime status symbols than I was to the structures that had put some of the men and women I have met in prison. Control is complicated, so is complicity.

An SPS Salon[41]

In HMP Shotts,[42] a prisoner will spend the lion's share of his (it's an all-male prison) sentence. The middle chunk, the repetitive slog, the best years of his life. As a result of being in one place for many years, those who are able to engage with the educational unit can start a degree, a Masters, a PhD, and finish them. And still have years to go.

Together with criminologists and social science researchers from a number of universities, I have been attending a para-academic reading group in Shotts, and similar groups have been set up in a number of prisons across Scotland. In Shotts, the group is open to the prisoners who are the furthest along in their respective

---

[41] A salon is a gathering of people under the roof of an inspiring host, held partly to amuse one another and partly to refine the taste and increase the knowledge of the participants through conversation. These gatherings often consciously followed Horace's definition of the aims of poetry, either to please or to educate (aut delectare aut prodesse). (https://en.wikipedia.org/wiki/Salon_(gathering)). We aim to do both.

[42] 'Shotts prison was built in 2012 and is a prison for long term adult male offenders with a capacity of 553. The prison is situated in countryside south of the M8 motorway near the Lanarkshire village of Shotts. The prison seeks to provide a secure, safe, caring and productive environment, while providing opportunities for offenders to come to terms with their sentences and address their offending behaviour. Shotts also houses the National Integration Centre (NIC) within its boundary. The NIC holds approximately 60 adult male offenders who are in the initial stages of sentences of eight years or over and prepares them for eventual movement to mainstream prisons. It provides a supportive regime for those sentenced to life or eight years or over during the first six to nine months of their sentences'. (www.sps.gov.uk/Corporate/Prisons/Shotts/HMP-Shotts.aspx).

course of study, but in reality probably to anyone who fancies coming along, security measures permitting. The basic premise of the group is to quite randomly pick one or two academic papers or material of similar intellectual weight that no one is an expert on, to read and discuss. As we, the visitors, are the ones who have access to the internet, it is usually us that bring in the material, but at the end of every session, we discuss the next topic in as democratic a way as possible. So far, we have dissected Haitian Vodou, obesity, football, the creation of the universe, Palestine, romance, universal basic income, to name a few topics. Since the topics are picked out of the blue, the hierarchy of knowledge is halted for the period of time we are in discussion, and what's in the paper, and how it can be interpreted, remains the focal point. This kind of round table discussion so established and taken for granted in academia and in other sectors too, although it might be called something else (think tank, meeting, etc.) is something that is harder to achieve and take part inside a prison. To put personalities slightly to one side, to suspend certain differences, to politely argue, convince, listen and invite the possibility to be convinced in turn is a very difficult, but fundamental process. To circle a subject, no one is personally invested in, or an expert on, except for by chance, in the hope of shining a new light for entirely selfless reasons and everyone's gain is a powerful experience. I found it to be a forgotten privilege in the lives of those of us who spend our days outside a prison. To be heard and to have one's opinion respected is integral to the human experience and to the fragile value we assign ourselves. I suspect it's not always easy for a prisoner who has been sentenced to a long time, for committing a serious crime, to have their opinions, on whatever trivial/academic/personal matter, respected. Neither vertically nor horizontally in the official and unofficial power structures.

This is the 'recruitment poster' (paraphrased) that got me into the reading group:

A reading group…with a difference!
Academic Reading Groups in Prisons
Reading groups are an important element of the student experience, forming part of the foundation of building an intellectual community and fostering skills of critical enquiry and collegial interaction. Since July 2014 academic reading groups have been meeting in Scottish prisons. These bring together postgraduate students at Scottish Universities with mainly undergraduate students in prison who are working towards Open University degrees. Participants can come from any academic subject or discipline including arts and humanities, social sciences and STEM subjects. The groups meet monthly for two hours, and typically number around 8–10 people at each one, with a balance of inside and outside students.

The groups aspire to be peer-led and equal: selections of readings and the flow of discussion emerge from the group's own interest. No one is in charge, and all members should be motivated mainly by being part of a shared intellectual community.

Deepen your reading and analytical skills; have a chance to read exciting and important texts that inform your research; meet other students in your university as well as students from other universities; be part of a unique and supportive learning community.

[…]

I'm not saying the two hours the reading group come to Shotts, and elsewhere, are revolutionary, but it is a great feeling to be proving a point in action, by doing something that goes beyond reading and writing.

In the Salon, all of us are for two hours equals in a way that social structures, the class system, educational levels, geography of birth, luck and many other factors present in daily life, whether inside or outside prison, often prevent. All of us fumbling and uncertain, weaving in and out of guesswork and convictions, in the polka of people talking. All of us just human for a brief moment in time.

**The McMillan Round Reading Room, University of Glasgow
55°52′21.9″N 4°17′16.2″W**

An End

I have no concrete conclusion to offer. I won't be recommending anything to parliamentary committees or even to the SPS. If anything, I would like this reflective piece to shine a light on the liminal spaces we occupy knowingly and the ones we don't see, and more to the point, the liminal people, often the ones stuck in, or shuttled between, institutions.

Prisoners are kept away from the public eye, unlike medieval times when the punishment for a crime was often much more public – think stocks or the practice of chaining sinners to the church walls. This seclusion is part of the punishment, but it also widens the gap between outside society and the imprisoned. I think this sequestering sometimes makes it harder for those of us on the outside to come to grips with how fortunate we are and to recognise our own privilege.

I hope that by looking at the geometrical and the imagined circle, with sometimes personal eyes, sometimes abstract and philosophical eyes, I have contributed to the growing number of exciting writings on human, and carceral geography, and that I have contributed too to the hybrid, liminal, complex, rich and always evolving body of creative non-fiction.

I hope I have touched on conditions, and seats and scenes of power, on how small things can make a big difference when you have been stripped of all your power. Early in my research I heard Nick Hardwick CBE, the Chief Inspector of Prisons for England and Wales, speak. He didn't talk so much about legislation or to parole or not to parole, but he did circle in on details. In this case, the exact colour of a prisoner's towel: 'Grey, like porridge'.

In my work as a novelist, the other side of this work, this is exactly the kind of 'significant detail' I would focus on. As for Hardwick, the human connection struck me. The small sum and trouble involved in getting a prisoner a clean towel, and how much of a difference small things (for us out in free society) like a shower, deodorant, choice of food, fresh fruit, exercise, sleep – all the things we talk about contributing to sound mental health – would help make a huge difference within the walls. In the words of Dostoevsky:

> 'The degree of civilization in a society can be judged by entering its prisons'. (Dostoyevsky, 2004)

A circular argument
(Latin: circulus in probando, 'circle in proving'; also known as circular logic) is a logical fallacy in which the reasoner begins with what they are trying to end with. The components of a circular argument are often logically valid because if the premises are true, the conclusion must be true.

Part 2
The Out

A Circular Argument, 59–212
Copyright © 2021 Martin Cathcart Frödén
Published under exclusive licence by Emerald Publishing Limited
doi:10.1108/978-1-80071-382-620211022

Chapter 1

11.00 Sunday

It struck me that I didn't know how my niece's killer took his tea. Excusing myself to the girl at the till I jogged back to the car, stationary between pumps 7 and 9. Frank was fiddling with the controls of the radio. Classical, rock, panel discussion, rock, classical.

'Black, just black', was his answer. I nodded and started to walk back across the forecourt when I heard the electric whirr of the window.

'Actually four sugars', he said. 'If you don't mind?' Then he went back to trawling the airwaves.

Why him? The question echoed in my mind as I tried to pay, fumbling with the coins as if I was a tourist.

When I came back he had turned off the radio. Triangular sandwiches precariously balanced on our laps, a big bag of salt and vinegar nestled on top of the hand brake, Styrofoam cups of Tetley stewing, we sat in the car in total silence, my ears ringing. Frank prised the lid off his cup and poured in all six sachets of sugar I had brought back. Our eyes followed the traffic on the M77 as if we were at Wimbledon together.

I had thought it best to drive straight to Bournemouth and to avoid cameras and contact with the general, nosy public as much as possible. But after an hour of slow-moving traffic, us wedged in like sardines, my eyes were gummed up and my bladder was screaming for attention. So, despite my conviction that my ideals were more important than my discomfort, we had to stop.

I found it unthinkable to urinate in an empty bottle in front of Frank, though I was sure he had seen worse. Part of me didn't want to pull over anywhere too secluded, didn't want to leave him alone in the car where there were no witnesses. The same witnesses I was trying my best to avoid. I was balancing on a silk thread, spun by myself, suspended over a gorge of unthinkable proportions. Best not to look down into the abyss, I kept telling myself. If nothing else, stopping meant we were now stocked up on Yorkies.

I handed my cup to Frank and turned the key in the ignition. My sister's purple Twingo from 2003, with ripped upholstery due to her persistent love of cats, reluctantly came to life. Making sure the headlights were on, and that Frank was wearing his seatbelt, I pulled away from the floodlit sanctuary of the petrol station. After I found the fifth gear, which I don't think the car had seen many times in its long, sedate life, and settling into a monotonous hum, Frank placed my tea in the centre console. For a while I was busy overtaking lorries that had emptied Polish food and Dutch flowers onto Glasgow, and were now returning to the continent.

Frank asked if he could turn on the radio. I nodded and said 'Radio 3', and we were instantly rewarded with a sonata   the soothing voice of presenter Katie Williamson occasionally interspersed with strings, bringing a certain gentleness to the male bonding experience. I was blinded by oncoming high-beams when Frank turned to me, and all I saw was his big fist and his wide wrist tattooed with the face of the Madonna. He slowly crushed his now empty cup, looked me in the eye and said, 'Thanks for this'. I wasn't sure if he meant the tea, the lift or the whole insane, complicated, awful matter. Before I had time to formulate a question, he said, 'Mind if I sleep? I always get tired in cars'.

'Sure', I said, thinking it odd he would ask for my permission. We had talked vaguely about the journey ahead of us and he had agreed that the stupidest thing for him would be to go straight to his family, where he would be captured immediately. I was an unknown quantity for the police, as impossible as a chance encounter. The fact that I was taking him to somewhere unconnected to his previous life was also a bonus, he had quickly agreed. At the time he didn't ask what I was getting out of the escape, and I don't know if I could have explained the circle of anger and guilt I had living inside for such a long time either. In the letter hidden in the tunnel I had said I would drive the escapee to safety, no questions asked, and for the moment that seemed to satisfy Frank. Looking at his familiar face I felt both queasy and elated.

Making sure the needle stayed well under 70, and looking out over the undulating landscape, I soon heard him snore. In sleep as in life he seemed calm and unbothered. And I'm sure I looked composed too. Only my breath, heavy with the fumes of violent vomiting in the stall at the service station, and my racing pulse, were indicators we weren't just colleagues returning from a printer cartridge sales conference.

For a minute I considered crossing the central reservation, to slip through one of the gaps reserved for emergency vehicles. To swerve straight into one of the oncoming lorries. How quick. How easy. Instead I concentrated on the steps ahead, taking one at a time, like I have for many years. As the miles sang underneath the balding tyres, the odometer turned from a three to a four. I smiled when I thought Katie smiled, and swooned when she did as she dissected a short piece of Sibelius. I would have wrung my hands if I hadn't been so intent on holding the wheel at ten to two when she told us the moving story of Jenny Lind and Mendelssohn. Then Frank moved and I flinched.

I opened my window an inch in an attempt to dry the cold sweat gathering on my forehead from the excitement, the fear, the fact that my bowels were in an unreliable state. It helped a little, so I turned the heater on to max to counteract the cold September air rushing in. By nature, and trade, I'm a careful person, but not since passing my driving test in 1961 have I stuck so closely to the rules. If I got caught speeding or not indicating properly, the paragraphs of the Highway Code would be the least of my worries.

Reaching for my cup I felt a pang in my elbow. Years of squash have damaged the cartilage. I shrugged into the seat and tried to calculate how much longer the drive would last. At the moment we were on the motorway but my plan was to use predominantly A and B roads. This was a base line rule, which would be reconsidered if and when the need arose. We had only just left Glasgow but heavy traffic had slowed us down, hence the rest, and we had furthered the delay with a cup of tea. My calculations quickly floundered, the South Coast was still far off.

Frank was mumbling in his sleep but I couldn't catch what he was saying. Either way I'm not sure I would have wanted to know. He let out a long sigh. I could smell his breath and opened the window a little more. Made a mental note to buy a bag of sugar to keep in the car. Less conspicuous that way.

In an attempt to put some distance between us and our silent, concrete Perthshire ground zero, I decided to initially ignore my own rulebook, and use the motorway. We could have stuck to smaller roads and quieter resting spots from the start, but 'safety in numbers', 'hiding in plain sight' and other expired TA jargon told me to use cash and anonymous service stations: to travel swiftly but not carelessly. There would be enough time for us to be alone, but for now I thought it best to stay on the verges of society, drinking tea, driving. A double-act of bad decision-makers.

Chapter 2

11.50 Sunday

An hour or so later he was awake but he was saying very little. Mostly gazing out the window, possibly shocked by a world which moved, racing past his face, as opposed to the dormant view he would have been yoked with in prison.

'Why?' he asked all of a sudden.

'Not now', I said. 'Patience'. He shook his head, but as I was busy overtaking a Volvo 343 on its last legs, I couldn't address his reaction. Once we were back in the left hand lane, he seemed happy to be quiet, which was good. It was too early to lay bare my intentions and motives.

Avoiding my face in the rearview mirror while keeping an eye out for blue lights I tried to formulate a line of enquiry to straddle the everyday and the bizarre. Words that would escort the elephant in the cabin out of sight. To address the coincidence of Frank being *Frank* would maybe dispel some of my anxiety. Instead I ended up chewing on my bottom lip, and was even on the brink of asking him if he had any Vaseline, but stopped myself in time. The miles rolled by, oblivious to my plight and chapped lips.

The roads were still busy, the fields brown and green in equal measure. Old brick buildings were making way for new corrugated mega-sheds. Obsolete gas works would soon become arts centres or malls. Neither the economy nor the weather could make its mind up.

The rain made me glad we had settled on a coat with a high collar for my sister. She had phoned quite out of the blue a week earlier and said she wanted to meet up, a request as rare as Halley's Comet.

'Is there anything on your mind Janice?' I had asked.

'No, not really. Can't I just see my little brother?' She sounded tired.

'Of course, I didn't mean... But is there anything you need help with?'

'No, just a cup of coffee, some company for an hour. I'm tired of going to work, I'm tired of sitting in my house, and I am tired of the bus journey between the two'.

'That's fine. You have every right to be worn out. It's not even been a year'.

'A year next week', a croak in her already reedy voice.

'I know'.

When she called I had been at home, in my dressing gown trying to decide whether to go to Morrisons or Sainsbury's for my groceries. Sainsbury's is nicer, and a bit dearer, but at Morrisons there's a very affordable café and I could get breakfast and lunch there. They never mind you sitting for a while so if you can stomach a late breakfast and an early lunch you can feed two nutritional birds with one stone.

'So, how about Friday?' she said. 'Somewhere in town'.

'Isn't town really busy then? There seems to always be some sort of sale on'.

'That's why I'm going', she said. 'I need a new coat. Not a winter coat, but an autumn one. Summer is definitely over. I can feel it getting colder every day'.

'Can't help you there I'm afraid. You know how colour-blind I am'.

'No need. Coffee is fine. Shall we say quite early to escape the crowds?'

'Fine. Just not too early'. I've never been a morning person. Always happy to burn through the night though.

'They do a breakfast deal at John Lewis', she said, as if she went there all the time. And maybe she did. These days I knew very little about my sister.

Reluctantly, and only because she was my sister, I agreed to meet her at the eye-watering hour of nine. I hadn't realised she slept so badly.

Once we had both penciled the date into our mental diaries we talked about the weather and taxes and the election, without agreeing or disagreeing, until she said she had to go. I got the feeling she had wanted to talk about more important things, but hadn't been able to raise them. There had been little gaps between sentences where she had fallen silent. Or maybe she was watching TV? At one time I had known what she thought, but not anymore.

I ended up going to Sainsbury's. Not sure why, but I'm glad I did because they had own-brand baked beans on 2 for 1. Just outside there's a McDonalds where I got brunch. It all worked out in the end.

* * *

The John Lewis café was beige and its population fawn or mauve in equal measures, roughly divided down the gender line. There was a slight favour in the number of women as demographics don't lie. The tables were almost at capacity, the mess hall brimful of people too aged to sleep. I was a few minutes late. I presumed Janice would be present and correct already, so I stood in the middle of the big room and looked around for her. Like a lighthouse with a beam trying to break through a thick fog of old folk. My eyes strayed over octogenarians hunched over teas and Battenbergs, sucking at false teeth.

I'm not like them. I happen to be retired too, but of a different kind. I've always been quite the stirrer. I wear bright ties. I drive fast. I go without socks in my buckskin loafers. I'm still connected to the cultural life of this city and wouldn't have been caught dead in this overpriced mausoleum of a café if it hadn't been for my sister's explicit request. I took another slow spin, taking in the lavender paradise full of pre-war home comforts. Still nothing. I walked down one aisle and gazed out the large windows overlooking Buchanan Street. My mini tour took in the servers' station and the raised islands with three or four tables. I could appreciate the light and the sound of china soaked up by wall panels and the well-worn carpet. The effort to cram in as many punters as possible without making it too apparent, combined with the birch-effect chip board and wipe-down vinyl, was effective but faintly depressing in its lack of ambition.

I saw movement out of the corner of my eye and my first thought was that someone was having a heart attack, falling off their chair.

'Here, Cecil. Here'.

I must have looked past or through my sister at least three times in my sweep of the room. She had aged terribly since Jennie. I realised I should have made a point of seeing her, but the months had slipped by.

'Hi Janice, sorry I was a thousand miles away. What can I get you?'

She wanted a cappuccino in a glass, but nothing else.

'Got to watch my weight', she said.

'Why?'

'Don't know really. It's the done thing', she said and smiled weakly.

When I came back with a slice of millionaire's shortbread and two coffees she had forgotten about her promise. She promptly got a knife and cut the cake in two unequal halves, put the biggest one on a napkin in front of her and spread another napkin in her lap. She sipped her coffee and I drank mine. As I had been summoned from bed by her early morning agenda, I felt it was up to her to lead. But soon our cups were drained. Janice used her ring finger, empty since Christmas 4 years ago, to press the last crumbs of shortbread into a little Mayan temple of sugar before transferring the whole structure onto her tongue. I looked away. Tried to gauge the clouds, but there was no way to tell which way it was going to go. Rain now or rain in a bit. When I looked back Janice had folded her napkin into a miniature swan and was working on mine.

'I still see her you know', she said.

'Who?' For a fleeting moment I thought my sister had maintained an extramarital affair with a woman, and that this woman was the cause of the divorce.

'I still see my little girl. Getting on a bus, washing a special bra in the sink, warming up out on an athletics track. I go past Hutchie quite often and I always think I have seen her'.

'Jennie? You see Jennie?'

Janice nodded and looked down on her hands which had now completed my swan.

'And does it scare you?' I asked, not sure if people still attended séances.

'No. It's not like that. Not in a ghost way. Just memories being played out I suppose'.

'Have you spoken to anyone?' I asked, relieved she didn't want to hold hands over a Ouija board.

'I'm speaking to you'. She took a deep breath. I won't speak to Ken. I saw him at the funeral and so did you. That was enough for a lifetime. Still can't believe he brought that woman along'.

Keen to move Janice away from the subject of Ken, I racked my brain for other avenues to pursue.

I had loved Jennie, but not seen her much since she was a child. I realised I hadn't thought about her much since the accident. It was too much to consider, so I didn't.

'More coffee?' I asked, half rising. The café was a cacophony of cups set on saucers and the volume of the hall was steadily increasing due to hearing aids failing their owners.

My stomach was rumbling and I realised I should have bought more than shortbread. Half a piece at that.

'Don't you see Mum or Dad sometimes?' she asked. 'Doing things, or, I don't know, peeling an apple? Remember Dad used to eat the whole thing? Core and all, and Mum would always make a face'.

'I remember them. Snippets of conversation, certain movements, Christmases, the Norfolk holidays. But I don't *see* them'.

'Well, I still see Jennie and it breaks my heart. Every day'.

'Me too Janice. Me too. I'm so sorry'. I looked away in case she felt like crying. I have always felt that crying is a private matter.

Once she had recovered a little she said, 'I wanted to ask you if you wouldn't mind coming over sometime next week to help me clear out one of the rooms upstairs?'

'Jennie's?'

She nodded, done with swans, and rolled her napkin into a child's cigarette.

'That's a big step, but of course', I said.

She looked out of the windows. It had now started to rain.

'I'm thinking of getting a lodger', she said.

'Why? Are you short of money?'

'I'm fine. I could use the extra, but it's more for company than anything else'.

'I wouldn't be too keen on that'.

'You've always been more of a loner than me', she said. 'I'd like to give it a go. There are a lot of students looking for somewhere in mid-September so it'd be good to have it cleared out by then'.

From the pocket of my sports jacket – slung almost nonchalantly over the back of a chair, unlike the oldies' carefully folded coats – came the sound of Johann Strauss the Second.

'Hang on Janice. Sorry'.

I started a one-handed grapple with my jacket. The first two signals passed, the third too, and by the fourth I had located the phone in the inner pocket where I never usually put anything. By the fifth I was looking at a long, strange number. I decided to answer, if nothing else to escape my sister's tears, however justified.

'Hello, Cecil speaking'.

'It's Frank'.

'Hello, Cecil O'Malley here. Could you speak up a little? The line is quite bad'. I racked my brain for Franks but came up empty.

'I'm in Stirling. At the bus station'.

'Great. I'm at a café in Glasgow'. I said, voice dripping with irony. I was sick of these cold-calling quacks. 'How can I help you?'

'Hang on'. There was a shuffle on the line and what sounded like a brief struggle with a zip or something. Then the voice said, 'Griffin'. I felt sick, in an almost good way. 'It says here that's the code word', the voice continued.

Putting an index finger in the air I stood up and walked away from Janice.

'Are you recently...' I took a deep breath searching for the right word, *liberated?* I asked, voice now trembling. The voice on the other side of the line said he was, and all I could do was to stand by the servers' station and nod. The waitresses must have thought I was mad. I realised the man on the other side of the line couldn't see me and said, 'Ok, let's get you out of Stirling quick smart'.

'Good', was all this man said. This Frank. The line went quiet, apart from an atmospheric hiss, coming and going like waves on a shingle beach. I took a deep breath.

'Ok', I said. 'Are you listening?'

'Yes'.

'This is what will happen. Have you got the information pack in front of you?'

'I do'.

'I've got a couple of things I need to sort out. Do you think you can make it to the rendezvous point, that's "A" on the first photocopied map, by 10:30?'

'You mean the bus station in Glasgow?'

'When you put it like that it sounds quite pedestrian – but yes'.

'I don't know when the buses leave but it seems busy enough here'. His voice was deep. By all accounts English was his first language. Quite a heavy local accent, but not intolerable. 'Hang on', he said and disappeared from the line. A couple of breaths later he came back. 'I checked the board. There's a bus leaving in ten minutes'.

'Great. Grab something to eat, stay low and I'll see you later'. I thought for a second, then said, 'I'll be waiting by the stand you come in at, wearing a hard hat and a hi-viz jacket'.

'Magic', the man said, sounding amused for some reason. 'Seems like this is my best option. Unless you're weird, or the police'.

When I didn't say anything he said, 'See you after', and now I heard just how local he was. Then he hung up and for a couple of minutes I couldn't speak. The pulse in my ears was drowning out all other sounds so I pretended to be on the phone while I worked out what to do next. Once I had an idea I made a big show of hanging up. I walked back to the table where Janice was leafing through a catalogue. My world had started turning faster again and all she could do was to look at pages of Denby casserole dishes in all the colours of the rainbow.

'Sorry', I said. 'That was my mechanic. He rang to tell me I need an emergency MOT. Apparently I've expired..

'He rang you this early?' she said barely lifting her head from the pages.

'He's very good', I said. 'But I have to drop the car off today. Tomorrow will be too late. He's going away on his honeymoon and I'll get all sorts of fines'. I scratched my chin, as if I was thinking about what to say. 'Did you drive here?' I asked. I knew she had.

Janice nodded and said, 'I'm happy to follow you to the garage and then give you a lift home'.

x'We can do better than that. I just realised I never got you anything for your birthday and I'm going to ask you a favour, so if you can pick a coat in ten minutes I'll pay for it. How's that?'

'Well, I like to take my time with these things.'

'Live a little Janice.'

'It's alright. You don't need to', she said.

'I want to', I said, a little too loud. 'Also I'd like to borrow your car for a day, you always take the bus to work and back don't you?'

She nodded and put the catalogue back in her handbag.

'Great', I said, relieved she wasn't set against it. 'So once we've got you a coat, I'll put you in a pre-paid taxi and you give me the parking chitty and keys. I'll drive to my mechanic, he's very central. I'll walk back here and pick up your car and drive myself home. I'll bring the car to yours tomorrow or so'.

'Sure, that should be fine', she said, her mind probably racing with coat opportunities.

'Come on then sis', I said in a rush, the words stumbling on each other. I had never called her 'sis' before. 'Let's get you a coat, and get out of here'.

* * *

Once home I decided I had 10 minutes to shave. Despite my shaking hands and a solid everyman's reticence towards my mirror image I cut myself only twice. I quickly patched up my throat with newsprint just like my dad used to. I chose a clean shirt and a sombre tie, a comfortable tweed jacket and a pair of designer jeans I had worn long enough to soften.

Despite knowing exactly what I needed and consulting the laminated packing list I made up years ago and kept on a 30 mm nickel-plated key ring hanging in the wardrobe, I packed and re-packed until I was completely happy. I put the five clearly labeled suitcases by the front door where they looked at me expectantly, like dogs needing a pee. I wasn't hungry but forced myself to eat a lump of tuna mayo on brown and then brushed my teeth and put the toothbrush in the bin. I had packed a new one for the journey.

While packing I found myself thinking back on the events that had brought us together – me and the Frank I was meeting in just over an hour. It was many years ago and I had made sure not to dwell on the past in an unhealthy way. But now, with my calculated windfall about to appear in the seat next to me, I allowed myself to remember how the Scottish Home and Health Department, with Euan Kerr-Henley appointed as head architect instead of me, had stolen Cromlix from me.

Even in the 1980s I was never a total hedonist, but I had enjoyed life before the millennium. Now some of that excitement was coming back. It was almost too much to comprehend. A couple of days of medium discomfort would be a small price to pay for revenge and the flutters I was now experiencing. I just hoped that circumstances would allow for a bit more comfort that sleeping in ditches, eating gruel out of a mess tin and drinking rainwater out of a helmet, but I couldn't be sure.

One of the last things on my mental checklist was to phone Janice. Luckily it went straight to her voice mail.

'Hi, sorry', I said, 'one of my dressers has just collapsed, but I've found a new one at Homebase. Unfortunately, it's not available until the day after tomorrow. Would it be ok if I hung onto your car for a couple of days? Thanks'.

I hung up and turned off my phone. I didn't want the satellites tracking me so plugged it in by the toaster. That way any triangulated phone records would show that my phone, and by extension me, had been home.

I had been squirreling money away for years in preparation for this moment. Always getting £10 more than I needed out and immediately folding the note into a triangle to stop me from using it. The little triangles reminded me of the Tetra packs of milk we used on car journeys to Lowestoft as a family.

I had amassed the little triangles in a khaki bum bag in the wardrobe. No good leaving a trail of card transactions, no good making a great big withdrawal for the authorities to draw conclusions from. Like an intrepid explorer from a jumpy newsreel I cocked an imaginary pith helmet and buckled the bum bag. It was bulging with about three grand in cash.

I found myself whistling while putting my miniscule flat in order. I got the life jacket out of the hall cupboard and swaddled six bottles of white, kept cool in the fridge for as long as possible, in a blanket together with a pair of woolly socks. I got two baseball caps down from the shelf, one 'Cape Canaveral' and one 'New York Yankees'. I thought my guest could pick his favourite. If the hats made us look like tourists so much the better. Transience is a great cloak of anonymity.

I threw it all in a bag for life and added a box of old Malteasers. I put this last little pile of things between the storm door and my front door and went back into the flat for a last once-over. I checked the latches on the windows, the boiler, the dripping tap in the bathroom – I always keep a flannel underneath to muffle the drops – and the fridge door one last time.

I went down to the car with the first load of suitcases. Luckily no neighbours felt like talking today and soon the five cases sat snugly in the small boot of Janice's car, covered with a tartan blanket. I put on a pair of overly big sunglasses and set off, hands shaking so much I had some trouble finding the indicator, instead surprising myself with a violent couple of swipes of the wipers.

I decided to take a longer than necessary route to the bus station. Pulling over by the SAAB/Jaguar showroom on Maryhill Road, I felt I was coming full circle. There was a little chemist on the other side of the road and I ducked in for a last minute addition of two bottles of clear nail varnish.

'Hello Frank'. 'Welcome to the free world Comrade'. 'Bonjour. Comment allez-vous?' I practiced out loud in the car in preparation, until I got to Killermont Street. I pulled into the Concert Square car park, just by the bus station, with time to spare.

* * *

Now he was here, sitting slumped against the window of my sister's car, traveling along at 68 mph, oblivious to the world. Exhausted from breaking his chains, link by laborious link. He was the minotaur of my personal Knossos, but his mind had freed him.

Chapter 3

12.20 Sunday

It was only a few hours ago, but already our first meeting felt distant. I had been leaning against a metal railing, my posture masking my excitement, as the Stirling bus pulled in.

He was first off, eager. Big, unassuming, normal. Just some guy, newly woken from a bus nap, wearing the overalls I had provided. Putting on the same hard hat, lanyard and padded jacket I was wearing, marking us out as different, and as brothers.

He looked up. I knew him. And suddenly an oversized ice cube pushed its way down my throat. No, it couldn't be him. No, no, no! The coincidence would be too much to believe. I looked at my feet, detached from me as I could no longer feel my legs. I took 10 deep breaths; a technique I had picked up in Somerset. Once my breathing was less laboured I realised I was being tested. Nevertheless, I felt like I was falling off a sky-lift. I started to struggle out of my foreman's jacket, but quickly got tangled in the lanyard. My white hard hat fell on the ceramic tiles with a loud clang, blowing my subterfuge.

He saw me. Raised his hand, like a friendly donkey had come up to lick his hand. Nodded, as if we were old buddies. As if we had done a hundred of these hi-viz jobs together.

'Fuck'. The kind of language I never use, slipped out before I could stop it. All my planning would not be for naught, this I immediately promised myself. I would not jeopardise the mission due to some flawed social construct of guilt and innocence.

I would prevail. But what were the chances that *he* of all people would solve the riddle I had set in concrete? There was no one to answer that question. My mind was an anthill onto which someone had poured Coca-Cola.

Man up Cecil, I told myself and went over to greet the man, patting my helmet down onto my head. I could tell that he didn't remember me from the trial. He flexed his shoulders, and in a few strides he was right in front of me.

He hesitated. Pulled both his hands down his cheeks slowly. 'Are you Griffin?' he asked, looking out over the row of bus stands. Not meeting my eye.

'Yes. Well, I'm Cecil', my voice a stage whisper. 'You must be Frank?'

He nodded, visibly uncomfortable with his name being spoken out loud, then asked, 'What now?'

'Now we drive', I said. I gave him a banana and a Galaxy bar I had bought while waiting for the bus to come in. I swallowed a bit of phlegm that had come up and walked off, half hoping he wouldn't follow me, half hoping he would, and unsure of which of the two halves were the biggest. I tried not to look like I was in a hurry, or to dawdle. People, me included, hate builders who look like they're slouching. The soft whoosh of the sliding doors closing behind us was not unlike a breath. A first or last breath.

I was sure I had left the car on the second floor, but the shock of Frank had made my mind a little muddled. 'You did this to yourself,' I thought, trying to locate the car in the multi-storey, Frank's shuffling steps close behind me on the concrete steps. The walls of the stairwell floured with smuts and adolescent obscenities.

We were about to elope on a flying carpet, woven from an old mixture of pride and penance. I thought I had accounted for everything, but the known unknown of the prisoner's identity had managed to surprise even me.

By the third floor I was thinking back. The hit and run a year ago. The witnesses and the CCTV hunt. The Golf with a cracked headlight and a girl-sized dent in its front left bumper. The car was found parked, still running, in a housing estate not far from the Saltmarket and Gallowgate. Close to where Jennie must have stepped out without looking. Where she stopped forever. They found a man in the Golf. Not drunk, not jacked up. Just on his way home from work, just sobbing uncontrollably.

In court he had been more composed. I had been there, standing next to my sister. It was the first time I had seen Janice's ex-husband in years. I must have seen him at the funeral but I don't remember anything from it. He had lost weight and grown a salt-and-pepper beard. It suited him. After a very short deliberation Frank was led away. Never to be seen again, I had thought.

Eventually I found the Twingo on the fourth floor. I unlocked it and we got in, putting jackets and hardhats in kitbag #8 propped open on the back seat, never to be used again. In the same instant I pushed my excess emotional baggage under and closed the lid.

I decided to treat Frank like a house-trained tiger, an entity to befriend and be wary of at the same time, sitting next to me in the cockpit of the car. The next few days would be a litmus test of my true self. Properly executed, this trip would be my first ever, genuinely generous act. Armed with my kit lists and fueled by PG Tips I was sure to succeed.

* * *

We passed a long row of lorries when the rain suddenly increased from soft sprinkle to downpour. The sound of it woke Frank. I glanced at him and at first it looked like he had no idea where he was. Then he smiled. As if the weather was a blessing and not a curse. And for our purposes it was. Fewer people out and about, less easy to see things and faces clearly. Switching on the windscreen wipers I thought the rain water looked slow – thick somehow. It must be getting cold.

'Wish I'd checked the tyres before we set off', I said. 'I remember some kind of rule about sticking a coin into the thread of the tyre and if you can't see the Queen's tiara you'll be fine in sleet'.

Frank nodded. I don't think he knew what I was talking about. Neither did I in all honesty. I was just filling the air. I slowed a little and pulled into the left lane, letting faster and better equipped cars overtake.

'Where are you taking me?' Frank asked, his voice flat, his eyes curious. 'In the note it said that I had won a prize and that you'd whisk me away to France'.

'Well, at least we are going to Bournemouth', I announced proudly, as if the seaside town was the Vatican and Shangri-La rolled into one.

'I don't know anybody there', he said.

'Neither do I', I said and shrugged my shoulders.

'Where are we going after Bournemouth?' Frank asked.

'Eventually to a little place on the west coast of France'.

It's the same Atlantic Ocean we have at home but somehow it is so much nicer in a different country. The first time I was over in France I was looking at prisons, and so to be going back to the Continent for the concluding part of Cromlix felt logical.

To fill the silence, I said, 'This is my third trip down'.

He just nodded.

'The first time it was reconnaissance', I continued. 'The second time to stock the depots along the way with useful things. And to enjoy myself. I have been a hard-working, tax-paying man all my life'.

'Me too', he said.

'Sure, but I had just retired. So I wanted to travel a little. See the world', I said.

When he didn't say anything I asked, 'You like traveling?'

'We traveled a fair bit as a family and before all this I had my own business. It took me to some interesting places too'.

'What did you do?'

'I rented out heavy machinery. Pavers, diggers, drills, a couple of trucks and vans, that sort of stuff. I used to have a pretty nice office in Bridgeton'.

'What happened?'

'Accidents, nasty people, money. That's what happened'.

After a long time of his staring alternately at his wrist and out the window he asked, 'What did you do before you retired?'

I turned to see what he was up to, but the question seemed genuine enough. Then the road surface demanded my full attention so I said curtly, 'I built houses'.

'You a builder? No offence, but you don't look it'.

'Thanks'. I smiled. The years of squash had helped keep a stone or two at bay.

'I was an architect. I was the one who devised large parts of Cromlix', I couldn't keep the pride out of my statement. Even after all these years. 'Still am, I suppose. I get the RIBA newsletter in the post every month'.

'What did your dad do?'

I thought that was an odd follow-up question, seeing that I had designed his incarceration and his freedom, but decided to answer truthfully.

'He worked in a factory'.

'Did he own it or something?'

'Not quite, he was a foreman'. I had to execute two tricky manoeuvres on the slippery road while thinking about my economic history, something I try to avoid.

Despite making some money in the 1980s, then losing it, I think of myself as working class. At least I come from solid working stock. Before I was born my dad was at the docks for a while. He later became foreman at the McVitie's factory at Tollcross. Eventually he got a job with the Union, where he became quite close to being the head honcho. Then he had his first stroke, and had to stop working. By then we had moved to a bigger house and he made sure I could go to university. The first person to do so in our family.

Frank leaned forward a little, one hand on his seatbelt, trying to gauge the clouds by the look of it.

'He died almost twenty years ago'. I said.

Frank nodded twice, 'Sorry. Were you close?' he asked.

I decided to be honest. As the core of the project was full of Faust's 'Schall und Rauch', I felt it was best to be honest. In the confines of the car at least. I knew I was nervous and blabbering a bit, as if I had had too many spritzers on a sunny day, but couldn't help it.

'Yes and no', I said. 'I'm both close and quite distant to all members of my family. My sister is a lot older than me. This is her car, by the way'. Frank looked around the sparse interior and nodded. 'She had almost moved out by the time I was five or six'.

As I was the host I continued, 'I think I became an architect because I was bored and lonely. Both my parents worked, my mum was a teacher, and early on I was given a key on a shoestring to put around my neck. The teachers called me Latchkey kid, and for years I wasn't sure what it meant, but I thought it sounded like Sundance Kid, so I was pretty chuffed'.

I laughed at the memory and Frank joined in. 'I'd let myself in make a cup of tea with milk and two sugars and settle down to play with blocks or Meccano'.

Frank sat back in his seat, his meteorological curiosity seemingly satisfied.

If it hadn't been for the sudden journey and its heightened emotions, the floodgates of my subconscious would never have opened. I had spent a long time and a lot of practice restraining myself. I am fourth generation West of Scotland, not prone to tears.

'I used to have a huge box of Meccano', Frank said. 'I remember building one of those double-decker trams, and hanging it from my ceiling on fishing lines. Then one day it crashed down and hit my brother in the head. He still has a scar', he laughed, a deep rumble.

'I never made any vehicles', I said. 'Just houses, bridges and statues and things. In hindsight I was just playing, but at the time I was deadly serious. In the evenings I would hold exhibitions and talk about the buildings. I think my parents felt bad for being away so much and since I was in essence an only child, they often humoured me'.

Frank looked out of his window. The rolling hills, wind turbines dancing and his silence threatened to propel me into my own melodramatic reveries.

'So you made the tunnel?' he asked. Matter of fact, like I had expected. Philosophising is a luxury not afforded everyone.

'I think it was a bit more than a tunnel – but yes', I said.

'Thanks', he said. I thought there was more coming, but he fell silent and I decided not to push him. It was a strange situation, possibly the most surreal I've ever found myself in, and it was mostly my doing.

'There's nothing unplanned or accidental about this part of the city', I said. 'Look at that row of houses, for example. Reddish brick, fake timbering, PVC windows. An awful bungalow belt in various degrees of low and deceptively high density. All planned and just right. No deviation. Cities and nature left to their own devices are good at throwing up in-between bits. Conurbations and suburbias not so much'.

I cleared my throat and said, 'Human minds need chance or they wither', to no applause.

The rain had turned soft again, buckets of it sloshing over the windshield. I had the heater on full blast. It reminded me of family holidays. Looking back to a time when life was homework, scabby knees and building blocks, maybe I was still trying to recreate those quiet afternoons of serious play before my parents came home? Forever the nine-year-old, busy with construction, and then showing off.

I had kept up this folly through my working life. Before I retired I would tell my PA not to let any calls through between two and four on a Friday. Then I'd make myself a cup of milky, sugary tea and settle down to work on structural, or more artistic, problems. Real or imagined. For a dreaming architect they are both the same really. My Friday drawer was soon filling up with revolutionary ideas, never to be realised.

This might be my last trip, and if there was a rational force following us I had reasoned a few irrational choices might throw them off the scent. In order to shake off anyone trying to plot our journey from fragments of registration plate CCTV footage, I had made space in the itinerary for planned anomalies and known unknowns.

I had chosen the M77, slightly longer but a lot quieter than the M8. After Kilmarnock, we would head for Dumfries, later joining the motorway by Gretna. For no reason other than curiosity I had thought we could go through Moscow on the way down.

Chapter 4

13.00 Sunday

We sped by a golf course and it made me think. Back when my swing was still fluent I was pals with some boys high up the Scottish Office and elsewhere. One of my closest chums was a guy called Stewart who I played with at least twice a week. I remember this one time while changing from loafers to golf shoes, I saw him come over to my car at a half-run. That was something rarely seen in the more sedate Cawder Club members' car park. As soon as he caught his breath he started telling me about the problem he had with this prison project. We almost missed our tee-off slot. On the third hole we let a couple of pairs pass us by while he explained further and by the fourteenth I had made a proposition.

Sitting on a high stool in The Nineteenth Hole, having made sure I lost the game but paid for the drinks, I waited while he made a few phone calls in the lobby where there was a row of pay phones. I had fed him broken tea biscuits all through primary school. His family was always short of money, and he had been a scrawny boy. Now he was feeding me work. And he wasn't scrawny anymore, *au contraire*.

When he came back from the lobby, we shook hands and I called my secretary and had her fax over a contract to Stewart's headquarters at St Margret's House. Then we got a bottle of bubbly in.

The memory made me wonder if Frank had ever had real Champagne. When we made it to the coast I thought I might treat him to a bottle. At least Cava. The rain made it difficult to see much beyond the road and I was afraid we might aquaplane on my sister's worn tyres. I settled in behind a reliable sort of car, a Focus, the Titanium edition, and relaxed a little.

After the meeting with Stewart, I had toiled for a couple of weeks to submit a first draft of my plans for Cromlix. Since I had the contract I knew I would be able to bill for the time spent. In the meantime, the board members all fretted in their borrowed seats. Stewart was more antsy than some of the others. He kept calling me to ask how I was getting on. Apparently not all of them were on the same wavelength as him but they all knew it was too late to go back on their decision and they knew the guillotine of votes would soon swoop down on them. I wasn't too worried. Contracts last longer than board members.

I made sure I kept them roughly up to date. For a while I was part of it too, just not in an elected way. By the frequency of Stewart's calls I could tell the committee was getting desperate. Elections were looming, and strangely enough the coffers were bulging. The money earmarked for a new prison had just been unearthed and it was important that they made headway. Both to secure the future flow of funds, and to make sure they could show real progress before the press got hold of the numbers.

Initially I had been happy at my architectural practice. I spent my late twenties doing little projects here and there. A few bigger ones when I felt ready. Then the 1980s rolled around and I found myself being much more ambitious than I thought I was. I wanted money. I wanted to make an impression. Not only on people, but also on the city, and on the landscape. I did a couple of high-profile jobs for two big companies and then I was asked to help the Scottish Prison Service Headquarters, and more specifically the Building and Engineering Division, to design a prison. Well, Stewart asked, and I presumed he had the authority to do so.

Choosing to put myself forward for Cromlix and choosing to undermine its foundations, literally and philosophically, were the two choices which had put me and Frank together in the car.

I was sure the funds for the proposed prison were some kind of Whitehall hand-me-down. No one in the sitting department board had that kind of clout, but I had long ceased to dwell on where money came from, and where it ended up. Someone had told someone, who had told me to get on with it. In my own practice I was involved as little as possible with the debits and credits. As long as my invoices were honoured I was content to let other people do the parliamentary cattle wrangling. Why the prison had to be built outside Cromlix I didn't know, or care really. Maybe because land out there was cheaper than closer to the cities? Maybe someone high up in Perthshire had lost a bet?

The left indicator of the Focus in front of us lit up, its broken prisms signaling change, pulling me back to the present. Unfortunately, the driver took the exit for East Kilbride and I was now slightly lost for a trailblazer through the water. I didn't want to go any faster, but slowing down didn't make any sense either. Luckily a few folk came onto the motorway from the A726 and I was able to latch onto a Yeti, one of those boxy cars for people who think they transport a lot of stuff but actually don't. I was still committed to not using motorways, but in my mind the M77 wasn't a real motorway as it soon peters out into the A77. I was keen to leave Glasgow behind, and happy to be more *laissez faire* once in England.

I looked at my hands on the steering wheel, the tremble almost visible. Now that I was embarking on my pilgrimage to the Port Authorities cabin on the dock where foot passengers for the Jersey ferry parted with their escort, I was hoping that some memories would leave me be forever. Part of my penance would be to temporarily allow myself to think back on some of the events that had put me in the car with Frank. These recollections would be counted off like red and black beads on a well-worn abacus. The miles my Ave Marias. My belly rumbled loudly and Stewart, always hungry, came to mind. My mind was trawling a 1996 seabed.

'In the wrong hands these figures could easily sink us all', Stewart said one lunch over drinks, and all the guys, including me, nodded. He continued in a jovial tone, 'But no one apart from us knows, so if we go down I will find the person who ratted'. He looked around the room, slowly finding the eyes of every man, before raising his glass with a loud, 'Cheers'.

There were overdue promises and misspent research grants to be swept under the carpet. A lot of money had been spent, and that wasn't including all the drinks, restaurant bills and overnights. The wad of expense claim sheets some people handed in were as thick as novels.

There were trips to foreign prisons for a lot of the members of the committee, paid for by the taxpayer. Always to safe, sunny countries. No one was interested in the penal structures of Siberia or the Democratic Republic of Congo. I hadn't gone to Isla de Pinos in Cuba to look at Panopticons, but someone had. Instead I was stuck in Glasgow looking at secure sewage systems. I was working on getting an invitation from a friend of a friend's brother, a prison warden from outside Nantes, but it was looking unlikely.

A week later Stewart rang. 'Cecil', his voice on the phone was snappy, 'we have looked at your plans and we would like you to come in and present them. A formality really. How's Monday?'

'Monday's fine I think. I'll call and change my tee-off for a later one'.

'Good man', Stewart said and rang off.

In those days I was half pathos, half profiteer. It was a good dichotomy to cultivate in my line of business. Something big was happening, I could feel it. I remember shivering the whole way home from my office afterwards. It could have been the vodka tonics. They were very cold.

* * *

For the thousandth time I checked my speed. The orange needle was still quivering just under 70. The Yeti just ahead of us.

I was the perfect man for the job, but not for the reasons Stewart thought. In my spare time, or my spare time at work, which I usually billed for, I had been working on plans for the perfect prison for years. A place where people like my uncle could reside, and be punished, but not suffer unnecessarily. An ideal institution where inmates could walk the fine line between pain and boredom, between bettering themselves while also making sure they knew how displeased society was with them. I kept these plans in a drawer in my office. More than any infidelities this was my most guarded secret.

We were just passing Fenwick, where the M77 becomes the A77. No big difference, but people always seem to become confused by the change. This means they slow down, and I was forced to do so with them, despite knowing exactly where I was going. For the first time in a while I took my foot off the gas and changed to fourth gear. A lot of confused tourists in rental cars were trying to make sure they ended up at Prestwick. With the weather we were having I could tell they were desperate to go back to Barcelona or wherever they all came from. I was just as desperate as them to get away from Glasgow.

'Could we have a beer later on? Depending on where we stop'. Frank said, turning an honest-looking face to me. Like a beagle asking for a biscuit. 'I've been in for about a year, not completely dry mind. But a cold beer in my own time would be amazing'.

'You can do whatever you want. Just, please, help me not to drink. I'm pretty jumpy as you can imagine', I said.

It had been years since I had a drink, but I felt dizzy in the best possible way. I knew I was stepping over all kinds of personal boundaries men of my age, and his, should adhere to, but I didn't care. It was the same reckless feeling you get when you start on the second bottle.

'Don't worry', he said. 'I've got a few pals who are struggling. Drink's a bastard'.

'There's some nonalcoholic wine in the back. It's ok, but not great. I still miss the taste of a good, chilled Chablis', I said.

'Don't think about it. It'll only make it worse. Here, have a Yorkie', Frank said. 'I heard somewhere that it's the sugar you're addicted to more than the alcohol'.

I wasn't sure what to make of that, but I said, 'Sometimes I think I should have stuck to Meccano. My job was my downfall. It made me a drunk against my will'.

In the fields cows, in the air crows and a helicopter. At first I thought it might be watching us, but to my relief the helicopter soon turned away, heading north. I then saw that it was yellow, part of the squadron of flying doctors. It could have been anything really; a last-minute kidney transport or someone with a complicated fracture from falling off a slate roof on Arran, a prematurely born child in Carluke, late afternoon pilot school. I didn't care as long as it wasn't a thermal image camera pointed at us by the police.

'How are you feeling now that you're out? I hope it wasn't too traumatic for you. At least not the building'.

'It was fine', he said. Not sounding grateful in the least.

'At the time when I designed it I thought the best thing would be to build a lenient prison'.

'You built the whole thing? Not just the tunnel?' he asked, incredulous despite everything that had happened.

'Almost all of it'.

Frank nodded and waved to a long row of cows lined up. There was no way they could have seen him.

A bright red Lotus Elise sped past us. A woman who looked like she had just started uni, driving with one hand. Confident as anything. We both followed her with our eyes.

The car reminded me of Stewart. He used to drive something similar, something clearly the result of a crisis and more money than sense. Last I heard he was marrying someone half his age, in Nassau. Completely tasteless. He always was.

Despite the time that had passed I still hated him. What he, and the others too, did to me over the prison contract, was unforgivable. He knew full well I had invested much more than just the hours I billed for, but still he let me down. He wasn't there for the presentation, even though it was he who had asked me to come. I thought he would be on the committee but he had resigned from it not long before I was due to present my ideas. Hours before in fact, but never thought to let me know.

'Watch out!' Frank said sharply.

A van full of students and suitcases was veering into our lane, and I leaned hard on the horn. They never saw me, or heard me. I could see they were all singing along to music. Once they settled into the left hand lane I downshifted and the RPM metre shot up like a space rocket. The whine of the engine as I floored it in fourth was both deafening and delicious. I sped past the oblivious youths and settled back into a more sustainable pace.

Bending the law tickles but breaking it seemed unnecessary. Working your way through paragraphs, and deciding which are applicable to you, is something I realised long ago can have personal benefits. Both as an architect, and as a civilian, I learnt to navigate the sometimes stagnant waters of small print. Nothing wrong with that. That's what the French Revolution was all about. Bringing down the elite to the eye level of the public. Making sure the clauses applied to all classes, not just the people who came up with the laws in the first place. I had managed to build a loophole and Frank had crawled out through it.

Despite my mounting curiosity I didn't want him to him feel like he was being interrogated by his liberator. It was still early days, and as I had made a conscious decision to treat him as a function first and a person second, I was happy to hold my peace. I could have felt ill at ease, but I was determined to let my ideals lord over my emotions.

Frank had returned to gazing out of the window and I didn't blame him. I had no idea what was going on inside his mind. I expect he was shocked. For his own reasons he must have decided that my wider plan and obvious flexibility was enough for now.

I had thought he would be happier but maybe stoicism is what you learn in prison and maybe that was a trait he had decided to hold onto for the time being. I continued licking the sores of my memory – Stewart's pudgy face and too strong eau de cologne. Euan's ridiculous pointy two-tone shoes and his cowlick held in place by mousse and the regular flutter of his right hand.

The van full of students shot past us doing at least 80. Then the red brake lights lit up and they veered off for the airport, tyres protesting.

Chapter 5

14.00 Sunday

By Ayr I turned off for Cumnock. This wasn't the fastest way south, just one of the slightly illogical choices I was trying out. The A70 is relatively quick though and it's exactly the kind of anonymous road I had decided we should use as much as possible. A van flashed its headlamps at me and for a moment my heart was in my throat. Then I realised I had flicked on the high beams by mistake. The blue icon was oddly placed on the dashboard and hadn't caught my eye. It was as if the Twingo knew its owner wouldn't usually venture outside in the hours of darkness.

The flat fields and stone houses we soared past looked virtually unchanged since feudal times. Then my bucolic fantasies came to an end. The Waste Management Service at Barr had nothing to offer in terms of diversion. I looked out the other window instead. Past Frank's hewn profile. The rain had stopped but I presumed it wasn't long until the next shower.

'Fancy another cup of tea Frank?'

'Sure', he said, unmoved, as if he was above sustenance.

I had spotted one of those trailers that taxi drivers and scaffolders buy their lunch from and thought that would be safe enough, if we parked some distance away. I didn't need the tea, but I did need the fresh air and to stretch my legs.

'Have you got any cash?' I asked. 'I've only got big notes and sometimes these roadside people get a bit annoyed when they have to break big notes'.

He rooted around in his pockets and produced two grubby tenners and a clean fiver.

As we pulled into the car park Frank blurted out, 'Why are you doing this?'

'I'm starving', I said.

'No, I mean this whole trip'.

'Revenge', I said, then pocketed the car keys and jumped out.

Walking across the drenched gravel I quickly decided I was man enough for the balancing act, but only just. I knew what he had done, but he hadn't recognised me. It was an added knife edge to an already precarious situation.

To overcome my doubts, I got us big cups of tea. As an afterthought I bought two egg sandwiches as well. On white, as that was all they had. If Frank preferred brown, then having white bread would seem a little like a treat. A holiday exception.

I took a deep breath. For the first time in many years I felt alive. I had been safely tucked up in my office at Park Circus and then in my little flat on Hayburn Street, just off *metropolitan* Dumbarton Road, bloody estate agents, for so many years. Although the situation was morally dubious and dangerous, I was bent on enjoying this road trip. I even got us fizzy drinks. It was something I hadn't had for years. Barrs Cherryade and Cream Soda was all they had. Even this departure from any kind of lemonade norm felt refreshing.

Strolling back to the car I found myself whistling. The rain had stopped and a weak sun was breaking out between low clouds. In a few hours we'd be traveling under the cloak of night. I was in shock, but I was enjoying it too.

The rear windows were steamed up. When I got to my door and looked across I saw that Frank was gone. My heart stopped. Before I knew it a trickle of wee worked its way out into my pants.

I stood up and looked around, lost to the world for what felt like an eternity. All this work for nothing? All this work for him to just wander off at the first possible opportunity? He would be making a mockery of my program. Bournemouth, Jersey, Saint-Nazaire; that was the jaggy longitude line we were migrating along. If that was to end in East Ayrshire, I would feel like a travesty of a man.

If he had decided to jump ship outside Ochiltree, he was no longer my responsibility. But who would find him and who would he tell about my involvement? At least when he was with me I knew he hadn't been caught. And if we were captured together I was fairly certain that my reputable past and good enunciation would get me out of trouble. Despite lacking a flashy suit or an expensive car, the way I sounded and the job I had held for so long were the cornerstones of my respectable image. I reasoned it'd be harder for Frank to blend in. Not everyone can hide where they come from. Accent, manners and tattoos tend to stay with you.

I was part of the establishment, at least in the eyes of the establishment. Besides, the hostage is always innocent, whether he is the driver or not. I had been looking forward to the trip though, and ticking the box of Bournemouth.

I put the sandwiches and drinks in the car. I tried to think about the next move. Should I call the police and exonerate myself? Strike back first or turn the other cheek? I felt certain no judge would be able to decipher my blueprints, and even more complex motives, but I would rather not come up against the system. Caught or not I'd rather keep my reasons under the radar.

I heard a sound behind me, hurried steps on gravel. I spun around.

'Sorry. I was bursting', Frank said, brandishing a lopsided smile.

I pointed him to the food and went over to the bushes, relief pushing on my bladder. Over the years, a lot of wine has passed through, and in many ways my pipes are older than the rest of me.

Back in the car, fan working away the condensation from our steaming cups of tea, I kept the motor idling while we tucked into our sandwiches. I have been told off by community officers before. Apparently an idling motor is the devil's workshop. But I thought it was safe enough in the countryside. To mask the sound of slurping and chewing I put Radio 3 back on.

I roughly massaged my face and revved the engine a couple of times to get more warm air into the system. Beyond the windscreen, sable clouds. September as impossible to predict as any other Scottish month, but sometimes more so. In a few hours the crest of the moon, hidden or not, would be peeking up over the tree line. By then we would be far into the safety of our allegorical Sherwood.

'We'll get to why we're here Frank. There's still a fair way to go', I said in answer to his quiet. I looked at the people packing up the stall we had just bought food from. It looked like a simple, happy existence. One that had been denied me. And Frank too I presumed. 'Of course you're free to leave whenever you want', I said. 'This is just one option for you. Possibly the best one, but either way I don't want to force you into anything'.

'So far so good Cecil. Is it ok if I call you Cecil? I had an O'Malley in my year at school. Never liked him. You're different though'. He took a bite of the sandwich then grabbed both cans. He held them up for me to choose. I picked the Cherryade and he nodded, seemingly satisfied. On the radio sweeping strings, in my mouth the strangely comforting taste of cherries.

'This is the best food I've had in ages', Frank said. 'I know it's just your normal sandwich but sitting here eating it in my own time, with a cup of tea is just great. So different from inside. If nothing else comes of this whole thing, at least thanks for this moment Cecil'.

'You're welcome', I said, glad that a sandwich could make such a difference. 'A stitch in time and all that'.

I handed Frank my can and put the car in gear. Once we were out on the A76 I took a long drink of the tea, almost scalding my tongue as I had forgot to put milk in.

A pack of motorcyclists wearing hi-viz sped past us and I stopped breathing for a little while. At a glance they looked like an overweight JFK motorcade. Then I realised they were no kind of authority. They were just middle-aged men larking about on expensive toys in the rain. The road was straight enough and lightly trafficked and I didn't want to disturb Frank while he was enjoying his sandwich so I kept quiet and let Pyotr Ilyich Tchaikovsky fill the air between us.

'So you've got no work to get back to? Is there at least a wife wondering where you are?' Frank asked after neatly depositing his tea bag in the sandwich bag.

'*No, je suis tout seul*', I said with a certain flourish. 'I'm a free agent'.

Frank snorted a half-laugh through his triangle of bread. I wasn't sure why. Either he thought it was funny, or maybe he thought I had been misled. I decided not to pursue it.

* * *

Stewart had said that my presentation on the Monday was nothing more than procedure really, the contract was mine. When I was told by the committee that the contract was no longer mine I came apart at the seams. When I realised there was as clause stating that they owed me 20% of the total budget up front, whether the project went ahead or not, I tacked myself together, ready for war. Stewart had put together the contract in a rush, and he was terrible with his own money, let alone the taxpayer's. While this was going on I lost the house in the unavoidable divorce but I minded less than I thought I would. Eventually I managed to get on the team of architects, under Euan, but soon also undermining him.

Chapter 6

14.36 Sunday

Frank crunched both of our cans and put all the rubbish in the bag and tucked it in by his feet. Then he looked out, rubbing his hands. The car was warm but the day outside, now that the sun had gone down, was drab and inhospitable. We were aiming for Dumfries. To begin with.

At the side of the road, a long row of school kids of various ages. Waiting for something or someone. In my day we were never out before 3 o'clock. It looked like they had been out for the day. Maybe they were the children of busy parents who had to work while their kids went to after school clubs? Maybe they were orphans who had escaped a horrible matron? I knew very little of the comings and goings of children.

'Have you got a partner, a family?' I asked now that he was done eating.

'I've got four', Frank said, more to the window than to me. 'One of my own, and my second wife had two from before'.

I immediately regretted asking.

Frank continued, 'And then she takes care of this boy with autism four nights a week. Though he's not really ours the other kids think of him as their brother'.

I burnt my throat swallowing too much tea. 'My God. I'm sorry. This trip, this, I don't know, this escape. Maybe it's not right for you at all. For some reason I presumed that you were on your own'.

Frank nodded. 'It's difficult, but it's for the best. They were coping on their own while I was inside, so this is no different for them really'.

'You can't contact your wife', I said. 'I'm sorry but you must realise that'.

'Of course I do. She usually comes on a Wednesday anyway so unless they tell her before then, and knowing how useless they are they might not, she won't know I'm out'.

'Really?'

'Or if they know they might not tell her. Messages, even really important ones, go missing all the time. It's part of the power structure. Or they might think that if she doesn't know she can't help me'.

A straggler on a motorbike, a huge cross-eyed eagle and *Suzuki* stitched onto the back of his yellow vest, sped past.

'This is all my fault', I said.

'I chose to follow the instructions. And it was pretty nasty inside. I have a better chance of making things all right outside'.

Without knowing it Frank had deployed scorched-earth tactics as he retreated out of the prison. His chance was a one-off; the clues were metaphorically burned after they had been read. I was pretty sure there would be no copycats.

I opened the window and poured out the rest of the tea. It left a thick brown coating on the door of the car. I was confident it would rain soon enough. The electrical purr of the window going up was the only sound in the car, and when I turned to Frank he was ready to receive my cup with the rubbish bag. I looked at the odometer, and for 7 miles we drove on not saying a word.

'What about you? Do you have kids?' he asked.

'We never had children'.

'Sorry', Frank said.

'I was too busy. I didn't miss them at the time'.

'Have you had yourself tested, you're not sterile?' Frank asked, candid as anything.

'No, I'm very capable'. Up until not long ago, I never had any issues on that front.

'That's not the same', Frank said.

'I know. But maybe Maude was. Is'.

'Did she not want them either?' he asked.

'Not too sure. We never discussed it properly. We had our own things going. Work kept me pretty occupied'.

In a field a flock of landlocked seagulls took off and for a short moment they were keeping pace with us. Then they veered off. The logic of birds, impenetrable.

'How much longer?' Frank asked. We had just overtaken a passel of moto-rhomes, all in the same colours, the big star-spangled banner painted on the sides of at least two. All for some reason doing 40 mph.

'A few hours still. Today is a big day. Distance is key. Sleep if you want'.

I don't know if he slept or not but he turned to the window and closed his eyes. I looked down on the speedometer and realised I was well over the speed limit. I wound down the window a little and slowed down. Plodded on through the countryside.

The radio, its Traffic Announcement function activated, came on and woke Frank. *An incident on the A76 by Gretna Green... Overturned lorry and long queues...* This meant police and slow going. I pointed to the glove compartment and Frank got the road atlas out. I pulled over and turned on the dome light. Together we pored over the map. The detour we decided on involved a turnoff at Annan, and a series of B-roads traversing the country.

I found it comical that we would be scouting the border, West to East for the best crossing. Like we were cowboys in the films I watched growing up. I was

Gary Cooper in *High Noon* and Frank looked a lot like the quarterback John Devine, from *Stagecoach*. I didn't tell him this.

With Frank reading out instructions, 'Left here, right here, no sorry left', we plunged deeper into the night and into the countryside. I wasn't going very fast, but I felt like a rally driver being read pace notes over an intercom. Frank could have led me anywhere. Off a cliff, into the dark woods. To one of his friends, if he knew anyone on the Solway coast.

Eventually, after a very long time, as we were not the only ones going south who had thought of circumventing Gretna, we joined the motorway, and sped across the border.

'Welcome to England, Cecil', Frank said and I smiled. We chinked imaginary flutes and over the airwaves Katie Williamson, miraculous in her marathon ability, smiled too as she purred about Maurice Ravel. I was beginning to doubt that she was a real person. Maybe she was more of a Classical Bot, or at least pre-recorded for the pleasure of the listener?

This would mark the end of motorways unless it was absolutely unavoidable. There are more CCTV cameras per capita in England and more people to control. With Frank being a Glasgow man I presumed the authorities would concentrate their efforts on the wider city area, his home, known addresses, and not the banks of the River Esk.

'It's nice going abroad sometimes', I said and turned up the radio which was playing Boléro. I used to be more clued up, but these days my ideas about devolution, jurisdiction and extradition were vague. Either way, leaving Scotland felt like a milestone.

Chapter 7

14.53 Sunday

We were approaching the outskirts of Penrith, still mainly using A roads, and B roads when available. So far the A6 had proved to be an unexpected gem. Picturesque yet empty, the adjacent motorway draining it of traffic. Radio 3 was playing a pretty challenging piece of music. Not for me, but for a novice maybe. I could see Frank fretting, but I wasn't sure whether it was the music, or the fact that we had been cooped up inside the car for a while.

'What's this Cecil?' Frank said closing the lid of the glove box with his fist. It had a tendency to flip open. It must have hit him in the knees a hundred times already but he hadn't noticed the small CD holder till it fell out onto his feet. I had labeled it *Cromlix*. I made a mental note to get some tape to permanently close the glove box.

'A collection of compilation CDs I made for this trip'. I overtook a huge John Deere. 'Years ago'.

'But you didn't know who you were going to take with you. Or what music they would like'.

'Everyone likes classical music', I said, raising my hand to the tractor driver who had veered helpfully.

'Or at least it's so bland that it's hard to mind it', Frank said waving the box in the air, as if weighing it at a market stall.

'It's not bland if you have the intelligence to listen properly', I said. 'It's the highest human achievement after all, at least within music. Outwith music there's architecture of course, Vitruvius' ideas, St Basil's Cathedral, and now Cad-Cam I suppose'.

'There are more important things in life than fiddles and buildings', he said.

'Like what?'

'Being content'.

'Perhaps, but listen to this'. I turned the radio up a little, and though I was not particularly fond of *Symphonie Fantastique*, as it's a bit bombastic, the point was still valid. 'This is eternal beauty. It transcends people and time'.

Frank nodded but put the box back in the glove compartment.

'This, for example, is Berlioz', I said, and superfluously pointed at the radio. 'He is featured on the first disc. There's nine CDs in total in the box. I made them so I could explore composers unknown to me. It's a list from A to Z'.

'To educate whoever you would be traveling with?' Frank said.

'Or at least enlighten them. It was also a way to challenge myself'.

Soon we were going through a series of roundabouts. Like mould spores blooming exponentially. The roundabout is apparently the best way to spend council funds. Measured by lives saved in relation to pounds spent. But how tedious to have to slow down, look over the shoulder, indicate only to speed up and endlessly repeat.

'So is there a CD player?' Frank asked.

'Turns out my sister only listens to radio', I said. 'I should have known; she is a bit of a Luddite'.

'Sure', Frank said and looked at my loafers.

'There's a tape deck but no tapes. Remember when you could buy tapes at petrol stations?'

'So now Radio 3 is enlightening you instead?' he said.

'I enjoyed making the selection, so something good has come out of the CD fiasco. Katie Williamson doesn't present in alphabetical but I still like her'.

'If we weren't running away we could call her and suggest that to her', Frank said.

I couldn't tell whether he was joking or not, but it wasn't a bad idea really. 'I might get in touch with the BBC once I come back from the journey. I can easily make up a *nom de plume*', I said.

In some sort of celebration of reaching the last in the series of roundabouts I must have forgotten to indicate properly. Turning left to exit I was nearly run into by a white van. He honked a long plaintive Transit van note, and sped by with his middle finger erect and limp fag in his mouth. I was suddenly glad I had a big, possibly dangerous, man in the passenger seat.

Once my pulse had settled and I realised the van man probably wasn't the kind of person to write down a number plate and report it, I asked, 'What kind of music are you into Frank?'

'Thin Lizzy, YES, old Genesis, that kind of thing. A bit of Led Zep, Sabbath, Deep Purple, you know'.

'Sounds like you're a bit stuck in a time capsule', I said.

'Forty years isn't exactly long ago. Mozart died, what, two hundred years ago?'

'But his music is immortal in a way that Freddie Mercury's isn't. We can't listen to rock, I'm tense enough as it is without a queer man in leather shouting about the devil at me while going 70 miles an hour', I said.

'I know what I'd bring to a desert island. And it's not Vivaldi. But don't worry Cecil. I won't demand we change station. Classical is fine'.

'There's a CD player where you're going. You're welcome to take the nine compilation CDs and of course you can listen to whatever profane noise you fancy. Just not too loud. I don't want the neighbours complaining', I said, involuntarily raising a finger.

'At least this kind of music is good for sleeping to', Frank said and placed his head on his stretched-out seatbelt.

'Well, maybe you will get it subliminally', I said as Berlioz leaned into the Fourth movement, the *Marche au supplice*, or *the March to the Scaffold*. I smiled at the irony as Frank and I marched along at 60 miles an hour. Hopefully away from the executioners though.

The road lulled me into reveries. When they robbed me of the contract and my idea of a Good Prison became impossible to carry out, I quickly rejigged my plans.

I spent a hazy weekend going over the blueprints Euan had submitted, printing them on tracing paper and working out how to string together the escape route.

In my office, and later in my flat, I kept a separate folder marked, *Cromlix Backwards Quality Control*. For my designed faults to work, the quality of the workmanship had to be top class. If I had known a joiner who I trusted enough I would have contracted him to build the faults for me. But the blueprints had to look legit, and the semi-competent contractors carried out my work fine, if not perfect. In addition to my faults there were thousands of undesired faults, some unforeseen, others not.

From my research on secure sewage I knew there was a pipe under the prison but I wasn't sure how much water it transported. Initially I planned to get the Unknown Prisoner out of Cromlix through an underground river. This would require a submarine, a baptism in used-up water, and once my prisoner emerged he would be a new, forgiven man.

I soon realised it was too complicated. On the brink of some despair, I rang the waterworks and found out that the cloaca under the prison was more of an overflow storm drain than a working part of the waterworks. It was over-dimensioned, underused and almost forgotten. In short it was perfect. If I could only get him there, my prisoner would be able to walk out of the pipe, risking only damp feet. My plans for a floating sarcophagus had been for nothing.

After that I focused on the Exit Kit in the tunnel. I put in a knife, nothing huge or deadly, a tool more than anything else. It would also be useful in case there was more than one escapee. With that in mind I put in a 10p coin to flip. I knew I could only take one person with me, and I taped a note to that effect in the lid of the kit. I was also clear about the disposal of the knife. I didn't want some guy with a record walking around with my blade in his pocket. I had even supplied a little weighted canvas bag and directions to a drain not far from the exit point.

I put in a change of worker's clothes including coveralls as they are more flexible to differences in weight and height, and a Hi-Viz vest with a made-up contractor's name on the back. I put in a hard hat and a card on a lanyard with a name but no photo. In a last act of generosity, I put in 50 pounds in notes as well as some change for a cup of tea and the paper.

It felt like a long time ago, and I knew I needed to be in the immediate circumstances for the mission to succeed.

As we crested a hill and got a look at the landscape and the road ahead I could see that the traffic was gridlocked for miles. We would probably end up crawling forward next to the angry man in the white van for hours, as is sod's law. Staring into the rearview mirror I found us a gap and managed to squeeze into a lane veering off, taking us into a retail park. The jolt of the speed bumps woke Frank up.

'Need anything from Block & Quayle?' I asked as we came to a stop in a secluded parking spot.

'From where?' he asked and rubbed his eyes.

'B&Q'.

'Not that I can think of', he said without lifting his head from his seatbelt pillow.

'Great. I think I have everything you need anyway. I'll just go in and grab a coffee and a few things, won't be long. Do you want one? Black with a couple of sugars?'

'No more coffees, please'.

'That's fine. Sleep if you want'.

We didn't need anything and shouldn't have stopped at all, but I was guided by chance. I was navigating under uncertain stars, for amusement and safety. With the traffic jam ahead of us my plan was to get a hot drink, maybe a spare petrol tank for Frank's dinghy and then retrace our steps through the maze of roundabouts until we found an alternative route south.

It was still a long way off, but I had always fancied driving across the Clifton suspension bridge in Bristol so we might head south-west before south-east. Maybe if I had been called Isambard Kingdom Brunel instead of Cecil O'Malley I would have accomplished similar triumphs, some kind of imposing landmark across the Clyde. Putting that thought aside I went through the automatic doors into DIY paradise. Into the welcoming, lukewarm nursery for retired men.

Walking around the aisles, a kind of two-by-four flâneur, I sighed happily. Things were going roughly to plan. It was nice to be out of the ship of fools on wheels I was commandeering, the vessel filled with an odd congregation of two, united in nothing but the madness we were both affected by.

The great thing about the car, and one of the cornerstones of my plan, was the easy intimacy of being seated in close proximity, but still not facing each other. In a car you're restricted in the use of body language, and not required or able to establish eye contact. It's a safe place, full of outside distractions if needed, and as private as a parlour if that's better. Close to death whirling past in the form of asphalt and other cars, by unfortunate chance and the mistakes of others, disaster only millimetres away, which I find subliminally sharpens the mind.

I came out of B&Q with a combination padlock, another silver foil emergency blanket and a sub-par coffee in a flimsy paper cup with no lid. I put my drink on the roof and the things in the boot, keeping my head down in case someone was watching. When I opened the door Frank woke up, but only to check it was me. He went back under the surface again, like a cat on a window ledge.

After performing all the required gestures of indicating, being in the right gear, not going too fast or too slow, I was soon back in amongst the round-abouts, heading for an alternative route. A digital GPS had been out of the question. Too predictable, too easy for the satellites to follow. Instead I had a box of Ordnance Survey maps for the areas we would be passing through resting in the rear passenger foot well. Paper had worked for Napoleon and it would work for me.

Chapter 8

15.30 Sunday

I was starting to appreciate my sister's car. Exactly by not being personal it was helping me, like a hotel room. While we were in it, the car was a place, a safe haven. As we traversed the country it was a fluid thing too, a non-place I suppose. Never one thing, never static.

We would be passing through places of importance to other people, inadvertently touching peoples' lives, but still we would remain trussed up in the same lilac interior, regardless of the outside. The Twingo, with its puny engine and insensitive controls, had been transformed into a vehicle for change and transformation, exactly by remaining the same.

I missed my own car, which in every sense was superior. But following in the footsteps of the brave men and women who won the West I settled in and focused my mind on loftier things than the lack of proper climate controls.

I thought he was sleeping, but suddenly he turned to me and asked, 'Why did you do it? Why did you construct the escape hatch?'

Frank was the lowest common denominator between me and Cromlix. Also, who was he going to tell? I deliberated whether to tell him exactly why, then decided to follow my gut feeling which told me that this might be the last ear I would be able to bend.

'I was so angry with Mr Patterson, Stewart and Euan and the whole machinery', I said. 'I was maybe deluded but I think I was right on principle'.

'On principle maybe', he said.

'I wanted Cromlix to be a human place'.

'It's just a holding pen', Frank said and I knew he was right.

'But it could have been more than that', I said, softly beating a fist on the steering wheel.

I felt myself flushing with the same anger that fueled me so many years ago and opened the window a little, then closed it. I made a mental note to buy something like a magic tree car air freshener, but something more subdued and classy. If I got something a bit manlier than the rest of the car, like a sheet of Black Ice or a fifties bomber pinup image smelling of Fahrenheit aftershave, it could dangle proudly, displaying our leanings and intentions to the world. A small totem to stave off any shadow of suspicion cast over our masculinity.

Frank sat forward in his seat, but remained quiet.

'As an architect, the brief for a prison is an impossible one', I said. 'Even if the building is great the system inside will always verge on the edge of collapse. It's not easy to make a good building when the end user, the prisoner, hates it. Also, there's no funding for anything'.

Frank nodded. I wasn't sure what that meant.

'If nothing else the hatch was my revenge', I continued. 'I wanted to reward the person clever enough to read the signs. Give something back to society'.

Frank leaned back in his seat. 'That's pretty weird. I mean it's great for me'.

'I didn't think the escape route would ever see any use', I said. 'I remember thinking that surely no prisoner would be clever enough to work out my stratagems. No offence'.

'None taken', he said and smiled a full set of teeth. Happy to prove me wrong. And for once I was happy to be wrong. It was a strange, unusual feeling.

'I also never thought that Euan and the others wouldn't notice me doing this under their noses. I guess it took a couple of years to build it, and he was less and less involved. Despite overcrowding elsewhere, the prison was empty for ages before being populated, so to him it was a done deal. For me it was alive. Still was until you came out'.

For some reason Frank counted his knuckles. I wasn't sure if he was working out which months had 30 days and which had 31 or if he was just checking their condition in case there was a fist fight coming up.

'I was quite surprised that no one worked their way out of my Ziggurat for so long'.

He just nodded. Seemed he had arrived at eight knuckles.

'Your bosses never suspected anything while you were constructing the tunnel?' he asked after a mile or two, a confessional priest at ease. The centre console, an imagined latticed opening, separating us.

'Well, they weren't quite my bosses, but anyway, they were in a great hurry and I was a highly functioning alcoholic for most of the time. To me it was a joke behind the teacher's back. I wanted to prove myself smarter than them'.

'I guess you won', Frank said. He folded his hands in his lap, fingers interlocking like a timber lamella. 'We won'.

'We'll see', was all I could say.

Overtaking a long row of caravans towed by people my age in reliable and very clean Škodas and Toyotas – tissue box and rubbish bin present and correct – meant pushing the Twingo to its limit. Luckily the road dipped and I could ease up on the throttle a little and still accelerate. We had settled into a comfortable pace on the A6, soon passing Tebay, arguably the best road side services in the north of England, if not in the whole of England, or indeed the Kingdom. It wasn't for us that day, but I made a mental note to stop there on my way back, the phantom taste of a sausage roll on my tongue.

I knew the stretch south from here to about Kendal quite well. It was my preferred England. I like anything north of Preston or west of Southampton. Here there was still a bit of humanity and nature left. The rest has died twice. First in the industrial revolution and then it was eaten up by bankers and staggering house prices.

London is different. I used to love it when I was younger. I used to invent all sorts of reason why I had to go down. In the daytime I was a tourist, in the evenings a monster. After a couple of days, the hangovers would catch up and I would have to spend a day or two sleeping in my Fitzrovia hotel room, slowly recuperating. The old me, the cocaine-snorting me, had adored the clubs around Old Compton Street and the glitz in the air back then.

The capital was full of odd architectural elements piled on top of each other by history, or uncomfortably married by cowboy builders. I used to go around with a camera and collect voussoirs, arc-boutants, lunettes, pilasters – my favourite fake, and in a sense the basis of my prison idea – and porte cochères. There was one in Pimlico which was the backbone for the jutting out roof of the entrance at Cromlix. By designing a tunnel, I was just exploring material through density, and through porosity, like any good architect should. Not just encapsulating air in cubes for living.

'12 years', Frank said, breaking my reveries of the Lake District. 'I couldn't have done it'.

'Is that how long you got?' I asked, innocently.

'I would have ended myself long before then. It was my family that kept me going. It's a double-edged sword. Seeing your kids and the pain of not seeing them, both helps and makes it worse. But even with a reduced sentence, and parole and all those things, I couldn't have hacked it'.

'So I suppose whatever happens, this outing might be for the best?' I said.

He clenched his fists and beat a little rhythm on his thighs. 'I'll make sure to get shot if they find us', he said, and I hoped he was joking, but couldn't be sure.

'I'm not so sure about that myself to be honest', I said once I realised he wasn't going to elaborate.

Frank coughed and said 'I was shunted around three prisons. That made it feel both shorter, as there was always something changing, and also longer, because I never understood what was going on. There was never anywhere to settle in, to make my own. I never got to know anyone. I never got the hang of the various systems', he said.

'Systems?'

'There's the SPS, the prison system. The police, the courts, seeing your lawyer, social workers, all that stuff'.

We overtook a recovery lorry pulling another recovery lorry, and I think we both sniggered a little.

Frank's face went blank again and he said, 'Beneath, no actually, above, is the prisoners' system. It exists in between, fills all the spaces where official systems can't cope. Like the bits of land you were talking about before'.

'Maybe', I said.

'You might think that you'd be able to hide away in your quiet corner, just work out a way to deal with the boredom and the lack of stimulation. Just bide your time'.

'That sounds horrible', I said and shuddered.

I thought about twelve years while looking at the sign for The South, but decided to not say anything.

'You have to assert yourself, prove yourself tough in all kinds of stupid ways. Piss people off enough so that they don't mess with you, but not so much that they want to ram a toothbrush down your throat in a quiet moment'.

'Or spit in your food?' I asked and he just nodded in a tired way.

We went past one of those pseudo-places of no character or use. I tried in vain to locate landmarks or some sort of sign telling me the name of this failed example of town planning. By the looks it was another brick and pebbledash hellhole. Its only highlight a Sainsbury's and a closed library to throw cider cans at. A place, like so many. Too built up to be rural, too far away from cinemas to be urban. Too far away to commute to and too bulldozed and tarmacked to be tranquil. I thanked my lucky star I had remained in Glasgow proper all these years.

'I thought you were safe inside, that they had CCTV everywhere', I said. I had been happy in my belief that everything inside was recorded for posterity and proof.

'Doesn't matter. And also they don't. There are plenty of blind spots, but you must have the eye to see this. Some of the guards are more vigilant than others, some couldn't care less. But the guys inside know every square centimetre of the place and know how to work any room to their advantage'.

'So how come you were the only one to make it out?'

'How do you know there weren't more of us?' he said.

'Were there?' I asked, pulse speeding up. Then I forced myself to calm down. It was a rollercoaster lasting four seconds.

Frank didn't say anything and I was staring down the road ahead of us.

'I think I would have heard about it if there had been a huge jail break', I said even though I hadn't been listening to any news since he joined me in the car.

'How do you know I didn't kill a couple of guys at the door, with the knife you put in the exit kit?'

A big Lexus pulled into my lane, a whole panel of brake lights blinding me, only to turn off, while I fumbled with the gears. Down to third from fifth, which was quite a feat actually, then working my way back up, without revving too hard, to our steady pace in fifth. I cursed the driver of what was essentially a dolled up Toyota. The Japanese Emperor's new clothes.

Once re-settled into our normal march speed, I asked, 'Did you?' My heart beating in my throat again, a precipice opening before me. 'With the knife?'

'No', he seemed almost offended. 'I've never laid a hand on anyone in my life', he said with absolute conviction and I couldn't work out if he believed himself or was just a really good liar. I had once been pretty good at it myself.

Presenting improvised ideas to big clients with absolute conviction takes a certain talent.

'Why you Frank?' I asked.

He bit his lower lip and said, 'I've always been a quick learner. Even in school I was good, then I had to leave to work and do all sorts of other things. I used to love languages, and the blue colour was almost like a language'.

I could only smile.

'How's your French?' I asked once I had been overtaken by a huge Wide Load trailer.

'I've never been to France but my French is fine actually. I used to watch a lot of French films when the kids were young. Peter had nightmares and he used to fall asleep on me on the sofa, so I couldn't really move or he'd wake up'.

I took a deep breath and asked, 'You didn't kill anyone did you?'

'No. I told you'.

'Just making sure', I said as sternly as I dared. 'I hope there are no others escaping. It would shatter our schedule if this became a large-scale Interpol manhunt'.

'I didn't tell anyone about what I was doing. Thought it safer that way. I didn't make friends so I didn't see the point'.

I was finding it difficult to get a comfortable grip on the strange, possibly French-styled, steering wheel. It had two prongs, at 3 and 9 o'clock and a slightly larger one at the bottom of the circle, but there was nothing in the upper middle. This space, this nothingness at 12 o'clock was disorientating. Other than that there was almost comically little to adjust in the car. The dash consisted of two vents, like the eyes of a child's owl toy, three buttons, a mediocre stereo without Dolby audio noise reduction and a shallow bowl for tapes or cigarettes, neither of which we used.

'I was still fresh in', he said. 'That's why I was able to follow the signs'. He coughed again. 'A lot of the guys have been in and out since they were sixteen, and now in their fifties, that's all they know. They hate the system, but also know how to work it, so they have lost the ability to think laterally'.

'I see', I said.

'It's not always a career in crime, but one or two outbursts which put you in jail. Even for a long time'. He looked out but I don't know if he saw anything. 'Sometimes it's just a stupid, stupid mistake. Or an accident'.

'Accident?' I asked, incredulous. However faulty the judicial system of this country was I still believed in it. I still believed it would take a little more than a mistake to get 12 years.

I was moving my hands on the confusing steering wheel. Round and round searching for purchase, but it was too hard to come to grips with.

'I hadn't had time to turn off my brain the way some guys have to. If you were always alert you would go mad, there's so little stimulation'.

'I always thought I would get in good shape, read the classics', I said.

'Most people think along those lines, but you run out of steam pretty quickly. Also the library was rubbish and the gym was always closed for refurbishment'.

The smell of cat which had lingered in the car up until now was slowly being masked by the odour of food and I suppose our body smells. I tried to keep the window open an inch or two whenever I could. I had never liked my sister's cats but luckily they seemed to either run away or quickly fade away in her care.

'I hadn't thought about that'. I said, almost missing the chance to read Wordsworth and do a 100 push-ups a day. My hands were still searching the dash to my left for things to adjust. The wind from the small vents was either a bit warm or a bit cold, but neither temperature setting was very effective.

'Unless you're used to it, the culture shock is mad when you first get there', he said. 'It's like being in China on your own, but everyone drinks Irn-Bru and talks like the people in your local shop. So in a way it's worse because you're not expecting the shock like you would if you were really going abroad'.

'So you would have preferred going to prison in Turkey, where the culture shock would have been more expected?' I said and adjusted the direction of the vents from *Face* to *Face + Windshield*. My eyes were getting a little dry.

'That's not what I mean. But the talk about bettering yourself, education, rehabilitation and forgiveness is maybe a waste of time. All the training and workshops, all the hoops you have to jump through to get out on time, are useless for a lot of people. Me, and people like me, don't need to be rehabilitated. We might have made one huge mistake, but we are more likely to get worse being stuck inside. I'm not saying there should be no punishment for crime, but after 7 years or so you're not getting any better. If you've not learnt your lesson by then you never will. I'm not saying victims or victim's families would like us to be out any quicker, just that some people could return outside a lot quicker than they are at the moment'.

I stopped breathing. Had he recognised me? He didn't continue, so I decided he meant just in general terms. I forced air into my lungs and overtook another caravan probably heading for Windermere. I was having trouble breathing and wound down the window as far as it would go. Then it started to rain and I had to put it up again.

The action of doing something had made me remember how to breathe again. I made up my mind to let the matter rest for now, otherwise driving would become too dangerous.

The blueprint had stipulated a generous gym and a library. I wanted to call it the *Athenaeum*, but Euan found it too hard to pronounce. It had been up to someone else to populate these spaces with dumbbells and books. It was another good intention turned sour by the last 10% of execution.

Frank pointed at a huge bird and I started racking my brain. It could have been a hawk or a buzzard, but Frank said 'Kite', with some finality.

We had passed signs for Manchester. Later I would make a choice between toll road or not at Birmingham, unless we could find a suitable A road. I would have preferred to use A-roads exclusively, but decided not to make up my mind too far in advance. Later I would face the M6/M5 or M40, which I might use to make up some distance. The best rule is to not always stick to your rules.

'What happens now?' Frank asked quietly.

'Once they find that you're missing they might find the passages. Or not. And if they can't find the way out they will scratch their heads for a while. Then I don't know'.

He nodded.

'They might just tell the press you've escaped and supply them with a mug shot', I said.

'But the blueprints are available if the police wanted to see them?'

'It would be very difficult for someone external to link up the passage on paper alone', I said. 'I have a master copy but it's well hidden and full of code only I could decipher'.

'But someone used the passage. That incriminates you, doesn't it?' he said.

'I might be able to wriggle my way out of it if it came to that', I said. 'I made sure it looks pretty circumstantial. Think about it like this: An axe is innocent till used, and stays innocent until someone decides to use it in anger. Likewise, the passage is an inanimate object which can be used in more than one way. I suppose I was the one who supplied you with an axe to chop your way out. I provided a map, but you were the one who used it'.

I had worn gloves while crawling around inside the tunnel, though any prints could probably be explained away quite easily.

I was looking at the road as much as possible, and thinking about Janice as little as possible. I was practising being both being aware of Frank and avoiding his gaze as much as I felt was socially acceptable. He moved his head. It might have been a nod in agreement.

Chapter 9

15.50 Sunday

The little A685 was snaking across a beautifully hilly landscape, with the relative metropolis of Kendal waiting for us somewhere beyond the horizon. In my calculations we couldn't be far off. We were scheduled to sail past the little stone heaven soon enough and I contemplated stopping to stock up on Romney's Mint Cake, but to my disappointment we hit traffic.

Crawling out of a smaller roundabout, which led us straight into a bigger one, we were suddenly corralled by Highway Maintenance. The strong arm of the council, whichever council, borough or local authority we were in. I wasn't sure exactly where we were – which was a good thing, as that probably meant no one else did either.

Outside: *Follow Diversion.*

Inside, I looked at the digital clock set in the dashboard, it said 15.51. The '15' lending a certain continental flair to the French car, which a simple '3' wouldn't have pulled off.

On our left, a hulking crane with *Ainscough* written in large blue letters on it, leading the eye up to its head. It had just lifted a series of concrete structures, possibly part of a jigsaw for a bridge foundation, but I was no engineer so couldn't tell. The wide pipes chained together were swinging a little in the rainy wind – overweight ballerinas rehearsing one last time. Tearing my eyes from the spectacle, beautiful in its functional aesthetic, as the car in front eased away from us, I turned to Frank.

'You know I spent the night once in that culvert'. I hadn't planned to tell him. It just came out.

'Why?' he asked.

'I was there to check on a couple of things. It wasn't the first time, but this one time the sirens went off. It reminded me of those wartime air raids you see in films. It must have been early June, don't know if you remember, or if you were even in Cromlix at that stage, but there was a lockdown. I don't know why but I was too scared to move'.

'I remember', Frank said. 'Some idiot stuck two biros into a wire and started a fire with his bedding'.

'Why?'

'Who knows? Boredom. Drugs. Issues? The scheduled visits from his girlfriend had gone off the rota somehow?'

'What happened to him?'

'Nothing. A couple of guards ambled in with buckets of water. The guy *fell into the bed frame'*.

'That's terrible'. I said.

Frank shrugged his shoulders. 'He kind of deserved it to be honest. The whole wing lost recreational time. That got the guy bruised up too, but actually less than I thought. He was always a bit nuts and people kind of go easier on someone like that. If they do it because they're confused and angry or whatever rather than being dicks, people are usually nicer'.

'I see', I said. And realised that if worst came to worst and I was apprehended I could always play the mad card, if it meant clemency.

Follow Diversion

While we waited, still surrounded, the car rolling in neutral, men in orange overalls finished putting up signs and gathered around for a cup of tea. As we approached one of the older men gesticulated wildly. A deranged conductor of traffic waving us past – anything to not disturb their tarmac séance.

'What were you doing in the pipe anyway?' Frank asked once we hit 10 miles an hour.

'Some last tweaks', I said. 'Just making sure everything was still intact, nothing blocked or missing, that sort of thing'.

We were being diverted onto a smaller road, which chimed with my desire to avoid the all-seeing eye. The prying, hunting gaze of authority which didn't yet have the resources to watch every small road in the country. I was banking on that hunch.

'That's the weirdest hobby I've ever heard about', Frank said. 'What's wrong with fishing or Countdown?'

'I like to keep my mind busy. For peace of mind I'd go back to Cromlix every now and then. Sometimes on official visits, *upstairs* if you like. I quite like the governor and she was always happy for me to walk around with one of the guards, knock on walls, measure damp levels, check sockets and joists. I would alternate this with visits *downstairs*. It gave me a chance to make sure everything was still in order. And it gave me something to do. To be honest being retired is a bit of a drag'.

'But you set it up when the prison was built? And no one had found out I presume. Or is this not your first trip?'

'This is my first and my last trip', I said and I meant every word.

We rolled past a man leaning on a spade, smoking. A landlocked ancient mariner with a thousand-mile stare, and a cloud over his head.

'So you would crawl into a prison in your spare time? Like a backwards escape?' Frank asked.

'You could say that', I said with a chuckle.

'How far in did you get?'

'All the way in. I crawled through the cylinder to the fake ceiling over the entrance and then inside the walls, like a rat, all the way to the laundry. All the way to washing machine number 14. Well I was beneath it. I never surfaced inside'.

'You're crazy'.

'You're free'. I said.

We were soon stuck behind a crew sitting on the back of a pickup truck. *This vehicle is limited to 60 mph* a sticker said, and I was glad we were nowhere near even 20 for the sake of the boys on the back. Glassy-eyed and quiet, asphalt soldiers waiting to be deployed somewhere. Wearing their livery like hardened militiamen. Each with a personal touch or minor sign of neglect marking them out as special in some internal or external way. A tear, a badge, a hoodie worn inside out.

'There was always something to check', I said. 'I tested the rope ladder down the drain and made sure the key to the lock by the pipe exit was still taped in place', I said. 'Made sure no vermin had gotten to the things in the backpack'.

'I liked that touch', Frank said, opening his eyes. 'It was almost homely. Like someone's mum had packed a lunch box for school. Everything was perfect. The hi-viz jacket, the lanyard, the knife, the packet of fags and the miniature Highland Park. The wellies and the tracksuit bottoms. I remember changing there in the light of the moon, a drink and the first fag since I was a teenager. I still didn't like the taste, but it was amazing to smoke it in my own time'.

'Glad you liked it', I said.

Follow Diversion

Soon we were stopped again. Eventually one of the men flipped a huge lollipop stick from STOP to GO. The queue of cars tentatively crept forward, and soon we picked up speed a little. Outside the car, rolling hills and HGVs staying in low gear passed like a theatrical backdrop. A collage of signs, toppled cones, people-carriers full of sweaty children and battery-powered traffic lights.

'I knew I was in a hurry and every fibre in my body wanted to run but I stood still and just enjoyed the moment. No one was going to tell me the break was over. I put my prison clothes in the backpack and set off. I had to remind myself not to whistle'.

'That would have been a bad idea'.

'I felt like an adult Tom Sawyer'. Frank smiled.

'Mark Twain you mean? The walking hobo?'

'Yes, Tom Sawyer'.

'I'm pretty sure the boy's called Mark Twain', I said half-remembering a pub quiz.

Frank looked at me then shrugged. "Either way, emerging like that was incredible'.

I couldn't hold back a smile.

Follow Diversion

We were directed towards the A-road we had left. Our path still determined by red and white traffic cones in endless lines, like a row of traditional barbers.

Frank looked out and said, 'At that time I didn't know how far away from the prison I was. For all I knew I had walked in circles and come out just outside the gates. My heart was beating so hard I was afraid people might hear it a mile off'.

'It's about a mile away. Not far from a big water works, where you could conceivably have been working', I said.

'No one questions a big man like me wearing a hardhat full of logos'.

'I wouldn't. Regardless of time of day'.

'I walked for hours. But with your map and the shortbread it was fine. Oh, I almost forgot. There was about fifty pounds, and I've spent some of it. When can I pay you back?'

'No rush. When you get money from somewhere we can talk about it. Till then don't worry about it', I said.

Frank turned the heater switch to our feet. It made very little difference. Then he asked, 'You said before you spent the night inside Cromlix. Where did you sleep in the tunnel? As far as I remember there was a trickle of water flowing in the pipe'.

'Once I realised I couldn't leave I made my way upstairs, to where I had made sure to put in a couple of double walls. Euan thought it was for extra insulation, *for a healthy airflow around the Rockwool*, I think I called it. I wasn't sure how the lockdown worked or for how long it would last, but I felt safe enough inside the wall'.

'Where?' he asked.

'You remember that long walk where it's a kind of a left, right, left, right pattern of cavities? I called it the *chicane*'.

'It was a terrifying walk. I always thought someone would jump out and strangle me. So many little corners to pass', Frank said and shuddered visibly.

'That's a shame. We tried to make it interesting. Not scary. Either way the space between the walls was empty at that point'.

'Why was it not full of stuff?'

I sat up and cleared my throat. 'I made sure to go over budget before we ordered the insulation. In the end we had to scrap a lot of the Rockwool. I thought Euan would be upset but when we talked about it he felt it would be an added bonus if it was cold and draughty. That the inside climate would be a punishment in itself. An extra dimension to your sentence'.

'I was never cold inside', Frank said. 'If anything it was overheated. Stuffy. Like all institutions. They just leave the radiators on full blast and close all the windows'.

'There was no coherent system for regulating the air flow or temperature. That was part of the design'.

'Yours or his?' Frank asked.

'His', I said quickly. Mostly because it was true, and also because it wasn't entirely true. I had to give it to Euan. He didn't care for looks, but he had been very efficient. If cruel. 'In his mind a prison is not a place for aesthetics or function. It's just a cube that holds people. The cheaper the better'.

'Incredible', Frank said and sighed.

I had spent years looking at sketches by Alvar Aalto, FLW, Niemeyer, Pei and Saarinen, and at one point made enquiries to the deed poll office about changing my name. It seemed like the added letter added a certain *je ne sais quoi*: Ceecil, Ceciil. In the end the Scottish Home and Health Department's machinations and lack of proper budget rendered my ideas null and void. My extra vowel never materialised.

Red cones and the yellow and black diversion signs were still keeping us right. I forced the car into third gear. It was too much, and I had to come straight back into second.

'It wasn't just to be cruel though', I said. 'Have you heard about the riot temperature scale?' I asked.

'Nope'.

'Apparently most riots kick off when the outside temperature is between twenty-seven and thirty-two degrees. Below that people are less likely to, above it gets too hot to be angry. The worst thing is a steadily increasing temperature. Something about serotonin being released. We would have liked to keep the temperature in the mid-twenties, but the Union wouldn't have it, said the guards would suffer in the heat. Not even when we said we would install water fountains for the staff did they agree with us about the safety in having a sufficiently over-heated facility'.

'So the temperature was kept steady, and hot? And we were continuously served tea and asked to wear long-sleeved jumpers. Always kept sluggish and dehydrated'.

'That's possibly part of it. I'm not sure what the SPS's line of thinking is. All I can take responsibility for is the way I intended the building. You see, some of the walls were scheduled to have insulation in them but in the end none of them had any. I thought it would be cold but it was quite warm and snug, at least inside the wall where I slept before the lockdown was lifted. It took absolute hours I remember'.

'You walked around inside the walls while that was going off? Then you spent the night in the chicane?' Frank said, eyebrows high in his forehead.

'Yes. It was terrifying and exciting'. I said, shuddering a little at the memory.

'But that's just by the guards' staff room'.

'I know. But it was the warmest, and straightest place I could think of. And though it was close to the staff room I thought it'd be empty quite a lot of the time. I presumed they'd be out patrolling most of the night'.

'I don't know. They have pretty generous breaks', Frank said.

'Sure, but they still work more than they are on break'.

'Don't be so sure'.

'Either way it was fine', I said. 'Quite toasty. I had my jacket for a duvet and my backpack for a pillow. It reminded me of the few times I had gone along to the scout things my dad wished I was more interested in'.

'I must have walked past you on my way to breakfast'. Frank laughed.

'Probably. I meant to get out first thing in the morning but I had a long lie. By accident'.

'By accident?' Frank asked.

'Well, I had a scare around midnight when my phone started ringing'.

'Imagine hearing that inside the walls', Frank laughed, louder this time.

'Luckily no one did. But I turned off my phone and the alarm I had set with it'.

'That's mad', Frank said and smiled.

I nodded. At the time I had been exhausted from jangly nerves. I slept in, till about nine thirty, something I hadn't done for years. Not since I stopped drinking. Once I was awake, I crawled out.

'I made everything ready for the lucky winner of a one-way ticket to Bournemouth', I said not without pride.

'Great', Frank said and once again tried to adjust his seat for more leg space.

Driving through endless sets of road works had made me think about the hierarchy of hardhats. Ordered either by colour, usually going from lighter to darker as the wage brackets descended into minimum wage, or wear. The men at the top of the pecking order usually wear new hardhats while the older hands, or the pimply boys just out of school, wear battered ones, maybe even hand-me-downs.

Frank turned to me, 'So what happens when we get to Bournemouth?'

Relieved to be deep into England I now felt happy to talk about this.

'That's where we part ways', I said. 'There's a ferry to Jersey which leaves twice a day, so I'll drop you off at the terminal'.

'I didn't bring my passport', Frank said, and I wasn't sure if he was joking or not.

'It would almost have been worse if you did. If you're a wanted man, that's all the proof you don't need. Besides on the ferry you don't need to show ID. It's like going to Millport or something. Just a bit further'.

'I don't know anyone on Jersey. Isn't it expensive, with all the tourists and it being a tax haven?'

'You're not staying. The last time I was there I bought a five-foot dinghy. A little Pioneer with an outboard. It's locked up with a chain and padlock in St Helier not far from where the ferry comes in. I'll show you on a map the next time we stop, and I'll give you the combination for the padlock once we get to the ferry port'.

'I can't tell if you're crazy', Frank chuckled. 'Have you escaped from some sort of hospital to do this?'

'No', I said. 'I can assure you I am perfectly sane. We've accomplished everything I have set out to do so far haven't we?'

Frank nodded.

'Have you had any doubt in my abilities or my secrecy?'

He shook his head.

'That's the spirit', I said. 'Think of me as a pilot. I might be in charge but I have as much to lose as you, the passenger'.

'I'll be in no more trouble on Jersey than I already am, so screw it, why not?' Frank said and smiled vaguely. Seemingly satisfied with my itinerary.

After a while the truck in front of us pulled over and we were directed back onto the road we had been forced off. Narrowly avoiding my face in the rearview mirror I went through the gears all the way up. At 58 miles an hour the car gave a low, unpleasant rumble that made me feel slightly nauseous. The reverberations, the standing sound waves in the car must have caused something to happen to my inner ear. I had read things about experiments that the army conducted with sonar frequencies. Supposedly they found a way to transmit a note which made people lose control of their bowels. It would be a very effective weapon in warfare. The initial shame and inconvenience, as well as not being able to keep any food, would quickly decimate an enemy.

The Twingo at 58 felt like it was a giant tuba playing this brown note. I pressed the accelerator a little, making the needle jump just over the 60 mark. At 62 the car gave off a mellow hum. As if it had been manufactured to resonate to whatever vibrations the tyres gave off at that speed. I decided to risk being just over the speed limit. I had heard that carmakers err on the side of caution when they calibrate speedometers. For the sake of the consumer the instruments lie a little. You have more petrol than you think, you drive slower than you think. The machine you're in censors what you are allowed to know.

'Why are you doing this though, what's in it for you?' Frank asked after being quiet for a few miles.

'I enjoyed putting together this bespoke route', I said. 'And now that we are here I am keen to see how it works out'. I wanted to move away from the esoteric aspects of my decisions, feeling safer in logistics.

I said, 'There's a suitcase in the boot with a life jacket and an empty petrol can you can fill up at the little marina. There's a sailor's jacket for a more likely story in case you're picked up by the coastguard. There's food and a waterproof flashlight too. You told me about your French earlier. That's great, fortune favours the brave and all that. You've got intellectual resources. I am merely providing you with material aids'.

'This whole trip so far has been like being on a cruise for retired people. Someone's thought of everything', Frank said and smiled.

'*For pudding you have a choice of custard and prunes or millionaire's short-bread*'. I said in my best camp steward's voice. He immediately picked up the baton and said,

'*This evening's entertainment is a Donny Osmond tribute act. Bedtime at eight thirty*'.

Chapter 10

16.16 Sunday

We racked up the miles. The right-most digit of the odometer slowly ticking over, from six, to seven, to eight. I found myself relishing the bad quality of the sound proofing, the abominable ride and the uselessly low torque of the car. Its inadequacy kept me connected to the mission.

Thinking back on the research journeys I had undertaken on my own, and how soon we would be in the south of England made me realise I had so much to teach Frank before we got there. I turned down the music and said, 'Listen. The crossing'.

He sat up.

'If the weather is rough you will just have to wait on Jersey', I said. 'You have to work out the tides. The engine is fine for crossing, but you might run out of petrol if you spend hours struggling against the tide on both sides. But don't worry, it's a really nice island. There are always old guys hanging around the harbour who love a chance to talk about the tide and where to set off from and all that'.

'What do I do once – if – I make it to the other side?'

'Once you're on dry land in France, drill two small holes in the bottom of the boat, then you tie the handle of the outboard to the side of the boat so that it points in a straight line and just send it back out into the channel'. I nodded in encouragement. 'Got it?'

'Yup', he said.

'I've super-glued a compass to the top of the outboard, if you're able to pry it off do that, if not, it's no big deal'.

He nodded.

Spurred on by his apparent competence I continued, 'In the suitcase in the back is a dry sack full of stuff you might need on the other side. Euros and a dry change of clothes in case you have to swim the last bit. You can swim can't you?'

'Yeah. I rented out dinghies in Balmaha a couple of summers when I was younger'.

'Great. Also, people swim across all the time'.

'They are professionals smeared in goose fat. I couldn't do that', Frank said.

'It won't come to that. My plan's too good for you to end up in the water'.

We sat in silence for a little while. Maybe he was thinking of the great expanse of water, the arm of the North Sea between us and the continent? Maybe not. I was thinking about how the Twingo's accelerator pedal was placed too far to the left for a comfortable long-distance driving experience. The difference between doing the trip in the little purple car compared to traveling in my own agile sedan was astonishing. The Swedish Aeronautics company had provided me with all my automotive needs for years. This included a seemingly strange, but actually very clever placement of the ignition in the centre console. This made it harder to steal I imagine and it also meant that your keys were not forever dangling into your thighs when driving. There was also a nifty dimmer switch for the instrument panel, highlighting only speed and nothing else to distract you from the driving. Fit for a fighter pilot, fit for me. Good for traveling in the eternal witching hour of motorways.

'Then what?' asked Frank.

'Patience my young apprentice', I said in a theatrical voice. I'm not sure why. Then I continued in my normal voice. 'Almost regardless of where you end up there's a smattering of small places on the French side. There are buses all along the coast, and the best course of action is to make your way to my house in Saint-Nazaire'.

'Your house?' he turned to me. 'You want me to stay in your house? I'm not sure I want you to know where I am. You know, I appreciate all you're doing, and all this planning is impressive to say the least, but I'm not sure about being a tenant in your house'.

'Surely that part of the plan isn't the weirdest bit?' I said. 'Don't worry, I won't be there'.

'Where will you be?'

'In Glasgow with a pint of Coca Cola and a big grin on my face'.

'I'm still not sure', Frank said.

'I understand, I really do. All I'm saying is that you'd be more than welcome to lie low in my house. It's a roof over your head if nothing else. I don't know if you're any good with DIY but there's plenty to be done on the property. And I'll pay you the same as I would pay any tradesperson. To get you back on your feet if nothing else. Idle hands, devil's workshop and all that. Also, it's a way to funnel some clean Euros your way'.

'I can paint and do a bit of joinery, but I'm not great to be honest'.

'It's not charity. I need some work done and I might as well pay you as anyone else. It also gives you something to do. And contacts and authenticity. I've spoken to the neighbours and the people in the local shops, and they know I've bought a house, and so it's not weird for someone to turn up and do some work on it. Less suspicious than if you were just staying, not doing anything'.

The last time I drove well above the speed limit, going south for a recce, less committed to staying on A roads and more keen to get to the ferry port. Back then I had been totally isolated from the wind and the weather, comfortably cool and just warm enough in my SAAB. The big arms of the windshield wipers effectively slushing away unwanted precipitation. I have no idea what the weather was like that time, that's how cut off from the elements I was.

'I could be a tourist'. Frank said. 'Wouldn't that be easier?'

'It's a small place where they don't get a lot of tourists, and though my place is fine to stay in, it's not ready to be rented out to any holidaymakers yet. Maybe in the future'.

'I see'.

'I've left a spare key with a Madame Morvan. She runs a little bakery not far from the house. You can tell her you're my son if that helps'.

Frank turned to me quickly, then said, 'I'm happy just being a joiner. Though it seems pretty far for a handyman to come. I'll just make up my mind if I get there', Frank said.

'You'd be surprised at what some of the expats do. They tend not to trust the local population for anything, let alone new skirting boards'.

'Sure', Frank said.

Now in lock-step, marching south with Frank, a man who had also been cut off from the sensations of weather for a long time, I was acutely aware of the conditions in the Twingo. I had to be vigilant, couldn't let my attention drift the same way as I was able in the SAAB with its award-winning ABS brakes. I missed the meshed back support and sugar-dusted travel sweets in the glove compartment, easing the discomfort of travel.

'There's money in a tin in the kitchen', I continued. 'Enough for food for quite a while and enough to contract a plumber and whatever else needs doing that you don't feel up to yourself. I've made a list; it's pinned up on the wall by the cooker. You might have to reconnect the gas'.

'And if I don't think that's a good idea?'

'Well, there's a barbeque you can use, or I suppose you can eat at one of the two restaurants, but then you'll run out of money much faster'.

'No, I mean staying at your house', Frank said. 'Exchanging one prison for another'.

'All this is voluntary. I'm happy to pull over right now, and you are free to get out at any point. I'd rather you didn't to be honest, but that's only because you might tell on me if you're caught'.

'I'm not a snitch', he said, eyes dark.

'I'm not saying you are. All I'm saying is that I am offering you these various things, and it's up to you what you choose to accept. If you stay in Bournemouth, or on Jersey, or go to Turkey via France, or to Guatemala, that's fine with me. And if you stay for a bit in the house and don't do anything that's fine too. Just tick off on the list if you do fix things'.

Frank looked at his hands. 'How do you know I won't tell them about you if I get caught?'

'You just said you weren't a snitch'.

'I'm not. But if it bought me fifteen years to give up my accomplice I would seriously consider it'.

'It cuts both ways. I can phone the police at any time and tell them I've got you in the car. Also, accomplice is maybe a bit strong. If anything I would settle on Mentor. Maybe Liberator. It has a nicer ring to it', I said.

'Whatever you want to call it, it'd still put you in prison', Frank said, palms turned upwards.

'It's quite plausible I was taken hostage by you. My diction and background will unlock a lot of doors that will be closed to you. No offence', I said.

'None taken. For starters you don't have a skull with bleeding fangs tattooed on your chest I take it?' he asked.

'No. Do you?' I said.

'No, just this one of the Virgin Mary, which I kind of regret, but also forget that I have', he said. He turned his wrist over like it was the first, or the last, time he was looking at the face of Jesus' mother.

'That's one of the things I also have in the back, concealer', I said, happy that I had thought of pretty much everything.

'Make-up?' Frank said, and turned around to look behind him, as if I had brought vats of the stuff.

'Just in case the escapee had loads of tattoos. I mean you can wear gloves and a polo neck and all sorts, but it's harder to cover up a spider's web coming up to your eyebrows'.

He smiled. Across his face a fleeting resemblance of the Virgin and the other great image of mystery; Mona Lisa.

'You will just have to keep your hands in your pockets a lot', I continued, looking first into Frank's eyes, then into the teary ones of the Madonna tattooed on his left wrist, her face just peeking out.

I tried to spray screen wash to clear some of the insect debris from the windshield, only to realise the reservoir must be a lot smaller than the one on the SAAB. There was more in the trunk but I didn't feel like stopping and so far I was able to see through the flying graveyard in front of my face. Years ago someone had told me to put a splash of vodka into the reservoir, apparently the alcohol cuts a lot of fat, but I didn't trust myself enough to get even a small 5cl bottle of something *triple distilled, ten times filtered*, and not drink it.

'Did you have any trouble the last time you drove down?' Frank asked.

'No but I had a much more reliable car than this. The difference between this one and my SAAB is the same as camping and staying in a four-star star hotel'.

'You mean this one is cheaper? Is that why you're not driving your own car?'

'Not really. Petrol is petrol. I mean with camping there is a sense of adventure and a certain kind of heroic discomfort. Being in touch with nature and in some danger, even if it's just at a campsite. My SAAB is comfortable and it has a turbocharger and the Griffin package I bought as an optional extra when I got it. Back when commissions were many and not so far between. Before I retired'.

Frank nodded and looked out of the window.

The Twingo wasn't quite horse and cart but the image of me as the Pony Express and Frank as the package which had to get to a certain destination for a certain deadline appealed. It wasn't as bad, or as honest, as walking: *You'll take the high road and I'll take the low, and I'll be in Bournemouth before you.* To be hung, and never see your loved ones again. Putting away the gloomy image I started to look for a turn-off.

I had developed a certain way of getting onto an exit ramp. I would slowly overtake a lorry and once I had overtaken it, I'd turn sharply as late as I could, still in the 'shadow' of the lorry, and come off the motorway. Hopefully confusing any followers enough to buy us time to disappear onto one of the smaller roads. I didn't think anyone was following us, but I thought it wise to adopt safe habits. This time a huge orange monster from Sainsbury's provided cover.

As soon as we were off the A6, just north of Bolton-le-Sands, I saw one of my new favourite signs. How the world changes once you stop working. The unassuming brown ones were now a great little distraction, meaning there was a tourist destination within striking distance. A stone circle, a decrepit factory, a steam railway run by volunteers in funny hats. This one was leading us to Charton

Old Rectory. The brown signs had led me to quiet places of interest many times in the past. Ones with tired parents and busloads of rheumy-eyed retirees. They were as good a hiding place as any other.

'My first car was a Mini Cooper', I said as we were driving behind one of the reincarnated ones. 'My uncle gave it to me to look after when he went away. He had left it sitting in his garage for years and when he passed away it cost me a whole summer's worth of extra shifts to get the car rolling. It was the most expensive thing I had ever owned and it broke down every two days or so but the sense of freedom that comes with your first car is priceless'.

'I've never really been into cars'.

'This Twingo reminds me of the Mini. Basic, but not in bad way'.

We pulled into the rectory car park and I got out. It was already half past four and my back was sore as anything. On the ground was a rubberised glove. It looked swollen, like there was still a hand inside. Maybe a saint's hand, dropped in a sacrilegious robbery? The wind caught it and under it lay what looked like a porcelain eye. I prodded it with my foot and it turned out to be a sweet. Who would buy an eyeball for their child to chew on? The same kind of parent that takes a child to a rectory ruin for a treat.

When examined closely the detritus of us all is quite confusing. The glove was coming my way again on the wind and I walked over to the other side of the car park where a plastic hubcap was nestled in some sort of thorny shrub. Manufacturers no longer even pretend that the covers look like they are made of alloy or magnesium, let alone chromed steel. Using the hub cap as a tray I added a Styrofoam cup from the car to the pile of artefacts that had gathered at my feet. I built my cairn of relics, then placed the tray back in the bushes and went over to Frank who was reading a plaque, squinting.

Chapter 11

16.50 Sunday

We ambled around in the ruin for a while. The café was just closing up so I got us reduced scones to go, and we ate them on the grounds. When I spotted bats whirling I felt nature's clock was telling us to move on.

While Frank was in the loo I had time to stand and think about something not directly connected to the journey. Well, connected, but more to the goal than the road. I made a mental note to send Madame Morvan a postcard if I could pick one up from a service station. I didn't have her address but I knew the name of her bakery.

The first time I saw her I was lost in one of the inexplicable aisles of a French supermarket. I had just helped a dead man's daughter and I was drunk on wine and opportunities. I had made a verbal offer on a house, a new life, and everything seemed possible for a change.

Madame Morvan's eyes were the colour of leeks. Her hair like a coconut or a Chianti bottle's straw cover, stained by wine and time. A strand or two was going grey. Her hands, no ring on either finger, I realised I had quickly checked, poking every single avocado on display. Apparently none were good enough. I didn't know what to do. I had never even tasted avocado, had never seen the need to, let alone prodded and disqualified one, but I walked to the vegetable display where she was standing. I had to.

'Excuse moi... Comment... Les avocadoes?' I asked.

'English?'

'Language yes, but Scottish'. I pretended to look at the long rows of peppers. 'How do you know?'

'Sorry?' she said, an accent of course to her English, but a charming one, and at least she didn't seem to instantly hate me for not knowing her language.

'How do you know which one to go for?' I asked.

'I don't know. I just like poking them', she said. Her words quick like petrol fire.

'That's crazy. What if they see you?' I asked, looking over my shoulder.

'Who? The Carrefour police?' she said and laughed. It was the best sound I had heard in years.

I told her I had just promised someone local I would buy their house and she told me she lived not far away. She ended up giving me a tour of the supermarket. Showing me the best frozen bits and the cheapest rice, which of the two surly men in the charcuterie to speak to first, that sort of thing. I ended up telling her all sorts of things about myself. Must have been the Claret. Also she had a fabulous smile, two dimples, white uneven teeth. One huge earring, some kind of feather, nothing in the other ear. I carried her things to her car, and we ended up having coffee for ages in a little café across the road. As she got up to get her third coffee I called home to arrange with a solicitor to see me about the French house the minute I got back to Glasgow.

She came back and told me she had to go but that I could call her when I came back. Her name was Genevre Morvan, just the sort of woman I would never have talked to if I had stopped to think about it. I was no less of a psychologist than to realise she was the complete opposite of Maud.

Frank came back from the loo and we got in the car. It felt well rehearsed by now. It was darker outside but still just about light enough to not use full beams. We had walked around the ruins for longer than I had planned but it had been nice to get some fresh air after being cooped up in the car. If it hadn't been for the swooping bats we might have stayed longer, but as it was the Grand Tour had to go on.

'Ready Frank?' I said, louder than I had intended, as if we were saddling up. He just nodded and reached for the seatbelt.

Yellow lights were flickering down on the road signaling road works or a gritting machine going slowly. Maybe a wide load, someone's house being uprooted and moved to a more scenic location? Maybe a specialist crane hired to erect a statue of someone recently deceased? Luckily it was easy to find the correct road again. It came in a few different guises, but between the A65, the A6070 and the Old Faithful, A6, I felt we were in safe hands.

We droned on in silence for a while, almost too comfortable. Soon my mind was going this way and that.

'Want to grab the AA map Frank? It should be in the pocket of the seat behind you'.

'Sure'.

'We've been on this road much too long', I said. By now I hoped that he was aware of the strengths of my seemingly haphazard navigation.

'It's only been twenty minutes since we stopped'.

'That's beside the point. We are going south in general but I'm happy for you to call the shots for a while. Now, where do you want to go?' I asked, letting the copilot have some time in the limelight.

'I don't know. I don't know England'. Frank said and looked out on the road, as if the tarmac was different here.

Involuntarily I looked out too, but there was nothing to note. The road was the same as anywhere. It was taking us through an area with houses dotted about. A stretch without any kind of grace. Seemingly populated out of geographical, or geopolitical necessity. Maybe there were only so many hectares to support whatever kind of farming they had traditionally been involved in here. Now they all commuted somewhere.

'Fine', I said. 'Just keep us going south in general, and if anything west too, but that's less important at this stage, as long as we use a different road for a little while'.

'Wouldn't it be better to press on?' Frank said. Squirming a little in his seat. Looking in the rearview mirror.

'This is what will throw them off the scent', I said, surprised at his question.

'What? Stopping for scones and clotted cream in heritage centres?' he asked, but I couldn't make out if he was joking or not.

'We can't starve ourselves. I didn't hear you complaining when we ate'.

'Do you think they're onto us?' he asked, his voice quite high.

'Probably. Just presume the worst. I always have, always will'.

'That's no way to live', he said and gave me half a frown.

'It's the only way I know how to. And I'm too old a dog now to change', I said not without pride.

'Have you seen any police?' he asked.

'I would have told you if I had any concrete suspicions', I said.

'I don't think they would stand around waiting to see what we were up to', he said.

He made a gesture of a sniper, sighting down a long barrel, but smiling at the same time. A little like he was a cowboy in a back garden game. 'They'd move in with tear gas and all kinds of paperwork letting them shoot us on sight', he said as if he knew what he was talking about. And maybe he did. Despite what he was telling me I couldn't let myself be too sure of his real identity and more importantly, his real motives for letting me motor him around the country like this.

'Speak for yourself. I don't see what danger I am to society', I said.

'I don't think our deaths would spark any riots like that guy down in London, so I'd be surprised if they even thought twice about it', he said.

'The Royal Incorporation of Architects in Scotland might have a thing or two to say about my assassination'.

'Are you a member?' Frank asked, and it wasn't the first time I was annoyed at his childlike ability to strike at the heart of matters.

'Not as such', I said, 'but I think my Rotary club would be up in arms about my death. Especially if I was shot point blank. I'm certain they'd put a picture of me on an easel at that month's get-together. A thick gold frame with a black silk border I should think. Someone might play a requiem on the piano through in the bar'.

I would never tell him this, but I had never built a prison before. That's not to say that Cromlix was my first major project. In the past I had built wings of schools, a vestibule for a university library, an annex to a hospital, been part of the design for several housing schemes and a major canal and lock refurbishment. However, Cromlix was the one project where I had a real chance to make a mark. Both ideologically and structurally.

At the time of construction Euan was being spoon-fed big contracts, or small lucrative ones needing a lot of client contact time. At first that made me a little jealous, but I quickly worked out how to use his absence to my advantage. In the vacuum created by Euan's newfound status as a minor celebrity, which took him away a lot of the time, I found that I was quite powerful – just by being available.

Being my own boss and working right next to two nicely turned out secretaries were a few of the benefits of running a small, or rather *exclusive*, architectural firm. My role was consciously vague, but it meant I could sign off on a lot of the decisions myself. I had to go through a structural engineer for some of the things, but I knew him pretty well, and like me at the time, he liked a tipple. For Christmas I used to get him a bouquet of Glenmorangie and Talisker, but that was a long time ago.

Euan's idea for a prison was useful but horrible. Mine, which was never built, wasn't perfect but it was a lot better than his. I was anything but a follower of the Brutalist school of thought. The exterior of the prison I drew up, tentatively named HMP Heatherville, was inviting and as low as possible while still being safe. The lower masonry was shimmering in pink and white pebble dash. The walls were all to be lilac, the most Scottish of heath colours, shifting between slightly concave and convex, a further deterrent, and topped with a metal cylinder three metres in diameter. Less threatening than razor blades or crushed glass. As safe as barbed wire, science had shown, but less vulgar.

This slippery, chromed bar would reflect the light at dawn and dusk, lending a celestial rhythm to the day. The service entrance where goods and prisoners arrived was hidden in the back. At the front a glass veranda-like reception for families and staff, possibly a café. I wanted HMP Heatherville to feel like a mall or a college, not an institution. It would have a nice car park and on an unused bit of land a birch copse and a play park.

'Is Rotary a bit like the masons?' he asked.

'Not really', I said, swiftly coming back to the reality of the car. 'It's business and golf and a lunchtime pint. And we raise funds for good things. Polio vaccines and building wells, that sort of thing'.

'When was the last time you went?' he asked, again consciously, or subconsciously prodding my conscience. It was as if he knew that my meeting suit didn't fit as well anymore. So what, I had put on a little weight. The breakfast-lunch combo at Morrisons hadn't been very helpful lately. Squash just wasn't possible anymore. I was still happy in my favourite Versace jeans though.

'It's been maybe two years. I don't drink or play golf anymore, so some weeks I just don't see the point', I said. 'And I don't do much business either I suppose'.

Frank just nodded and looked at the wild fields outside.

'Let's just avoid getting shot', I said with as much finality as I could.

Chapter 12

17.20 Sunday

'Frank, how are you getting on with that map?' I asked when he showed no signs of finding us route alternatives.

'Hang on, I don't even know where we are', he said and looked out.

'We'll find it. I'm taking this exit, you can work it out', I said. Every car journey needs a strong, resolute mind.

'What did the sign say?' he asked while leafing through the road atlas.

By now we had passed it. 'I don't know, I'm driving'. Outside a grey ocean of cold grass and concrete crash barriers. 'Have you got it?' I asked.

'Give us a minute. You've been banging on about your stately funeral', he said.

I pulled out to overtake a camper van which was belching blue smoke only to have to duck back into the left lane as I was almost rear ended by one of those faux rally Subarus with golden rims and a thousand spoilers. The chump driving it didn't even see my masterly manoeuvre. He just sped past us, head nodding in time with some horrible music, probably the kind created by robots high on ecstasy tablets.

Once I had put the camper van behind us I said, 'I'm not asking for much. I'd be glad if I ended up in the ground, that's all. Not strewn to the fish at sea like some kind of terrorist'.

'You think the government fears your grave would become a shrine if it was on land?' he asked, still looking at the map in his lap.

I just shook my head and pointed to the box behind his seat. He started rooting around for the OS map corresponding to our position.

'If I could decide myself I'd have something up behind Glasgow cathedral. *A Metropolis always carries within it a Necropolis*. I think that's Milton, or Schopenhauer. I've always liked that place. Used to go up there with Maud before we were married'.

'Isn't the Necropolis more like a museum?'

'Don't know, but I assume it's oversubscribed anyway', I wasn't entirely comfortable talking about the exact arrangements for the disposal of my body.

'Right. I've got it now', he said as we passed a signage cluster of place- and road names. 'We are just past Dolphinholme. If you go straight at the first roundabout and turn left the second that should take us to an A-road, presumably the one that the motorway has replaced. It looks quite straight. Then there's a B-road, a snaking one that looks like it goes up some pretty steep hills. Just the kind of road you seem to like'.

'I'm doing this for both of us', I said.

'I know'. Again that half frown.

'Just hope the inclines aren't too steep. Not sure the car could handle that', I said. We could both lose some weight.

'This diet of Yorkies and white bread isn't helping. Not that I'm complaining, after prison food anything is a delicacy', he said.

'Let's try that B-road. You can always get out and push if it gets hairy', I said.

Frank just grunted and turned to read the signs of closed down factories. Carpets, concrete, rubber shock absorbers. All moved to sites elsewhere. We were traveling through manufacturing ghost towns for a while, but as we came further away from the main road artery the country came alive again. Not with crowds and productivity. Just with bird song and quiet folk going about their business. Zimmer-framing their way to the Co-Op. Walking a reluctant poodle.

Shifting down into third, a gear and resultant speed the car always seemed the most comfortable in, we rolled through polite villages and mock Tudor market towns. The road led us into a valley and soon the radio started coming in and out, a sound almost like waves breaking on the shore as the strings ebbed out and static overtook them. Radio 3 was playing Arvo Pärt so it didn't really matter if we missed some of the music as there was no melody or structure to hold on to anyway.

We had just left a huddle of houses when a black shape shot out of a hedgerow. There was no time, absolutely no chance for me to turn the wheel before we went over it. The left wheel juddered a little, as if I went up on a kerb when parallel parking, and then we settled into the road again.

'Stop the car Cecil', Frank said.

'I'm sure it's fine', I said.

'Stop the car'. His voice steely.

I started to pull over but didn't put on the hazards as someone might stop, thinking we needed help. It was better if any passer-by thought we had just stopped to take a piss. No one parks up to look at two old guys peeing.

Frank was out of the car before we had even stopped properly and he half-ran back, in his oversized way, to the place where we had heard the thud.

'It was an accident Frank'. I shouted, breathlessly running after him.

'It doesn't matter what it was'.

'Look, I'm not too happy stopping. People might see us', I said loud enough for him to hear, but not loud enough for it to sound like we were having a fight if anyone was listening.

'You never seem to mind stopping at ruins or RSPB places', he said, taking long strides.

'That's different. Lots of people stop there', I said, hoping he'd see sense.

We approached the shape and I realised it was a cat. Its back legs were crushed and the spine looked more bent than even a cat could handle comfortably.

'Let's just leave Frank. It's dead', I said.

'It's a tom cat', he said quietly.

'How do you know? Cats just look the same regardless of gender', I said.

'We had cats growing up. This is a male'.

'And he's dead so let's go..

'Look closely. He's breathing', Frank said and bent down to see better.

'I'd rather not. Either way it can't be long now'.

'We can't just leave'. Frank said.

'It was an accident', I said and threw my arms out for extra emphasis.

'There's a collar and a name tag. Maybe there's an address?'

Frank reached out and at first there was a hint of hostility in the cat, an attempt to raise himself up and sneer, but Frank put a big hand on the cat's head and it seemed to relax. Frank detangled the tag from the fur and turned to me.

'His name is Quirinius', Frank said.

Frank stood up and looked back up the road. 'We should go back to the village. With a name like this we should be able to find the owner. I know it was an accident but closure and a kind word goes a long way. A lot of my cats ran away. Or at least I was told they ran away. My mother used to call it Cat Holiday when they disappeared'.

'You can't show your face, and I don't want to do it', I said.

'We have to. This is someone's loved family member. Some little girl's best friend'.

'Then they should have kept the cat inside', I told him, desperate for him to see sense.

'Cats wander. Doesn't mean it's ok to kill them willy-nilly', he said.

'The best thing would be to drive away and forget all about this. Being out here on the road it could have been hit by any car'.

'But it wasn't. It was us', Frank said.

The cat started to vomit and shudder. It was horrific. Frank bent down again put his hand on the cat's head and that seemed to calm it down for a second or two. Then it started screaming, the sound of nails on a blackboard. That was the last straw for me.

'Frank, I'm leaving', I said. 'You can stay here if you want and take a train to Bournemouth. I could meet you there. That part of the deal would still stand even if you chose the cat. Or you can go wherever you want'.

'It hasn't got long to go. Give it a minute or two to die Cecil'.

'It could be ages. As far as I know you're not a vet', I said.

'Look at the breaths, they are coming slower and slower. Its eyes have gone dull too'.

'I'll be in the car', I said. But I couldn't move, glued to the spectacle of the cat's spasms.

Frank looked up at me. 'Cecil, help me find something hard'.

I shook my head to show how I felt about the whole thing but I stepped down into the ditch looking for a fist sized rock to wrestle out of the mud, but I couldn't find anything worth using. When I came up my suede shoes were caked in brown leaves and dirt.

'I'll get the jack from the car', I said. 'It's the best I can think of, but I'm not doing it', I said and stalked off back to the car, carelessly parked at the side of the road.

Once back I handed him a compact, foldable of jack I'd found in the boot.

'I'm sorry Mr Cat. Mr Quirinius', Frank said to himself and then swung the jack down hard onto the cat's head. It didn't work. The cat let out a groan and Frank hit him again and again until the cat stopped sounding like a broken hoover.

'Happy now Frank?' I said once the cat had been still and quiet for half a minute.

'Not really'.

'Can we at least go now?' I asked.

Frank had tears in his eyes and there were spots of blood on his right hand. He turned and threw the jack into a field. It sailed like a bird for a second then landed in the coarse leftovers from the wheat harvest. I grabbed the dead cat by the nape of the neck to swing it into the ditch but Frank stopped me with one look. He took off his shirt and wrapped the cat in it and then jumped over the ditch. He walked over to a stone wall and put the feline corpse inside it. Once he was done it looked like he crossed himself. He carefully replaced the stones and closed the hole. Only then did we go back to the car. I felt as if the Holy Mary on his wrist was looking at me with stern, wistful eyes.

He wouldn't speak for miles and miles. Just looked at the map and pointed left or right whenever we came to a crossroads. As we emerged out of the valley up onto the hills and a kind of moor, the radio kicked back in. The stark Estonian music from before was still playing, only now it seemed much weightier. We could have dug a shallow grave, or put the cat in the back seat wrapped in a coat, for a proper burial in land or at sea later on. We could have syphoned petrol out of the car and cremated him. We could have scraped the ashes of it into a sandwich container and spread the remnants of Quirinius somewhere he would have been happy to tether his afterlife to. But we didn't. We couldn't.

When we made it to a place called Dunsop Bridge we turned south, but despite the stunning scenery it was a very long way to get to the B5269, where I could speed up a little. After half a lifetime we were able to rejoin the A6, just by Preston. Pootling along tiny roads I made up my mind not to go any smaller than one or two digits on the B roads.

'We should have found the owner', Frank said quietly, but loud enough for me to get the message.

'I know Frank. Under different circumstances we should have. Maybe I'll come back this way on my return journey to Glasgow'.

'If you're coming back'. Frank said looking out his window.

'What do you mean? Of course I'm coming back'.

Chapter 13

17.50 Sunday

Not having Frank to talk to, as he was in a huff, made me think once again about the Twingo and how it was quite different from my own choice of vehicle. First of all, it was lilac and not pewter like the SAAB. The little car was full of cat hair and the back seat was more like a pin cushion than the sprung sofa it should have resembled. The two front seats had off-the-shelf covers I bought for my sister a couple of years ago. I had been stumbling around the aisles of B&Q looking for bolt cutters and duct tape for Cromlix and polyfilla for my rented kitchen as I had kicked a big hole the kitchen door. The tinsel and the manic music made me realise it was Christmas and my eyes had landed on the seat covers I was now enjoying. Without them we would have been stopping even more frequently.

I was tired and Frank was soon sleeping again. My eyelids were getting a little heavy too so I decided to look for a rest stop. When one came along I gathered enough momentum on the slip road to be able to coast into the car park in neutral, before cutting the engine completely well before I slotted the car into a space. That way I hoped Frank wouldn't notice the difference in sound and motion so much, and he might go on sleeping, like the big toddler he sometimes resembled. I stepped out and did one or two quick lumbar stretching exercises.

We were just south of Bolton and hardly anything was natural despite the fact that we were overlooking a pond with fat geese and a shaggy bunch of trees. There was a squirrel raiding the bins by the toilets, but it looked hopped up on candyfloss and hardly counted as part of nature. I looked at the stand of trees, some kind of willow. Imported by the looks of it.

It got me thinking about my copse by Cromlix – or Heatherville as I had named it back then. The prison ended up being concrete grey of course, and not the gentle colour I had wanted it to be, and there was very little boscage for a visitor to enjoy. The prison ended up Brutalist, and not humane like I had hoped but not budgeted for.

It wasn't without irony that I was now traveling in a lilac car, roughly the same colour as I had prescribed for the outer walls of the prison, with a prisoner. In a self-imposed cell with a weak combustion engine, moving over space as well as time. In a cell there is movement over time, not much movement in geographical terms. The criminal element is captured in time as well as in space. I had shattered the albumin that had held Frank and now I was weaning him back onto geographical movement.

I had left a note for Frank who was sleeping in the parked car, and I could see him from where I was standing, so I wasn't too worried. I had learnt something from the first stop outside Ochiltree. I turned and looked at the geese. A wing-clipped armada dipping in and out of the pond snapping after scraps of sausage roll and ejected Chewits.

I turned back to look at Frank. His mouth was open in childlike abandon. Total trust, or total lack of care, I wasn't sure which. I wasn't hungry but I knew I should get something to eat, or at least to drink. I found that I had nothing to do with my hands. At home I would have fiddled with my phone but on purpose I had left it turned off, plugged in by the toaster. Satellites and echoes from masts, triangulations and words eavesdropped in the dark, were part of my phantoms. I didn't want to get caught in the nets cast by acronymed government agencies. In my mind there were spinning wheels of one-inch tapes recording every word spoken across the country. A huge call-centre full of young people, a hand raised into the air to catch the attention of a supervisor as soon as certain words, phrases, or names were mentioned. I wasn't sure how I was surveyed but I was sure I was.

I had my money belt stocked full of money, £2,036 in old bills, one being a £1 note, the one with the ramparts and mini Pantheon on, which I had kept for good luck. I totted up a mental tally deducting petrol and sustenance from the nest egg I had amassed over the years. Cash is king and cash is cloak and dagger. I had left all forms of ID, including my debit card, and the credit card without much available leeway these days, in the kitchen drawer at home too.

I left the dirty geese and walked towards the bright lights. I got us Whoppers and chips, a big Coke and a forest fruit pie each. For an extra pound I got us *MintyMintyFresh* chewing gums with the meal, some kind of promotion. I thought that might ease the strain we were putting on the car's interior smell. Luckily the girl serving me seemed devoid of emotion and didn't seem to register my face as she took the money. I wanted to tip her for her anonymity curtesy, but realised that might make her remember me.

It was just after 6 o'clock so it wasn't illogical that I was beginning to feel drained. From the nerves churning away and from surreptitiously looking over my shoulder. From evaluating Frank, especially in the light of the aggression brought on by Quirinius. Endless cups of stewed tea weren't helping either.

When I came back to the car Frank was awake, though his eyes were still crusty and it looked like it would have been better for him to sleep on. The car park was almost deserted and I beckoned him out of the Twingo, as if I was a tamer and he a sleeping lion. Was I slowly putting my head between his jaws?

We ate our burgers in silence, sitting on the bonnet like washed-up matinee stars. The Whoppers were the normal sugar-coated cardboard but at least the food occupied some space in my stomach that might otherwise have been inhabited by stress. I knew I should have worried but I was happy, my feet resting on the front bumper. Wilfully trapping myself in a bubble beyond clocks. At these feeding stations marooned along the road network time was suspended. We stopped, so our progress stopped. Anyway, the vending machines and outlets we made use of were open around the clock, undermining any natural rhythm to the day, further confusing the traveler.

'Here, Frank, while we've got a couple of minutes', I said once we had finished our burgers. I opened the trunk and rooted around a little before I found the bag from the pharmacy on Maryhill Road. I held up the two little bottles proudly.

'Nail polish?' he said.

'I should have put it on before we left, but forgot in the rush'.

'What are you on about? All this talk about dresses and make-up is weird', he said.

'Don't worry. I'm perfectly heterosexual. This is for the car'.

'Can I eat my pie first? I'm still starving', he said pointing at the brown bag.

The car park remained empty so I wasn't afraid of being spotted. The wind picked up a little, and it was the harbinger of winter. We opened both doors and sat in our seats, with our feet on the ground, in perfect symmetry, and ate our pies. The resident squirrel eyed us but quickly deducted we were either too hungry or too broke to give him even a morsel. On the radio 'I say a little prayer' came on.

I feared Katie was losing her touch, then realised she might have been succeeded by a different disc jockey by this time of day. I rarely listened past six in the evening. It had never really struck me to think about her working hours and what kind of contract she might be on. If she was part of the furniture or freelance, recording her programs from a little house in Portree or a busy flat in Stevenage.

Once we were done I threw Frank one of the little bottles I had bought just after paying for Janice's hideous coat. 'Slather on as much as you can on the reg plate'.

'Why?' he asked.

'It's a trick I've read about. Apparently if your car is being photographed by traffic cameras, this shiny layer will help confuse the picture. In the dark the reflection from the flash should render the photo almost illegible'.

'Really?'

I shook my bottle like a maraca. Like one of Aretha Franklin's backing singers would have. 'It's worth a shot'.

'Why doesn't everybody do this?' he said smiling.

'I'm not everybody'.

Frank shook his head, and absentmindedly hummed along to the music.

'Anything else before we start?' I asked, half in jest as I was really full and thought that he must be too.

'Can I have a cup of tea? Just black', he said, face straight.

'Anything else. To eat?'

'No thanks. Actually can I have an extra-large mocha instead, and a caramel muffin?'

'That's the complete opposite'.

'I know. I just forgot that I could make whatever choices I want to'.

'Within reason. Money doesn't grow on trees', I said.

'It's mad how quickly I was trained out of the small things once I was inside. Like having a latte instead of black tea or instant coffee', he said, almost nostalgic.

I was trying to pry the little lid of the bottle and just nodded, now happy it was windy as it would disperse the fumes faster.

'I know it's just a stupid warm drink but the whole idea of spur of the moment is removed from you. As extra punishment I think', Frank said.

'Let's get the coffees on the way out then, my treat. But *First work, then pleasure*, my father's motto'.

I thought it'd be quite quick but it took almost 20 minutes. The brushes were so small and crouching down in front of the car was painful. Frank worked on the back, apparently at ease with the manual task. I was still wearing my favourite Versace jeans and I didn't want to sully them by sitting down. They are quite light, kind of fawn. I should have brought along a selection of paintbrushes instead and we could have used tea cups for pots. Maybe coveralls and a set of kneepads? You live and you learn.

I was quite woozy by the time we set off. Looking out the window the world seemed full of adventure, shafts of light breaking beautifully on the windshield. I felt like we were knights endlessly pursuing our goal. Our journey was on par with the adventures of those men, looking for the real source of the Nile or Eldorado, not just a dismal walk-on ferry terminal in Bournemouth. If I had been alive a hundred years ago I would have been blazing trails in jungles or across the icy tundra of the far-flung north. As it was, I had made certain contributions to the face of Glasgow. Mostly in the form of buildings and by extension the city's cultural life in terms of the function these structures fulfilled.

The Twingo rumbled on and soon I realised I had forgotten to get Frank his muffin. My stomach rumbled too as the burgers had created space in me rather than filling it. Again I had been jipped. The sun had set over the low hills to our left. I presumed it was west but I couldn't be sure if we were driving south right that minute.

It was unusual but the temperature in the car was just right, the amount of wind coming in through the slightly opened rear windows not too loud but enough to filter in new air and expel foul odours and our carbon dioxide. After many hours of trial and error with the various vents and settings on the air control panel we had agreed that having the heat on, just past 12 o'clock on the dial and keeping the rear windows open between an inch and an inch and a half was the perfect middle ground between comfortable and fresh. As the evening light deepened I afforded us another mph or two of progress. Soon white cat's eyes began winking back at me.

Chapter 14

18.30 Sunday

I thought back to the beginnings of my involvement with the concrete juggernaut. On the Saturday before the presentation to the committee I slept in the office. On the Sunday I had breakfast in a greasy spoon, but couldn't eat much. I was too worked up about the prison, so ran back to the office to continue. Just after lunch I made an advance withdrawal from next Friday's bottle in the wine rack and made some last changes to the placement of HMP Heatherville. It was the most nervous and excited I had been in years.

On the Monday I felt so alive I couldn't sleep and I was up early. I showered before the sun was up, and it was May. My new cufflinks were hard to get through the holes of my stiff shirt. Maud was sleeping on the sofa. She liked falling asleep in front of the TV. I often came home late; the game shows kept her company. I remember thinking her general knowledge had increased since we were first married.

If she was awake when I came home she would tell me I smelled of wine. That was sometimes true, but most of the time not. If anything I smelled of chewing gum. I did sometimes have a glass of wine, either while drawing up the prison plans, or after, to wind down.

Sitting at the breakfast bar I inspected my nails. I felt like a builder, but un-calloused and clean. I put my coffee cup and saucer in the sink and removed the four bits of tissue paper I had used to stem the flow of blood after a close shave. I shrugged into my coat, put my rolled-up tie in a coat pocket and went out to the car. The meeting wasn't scheduled until 11, which was good because that meant I would have time to get hold of a miniature bottle to steady my hands.

I took the long route into town, pulling over by the SAAB/Jaguar showroom on Maryhill Road. Though I was perfectly happy in my 9000 CDE, I entertained the thought of trading it in. A bus trying to access the bus stop honked and I had to pull out into traffic again, middle finger out of the window.

I went and sat in a swanky café just off the Royal Exchange. I fingered through the plans and had industrial amounts of coffee. Then it was time to go.

Striding up the steps of St Margret's House two at a time, I held in my suitcase a whole host of sketches. With Stewart backing me I planned to lead the committee onto discussions on colour and minor changes. To make them feel like they had a say, and to distract them from the more revolutionary aspects of my design. I felt that the intrinsic flow and the modern irregularities were too complex for those paper-pushers to understand.

After all, and this I had tried to explain to Maud on more than one occasion, my shapely prison was destined to be one people would make pilgrimages to in the future.

'My *Wotruba Church*', I told her one evening, proud. Maud just nodded and returned to Interceptor.

The lobby of the St Margret's House was empty. I was early and sat down in one of the uncomfortable, commissioned chairs. I went through what I wanted to say, and how I would guide the audience of laypeople through the design.

'A formality really', Stewart had said, the contract already signed.

I had thought he would come down and meet me, but at five to eleven I gathered my things. On the way to the way to the conference room I opened my briefcase, smelling its new leathery interior and flicked through the colourful folders. Nestled between the pens in the rack of the briefcase was a small bottle of Cabernet Sauvignon I had bought for this occasion. The screw-top came off easily and the contents disappeared just as easily. My cufflinks were clinking against a brass banister as I inspected my close shave in the sheen of a panel, removing the last traces of paper from the cuts.

Some of the boys on the committee knew me. Some even remembered my dad. The red blood of a socialist is impossible to wash away, and that was one of the reasons, beside my obvious technical prowess and proven track record for suc-cessful project management, that I was the best man for the job. I had grown up coming to my dad's factory, eating all the broken biscuits I could stomach, and bringing home bags and bags for my friends at school. Especially Stewart.

I had been so busy inspecting the quality of my shave that I had forgotten about putting on my tie which was still rolled up in the pocket of my new wool coat from House of Fraser. Approaching the end of the corridor floor I pulled it out and whipped it on. As the door was opened by someone stepping out for a fag, I finished the single Windsor, as time was of the essence. Before I had time to ease the knot off my Adam's apple I was set upon by the committee members, all wanting to shake my hand and pour me instant coffee. At first I found it hard to breathe, then, as I struggled to remember the names of all the old boys shuffling towards me in an endless stream of bald heads and liver spots, I forgot about the anaconda around my neck.

I was directed to the head of the table without much preamble. As if I wasn't a carceral visionary, burdened with one of the breakthroughs of the century.

'Where's Stewart?' I asked.

'Not with us today', someone said.

I looked around the room, taking in the 12 men on the panel. They were all people I had met, or stood next to before. Apart from one or two they were pushovers – cattle easily herded. They were only interested in solutions, in results which kept them in their elected seats. I knew the game. The civic machine had put food on my table, and wine in my rack, long enough.

I remained standing. I had learnt that it inspires confidence and gives the speaker power. I bent down to unclick my briefcase, inhaling deeply. I ran my hand over the tubes of paper and the presentation folder. I unbuttoned my suit jacket, spread my arms and was just about to start my talk when someone knocked on the double doors leading in to the conference suite.

I knew everyone who was meant to be present was in the room and was mildly annoyed by this interruption. If it was a cleaner I would be stern, if it was a tea lady equally so. If it was a tea girl, I would be stern but mildly funny.

The double doors opened slowly, revealing an unknown man. He was young, not just younger than the men on the committee, but younger than me. His suit glimmered like a shark in tropical waters.

Scanning the room, I realised everyone else knew this man. One of the old guys, a Mr Patterson from the Building & Engineering Division of the Operations Division of the something rather, got up. I had given up years ago trying to understand the impossible organisational morass, and just nodded at him. Mr Patterson started pulling over a chair, breathlessly saying,

'Euan, just in time. Have a seat here next to me'.

This 13th man gave me the willies. I tried to undo the knot of my tie a little but my index finger got stuck somehow. All I managed to do was to make it even harder to breathe.

Euan had not brought anything with him. No notepad, no suitcase, no coat, hat, or gloves. This meant he either worked in the building, or was very warm. That he either knew everything about the project, or knew nothing at all, and was just here to listen.

I went into the presentation like a child into a steep waterslide. Once I was done the chaps ooh'd and aah'd a little over the blueprints I sent around while I poured myself another coffee from the urn. As no one was looking I made sure to add a dash of Cab Sauv from the second mini hidden in my suitcase. Some people say wine and coffee don't mix, and I tend to agree, but I was gagging.

I was just about to launch into a more informal discussion, some Questions and Answers as well as the inescapable praise, when Mr Patterson stood up, and said,

'Thank you so much for coming in today Cecil. I think I speak for everyone when I say that we thoroughly enjoyed your, hmm, visionary plans for the prison'.

"No bother at all," I said from the corner with the coffee urn.

Mr Patterson continued, 'You're more than welcome to stay for Euan's presentation, if he doesn't mind. I realise you might have other projects to get back to'.

'What will he be talking about?' I said, thinking I would let my pulse settle and finish my coffee, while listening to a talk about the future of the oil industry or something equally cut-throat. Only someone in business would wear what Euan was wearing.

'The proposed plans for the prison. Same as you'.

The room spun.

'Is Stewart coming at all?' I asked again, swallowing hard.

'He's no longer with us', Mr Patterson said with some finality.

I was too shocked to say anything. Before I knew it Euan was in full swing, showing slide after slide of graphs and numbers. He was more focused on the cost of things, and keeping it affordable, than I had been. He had a very sharp projector, which he must have set up prior, and his hand-outs were printed on thick, creamy paper. His presentation was so slick I took him for an actor rather than a competitor.

He presented the board with a completely square box, a prison with slits for windows and one entry point, same as the exit point. Even managed to dress up his monstrosity as something good. He showed them a perfectly symmetrical structure and presented it as a viable alternative to my prison. If a normal building is a machine for living, my prison was a machine for betterment. Euan's structure, a concrete dice with room for 300 prisoners, was an apparatus for punishment. A cheap one too.

I was too stunned to react and instead of doing anything I drank cup after cup of coffee. Once Euan came to the Q&A part of his presentation I excused myself, apparently to no one.

I stumbled out into the brash sun, the windows of St Margret's House reflecting the light in a way which only highlighted the soot stains. By now the lunch rush was over and it was easy to find a stool in a quiet bar.

By the third glass I felt no better, but at least a certain numbness was setting in. While writing my name in used-up wine against the back wall of the urinal I suddenly remembered the contract Jeanette had sent over in a rush. Struggling with the zipper of my trousers I ran back out, and made it back to Park Circus before Jeanette left for the day.

Together we pored over the contract and to my great relief it seemed quite set in stone that I was the assigned architect. That 20% of the fee would be paid even if the project never went ahead.

I celebrated by popping a cork and then called and left a message on Mr Patterson's phone telling him I was the chosen one. I had no idea why Euan was even presenting. And I had no idea what had become of Stewart.

I kissed Jeanette on both cheeks, got a fiver out of my wallet for a taxi for her, as it was now quite late and I still couldn't remember if it was her or Lise who had a kid, and ran out to my car.

In the morning Mr Patterson rang and asked me to come in and see him. By 11 I was back at St Margret's House. A freshly printed contract in my briefcase, a reminder of my rights.

'Where are the others?' I asked when I stepped into the empty room.

'They won't be coming today'.

'Any word on Stewart?'

Mr Patterson just shook his head and looked at his fingers, pushing down a cuticle with the back of a biro.

'We have chosen Euan', he said.

'But the contract, I mean, regardless of everything else…'

'Right now it's only really worth the paper it's printed on'.

'I…' it was difficult to breathe. 'It states that I will receive a fee whether you go ahead or not'.

He swatted the air, as if it was full of flies.

'Cecil. Listen to me. Stewart's no longer here to hold your hand. We have agreed to take you on in a kind of advisory role, a consultant if you please. That's your only option. Or you can go back to designing extensions'.

I hadn't realised quite how powerful Mr Patterson was in the scheme of things, I thought his department was some stuffy place where mediocre bureaucrats went to die.

'I don't understand'.

'We're on the same side here, and taking Euan on board makes perfect sense. If necessary, he can be the public face of the contract. You can still have some input if you fancy. We all know you're a competent architect'.

I had a sharp, steely taste in my mouth.

I tried to speak up, but again his hand shot up. He palmed the air, like he was trying to calm an agitated llama.

'I have a new contract here', he said, walking to the head of the table. I followed and he handed me a pen. Feeling sick, for the second time in 24 hours in the same room, I signed on the dotted line.

Chapter 15

19.00 Sunday

The Twingo was pulling us along. I had been through about 20 of the little white chits and my tongue was going numb but I seemed to be thinking less about food when my breath was *MintyMintyFresh*. I continued popping chewing gum in, sometimes adding cold coffee to further suppress my thought about where our next meal would come from.

Maybe I had changed his metabolism because soon Frank caved in and told me he was hungry. And luckily, or maybe he had seen a sign and received a subliminal signal, there was a Drive-Thru not 10 miles away. When we came up to the car park I thought the place looked like it was full of surveillance cameras so I made Frank get out before we entered the car park proper. He was to stand in a little grove and wait for me to return, and on the signal of my twice flicked full beam he would step out of the shadows and re-join me.

'Cecil, if anyone sees me they'll report me for indecent behaviour', he said, getting out.

'Why? If you need to pee surely you can be discreet about it? I'll only be a couple of minutes anyway'.

'You know what some of these truck stops are like. All kinds of tastes catered for'.

'I can't see any prostitutes', I said craning my neck.

'Doesn't mean they're not here'.

'The ones I've seen, you could tell right away what they were', I said.

'Have you seen many?' he asked, a smile playing on his lips.

'On TV. Get into the woods'.

'Just be quick. I don't want to fend off horny lorry drivers and I don't look like a hitchhiker'.

When I came back out of the restaurant with two steaming paper bags, Baconator Combos and Doctor Pepper, Frank was standing by the car. He was looking exactly as shifty and guilty as I had feared he would. What he had going for him was the fact that he was leaning against Janice's car in a proprietary way, smoking, the best excuse to stand still literally anywhere for any length of time. I don't know what we will do in a smokeless future. I suppose fiddle with our phones or implants until our thumbs are triple jointed.

'Where did you get that?' I asked pointing at the cigarette. 'I didn't think you smoked'.

'I found it on the ground. I didn't want to ask anyone for a light, so I lit in the car'.

'Did you force the lock?'

'No, I wouldn't know how to. You forgot to lock the car'.

'And the lighter worked?'

He just nodded and cocked the red tip of the cigarette towards me. The superheatable coil which seemed so out of its time in the car had proved itself useful for once. The orange bullet waiting to be discharged had saved us a little.

'There were all kinds of things going on in the woods', he said and exhaled a shallow breath. 'I couldn't stay'.

'I was only gone a few minutes, I said placing the paper bags on top of the car, in preparation for a roof-top picnic'.

'I saw at least three couples', Frank said.

At that moment we were blinded by a wall of white lights. A bank of sharp rays shot through the little woods. Outlining several people either throwing themselves to the ground or zipping up their trousers and casually walking off, stage right. The copse had been transformed into a drama school play, full of cheap silhouette work.

There was a roar of diesel engines and the lights dropped in intensity. Two white people carriers marked POLICE edged around the woods and into the parking lot. One from each side. They parked to the left and to the right of us in a bay not far from the entrance to the service facilities. Instinctively I pushed Frank down onto the ground. Luckily there was a Vauxhall Insignia parked next to us and Frank could cower in the gap between the Twingo and the hallmark middle-manager vehicle.

'Tie your shoelaces for a bit', I murmured out of the side of my mouth while I struggled with the lock. The stupid Twingo had locked itself and my palms were sweaty, slipping on the key. I felt the van drivers' gazes play over me. 'I don't want to die before I've seen York Minster', I said out loud, surprising myself. The sliding doors of the first van opened and five burly men stepped out lithely. Armed jaguars on two legs, visors pulled low, flak jackets tightly buttoned.

The doors of the second van opened up. The men who came out looked like grizzled veterans. Negotiators in stain-proof suits with police IDs swinging on beaded chains from their necks. They had less of a need to look imposing. You could tell that the entire state machine was behind them. They dry-washed their hands in the chilly evening air, rolled their shoulders like welter-weights, glanced over at the woods and spat, their saliva undoubtedly hitting whatever they were aiming for.

My arms were now up above my head and then they all broke out laughing. I pretended to stretch while I tried to work out what was happening. The two forces met not far from where I was standing and their rude jokes about the *dirty rabbits they had flushed out from the woods* and *pervs* was a balm to my ears. My heart was beating so loud I was afraid they might hear it. I could hardly fit the key into the lock, but I eventually managed to open the door. I reached in and pulled up the knob of the driver's side passenger door.

Frank was still crouching. Having another man kneeling so close to my crotch, in a place full of questionable activities, might be enough for an arrest regardless. I carefully looked down and was startled by the energy lumped together in Frank. He had killed his cigarette which was a smart move and now looked like a 100 m sprinter, quivering with energy, about to set off. I realised he had seen the police too and would not allow himself to be caught easily – if alive.

'Frank, crawl into the back seat, and stay low', I said under my breath. He got in and I realised there had been two bags of takeaway food on the roof of the car the whole time. The eagle-eyed investigators and snipers must have clocked it, I thought. No one likes Burger King enough to get a double portion. I got in, trying to look like I was not in any hurry and passed one of the bags back to Frank.

'Let's go Cecil', he whispered urgently from the back, but I sat still for a few moments even though my sweaty armpits and my mind was screaming for me to floor it out of the car park.

The drivers of the white Police vans now got out too. I presumed they had been logging miles or securing armoury padlocks. They were laughing, undoubtedly at their antics, at the full beams of inspection into vice. They filed into the eatery, following the strong arms and sharps minds of the law, and only then did I turn the key in the ignition. I didn't want it to seem like I was leaving just because they had turned up.

Indicating properly, I drove out of the car park as slowly as I could. Triple-checking the lights were on and hoping no one would notice how low the suspension was despite there being just one person in the car. I was thanking my parents for gifting me such a plain, unmemorable face.

'Do you think they saw us Frank?' I asked, once we were out of sight.

'They might have seen us, but they didn't recognise us. If they were looking for us we wouldn't be here now'.

'How many people in the woods would you say?' I asked.

'Maybe six or seven, I don't know', he said.

'Enough for two teams of riot police to turn up?' I asked as if he was some kind of expert. He had been in the care of the state and might know their workings.

'Too many. If they really wanted to do something about prostitution or whatever indecent exposure there is, they would make it illegal to buy, not illegal to sell. That would make some politicians sit up and take notice. Some might have to zip up and take notice', he laughed, a low rumble. 'Staking out a little wood by the roadside won't change anything. I'm sure they were just on their way home from something else, maybe they do this all the time'.

'It felt rehearsed somehow. Like they knew their roles', I said. 'Let's just hope it's their weekly joke on the repressed local population, starved of the affection of strangers'.

In a lay-by a few minutes up the road I had a look at the map and saw Liverpool and Manchester were the biggest cities nearby. Riots happen in big towns, not in the country. Same with strikes, demonstrations and most visits by foreign dignitaries. I concluded one of these was the reason for the vans.

'There's a lot of football violence in these parts', Frank said, and I nodded. 'Maybe they were just on their way back from a derby', he continued, and I was inclined to agree. With this in mind I drove in the opposite direction from these Meccas of disorganised sport, which is where I presumed the force was coming from. I wanted to be far away from civilisation just in case there were more of these humorous constables roaming the main roads. This meant going East for a good hour but once we were past Manchester there was a long stretch of quiet road. Such was the extent of my discomfort at seeing the police that I decided to temporarily abandon my principles and we joined the M62 not far from Rochdale.

I must say I felt for the lorry drivers and men in the woods. With any luck the area would soon be a designated Public Sex Area, and these enthusiasts would be left alone. It was a relief to think that the incident had nothing to do with us, but mainly with the stirred emotions of men in tight uniforms. Luckily I had always been able to work in smart/casual.

I had kept my food in the paper bag until we were safe and I can't recall ever having a more delicious cold burger and warm fizzy drink. Soon we were humming along at an unprecedented speed.

'I'm afraid we're going to have to go via York', I said.

'My geography's not great, but that's not on the way to Bournemouth', Frank said.

'I know. It's difficult to explain, but if it makes you happier it's the last thing they expect'.

'You're the driver, it's your car', he said. 'But the quicker I'm out of the country the better'.

'I agree. Don't worry, this won't add much to the journey'.

In the back Frank had buckled himself in with both sets of seatbelts. Once across his chest and the other across his thighs. He was lying in a foetal position, and soon he was snoring, his bag neatly folded on the floor. The adrenaline of the encounter soon ebbed and I felt sleepy too.

Sitting on my own up front, for the first time since driving the Twingo to the car park by Buchanan Street bus station, made me feel both lonely and generous. Possibly the closest to a parent I have ever felt.

Back before I was consumed by Cromlix I saw my sister and niece a fair bit. Janice went back to work very soon after Jennie was born, doing irregular shifts, and her husband was working long hours so on a Saturday I would sometimes offer to help. I remember taking Jennie out when she was little. She would sit in the pram and soon fall asleep – sometimes happily, sometimes crying. For better or worse I was probably a bit more wooden than her mum. I wouldn't give in and I didn't molly-coddle her, but I loved her. Especially when she finally slept.

I would wheel Jennie around and in my mind I sketched on improvements for my own projects or for famous landmarks. I would think up clever solutions to problems never posed as my bread and butter clients were a far cry from the Sydney Opera House, or anything else that required my skillset as a visionary architect. I spent years doing extensions and kitchens, ruining my eyesight on blueprints detailing whether cupboards were to open left or right. When I wasn't busy dreaming of improving the Kaufmann Residence, everyone knew the joke *Falling Water – Rising Mould*, I spent weeks submitting ambitious bids. Pepper-potted outskirt projects and humbler ideas of lit plexi-glass soffit solutions for private properties. At one point even a couple of community gardens and a light makeover tender for a mini retail park on Broomhill Drive, a career low point. All but a few were rejected.

The moving picture that the arc lights from the police van had painted at the resting place, using the trees for shadows, reminded me of long days in the Uni library. Drawing architectural plans with an imaginary sun present, for imaginary clients. The sun shining at an arbitrary 45 degrees onto the vertical and horizontal plane, the light always coming from the left hand side, casting shadows to the right. A western reading of the world, progressing from one side to the other. I got quite good at it. I was always good at make-believe, and this one was especially interesting because it involved messing with the whole solar system.

This forced and rigid perspective had nothing to do with how the building would look in real life, apart from maybe for a few minutes on a sunny day, but it was a representation the clients were after, not the real thing. The police force supplied their own sun, their own searchlight, and had painted a startling, temporary canvas.

I had some interesting ideas about sculptures as architecture for the prison. But when I tried to implement them I hit a *cul-de-sac*. For a while I wanted to set up a few free-standing structures on the walls of Cromlix. Ones that would cast significant shadows. And not unlike the effect of Stonehenge these shapes would come together at a particular time of day or even once a year to form either an image or a word of encouragement and emancipation. These sculptures would show time moving, while interacting with the eternity of the heavens. Euan and the others thought having climbable statues on the walls, just for decoration was a bad idea and I was inclined to agree with them when it was put that way. I was still a little disappointed in their lack of enthusiasm for what were in essence sundials for the twenty-first century.

The memory of being a temporary carer for Jennie made me even more determined to deliver my current package safely. My happenstance navigation had kept us safe so far, and if I started doubting my ability to make the right decisions we were in trouble. The course now reset by my inner compass, extending the journey, was hopefully further confusing Scotland Yard's bloodhounds. Heading for York, as my subconscious had told me to, felt right. Roaring politely along the back roads framed by rain and rolling hills, I felt the fear of the episode drain out of me, only to be replaced by an implacable *joie de vivre*. I opened the window and punched the evening air, whooping quietly as not to wake my sleeping charge.

Chapter 16

19.30 Sunday

For a little while I was not entirely sure where we were. Then I realised I had had too much to drink. When I pulled over just outside a little place called Facit to take a leak, Frank woke up. We were still a while away from Leeds, so I deemed it safe to stop. We had been eating and drinking at the same time, and it seemed his bladder needed emptying too.

He stood a respectful distance away, engaged, as was I, in one of the few purely mindless, yet satisfying acts left in the world. Also one that is entirely free. When we got back in the car I handed him a wet wipe, then started the engine.

The rain started like crystals on the windscreen. I didn't want to disturb the specks of water and light gathered before me. The wet diamonds grouped themselves into milky ways, forced into longish patterns by the speed, still about 58 miles an hour. A fancy Audi A4 overtook us. It was painted a matte black and seemed to suck out the remaining light, a black hole on four wheels. If I had been younger and good at sports, that's the car I would have wanted.

'What car did you drive Frank?' I asked. 'Before'.

'My wife used to drive a Golf. An old one, nothing fancy', he said, no hesitation.

'Was it red?' I blurted out before I could stop myself. I had been at the trial after all.

'How did you know?' Frank turned to me and I felt sweat gathering in the small of my back.

'Lucky guess. A lot of cars are red these days'. My pulse like church bells in my ears.

'Very lucky. Have you read about me in the news?' he said.

'Nope', both hands slippery on the French steering wheel.

'Maybe you have and forgot', he said, still looking at me.

'Maybe', I said keeping my eyes on the road.

'I was in a lot of the papers when I was sent to prison', he said. 'All the tabloids had something. Most of them just copied the information from some central text. Most of it was wrong. Including hard facts, which they could have checked'.

I nodded and looked at the numbers, each one in turn on the speedometer. The rain made the road look slippery, so I slowed down to 56. We were completely entrenched in middle England and the density of cars and housing had steadily increased from the sparser outpourings of the urban sprawl of the Lake District and the Yorkshire Dales. I had to concentrate a bit more on the driving than before.

'It's not a thing I'd wish for my worst enemy', he said. 'Having rumours printed about you for everyone to see'.

'But you were convicted for a crime weren't you?' I asked. 'Otherwise you'd not end up in prison'.

'The papers weren't interested in that. That was just something they glanced over. Instead they played up all kinds of theories about my "dark past"', he said, his eyes turning to the road.

I thought about the day Janice called me to tell me what had happened to Jennie. The accident-prone crossing, the hit and run, the red hatchback a witness had seen. I wasn't sure what to make of Frank, but 'Griffin' had been too long in the planning to abandon now.

On the fourth floor of the Concert Square car park off Killermont Street I had made sure to push my less rational, immediate feelings under. Then and there I closed the lid. Putting Janice and Jennie on the back burner was the only way this could work.

If I allowed myself to think about Frank as a person, rather than a function, all would be lost. I was still reeling from the shock from seeing him, *him*, step out of the bus at Buchanan Street, but had quickly decided to keep hold of the dizzying feel, an otherworldly sensation, like being abroad but still on home soil, to get me through the mission. I had to keep him in the philosophical sphere, otherwise nausea and guilt would ambush me.

The spray from the Audi ahead of us, doing sometimes 80, sometimes 50, contributed to the mass of glittering precipitation and regrettably I had to turn on the windscreen wipers, scattering the clusters of diamonds on the windshield.

'Do you have a *dark past*?' I asked.

'I didn't finish school and I am divorced', he said. 'But nothing before this'.

'Do people recognise you in the street? If they do, we are going to have to go deeper', I said, my mind racing.

'I'm no celebrity', he said. 'I kept my jacket over my head whenever we were outside. My solicitor drummed that into me. There was a courtroom sketch, but it didn't look anything like me'.

'That makes things easier', I said. 'I suppose in the olden days to forget and to forgive were closer linked. Now the internet never forgets'. I scratched my emerging stubble.

I realised he can't have had any access to the internet for the duration of his sentence. Unless he was checking his emails on a phone someone had smuggled in. I wasn't sure how Wi-Fi or 4G worked in a prison. Presumed they had blockers or something going. Before I could ask he said,

'No one's approached me yet'.

I just nodded. In a perfect world I would have had a plastic surgeon lined up to put him under the knife, but I had calculated the risk to be too big. Also I didn't want to be holed up somewhere while his nose wings and eyebrows healed up.

The silence made me remember what I was thinking about before we stopped to pee. I have thought of better windscreen wipers for years, but so far I've not been able to improve the design, but there must be progress to be made even in this trivial field. I had a couple sketches at home. Ones with a pivot halfway down the middle.

'One day at a time. That's what they told me at the group meetings'. I said and shuddered at the memory. These awkward sessions with people completely unlike me might have been the thing that saved me. It was a place I never wanted to go back to. Frank was quiet.

'I'll see my family soon', he said.

'Careful'.

'Don't worry. You're not part of it. I'm just grateful you decided to help me out'.

'I didn't decide to help *you* out. I decided to help one gifted individual out. It happened to be you'.

I thought it was ironic that the biggest success of his, and my, life would never be reported on. It wouldn't even be given a small article in the RIBA journal, despite being almost flawless.

I had literally set my ideas in stone and Frank would reenter society through the gateway that was my house in France, another stone structure.

I had calculated that it might not be the escapee's wish to go on a road trip with me. Not all drowning men wish to be rescued. There was potential for an unaided escape, but I didn't rate their chances, and I think the same person who had made their way out of Cromlix would come to the same conclusion. I knew Frank could have pocketed the money and left on his own, but he didn't. He chose to come with me.

There was no way, apart from the infrequent checks I made on the location, that I could have known that the drain cover had been opened from the inside. I considered wiring it up to some sort of alarm, but it got too complicated with batteries and transmitters. I didn't want to involve anyone else in my scheme so I just left clear instructions in a double plastic bag, taped high up on the wall, far away from any water.

Our outing into the unfortunate plains beyond Dolphinholme, our own Elysian fields, still played with my mind but I decided to bury the image of the cat and Frank's wet eyes. How he banged the car jack down onto the cat's head over and over. Together we had stared death in the face, and that tends to change a man.

'I'm just going to crack open the window a little', I said, opening it the width of a small whisky.

'It's not me', Frank said grumpily.

'What isn't?'

'The smell'.

'I'm sure it's just manure from the fields', I said.

Frank smiled, 'Just opening the window whenever you want to is amazing. Especially when you're used to spending all your time with other guys. Some who wash and others who don't'.

'Why wouldn't you wash? There are en-suite showers aren't there? I know I put them in the design. Don't tell me they have been relocated or something'.

Frank smiled, almost condescendingly, 'There are showers but some people choose not to use them. Some people don't think about personal hygiene. Especially when you're not meeting anyone new or strangers. You don't see anyone you care about, except for at visits if you get them, and not all guys do'.

'Weird. I think I'd still like to be clean', I said, trying to work out how long it had been since I had a shower. Packing the kits in my sister's car, hair still wet from the shower in my flat, seemed a lifetime ago.

'It's almost like a choice too. Like it's the last little bit of freedom', he said.

'What? Being dirty?' I said.

'Prison is clinical and it tries to be disinfected, as well as grim and dirty in other ways. It's another of those weird double things they use to play with your mind'.

'I tried to make Cromlix easy to keep clean', I said.

'It's like a train station I guess', Frank said. 'Somewhere between working and falling apart'.

'I spent years designing that thing'. I thought about my office drawers and long afternoons with milky teas.

'No offence. It's just used by a lot of people, who all hate the building'.

'The plan was to let in as much natural light as possible', I said. My go-to defence. 'People love light'.

'That's not the problem. And also you didn't build the finished product so don't blame yourself. Your ideas sound nicer'.

'I can't be blamed for people not showering can I?'

'There was never much hot water. I could never shift the smell of institution'.

'I know it', I said. The mixture of urine and chlorine, of desperation and baked beans, a nauseating cocktail.

'You could have put in better ventilation', he said, as if he had made a mental list of grievances toward my building.

'I tried, but they were so afraid of escape attempts that I had to scale down the vent pipes and shafts from 1.5 metres in diameter to 0.5 m, so that no one could crawl through'.

'I thought you said you used the blueprints for your own purposes?' he said.

'I did. Remember walking across a big gap on the second floor on your clandestine way out?'

'On a set of pipes?' he asked.

'Those were three 0.5 pipes set in cluster, making 1.5 metres worth of ventilation'. I smiled at the memory, 'A gangplank to freedom'.

The rain increased. The water on the windscreen had no longer had time to form starry patterns.

'So why was it still so smelly inside?' he asked.

'In the end there wasn't enough power in the air condition units to pump through enough for a building that size. It's not like airports and colleges are kept fresh just by open windows. Turned out it was really expensive to provide fresh air, which for most people is a free thing'.

'So it's another form of punishment?' he asked.

'The difference was a couple of grand. That was in effect used for a very nice unveiling ceremony. We had Tabitha Greaves and that guy off the telly, you know the one who does the weather sometimes?'

'Instead of fresh air?' he said, turning to me.

'The canapés were amazing. There was this one with capers which just blew me away'.

'So for that I was inside a box full of people's sweat and piss and farts', he said.

I kept my peace. Opting even to keep the radio off, listening to nothing but the noise of the road. It was a gentle hiss, like the gas heating up a pot boiling two eggs.

Ahead of us the bright lights of Leeds. From previous visits I knew it was going to be a bit of a headache to get through this Motorway City of the 70s, with high speed roads going straight through instead of a ring road. We had to get away from the M621 and get on the A643/58/64, or York Road. I wasn't looking forward to this untangling of the forty-odd year-old urban road vermicelli, but there was nothing for it. Pedal to the metal if we were going to make it to the Minster.

The continuous ebb and flow of adrenaline – self-inflicted or brought on by external events – was starting to take its toll too. I was exhausted from having driven the whole day. The lulling motion of the wipers sloshing back and forward right in front of my eyes didn't help with the onset of sleepiness either. Out of the dark, a car came shooting past, only to turn off, spectral brake lights like the Devil's eyes in the black night.

Chapter 17

20.00 Sunday

Once we made it out of Leeds, not without getting two turns wrong and being up on the chevron for three exit ramps, the A64 was a nice reprieve. Off toll, off grid, off piste into a new future for him and possibly for me too. Ears to the ground, eyes on the horizon. In the spirit of things I permitted Frank two beers from the stash in the boot, and he drunk almost all of the first one very quickly.

'Humour me Frank. I'm falling asleep here. How did you find the escape route?' I said, to avert his thoughts from the inadequate air ducts.

'I worked in the laundry, long shifts', he said.

He held onto both bottles, unsure where to put them.

'Once I realised the bright blue panel underneath washing machine number fourteen was really thin I got thinking. If nothing else, it would be a good hiding place for things. When you're inside that's the sort of information you squirrel away. It was quite a bright blue, and once I had clocked this panel I started seeing other blue bits dotted around the prison', he said.

I laughed, and told him, 'It was gypsum board, the thinnest in the business, painted with RAL 5005, Signal Blue, or in French *Bleu de Sécurite*. It was my little joke. And I presume you were thinking along the lines of the French Revolution, White: égalité, equality, Red: fraternité, brotherhood, Blue: liberté, or to you, Freedom'.

'Not really. If anything I was thinking about water, and thinking that all the water the prison was using had to be going somewhere', he said.

I smiled. If nothing else in our lives overlapped, at least this experience did. I had dug the rabbit hole, he had jumped in.

'I decided I wanted to take a closer look at the panel in the floor', he said. 'The old guard in charge of the laundry knew me for a "good guy", his words, and most of the time he left me to it. I was usually pretty conscientious. It seemed time passed quicker anyway if I did what I had to do and didn't think about it too much'.

He was still gripping the bottles, like microphones. As if he was holding a press conference.

'Once I started noticing blue bits of the prison it was like my eyes opened', he continued. 'It's like when you have your first child, just to realise that loads of people are pushing prams, but you've just never noticed. All of a sudden these blue bits were everywhere. Sections of the huge tube on top of the wall outside, the lower bit of the flagpole, a long fat line along the floor in the main corridor, which continued up on the wall near the guard's room'.

'That must be close to where I slept that night', I said, remembering the sudden fright when I heard my phone ring inside the wall.

'I guess', he said. 'It was lucky the guy in the laundry didn't know I wasn't very good with my hands. Once I decided I wanted to pry a little beneath washing machine number fourteen, I started telling him about my job on the outside and he seemed suitably impressed, enough to make him think I knew my way around machines anyway'.

'That's perfect', I said. 'You used your personal traits to increase the quality of your life. Truly upwardly mobile'. I knew I sounded like Thatcher but I didn't care.

'Maybe. Either way, one day I told him number thirteen, which was next to the one I was interested in, needed a new seal as it was leaking. He immediately started complaining about his sore back, which I knew he would, so I volunteered to do the job. He went to the stores to requisition a spanner, leaving an even lazier guy to look after us. This one always read both the Sun and the Record but would never lend his paper to anyone even when he was done. He called it SPS policy; we called it something else entirely.

The lazy guard sat himself down in his usual seat and this gave me a chance to look properly underneath the gypsum board. It was only when I saw the rails and the mechanic's creeper trolley peeking out from underneath the next section of the floor that it struck me that it might not be an accident that the board was fastened so shoddily. I threw in a pencil to see if it hit anything but I could hear it flying quite far into the cavity. I was aching to investigate further but I knew I didn't have time to do so. Instead I poured a bucket of water onto the exit pipe of machine 13, to make it look like there was a leak. I managed to put the board back just in time for the old guy to come back.

He called me over and told me he couldn't get hold of the spanner until next week and asked how bad it was. I said it wasn't as bad as I thought, that it was worse in the beginning of the cycle, but seemed to settle once the pipes were warm and expanded.

That made him happy, as he wouldn't have to fill out any forms'.

Frank finished the first bottle, swirling the last of the foam into his mouth, smacking his lips. He leaned forward, placing one bottle on the floor and his now empty left hand on the dashboard in front of him.

'After that I waited almost a week', he said. 'In case someone had seen me, if it was a trap. It was a crazy time. I ate almost nothing, to make myself slimmer. Stock-piled Mars bars to tape to myself like a suicide vest, in case I got stuck somewhere inside the building. I also tried to map and piece together the various blue bits of the prison'.

He opened the second beer with his teeth and took a long, deep drink. Wiped his mouth with the back of his hand. Then he continued,

'One morning, the Friday before I left, there was a new job lot of guards, which was great. This new batch of trainees were nicely clueless, and seemed to trust the system, so I decided to take my chances'.

He smiled, then said,

'I folded the three photos of my wife and the kids I had up on my wall and put them inside my pants. I have never been so excited and scared at the same time. Apart from when my daughter was born, but that's different'.

He turned to me and for the first, and possibly last time, in my professional life, I felt I was treated with real, *real*, respect.

Frank chuckled and continued, 'The laundry shift was four hours, starting earlier than any other job, and ending later, meaning we had lunch last, which made it a pretty unpopular job, which was great for me. I was the most reliable person there and was usually in charge of a couple of machines and left to my own devices.

As soon as I got in that morning I put on all eight washing machines and all eight tumble dryers, telling the new guards they needed an extra cleaning spin. Planning for the machines to cover any noise I had to make to open the panel.

I undid the screws with a plastic spoon. They were more placeholders than screws anyway and lifted the blue panel. I lay down on the trolley on my back, feet first, then I rolled half my body in. This meant I could fasten the blue board back over my head'.

'Great. All part of the design', I said. Happy that me and Frank had been on the same page. 'I made sure to leave enough space either side to enable that', I said, no longer sleepy, remembering the nerve-wrecking climb into the bowels of the prison to make sure the escape route was in full working order and the screws loose enough.

Frank laughed at the memory and continued, 'I was now sealed inside the tunnel and no one would look for me for the next 4 hours or so.

I didn't like my fellow prisoners, but I trusted them enough to not say anything if I wasn't immediately located. There was the bathroom, the dentist, a lawyer's visit, all sorts of reasons why I could be away from my work station. Anyway, on the inside anything different is as good as a holiday. Making the SPS look bad was entertaining if nothing else.

I hoped the newbie guards would believe in the security of the building. Trust their routines and their systems, more than their eyes and ears', Frank continued.

This was the most he had spoken since we set off. The beer seemed to help.

I said, 'I made sure the tracks were hidden from view from above and that there was a slight downwards slope to make the trolley roll better. To the world, and to Euan, this was just an emergency overflow channel which I put in to prevent flooding in case there was a massive leak in the laundry'.

Frank nodded. My most appreciative client.

'Once the panel was secured I set off into the darkness', he said. 'My hands feeling the way along the walls. I was still going feet first in case there was a drop, so it took me a while to realise there was a torch taped to the front of the trolley. I thought it was just some kind of lump but once the channel opened up a little I could swing around and when I turned it on I felt a lot better. It was only then I noticed the first note from you'.

'I hope the batteries hadn't corroded. I bought a decent brand', I said.

'Nope, they were perfect. They would probably have lasted a couple of days. Longer than me'. He wiped his mouth and continued, 'I made it to the end of the tunnel and found the ladder up to the top of the wall. There was a bit of a crawl...'.

'Twenty-one yards, almost to the inch'.

'...and then the floor changed'.

'You were about eleven feet, eight inches up in the air, same as the Berlin Wall', I said. 'Seemed a reasonable height to me. Trusted the East Germans had done their research. On top of the actual wall was the cladding and the slippery anti-climb pipe, hollow at parts, and solid at others, which put you a further four feet, nine inches above the ground'.

'Then down again, this time with a rope you had tied to a rebar sticking out', he said.

I remember planning that part of the prisoner's journey. I had thought it was enough to pretend to forget one tool box on the premises, two would have been pushing it. But no one asked to inspect my rope when I walked about with it on the site, and then I lost that too inside the Western wall. The rebars at that part of the journey was a perfect example of a designed fault of the highest quality. I had specified them to stick out, and the builders had blindly followed my orders. It was either that or screwing in mountaineering anchors with a fixed perpendicular carabiner and a rope, which seemed too risky.

Frank finished the beer and looked at me. I could do nothing but nod. He had been *inside*, he deserved a drink. God knows I would have had a couple, but I was glad I hadn't bought more than six watery German bottles for my guest.

My mind drifted back to the infancy of Cromlix. As it was no longer my project I had made sure that cost calculations and timelines collapsed whenever I could. In a clever way though. I was older in the game than Euan and knew how to piss off contractors enough to make them work slower, doing a sub-par job, that often had to be re-done, but not to annoy them enough to walk out on us. There was a fair chunk of money involved and complicated contracts so I knew it was unlikely that any of the contractors would give up no matter how obtuse I was. It was a fine balancing act.

Due to the more and more garbled construction process Euan was soon happy to hand over a lot of the day-to-day business to me. By then, as a result of the prison contract and his connections within the Scottish Office, he was also in charge of the big revamp of George Square and a couple of private Highland hunting lodges, so he was busy. Once he was out of the picture, the *starchitect* of the day, I reeled in the fractions a little. A greased palm here, a couple of kegs of beer for the thirsty workforce, a bunch of tickets for a Rod Stewart gig. It was easy to get the big contractors and the smaller builder guilds back on my side.

I was now in a much better position to implement some of the changes I had in mind. I told people they were improvements, alterations, meeting new EU standards, in preparation for coming legislation. ISO this and ISO that.

On paper, I made the parts of the escape route seem like separate bits, totally unconnected. Linked up they had resulted in a one-man cornucopia.

It was ironic that the public would see such a small part of the prison. The design could not be scrutinised by the people who paid for it. They saw a peel tower and a car park. Got a taste of the site rhythm, through a glimpse of barred windows, mainly stores and offices, but no more. I could have proposed more of an iconic skyline, like the Kuwait National Assembly, or the Fernsehturm, but I felt it would have cheapened the intentions.

These vanity projects are often the signs of a council, or nation, down on its knees. Both financially and in worship of the creative mind. I didn't want to do Norman Foster in chains, van der Rohe under the glare of CCTV. I wanted to do me, and the interred men, justice. At least until I decided to scuttle the prison.

'What if they had found out what you were doing?' Frank asked, once he had finished the third bottle I had allowed.

'On paper it looks innocent – if incompetent', I said.

Frank nodded, but didn't say anything. I hoped he realised Cromlix was the very opposite of an incompetent building.

'To be perfectly honest, I was terrified', I continued. 'It was the best time of my life. My heart was in my throat twenty four hours a day. My pulse was irregular and racing. I couldn't eat and I couldn't sleep. It was a bit like being in love, amazing'.

'You're nuts', he said. This time shaking his head and smiling broadly.

'Maybe', was all I could say.

I thought back to the heady days of infiltrating my own work place. The excitement was addictive and I was soon taking bigger risks. Doing silly things just to see how far I could push things. I brought in a couple of ladders which I 'forgot' to take out, I scattered knives and master keys on the premises, but since it was still a building site no one noticed.

As the prison ramparts slowly came up around me I started inspecting the inside of the pipes, ceilings and the double walls I had specified, all in broad daylight. Never a raised eyebrow. My job, my looks, my accent worked like an invisibility cloak. This made me feel untouchable. I was soon an adrenaline junkie, bringing in more and more ridiculous things to the prison site. Laminated porn, cash in double freezer bags, a couple of air guns, 10 or 11 boxes of Diclofenac, leftovers from a series of knee surgeries. While out snagging I scattered the blister packs over the premises like chanterelles strewn in a forest. No one ever asked me what I was doing. If anything my breadcrumbs were probably found and gobbled up by grateful men on both sides of the barriers of the law.

It got so far that in the end I broke into my old house in Bearsden. It was a great rush. I had a set of keys which I hadn't returned out of spite and one night I decided I would retrieve my old Meccano set which was still sitting in the attic. Needless to say it was the Chardonnay making decisions for me. I made it in, tiptoed upstairs and got the box. On the way out I had a quick look around the house but I couldn't sense the presence of a new man.

I had a quick look in the fridge and grabbed a chilled bottle, noticing she had come down a couple of rungs on the wine ladder since we separated. I peeked into the coat room and did a quick coat count, and got the impression that Maud's mother was living there. This cheered me up no end. Once outside I was shaking a little but the cold wine helped and by the time I walked down the hill to my car, clutching the big box of my childhood toys under one arm I was whistling happily. I wanted to use the main part of the Meccano set to build the guiding track for the mechanics' trolley leading from the laundry out to the main corridor of my labyrinth, but quickly realised it wouldn't work.

The car now smelled of beer. Pleasantly, almost like a bakery. I had never been too drawn to lager so it wasn't too hard to not take a drink. If Frank had been drinking wine it would have been more difficult. He reached back and fished out another beer, this time without asking.

'How did you get on once you were down on ground level', I asked. 'Out of the pipe and into the wall? Out of the cauldron and into the fire?'

'Fine. It was a bit of a squeeze, but...'

'Shit Frank! Shut up!'

On the horizon flashing lights, sharp blues and red. On either side of us inescapable crash barriers. I was fenced in. Going down a conveyor belt into the mouth of hell.

'It might just be an accident', Frank said.

'I think there's more to it than that', I said. 'It's a funnel. Shit, shit, shit. And the car stinks of beer'.

I was finding it hard to breathe. It felt like someone had forced a sock into my mouth and plugged my nostrils with sharpened wine corks. Between gearshifts, engine breaking to softly reduce the speed, I was clawing at my throat.

'Open all the windows Frank and get in the backseat. There should be a big blanket, pull that over you and don't even breathe until I say it's ok'.

The walls of the little car were closing in on me. Many times I had seen concrete being poured into a frame for a foundation, and now the car was flooding with the slush. The mass was creeping up, pushing out the air. Circling my torso like a semi-fluid boa constrictor, the animal vice closing around my neck.

Meanwhile Frank somehow squeezed himself between the two seats and was now folding himself up like a big, unwieldy turtle. If I hadn't been so scared it would have been very funny.

'Frank', I croaked. 'Are you done?'

'Take it easy Cecil, slow down'. I heard Frank's muffled voice from the back.

The lights on top of the police Land Rover were getting sharper and sharper the closer we got, piercing my eyes like needles. I tried to tell him to hurry up, but couldn't get my tongue out of the way. It was stuck to my teeth.

'Hide', was all I could say, but it came out sounding like I was drowning or as if I was trying to speak Danish.

I felt my heartbeats in my neck and groin, and I almost wished I had put on an adult nappy for this eventuality.

'I'm under the blanket', Frank said from the back. 'How far away are we? I'm getting cramps'.

'Sshhh. Not far'.

The long row of brake lights ahead of us told me we weren't just driving past a police car. This wasn't an accident or someone pulled over for speeding. My breathing was so laboured I thought I was going to pass out. One by one the cars ahead of us came to a stop. Then there were only three to go before us. One of the new Beetles, a Citroën Berlingo and a Fiesta.

Once the Fiesta drove off, it was our turn to roll up to the constable. Feeling as if I was about to die from lack of oxygen I punched myself in the midriff to force down air. Then I took my foot off the clutch, 100% ready to denounce Frank if I had to. I came to a gentle stop next to the police man. The officer, a young man smelling of quick spurts of supermarket aftershave, leaned in a little, friendly elbow on my window frame, and said,

'Are you ok? It's a bit cold to be driving with all windows down'.

'I'm just allergic. To cats. It's my sister's car', I said in a convincing wheeze. Before I could check myself I asked, 'What seems to be the trouble?' I had stolen his token line, and felt myself blushing.

'Flash flooding a few miles from here. Diversion. If you're going north keep right, if you're heading south, keep left'.

I'm going north'.

'Fine. Have a good evening and take care'.

'It's ok, I've got an inhaler', I said, ripping the little lighter stub out of the middle console, then sucking on it, like it contained Pulmicort. Luckily the officer had already turned his attention to the next car in line.

'Bye', I said to deaf ears, my voice that of a pubescent boy. I put the car in gear again and rolled off, calculating the risk of taking the opposite path to the one I had said I'd use as minimal. When I tried shifting to second I accidentally put the car in fourth and the car stalled. I had to stop, turn the ignition again and suffer being honked at by the car behind me. I was so stiff that I couldn't turn around to look at this enemy. Frank reached over and double-blinked the hazards and I nodded my thanks. Soon we were off, far away from the prying eyes of authority.

Once we had put some distance between us and the police I felt the blood drain out of me and I pulled into a small farm track. Then my vision gave up on me. I searched for the hand brake and pulled it.

I don't know how much time passed. I felt Frank climb out of the back seat, and heard him pull open first his door, then mine. He dragged me out of the car, and he put me down on the blanket he had been hiding under, placing a life jacket under my head for a pillow.

'Take deep breaths, I'll get you something to drink', he said.

'We made it through', I squawked.

'Here, the sugar will help', he said.

Slowly the concrete waters receded and I was soon up, sitting in the front seat while Frank syphoned non-alcoholic wine into a Sprite bottle, 80/20.

'I'm fine now. Let's press on', I said. Frank handed me a straw and Eminasin Verdejo gushed into me.

I had told the officer we were going north which in the general sense wasn't true, but because of my desire to see the Minster and the layout of the A64, I had inadvertently told the truth. I should have used the northern arm of the ring road to approach the holy city, but now we were going south on the A19. After consulting the map, I decided we should construct our own ring road. Using the A19/A63/A614/A1079 we would soon be back, now coming at York from the east.

For the first time so far I was worried that the trip was wearing me down. That the rigours of the road were stripping me of my usual devil-may-care attitude. Most of all I was worried we would run out of wine before I could stock up.

My hands looked strange and lobster-like on the steering wheel without the right set up of spokes to hold on to, but I managed to put the car into a comfortable marching speed. Powered by regular slurps, we were soon outrunning both distant and near memories of personal trauma. I was pretty sure the alcohol free wine either had remnants of alcohol in it, or else triggered a buried happy reflex in my system, because after just a few miles I was giggling to myself. There was nothing funny about the A63, but soon Frank and I were spluttering like boys thinking about farts and boobs in class.

Chapter 18

20.30 Sunday

By now Frank would be a wanted man. For that reason I kept looking in the rearview mirror, expecting to catch my breath. At first scanning for signs of the cavalry I was trying to outrun, later to monitor myself and my levels of tiredness. I was measuring the circumference of the black circles pooling around my eyes. For 20 minutes I was trying to escape my mirror image, whilst also trying to catch the creature looking back at me from the other side. To Frank it must have looked like I was having a drawn-out seizure.

All of a sudden the image laughed at me so I ripped the rearview mirror off the windshield and threw it out of the window.

Frank turned to me and asked, 'You ok?' his voice surprisingly level. I was suddenly glad I was traveling with someone who had explored the deepest caves of despair. Someone who had known extremis.

We needed the mirror to succeed, I knew that. It was just that I had caught my silvery twin looking at me funny, and in a panic I had decapitated him the only way I knew how to. Frank's voice broke the spell a little and I swerved over to the side of the road. This was one of the rules I had decided never to break. Instead, I was now sitting on the hard shoulder, ready to be caught. Frank didn't say anything, but I knew what he was thinking. I nodded, then opened my door and started walking back, searching for the place where I had chucked out the mirror.

I found it wedged between two rocks on the hard shoulder, and went down on my knees, about six feet away from the ribbed outer road marking. Half inspecting, half prostrating. The rearview mirror was only two hands wide but it scared me. It was sharp now when broken, but even in this secured state, on the ground, it carried itself with immense power. Wielding nightmares, simultaneously taking in the past and the future, as well as projecting the future and the past. A shiny slice of time dilation.

It had been a rectangle, but now it was broken and therefore had more than four corners. If I didn't pick it up it would soon be forgotten, stacked here against a rock. The gravel was digging into my knees so I lay down on my front. The mirror, with countless dust motes multiplied on its surface, was intriguingly useless although its basic function still remained intact. As an object it was still as potent as it ever was, but by being cast aside it had become roadside rubbish. The glass had come away from the plastic housing, and the black underbelly of the mirror was the opposite of its face. Dull, lifeless, never seen, commented on, feared or celebrated.

I came closer to it, snake-like, with my belly on the ground, but I didn't touch it. A thin layer of shiny foil was hidden within the glass. I needed to touch it, to connect with the man in the mirror, but I didn't want to use my fingers so I prodded it with my fist. I got even closer, to see if I could spot him.

Putting my tongue to the glassy surface I was surprised by how cold it was. It should have been as cold as the air. Somehow the piece of glass, which was once molten sand, baked in an oven as hot as the inside of a volcano, or Mercury maybe, was now the temperature of a loch.

I picked it up and as I turned the two hand-widths worth of broken glass over it became an armless cross, a mountain range, a tram from the future. I realised my left, right, top, bottom was now completely irrelevant. In handling it I caught myself. It jolted me. Scared me. The face staring back at me seemed unhinged and disproportionate. The image told me I needed to sleep and that I needed a shave. That's about the only time in my life when I need a mirror. Other than while shaving I try to avoid eye contact with the man who lives inside me. I looked again at the figure in the mirror, and he was shivering. It was clear I needed to pull my various selves together and get to Bournemouth.

I felt a hand on my shoulder. Again Frank asked how I was feeling, and again he had broken the spell a little. He helped me up, and I brushed off my knees. For some reason I handed him the main bit of the mirror, then I bent down to pick up two of the larger fragments as well as the plastic housing. The rest I left in the gravel, like a twinkling bouquet of roadside flowers.

'I've got some tape in the back', I said. 'I'll fix it once we're parked somewhere secure'. At the time I had no intention of fixing the mirror.

Once underway I sat and thought about the way communication signals are mirrored back and forward across the vast, dark wastes of the heavens, and about the interrogation rooms with secret mirror walls that Frank would have spent time in, and how similar they are. I felt happy that I had made the decision to leave my mobile phone at home. At the risk of being stranded in the case of a medical emergency I would rather bleed a little longer than be monitored by the state, at least while on the road with Frank.

After about 20 minutes or so, once my pulse had come down a little, a Twingo of the same year and colour pulled up next to us. It was uncanny, seeing a mirror image floating along like that at 60 miles an hour – a mirage from 2004. A man and a woman in the front seat. Both staring straight ahead, anxious to get to where they were going by the look of their clenched jaws. Then two blond heads popped up in the back seat. A boy and a girl, maybe three and five pointed and laughed at our car. The woman turned to look and waved, and the man nodded across the transmission tunnel and the road markings. A nod of mutual respect, driver to driver.

'The last time I was this far south was when I was rehearsing this trip', I said. 'Strange to think of this as the real performance. Let's make sure we're perfectly choreographed'.

'I'm not dancing', he said. Half in jest, half annoyed.

'I'm not asking', I said as quickly as I could. 'I'm talking about timings and luck and stealth, and the fact that we are in the grip of a society where everything is so tightly managed that it's easy to work out the flow of anyone going from A to B'.

'But no one apart from you knows where we are going. Even I only have a hazy idea', he said. 'I don't mind. It's like a strange dream anyway. Lately my life has been a bad dream, this is just a slightly better part of a rough nightmare'.

'Only I know exactly where we are going, partly for your own safety, but by now they know where you are going from. So working backwards from there they will soon have us triangulated', I explained.

'We don't seem to be in much of a hurry'.

'*Seem* is the operative word', I said. 'We are, you just can't see it. It's about *time* and *distance*, in agreement. It's about expectations, patterns, coded movements, known abodes, main arteries, transport hubs, gateways to the South, associates and ambitions. A whole number of parameters we're cleverly circumventing'.

'Great', he said. Not suitably impressed but at least not outright sceptical.

'When the hunter is larger than the quarry, the quarry has to be smarter. With the amount of cameras and RAM power available to the state, all this info is at the fingertips of a bureaucrat in Swindon or something. It's up to him to work out the code of our journey, and up to us to be one step ahead of him and his computer'.

'We could swing by Swindon and pull the plug'.

'Sounds good to me. You a trained hacker or suicidal electrician?' I asked.

'Nope. Just some guy who rents out heavy machinery', he said.

'That's why we are in my sister's car and not mine, for example. That's why I asked you to come to the bus station, as I knew it has very few cameras. That's why we need to take little detours or long-cuts, even double back on ourselves, things that no computer can work out. We need to behave erratically and organically, like only humans can. That's the only way we can outlast the surveillance'.

'But still get out of the country as fast as possible?' he asked.

'Yes. Be in a rush without seeming to be in a rush. Don't worry. We'll soon have you in France'.

The other car, the will-o'-the-wisp on wheels, was hovering an arm's length from us for a minute or two. Then the father floored it, and they sailed off into the future. My mind drifted to the past and France.

As a certified practitioner, my name firmly in the books of the Architects Registration Board, I finally managed to arrange a meeting with a French warden. In the end I was in and out of the prison, quite a small one on the outskirts of Nantes, in just under an hour. My French is quite poor to be honest, and it was even worse then. For technical stuff beyond greetings, food and board, it's appalling. Despite this I had waivered a translator. I wanted to have a pure experience with no human filters.

The warden had showed me two of the five wings. After that we walked around a bit in the yard and smoked cigarettes in the staff car park as it was his lunch break.

Obviously I couldn't take any pictures, or even sketch. All the blueprints were classified and so I couldn't take any solid information away with me. I asked to be allowed a cursory glance at the plans, but apparently they were locked away at a central hub outside Lille. To an outsider auditing my travel expenses, or the workings of the sitting Buildings and City Planning board in the council, it might have seemed that I went all the way to France to wander around a bit of a fenced-off field. But it was more than that. Some things are just very difficult to quantify.

I was meant to go to a structural conference later in the week but it was in Paris, or not even Paris proper, but out at one of these conference centres next to the Charles-de-Gaulle airport. Frankly I couldn't see the point. My French was below par, still is, and then there was the drive across half of France. I only had the rental car for a week and the warm weather drew me west towards the coast rather than east toward the urban sprawl of the capital. I can see now how it might have looked fishy, me gallivanting around spending funds, but everybody did it. Still do I presume. If it hadn't been me, it would have been someone else. And that someone else probably wouldn't even have gone on the prison tour. They would have headed straight for the golf course as soon as they stepped off the plane.

I wasn't elected. No one needed to see me. The taxpayer couldn't care less where I was. Whether I was in some stuffy conference suite, or finding artistic, architectural and engineering inspiration from more diverse sources. Hand on heart I was fascinated by the landscape, traditional rural building methods and the civic structures of the wider Loire-Atlantique area, and if that upset some people, so be it.

Outside the flimsy shell of the Twingo the mud-coloured suburbs of some far-off magnet of jobs and opportunities were gathering. The buildings coming closer and closer to the road, aided by sound mounds and barriers. *Prime retail land, Commuter belt potential, Excellence in Exurb.* A thick soup of buzz words displayed on estate agents' placards mounted along the road. In expectation of new developments. For the mortgages of double-income families with one dog, two children, three mini holidays a year.

We were driving past one or two unfinished fly-over foundations that reminded me of the road leading into Guémené-Penfao, a little town north of Nantes I had gone through in my rented car a long time ago.

'There's a wonderful visitor's centre in the national park just north of Saint-Nazaire', I said to him. 'Some of which spurred me on to design a certain bit of the plan I submitted for Cromlix. A really fantastic way to marry joists and a semi-opaque roof. I went there a long time ago, finding inspiration. You should visit it if you have a chance'.

'But your prison was never built, was it?'

'I didn't know at the time that I was going to be robbed. And humiliated', I said.

'How long were you away, *finding inspiration*?' His ironic voice somewhere between a teenager's and the voice of reason.

'Just over a week. I had a rental car for a week but extended the trip for a couple of days. For which I paid myself'.

'But someone else paid for most of it', Frank said, 'You realise normal people don't live like that?'

'You realise normal moderately sought-after architects in most major European cities live just like that?' I said, annoyed that he was so insistent on these emotional pinpricks.

'You know what I mean', he said sounding not unlike my long gone mother. I made a mental note to pull over to get him a Twix at the earliest possible place. His tone of voice was probably linked to low blood sugar.

'My neighbours at the time, their lives were exactly like that', I said. 'If not more glamorous. They would go to France to ski and not even have to pretend to work. 'Besides', I continued, 'the other people on the committee were luckier than me', I continued. 'I only got to go the once, and only to the mainland. There were people who went to Cuba, Argentina, Florida, New Zealand, a couple of times. Not all valid journeys, even by my standards'.

'By any standards', he said.

'I hear what you're saying, and to some extent I agree, but seeing something first hand, there is no substitute for that. And seeing how they do it in other societies and cultures, I think there is something to be said for that. Sometimes we can be quite blinkered in Britain'.

Frank just sat there in silence. More silent than just silent in fact.

'These were study trips', I said. '*You need to form an opinion to have an informed opinion*, one of my tutors at university always used to say'.

'He sounds like a dick', Frank said.

'He was', I said, thankful I wasn't a student anymore.

My throat was parched and I returned to the bottle. Held the straw between my teeth, and let the syrupy goodness trickle into me. Soon I had finished the Sprite and Eminasin Verdejo.

'Despite studying this hard, traveling to places and that, what you came up with in the end was a horrible, leaking, faulty concrete box full of unhappy people', Frank said.

'I didn't. Euan did'.

'I didn't mean *you* you. I meant the committee, or whoever signed it off'.

'I agree. Totally, and that's why I felt I had to undermine the powers-that-were'.

'In hindsight I could have spent less time in France', I said while waiting for a huge BMW 8 series to overtake, 'but the upshot is that while I was staying in Saint-Nazaire I stumbled on this old house. I think someone, probably an old man judging by the state of the house, had just died. Two women, his daughters I later found out, were carting stuff to a van. When I walked past they were struggling with an old fridge and I ended up helping them for a while. I didn't mind, I had the day off anyway. They were very pleasant, one of them had been an au-pair in London and her English was quite good, if a bit marble mouth, you know high teas and regattas, but she was nice. Once the van was full they brought out lunch and we got talking. It transpired they were just about to put the house on the market so I made them an offer on the spot. I think it was the Claret'.

'Who does that sort of thing?' Frank asked as the BMW finally passed us. Long wheelbase, tinted windows, diplomatic plates, a red and blue flag I didn't recognise. Slovenia, Slovakia, Liechtenstein? Either way it was another perfect disguise. Apparently the inside of an embassy vehicle is a piece of soil from the country being represented. In essence you could install electric chairs in the American fleet of cars and perform mobile, legal executions. I didn't want to do that, but I was jealous of the camouflage a foreign state would have provided.

'I don't know what came over me', I said, tearing my eyes off the BMW. 'I think I was thinking about their father, now dead, and how much nicer his end of days had been compared to my future ones, stuck in a damp flat just off Dumbarton Road'.

Frank just nodded.

I had since decided to name my holiday home 'Le Petit Trianon', in honour of Madame Antoinette's ambitious and idyllic time travel. I had a local artisan make a brass plaque which I displayed proudly on the right gate post. Several times I made plans to go to Versailles and Le Hameau de la Reine, but I never managed it.

Frank had unfolded the map on his lap. Finally, a team player.

'Left here, Cecil if you want to avoid the motorway', he said, now a tad more urgently. It was good to hear that he feared the surveillance cameras too.

'Sorry, yes, thanks. I'm trying to get into the lane'. I floored it and the car shot over into the exit lane, not far from the chevrons. For a smidge of a second I was Steve McQueen and the Twingo a Mustang 390 GT.

'I hope you realise how lucky you are, just being able to buy a house like that', Frank said once we settled into the gentler traffic of the A road. It was a pace we were more used to, a feeling like coming home and putting on one's slippers.

'It might sound more romantic than it actually was. It involved a lot of notaries and lawyers and hassle to be honest', I said.

'I didn't mean the paperwork. I meant the money'.

'It wasn't expensive. And it was money left over from the divorce. My wife got the house and I got a pittance in comparison. Sure, we got the house from her dad, but we were married and so I think by rights half of it belonged to me. I also worked hard for many years. She never felt like taking up a career, she was just home. Looking after the plants, unlocking the door for the cleaners, volunteering for a school fête once a year, drinking coffee with her friends'.

'I can't believe we're even from the same city', Frank said shaking his head.

'Mother Glasgow has a wide bosom. She is able to hold us all', I said.

We droned on in silence for a while. I had already adapted to using the side mirrors as the main one was lying broken in the back seat. I wanted to be able to see if there were blue lights coming up from behind, but I wasn't keen on catching sight of my face again, so the side ones were perfect.

'Remind me to get some super glue at the next service station, Frank', I said unconvinced, but he didn't answer. I thought he was maybe sleeping. He was feline like that. I turned up the radio a notch, Katie Williamson was back, her velveteen and possibly pre-recorded voice filling the cabin. I started to wonder how old she was, what she looked like. If there was any chance of going on a tour of the BBC building, maybe ask to see her at work in the studio.

Katie introduced a piece played by one of the new generation of Russian wonders and I took a deep breath, felt my shoulders drop. As Yulianna Avdeeva's fingers danced over the ivories in Chopin's footsteps my mind drifted. The black keys, the white keys, the blacktop, the white lines, the black keys, the white keys...

Chapter 19

21.00 Sunday

From Frank's concerned face I deduced that something was wrong. For what felt like hours, but was probably seconds, I tried to work out what it was. Then I heard a sound. A high-pitched, ragged sound. My tongue felt dry, like it was coated in sand, a dead halibut washed up in my mouth. I closed my lips. The sound stopped. I opened my mouth, mainly to breathe, and the sound started again. I thought at first something must be wrong with my ears. A while ago I had some trouble with my left Eustachian tube. I soon realised that wasn't the case. I thought maybe the car was making the noise but a look at the gauges informed me that we were rolling along at 60, temp fine, oil pressure fine, revs normal. Then it transpired that I had been screaming like a pig being slaughtered.

If my body had produced this reaction, taking pains to forge a shortcut past my conscious mind, things must be bad. The reptilian mind had broken out of its chains to challenge Homo Erectus. I had always lived the motto *Je pense, donc je suis*, but if I was no longer thinking straight, I was half dead.

This made me scream again and I only stopped when Frank slapped me. It was an open hand, not hard enough to hurt really, but it was effective.

'Thanks', I said, once I had caught my breath. Then I looked down and saw Frank's right hand holding the steering wheel.

'You fell asleep', he said.

I had somehow descended into a primal scream. It flooded back. The soft piano music. Yulianna's fingers stroking the keys. The black keys, the white keys, the blacktop, the white lines, the black keys, the white keys... I had been dreaming about prison. The noise of my tin cup rattling on metal bars must have been the little car going over the raised rib line to our left. I had been pacing my cell for the first time, panic rising, cup playing the cell marimba. I had been given 19 years, but had no recollection of the crime or any of the proceedings.

'Thanks', I said again, and took over the wheel. 'Let's get a coffee. Keep an eye out for a place to stop'.

For miles and miles there didn't seem to be anywhere to get a hot drink. I felt Frank looking at me but tried to ignore it. He had every right to monitor me after what had just happened. Whenever we caught slower cars I threw caution to the wind. There was no reason to go into fourth for overtaking, but the noise and the acceleration kept me awake. I was still shaking, and the cogs underneath us protested loudly, the noise of the whining timing belt embarrassing.

I was actually relieved when we we're caught in a queue stretching into the distant future. As part of a well-rehearsed act I handed Frank his hat and sunglasses in one smooth motion. It was past nine so people might wonder why we were wearing them, but I preferred looking like wanna-be celebrities to people seeing our faces.

I put on my pilot's shades, wide enough to cover half my face, and my Yankees cap. The Cape Canaveral one suited Frank better anyway. In our respective headgear we were now more invisible to the people in the adjacent lanes. Soon we came to a complete standstill and after 10 minutes I switched off the engine and went back to the boot for a multipack bag of ridge cut crisps I had bought the last time we stocked up on provisions.

When I came back I said, 'I guess we're stuck in here for a while, and we can't go anywhere', I felt the weight of the crisps and wondered how something so insubstantial could be so perfect. 'The car is a cell on four wheels really'.

'It's much nicer than that'. Frank said.

'Of course. But there are still similarities. We are two men lumped together in this confined space by chance. We don't know each other. We don't know if we're going to get on or fall out, but for our own reasons we have to make it work'.

'Luckily not all cells are shared', he said.

'Most of the ones at Cromlix are. *For companionship and community-building. To learn how to make compromises.* At least Euan and I agreed on that point'.

'To learn how to deal with a stranger's farts and how to ignore him sobbing on his kids' birthdays', Frank said in a flat voice.

'That's at least some kind of compromise'.

'My cell was empty apart from me'.

'Why?' I asked and opened what I felt would be the first of at least three bags of crisps.

'No one would tell me. I really didn't want to get to know anyone, and I really didn't want to share, so I kept quiet'.

'I thought all Scottish prisons were full', I said, looking ahead for movement. But the queue was a static metal snake.

'I have no idea', he said, reaching out for the big multipack bag. He started to deliberate over flavours. We were stranded, and expecting to remain so for a while. I wasn't sure if I could call Frank 'Friday' after Crusoe's only friend yet. Maybe soon, depending on how long we'd be marooned on the road.

Frank chose Cheese and Onion, my second favourite after Salt and Vinegar, but I didn't mind. I had almost killed us after all.

'You can sit in the backseat if you think this is too much company'. I said, half-jokingly.

'This I've chosen', he said, gesturing around him, smiling a sad smile. 'And I can sleep whenever I want to. I don't get car sick but I like to see where we are going, so I'll stay up here. Who knows when you'll need me to read out directions again. And since there are no cup holders you're always asking me to hold your cup'.

'Sorry. I think they put holders in the next generation of Twingos', I said, thankful he hadn't mentioned my recent more serious blunder.

'You've got the map, the plan and the car. I'm just the passenger. I'm aware of the hierarchy, it doesn't bother me', he said, choosing his next fix; Ready Salted, our least favourite one.

'Sure', I said. Thankful he had left me the last blue packet. I considered turning off the radio but kept it on at a low volume. I didn't think there was any risk of it draining the battery, but I turned it down another notch just in case.

I looked out at the sea of cars. I could sense the mixture of claustrophobia and companionship surrounding us. We were all in the same too-small boat. This particular stretch of the road network was not meeting our expectations or special requirements. Someone was to blame for this but it was too difficult to work out who. And if there was a who, they would have left their office about 4 hours ago.

Frank took a swig of cold tea and said, 'It would have been terrible to share with anyone. It was a tiny cell, luckily I was on my own'.

'I didn't think the cells were all that small'. I said. 'We made them bigger than regulations stipulated. On which side were you? North? Could you see the hills?'

'I could see some of the outside through half a barred window'.

'Half? Did the sun come up or down through it?'

'Up. Really early. And there was no blind. Instead I had a shirt stuck to the wall with these ridiculous Velcro tabs. I had to buy them like contraband from this guy who for some reason was allowed to go to art classes every day'.

Outside a man had climbed up on the roof of his big brown delivery van to better see how long the queue was. He too wore a hat and sunglasses. He didn't seem too troubled by the hold-up as he scanned the horizon, one hand further shielding his eyes despite the dark. He resembled a commander of a fleet momentarily lost. I suppose his boss in an air-conditioned office somewhere could see him stranded in a metal morass of cars, a winking dot on a digital map.

'What idiots', I said. 'They must have put in partition walls in the double cells I designed'.

'Does it matter?'

'The relatively spacious cells, and the easy companionship they would have afforded, was part of the deal I struck with the Scottish Prison Service Head-quarters and Mister Euan Kerr-Henley. But they shouldn't have put up walls without consulting with the original head architect. Euan, what a snake, he must have given the go-ahead without telling me', I said, fuming.

Frank, oblivious, just nodded.

I looked at the brown-clad delivery driver on top of his van. Maybe, like me, he had a human consignment. If so, I had to admit his disguise was more effective than mine. I cursed myself for not thinking of the postal option. But then again I wasn't so sure my Unknown Prisoner would have liked a long trip in the confines of an armoured van.

'Did you like the bars for windows at least?' I asked. 'I had them designed in the stylised form of a thistle, the Scottish symbol of the defeat of Vikings at Largs at 1263. Apparently a Viking stepped on a thistle and cried out, which gave them away. And that was the end of that brutal era'.

'I never knew they were meant to be flowers. Now I realise that mine was mounted upside down. So were most of them I think. The joke was that they looked like Hitler's dick'.

'How so?' I asked.

'One ball, and small', he smirked.

Suddenly, and with the internal logic only applicable to traffic jams, the cars ahead were moving. I panicked and as I reached for the ignition I spilled the entire bag of crisps into the wedge between my crotch and the seat. We lurched forward, the engine whining in first gear.

'There was bird shit on my window that no rain could wash off', Frank, unaware of the design intricacies, said.

I couldn't explain to him that this was because of a miniature parapet, inspired by a series of campaniles built in the fourteenth century, which I had spotted in France. On home soil they served as an overhang to the first floor. Apparently my idea of a demi-gutter hadn't worked, if it was keeping the rain off the windows too well.

'Sorry', was all I could say. It was too complex to go into. Especially now that I was revving too high for first gear but too low for second.

I yearned to graduate into a higher gear, but despite moving slightly faster, I couldn't. The river of cars was still flowing thickly. Keen to score a point, I said, 'The inside was quite successful I think. We approached the surfaces and cultural echoes in the building very differently from how most penal architects would'.

'I never noticed anything but walls', he said in a surly voice.

'I had some pretty exciting plans and thought long and hard about the *Message of Material*. For example, bricks symbolise home, so the corridors were to be part bricked. Some of the facility was to have textured concrete walls. Tying Cromlix back into its cultural heritage, crofter mainly. There's a rich history of iron ore and shipbuilding in this country, so if it had been up to me I would have left a lot of joists, rivets and welding work exposed. I also I sketched on a lovely, buff, sandstone-like façade. When I spoke to the governor she seemed very proud of all the potential local tie-ins and homages to generations past'.

'I wish I had known'.

'None of it was realised', I said.

Frank nodded, didn't seem surprised.

'Surely you noticed the upper walls in the dining room?' I said. 'At one point there was a flint mill not far from Cromlix, and we poured the concrete so that it would look like flint. Like it had been crafted rather than constructed'.

'I suppose I was too busy eating', he said. This time he sounded at least 80% ironic.

'Did you at least enjoy the viewing gallery? The scenery is quite spectacular, the hills and the weather systems can really put the fear of God into you', I said, finally moving into second, then quickly into third gear. Resolute not to feel disheartened by Frank's mediocre review of some of my building. Euan's building.

'They turned it into a stationary cupboard. It was brimful of lined paper for us. We were not allowed plain paper in case we somehow forged watermarks and letters from lawyers or the Queen demanding our immediate release. Despite a forest worth of paper, we were only allowed two sheets a week for personal use. My letters home were very tightly written'.

I tried catching up with the car in front but it was difficult. The Twingo, and I, were feeling tired after a long day. As I shifted in the seat there was a crunching sound from the spilled crisps. All I could think of was how my Versace jeans would now have a greasy stain stinking of vinegar where I needed it the least.

Frank continued, 'Couldn't you just have built something nice? Something plain and simple. Spent the rest on better food, better beds, better showers? On the things that really matter?'

'I was maybe too idealistic in my plans, but that's hindsight talking, not the potent courage of youth', I said. 'I agree with some of your criticism, but national and local government budgets don't really work like your own wallet. If you save on clothes you can go abroad, if you turn down the heating you can buy nicer tea bags, or whatever. We had money to spend on the building. The running was left to someone else. Those pockets of money are watertight that way'.

Finally, I caught up to the car in front of us. I had moved through the gears quite seamlessly. Soon we were humming along at our normal 58. Occasionally I flicked a swift backhand over and under my crotch, trying to get rid of every last sprinkle of crisp. Mostly I was trying to keep us on course in the aftermath of the queue as people were weaving and bobbing in and out of lanes to make up for time lost. I predicted it would take another 10 or 15 miles for the traffic to settle down, but in the end it happened faster. From the initial exuberance of calves set out to spring graze, we were soon locked into a more regulated dance with the other motorists. Most of them driving just above the speed limit, presumably hating the government for imposing on our freedom, wishing we were on Autobahn.

'So you put in all this thinking, and yet it became an ugly place', Frank said.

'Euan was right about one thing, whether he knew it or not. The ugliness is part of the safety. Brutal systems should be housed in brutal, and possibly brutalist buildings, even though brutalist has nothing to do with the English word brute. You know your French, brute is just raw, as in raw concrete and so on. But the theory still stands; stern systems in stern spaces. Otherwise the friction between expectation and reality would be too great to bear for inmates – and staff'.

Frank nodded in a non-committal way. I was no longer as shook up by the earlier sleeping incident, but, it was getting late. My mind drifted back to the origins of the brutalist form, Hans Asplund's Villa Göth, and Aleksandr Rochegov's embassy in Cuba.

'Can't the building change the system?' Franks said, breaking my concrete reveries. 'You have all these ideas about changing the criminal inside. Can't you punch upwards as well as downwards if you think the system is too brutal?'

A swarm of Japanese motorcycles, four green Kawasakis behind a black bike that said Hayabusa on its tank, shot past us. Frustrated riders pulling hard on their throttles, making their toys throb underneath them. The sound of a thousand sewing machines breaking.

'It's very complicated. There are a lot of stakeholders. A lot more than for a normal structure', I was blinking hard to get some moisture back into my eyes. 'For a house, it's a person or a family. For a bigger building, it's usually a company with a CEO. For a prison it's almost impossible to determine the amount of people with vested interests'.

'Did you try to change people?' he asked. I wasn't sure if hadn't heard my explanation or had just decided to cut to the core. It was pleasantly awful to travel with this, if not *idiot savant*, then at least *savant*.

'I tried to change the individual', I said, 'but not the powers that commissioned the building in the first place. And not the lawmakers, or the voters really. That was beyond me'.

Frank nodded. I wasn't sure if that meant he agreed or if that meant I had somehow confirmed his suspicions. I decided not to ask for his honest opinion on me. We were still far away from Bournemouth.

'I'm afraid we're going to have to make a detour', I said as the big brown van rumbled past in a purple diesel cloud.

'We've been taking a lot of those'.

'This is different. They were spontaneous, this one is necessary. I'm too tired to go on'.

'So what do you suggest? That we sleep in the car and set out for York in the morning?'

'I thought we could find a Premier Inn or something', I said. While talking about Cromlix, which I was an expert on, and could have had a PhD in if I had bothered, I must have missed the exit for the A1079.

For a while I was busy overtaking lorries. Soon we had continued far too long on the A614, and realised we were almost in Driffield. Blown off course by the second in command's slight ineptitude. If we had been at sea, I would have stripped him of his rank and his sextant. If driving was my responsibility, then navigating was mostly Frank's, but I decided to let the matter rest as it was me who wanted to go to this bit of the country in the first place.

Making the best of the situation we headed for the coast where I thought there would be more places to stay. In general, the population would also be more used to travelers passing through than in the landlocked towns away from the cities or the sea.

I told Frank to keep his eyes peeled for a Holiday Inn or a Travelodge.

'What about not leaving a trace? You'll need to pay by card. Remember our technician in Swindon?' Frank asked.

'Don't worry about money. You can't trace cash so easily. I've got that sorted', I said, still trying to be vague about how much money I had, and how I was carrying it.

'Fine, but they'll still want you to show ID in case you're planning to wreck the place'.

'I'm not', I said indignantly. 'I'm a very peaceful person'.

'Really? I thought you were a rock star', he said, chuckling.

'Funny', I said. 'I could have become a rock star had I wanted to but I chose engineering. I wanted my art to leave a lasting impression. And for my art to have actual use'.

Frank snorted, as if he had gotten something up his nose.

We left Driffield and entered the civil parish of Bridlington. No hen parties, no Brighton style riots. Just a slightly damp seaside town, and the salty wind coming off the North Sea. We fumbled our way through a sparsely built-up outlaying area. By the dog walkers I judged the neighbourhood to be neither upmarket nor rough. The size of the dog, and the shoes of its handler, are always clear indicators of class and aspirations.

'Still though, you might steal the towels', he said.

'Maybe a B&B then', I said, conceding a point.

'Some of them are less than happy about housing two men I hear'.

'We would get two rooms of course'.

'Of course', he said.

'My treat either way', I said.

We entered Bridlington proper, not that it made a huge difference, and drove toward the sea. After a couple of minutes, we saw a hotel that looked quite run down and would probably have had us, with or without ID, but the car park was full. I tried to work out if it was a wake or a wedding, but I decided to give it a miss either way.

Further up the road was a B&B and I parked up on the pavement, but I didn't like the look of the front garden. Too neat. These were the kind of people who would want to find out every little detail about you before letting you into their precious castle. With a sigh from Frank we pulled away from the curve and continued towards what was probably the town centre.

After a minute Frank pointed to a sign saying 'Lauriston Place B&B. Vacancies. No pets, no smoking. Open 10–10'. I made a note of its location and drove past. Casing it so to speak. Not far beyond it we came to a big car park for a swimming pool or something and I pulled in.

'I'll go and have a look', I said. 'I'm still not convinced. The anonymity you get in a hotel is a great cloak. The familiarity you get with a smaller place, which is usually why people choose a B&B, is not going to work in our favour. I don't really want people to see you'.

'I don't mind. I'll stay in the car', he said.

'It'll get freezing', I said.

He nodded and said, 'Leave the key this time. I'll pop the heater on every now and then'.

'What if you decide to drive off?' I didn't want anyone to spot us in the parked car. From the outside it must have looked like a lovers' spat, us gesticulating in the front seat. The gentle rocking of the suspension brought on by us shifting in our seats. Our bodies moving in tandem as we tried to disentangle ourselves from the seatbelts, putting crisp bags and hats in the back seat. The car park was seemingly chosen for an out-of-earshot fight and a clandestine making-up session. I was keen not to send out the wrong signals. I was keen not to send out any signals.

'If I wanted to leave I would have left by now. You're the best tour guide I could think of', he said.

'This is serious', I said.

'You don't have to tell me'.

'I'll be right back', I said, heart pounding.

He nodded and I saw his eyes spot the keys I had left in the ignition.

Chapter 20

22.00 Sunday

It was getting quite cold outside, some kind of blip, and I hurried back over to the car park. In the car, which to my relief was still there, Frank asked, 'How did it go?'

'Easy. Surprisingly easy. It was a couple, older, properly retired, and they kept talking about how quiet it is now with the new motorway. They feel a lot of traffic circumvents them. I told them I had lost my wallet, that I had taken a couple of wrong turns. For extra points I told them I was a retired engineer, they seemed the type to appreciate that. Anyway, they are happy to take cash. I even signed the register with a false name and address'.

'You're becoming quite the con man', Frank said.

'It's easy when it's for a good cause', I said.

I looked up into the air and it was pitch black. There were no stars to be seen and the nearest streetlight was broken and the one beyond that must have been a hundred yards away. For our purposes it was perfect.

'I'm just here to get my stuff. I had a quick look at the forecast in the paper while I was checking in. It's going to snow and might creep down below zero, so you'll die in the car'.

'I'll be fine'.

'I'm in enough trouble without also trying to get rid of a dead body, frozen stiff in my car'.

'I'll just get out and walk if it gets too cold', he said.

'I'm not sure if that's enough. Look, I'll open the window to my room and if you're cold you can just come in for a bit'.

'Like a teenage lover?'

"Frank, please don't. This is weird enough as it is'.

There was a sharp taste in the air. Like frost descending.

'Anything about me in the news?' he asked.

'I was trying to be discreet and read the paper from the back to get the weather'.

'Or you?'

'Less likely, but nothing as far as I could tell', I said. 'It was a local paper, the *Bridlington Enquirer'*.

A strong gust of wind shook the trees bordering the car park. A hurricane somewhere off Florida was throwing the weather systems into confusion in England.

'I asked for a packed breakfast, told them I had to hit the road early to get back to Doncaster. We can share it once we get underway'.

'Doncaster?' he asked.

'Don't worry. It's a ruse'.

'You never know with you Cecil'.

'Good.'

Franks smiled and said, 'Actually any coffee?

'Let me grab a flask from the boot'.

'It's like I'm the policeman and you're the criminal, and I'm here on a stakeout', he said. 'Could you get me some doughnuts?'

'*Sure thing pardner. I'll get you a pastrami on rye, easy on the mayo*', I said in my best NY cop whine. I got kit #28, out of the boot and walked over to the B&B. While I waited for the kettle to boil for Frank's instant coffee, I tried to warm my hands under the tap in the bathroom. Then it was time to scurry back out to the car.

Frank was wearing the two blankets from the backseat like a Bolivian poncho and wouldn't even open the door. He wound down the window as little as possible and accepted the coffee.

'Sorry there's no room at the inn', I said. 'But you can hang out in the fields with the shepherds until it's time to bring me myrrh and frankincense'.

He just nodded.

'Sleep well', I said.

Back in the room, I sat at the floor with my back to a radiator, drained. The carpet was cheap polyester, for medium to high traffic density I suspected. The wallpaper was neither here nor there. There was a wall clock, Roman numerals adding a certain class, ticking loudly over the bed.

On my own for the first time in ages I got up and inspected the room, my nocturnal investment. The walls behind the wallpaper were fine, nothing special, probably a skeleton of two by fours, clad with wallboard and painted, years ago. The coving and the skirting was adequate, the main light a dull glass half-dome. The ceiling was plagued by the plaster swirls that seem popular in certain bits of certain towns, but this pattern wasn't too obnoxious. It must have been put on by a rather subdued, or perhaps apprentice, Artexer.

After wandering around the room and turning the electrical radiator from *medium* to *max* I felt my shoulders coming down from their stressed position. I had kept my hands at ten to two for a long time.

I brushed my teeth, with the light off, and listened to the steady sound of Roman seconds ticking by. I untucked the covers from the bed and decided not to watch TV. After leaving the window off the latch I crawled into bed, and must have fallen asleep. I had meant to have a bath and review the next days' options, the AA road map spread out on the bed covers, but sleep must have crept up on me like a silent assassin.

I woke up with Frank towering above me and for a second I felt like I was falling off a ladder. He was dry-washing his hands, blowing on them. His face a strange rigor mortis. I glanced at my wrist. It was half one in the night and I had slept for three glorious, traffic-free hours.

'Give us that bedcover', he said. 'I'm so cold my cheeks have gone numb. I've been out walking for hours but my knee is giving me trouble'. I came to and started pulling on the covers. He wasn't about to pounce on me after all. Be still my beating heart, I told myself.

'Your knee? Did you fall over?' I asked crawling out of bed.

'Yes. When I was seventeen. This midfielder from Dundee Violet took me out. Broke my leg in two places. At least we won two to one'.

'Here, you take the bed', I said. 'My back is too sore. Sitting in the car, probably tensing up all day doesn't help. The bed is too soft'.

'Are you sure?' he said, putting his hands under the covers, presumably to thaw them out.

'Don't worry. I slept in most of my clothes so it's not unsanitary in any way.' I said buttoning my shirt.

'Remember I've been in prison?' Frank said, his lips still frozen from the blurry sound of his words. 'Sleeping in a bed that some other guy has slept in once is the least of my worries'. He looked around the room and said, 'Where will you sleep though? Don't go to the car. It's bloody freezing out there. Must be a couple of degrees below at least'.

'I won't. I'll just camp out on the floor. It's supposed to be good for your lumbar area'.

Frank got out of his shoes, folded the shoelaces into them, and placed them neatly halfway under the bed.

'We should probably be quiet', Frank said in a stage whisper.

'It's fine', I said, 'I told the people who run this place that I usually fall asleep with the radio blaring and they told me they sleep at the other end of the house and can't hear a thing'.

'I suppose that's the best thing to do if you have overnight guests all the time. Do you want to turn on the radio then?' Frank picked up the little white bedside AM/FM transistor.

'No, don't bother. Chuck down the pillow and the throw. I'll set an alarm for five thirty, when it's time for you to climb out again'.

My pulse wouldn't settle. Being woken up by Frank standing over me had surprised me a little and I could feel my heart beating irregular, heavy beats. A broken Big Ben. A faulty Orrery spinning, cogs coming undone inside me.

I had thought I'd be able to hear the invited intruder, that my hearing and sleeping awareness was closer to SAS than to SAGA. It was worrying that he had made it in and all the way to my bedside before I had even an inkling he was there.

After a sleepwalker's shuffle across the floor I located the door to the loo, and stood fumbling for the light switch for ages until I realised it was on the wrong side of the door. Only a cowboy builder would place it at the hinged side of a door and not at the opening side. The people who owned the B&B had clearly been had and if I hadn't been trying to be discreet I would have told them. Maybe I would on the way back? It was another thing to add to the list of tasks to accomplish on my return leg.

I turned on the bathroom light and was instantly blinded. Quickly turning the light back off again I waited until the pink and orange shapes dancing on my retina disappeared. Unscrewing the bulb to have a look confirmed my suspicions. Someone had put a 60-watt bulb in a housing meant for a max 30-watt bulb. No wonder I had been stabbed by the light.

I put the bulb back and turned on the light, shielding my eyes with one hand, and was shocked by the big mirror. I was staring back at me for a little while, the visual thread unbreakable. I inched closer to the graven image, slowly approaching myself. Age had kissed my beard with flecks of grey. I looked at my face as closely as I dared, careful to avoid eye contact.

The stubble was part of me and sprouting out beyond me. Out of me. The same little pinpricks year after year. Follicles producing the rasp, the chin's file. Even after my death, the 5 o'clock shadow will appear one last time. Shading my upper lip like dust or theatrical kohl. By then either gaunt, by circumstances or illness, or bloated by rich food.

'You ok Cecil?' Frank asked, standing just outside the door judging by the sound. 'It's been more than half an hour'.

'I'm fine'.

I washed my face and stumbled over to the blankets heaped on the floor. I lay there looking at the darkness of the ceiling for ages, unable to go back to sleep. Frank was wiggling around in the bed, like a dog preparing his cot. The memory of the proto-hound flattening a circle of long savannah grass to sleep on still present.

'You sleeping Frank?' I asked after a while of him fretting.

'I want to but can't', came the answer. 'I'm used to being squashed in the cell. This room is too big, and so is the bed. Maybe the car is better?'

As usual I couldn't tell whether he was joking or not. Since he was so recently escaped I realised confined spaces was playing on his mind, but as I had never been incarcerated myself I kept quiet. I thought about the room we were stuck in. It had a neutral smell, but still a smell. Of chlorine, spilled instant coffee, other people's feet and the owner's chosen brand of fabric softener. There was nothing offensive, but nothing inviting either. It didn't smell like a home, not even like a home away from home. It just smelled like a place. A space suspended in time for people going somewhere. The more I sniffed the more I became aware that now in the off-seasons there was a certain stale aroma to the room. And maybe the re-routing of the motorway that the owners had alluded to was forcing the room to turn itself into a memory.

It didn't help the odour of the room that two rather unwashed men with dietary challenges and a sedentary trip behind them were using it. I made a mental note to leave the window open when I left in the morning. That way there would hopefully be a couple of hours of air circulating before the hosts came to change over the beds, replenish the soap and fold the toilet paper into a point again.

'This room is about four times the size of the cell I was in', Frank said and tried to flatten his pillow, accidentally punching the headboard.

'Nothing about the ideas of Cromlix was accidental. In my master plan the prison was designed in the shape of an hourglass with a central meeting point in the middle. At the nexus where the sand, the people, would be able to move from one side to the other'.

'But yours was never built?'

'Some of my ideas were incorporated. Others weren't. Too forward-thinking at the time. Either way I'm talking mostly about the idea here Frank. Not the paltry reality'.

'Of course'.

'When designing the living quarters, I tried to follow the classical school. There's the golden ratio of course, and we had several prints of Fibonacci's shells put up in the common areas to illustrate this.

'Sounds good', he said. 'For most people I'm sure those measurements were fine. For me – not so much', he said ruefully. 'I've always been quite big and always been happy with that. In life it's not a hassle. If anything it's saved me a couple of times. But in my cell I really wished I was a smaller man. A bit like you. Just below average height, and quite slight'.

'I'm just taller than the average and I've always kept fit', I said, happy I could still wear the Versace jeans quite comfortably, though maybe the belt was one hole further out than before. I remember buying them in a boutique in SoHo and I could still see the colourful bag they came in. This must have been 1988, or actually 1989. It was between the opening of St Enoch's shopping mall and the fall of the Berlin Wall. What a year. I wondered if I still had that bag somewhere.

Back then I still had hopes of becoming the blueprint enfant terrible of my generation. I had some great sketches of a mixed-tenure village with artists' kilns and a canning factory. An inhabitable bridge – a series of belvederes cooled by the Donau, with convivial spaces provided by pontoons, manipulated by a hydraulic cantilever truss grid. My Friday drawers were overflowing with great, under-funded, ideas.

Frank interrupted my memories, and said, 'I got a headache from bunching up my shoulders all the time. From sleeping on my side as I couldn't get comfortable on my back or front'.

I felt that Cromlix maybe had a lot of faults, but this was one aspect we had looked into quite thoroughly, and said, 'We did some calculations and decided that the normal bed size at 6' 3" by 3' was a bit too generous. Since the beds were built in, flush against the wall, we reasoned that some of the wall area could function as bed too'.

'How do you mean?' Frank asked.

'Well, lots of people like to lean on something when they sleep'.

'Usually another person', he said.

'Well, a wall was the best we could do. And to that effect we made the room bigger by reducing the width by an Egyptian Royal Cubit, about 20 inches, and the length of the bed to a more suitable size, making it 5' 9" ½ – modeled on yours truly. Most people don't stretch out when they sleep so even if you're six foot a slightly shorter bed is perfectly fine'.

'Maybe for the designers who don't sleep in them', he said. 'Maybe for smaller guys like yourself', he continued, his joking tone now teetering closely to the edge of real critique.

I propped myself up on one elbow for him to hear me clearly and said, 'We reasoned that floor space was to be prioritised. Daytime is productive, you can better yourself, do exercises, study if you have floor space and a table and a chair. Sleep is just sleep'.

'Not for the people inside', he said. 'I'd say sleep is the most important bit. You end up doing so much sleeping and if you have bad night after bad night it really screws you up'.

There was no holding him back. Maybe it was the darkened room where we were devoid of facial expression, maybe it was the sensation of being freed from the car.

'So maybe there should be some sort of tier system of cell size, quality of mattress and amenities based on length of sentence and behaviour, and type of crime to some extent', I asked, a peace offering.

'I'm not sure what I think', he said. 'It'd be good if the cells felt more normal, more like a home of some kind. I mean you spend the nights there and a lot of the daytime too, more than you would in your own house, but it's nothing like a home'.

'So a selection of curtains and a choice of furniture? The option of re-arranging the layout of the room? A choice of wallpapers and a painter-decorator who can change things around to suit your requirements? If you have the money or if you behave?' I asked.

'I don't know if you're serious or taking the piss Cecil'. I was surprised and somehow happy he was now in the position I so often found myself with his comments.

For a while the world was silent. No traffic, no people. I had asked, and there were no other guests, which was a bonus. The owners were quiet, asleep or dead. No sound from a TV. My ears were ringing after being in the noisy Twingo all day, so it was nice to let my hearing have a little holiday too.

I decided not to go into my wider reasoning about his cell. The sliding scale of spaces which are to accommodate all our needs, from the toilet to the theatre stage, the Private – Semi-private – Semi-public – Public arenas which we all operate on, but a prisoner more so. By now I was quite cosy in my blanket and I put my hands behind my head. In my opinion the room at the B&B would make for a pretty decent cell. The size, and its stark functionality, the view of some nature, but mostly semi-urban nothingness, the cheap but hard-to-break furniture. The door could be supplied with a proper lock, and the window could be sealed shut, then the prisoner would have his whole world while the world outside went about their business. Maybe this was something failing B&Bs and hotel chains could turn their hands to? Halfway homes and re-entry points lodged in down-at-heel holiday inns and failing seaside towns.

I arched my back to look around the space. The B&B room was a dull, symmetrical shape, perfect for housing unruly elements. The enterprising hotelier, dealing with a smaller, mixed prison population, could probably mix high-risk, low-risk and normal guests. As long as the rooms were fitted with the appropriate locks. Some self-operated, some centrally controlled. A carceral cottage industry, Con-Air BnB.

In my drawers at home I had hundreds of scraps of paper dealing with the shape of a room. It didn't have to be a rectangle. There were so many shapes in the world. What were the possibilities of a round cell? An oval one, which didn't have a centre, or two centres. If one shape was better than the other, you could introduce a scale of rewards too. Then there was height of ceiling. How do you live in a room with a really high ceiling? Maybe 30 feet or more. Or one with a glass floor over a big drop? Then there was the view versus the privacy. How about a bay window, no window, all window? The possibilities were endless. It was just a shame that financial matters got between me and a genuinely interesting prison building. If jails were somehow status symbols in our society, the way parliaments and opera houses are, I think we could get somewhere with their function. As it is, prisons are little more than human pigeon holes – and designed with as much panache.

I made sketches, a series of quite nice watercolours which I framed, of what HMP Cromlix would look like in 500 years. As a ruin, all moss-clad and festooned with ivy, nibbled at by time's inconsiderate teeth. If Cromlix was destroyed I hoped some of the squares of concrete would be used as building blocks for future structures.

The images were still at the old house in Bearsden, I had forgotten about them until now, lying on the floor in the B&B. I would have to contact Maud about them, which tipped the scales into forgetting about the pictures again. I didn't think I would be able to work up the courage to break in again. Not in a sober state.

'It's so quiet out in the world. I had forgotten', Frank said. 'All the noise inside, even at night, occupies a big bit of your attention. At first it kept me awake, now I find it hard to sleep without it'.

I stood up to find a radio station. For a while we got music but the machine kept coming off the frequency. After the fourth attempt trying to make it latch onto pleasant airwaves I just left it, stuck on the white noise between stations. The long static wave breaking on an aural shore, the transistor's lullaby, put us to sleep.

I woke with a start. Someone was knocking on the door. For a second I thought the Police had finally found us. Acid from my stomach, the precursor of being sick, sprayed into my throat faster than a bullet train.

'Hello?'

The proprietor was telling me that my breakfast was ready to be picked up, and that it was 9 o'clock. I shouted a garbled thank you and tried to wrestle my way out of the blanket. I raised myself on one elbow but still couldn't see much. I got up, knees protesting a little, and once I had been to the bathroom I looked in the bed.

Frank was snoring and I had to prod him awake. At first it was obvious he had no idea where he was but as soon as he recognised me he rubbed his face and swung his big body out of the bed. Like a soldier ready to receive orders. He put on his shoes and walked over to the window, flung the curtains aside and started to open the window. Patted his pocket where he must have kept the car keys.

'Wait', I whispered as loudly as I dared. 'It's much later than we think. The alarm never went off. Wait here for a minute. I'll go out and speak to the couple about boilers or something. People love to talk about their heating when it gets a bit colder. I'll distract them long enough for you to get to the car'.

Chapter 21

10.00 Monday

Once I disentangled myself from the husband–wife team who were all too keen to show me their radiators, installed just over two winters ago, I made it back to the car. It was already running which was good for heat, but bad for cover. It must have been a windy night as a wedge of urban debris had gathered by the wheels on the starboard side of the Twingo. A deck of empty blister packs, glass crushed into an urban potpourri of greens browns and whites. Yellow and blue PET bottles, confetti from a Connor's birthday party.

A pale sun was shining and Frank was leaning against the car out of the wind.

'Let's go', I said.

'Just a minute'.

'Why? Do you need anything? The bathroom? I'm happy to wait'.

'No I don't need anything. It's great. Amazing not to need anything for minute or two a day'.

'I've never thought of it like that. Sounds a bit like homemade Buddhism if you ask me'.

'It got me through a few low points inside. Nothing spiritual about it really. Just stand or sit somewhere and tell yourself you don't need anything', he said and pushed himself off the car like a heavyweight pushing off the ropes.

'That might be hard', I said. 'It's the opposite of the 1980s, the era which made me who I am. I used to think 'I need *everything*.' It's that attitude, by extension, that has got me into this mess'.

I kicked the yellow bottle, and it spun. A carousel of additives and water. Ten years ago there would have been cigarette butts on the ground. Not anymore. Soon vaporising ampoules will litter our streets and squares like leaves used to. I thought about nothing for a couple of heartbeats. Then life flooded back into me.

'You know, I might try that nothing thing every now and then', I said. 'But now we really need to go'.

'I know. I just can't tell you how great it is to be in charge of your own time, even just for a minute. So different from inside where even your alone time is scheduled, based on some sort of psychological risk assessment scale. The guards count how long you've been in the toilet if you go there. And if you take too long the door will be unlocked from the outside. Regardless of your constitution'.

'In your cell?' I asked, looking at the bottle still spinning.

'No, up at education or at your workplace. In your cell you can sleep by the toilet if you like. Or need to'.

'Do you need the toilet now? There's a bush over there. You can be as long as you like. I've reached the age of plums and flax seeds so I understand. I won't count'.

'It's the small things like turning your face to the sun, I'm appreciating. It's amazing how powerful choice is. Like being able to have a breakfast with real coffee'.

'That's a real war time cry. *Less bark – more beans*, my gran used to say'.

'Once you've had instant coffee and lots of tinned foods for a while, an apple, or I don't know – mustard, gives you a head rush'.

There was a whirlwind playing with the litter around the car. The evidence of many cold hours spent by what I could only presume had been teenagers trying desperately to say things to each other. Sentences they felt compelled to say but couldn't bring themselves to utter. I wasn't totally excited about being retired, but I was glad I was no longer an awkward teenager. At least by now I knew how sex worked.

'I guess I take my freedom for granted', I said, trying to forget I really needed breakfast. Trying to forget we needed to get into the car and out of sight.

'On top of that you're a bachelor. You've got no ties', Frank said, looking at his left hand. Possibly where a wedding band once was. Lost, stolen, sold – I didn't know.

'Maybe', I said quietly.

'Although I realise you're not rich, you don't worry about a fiver here and a fiver there. By the looks of it there's always been enough for milk and bread. And cufflinks and stuff. That freedom is rare for a lot of people'.

'You make me sound like James Bond'.

'Well that's stretching it', he said, looking me over as if he was a casting agent.

'I'm a crusty old man, with no family', I said, again surprised by my own candour. 'I live in rented accommodation, and don't own much more than an eighteen-year-old SAAB'.

'I'm sorry. I didn't mean to…'.

'It's alright. Appearances can be deceptive'.

'They can', he said, looking down on his tattooed wrist.

In preparation for departure I circled the car. The Twingo, our mobile memento mori, was showing marks of use. Road grit had stained the bottom panels, the sidewalls on the wheels on the right hand side where I had done a poor job of parallel parking at a rest stop further north, were scuffed. The small rear windows were dirty and the nail polish was flaking in one of the corners of the reg plate. If it had been warmer, I would have touched it up. I offered up a silent apology to my sister for using her car, but means and the end were perfectly combined in the little vehicle.

'Let's go', I said once I had completed the circle. 'If you're done worshipping the sun that is'. I handed him the packed breakfast from the B&B people, got in and pressed the accelerator for effect. The Twingo whirring more than roaring.

'You're not that old. Or crusty', he said once he was seated and belted.

'Thanks. You've earned yourself an extra grande chocolate muffin at the next Wild Bean Café. Now let's go'.

Once we were back on the A614/A166, heading for York, a motorcade sailed past. Brightly polished masterworks of engineering from dead factories. Classic cars in full livery. Bristols, MGs, Sunbeams and what looked like an E-Type in racing green, followed by slightly newer cars, a Lotus in the upstart's yellow, a Jensen in incongruous Italian red. Chequered flag stickers and RAF roundels on several of the machines. Carefully applied labels from meets and automotive associations, stretching back into the past. An ambulatory concert smelling of two-stroke and leaded petrol, of elbow grease and copper paste.

It was a long nostalgic fanfare driven by men with white sideburns and nappa leather gloves with knuckle holes. It made me proud to be over 50. Over 60 in fact, something I often forgot.

'Last night in the car, freezing my balls off, is the first time I've been absolutely alone, no one knowing where I am, for ages', he said. 'With you away and all'.

'I'm always on my own. Always have been, since my Meccano days', I said.

'By some kind of choice', he said, following the Jensen with his eyes.

'A combination of choice and bad luck I suppose. My parents worked a lot. Architecture is mostly a quiet, solitary pursuit'.

The old cars kept a stately pace, not unlike a funeral procession for a well-liked if uncelebrated member of the House of Commons, an outdated display of dignity and pride. I wasn't old enough to join their ranks but I felt a stab of jealousy looking at their perfectly shaped cars, where leather, metal and patina made a pretty strong case for the fact that some things actually were better before. I highly doubted there would be people salivating over Twingos in the future, organising swap meets and fan mail lists to celebrate the little French tarte terrible.

'I suppose there was very little privacy inside?' I asked, thinking about the quiet afternoons in my workplace. 'We tried to design some in, but it's very hard', I said.

'You can't imagine what it is like to be watched all the time. Or at least feel like you're being watched. I wasn't doing anything illegal once I was inside. I wasn't selling anything, buying anything, planning anything, sharpening anything. I was just, I don't know, waiting. Surrounded by people happy to see the worst in me'. he said. His eyes no longer looking at the buffed machines parading around us.

'Weird that it's become this', I said. 'The removal of choice and privacy, and of course freedom, are the main ways to punish people. Not by inflicting pain like it used to be. Or sending people away to some spider-infested colony. I can't imagine it', I said, 'being seen all the time'.

'I don't think anyone can unless you've been inside yourself', Frank said. 'Also because the other extreme, the opposite of having people in your face the whole time is worse. Solitary confinement is a sure way to break people's minds'.

'Seems like we need one another, just not all the time', I said. 'I mean not you and me – people in general'.

One of the old guys waved at us, and at first my heart skipped a beat, then I realised he was just being friendly.

Frank waved back unselfconsciously, and said 'The whole punishment thing is complicated because everyone is different. Like my wife, she loves being around people. She works as a hairdresser, and her customers feel at home with her. Like she was a friend who just happened to be doing hair stuff. It's natural to her in a way it's not to me. I like people and I like being on my own'.

'So solitary would be a real nightmare for your wife?' I asked.

'It's an absolute nightmare for everyone, but I suppose different people would deal with it in different ways, and I would maybe fare better than her'.

I swallowed and looked at the dash. Everything was in order. Then I asked, 'Do you miss her?'

'Every second', he said. No hesitation. It was beautiful and scary at the same time.

'I never thought of family when I planned this', I said.

'I understand. I could have chosen to go straight home from the prison when I came out. Instead I made my way to the bus station in Glasgow'.

'I'm sorry', I said and I meant it. Frank's wife hadn't done anything but she was still being punished whether he was in prison or not.

'Don't be. It's better this way', he said, but he didn't sound too convinced.

The last of the classic cars sailed by. A white Ford Fairlane with a male couple sharing the front sofa. Canvas top folded back despite the weather, leather caps pulled down as far as they could go. They looked like silver screen pilots deployed to an exotic theatre of war. The whirl of spokes, the blue fumes coming out of chromed double-pipes and the innocent smiles playing on the faces of those grandfathers made me happy. They had been transformed into children, but with greasy hands and sky high insurance premiums. So what? It's not always best to leave your kids money. *You made it, you spend it*, I found myself thinking as I watched the old boys.

'Us going to York, that's my unavoidable, dreamed-up penance. But is there anywhere you'd like to visit on our way down?' I asked. Chance was still our best travel companion.

'When my wife first came here she lived in a little place called Sharpness. She always talks about it being really beautiful, but I've never been'.

'Where is it?' I asked.

'I'll have a look on the map. It's not far from Cheltenham, but by the water'.

'If it's not too far off the mark, I'd be happy to go there, I mean it's only fair, an equal count of wishes fulfilled'.

'It's not important', Frank said while flicking through the pages of the AA road atlas for the right page. 'Look here it is. Just off the M5'.

'What does that mean for us? What is the closest A road?' I was a little annoyed he didn't know our credo by now.

'Hang on'. He licked his index finger and finally found the page. 'A38'.

'That's fine. Let's see how we get on', I said. 'There might be a nice fish and chip place on the coast'.

I looked ahead of us. The men now on the horizon were bravely propelling their ancient craft toward a grassy field full of enthusiasts somewhere. To ale pulled out of casks, to pie and carburettors, to holy parts bins full of coveted nuts and bolts no longer manufactured.

We were quiet for almost 20 minutes and I realised he had never finished his escape story. I knew he had been inside the fake double wall, temporarily troglodyte. In what seemed to be a *cul-de-sac*, the most English of French words, but I wasn't sure how he had found the next cookie crumb made out of paint, the next clue in cobalt blue, which I had dropped for him.

We drove into a long tunnel, so long it had a name, Rowan Hill Passage. From all the insignias and blue and yellow signs dotted about the entrance I gathered it was built almost entirely by EU funding. It was well lit, a yellow phosphorescent light, which made me feel like we were entering a dream. We were all alone on the road and I quickly realised I had slowed down.

'How did you get on with the rest of the maze?' I asked, feeling the weight of the concrete semi-circle above us, and the hill above that.

'Fine', he said. I had hoped for more, but with the walls closing in I decided to concentrate on getting us back out in to fresh air. Maybe Frank wasn't keen on the enclosed space either.

The tunnel seemed to go on forever, so I turned on the car's lights. Soon the entire hill was weighing down on the little purple car. I was usually quite immune to claustrophobia, but the circumstances had upset my bedrock.

'One of the things that troubled me was the fact that the flag post was blue too', Frank said. 'I had spotted that earlier that week when I did nothing, but couldn't work out how that fitted in the route'.

I laughed at the memory of my paint-stained trousers and hands, and said,

'Well, part of my initial plan involved the flag post. It was to be hinged, about three feet up, and once folded it would have reached the outer wall, providing a long monkey bar to freedom. I would somehow have provided the key to whoever solved the riddles. They would have unlocked the mechanism, and swung themselves out'.

I made a monkey noise and Frank laughed. Just a little moment of fun. Then I continued,

'In the end I decided against it. It would have been too public. I mean I could have put a block of Semtex in a wall and wired it up to a button that said *Emergency Exit*'.

Frank nodded. The idea of a long escape hatch wasn't a stunt or some kind of ploy to make a point or for my own glory. It was an underground tremor along a logical fault line, the least I could do to get back at the Scottish Office. A more spectacular escape would have meant that there was no confusion or embarrassment on the part of the Scottish Office, the Police or the SPS, but this mere vanishing of an inmate bought us time. And it was the same successful principle we applied to our travels.

I continued, 'Telling people I was painting the flagpole blue meant I could easily bring in a lot more blue paint than was needed for the more decorative elements in the prison. Enough to create the signage you interpreted correctly'.

Frank laughed slowly and said, 'I think the tunnel was a better idea anyway, especially the painted arrows inside the walkway whenever there was a choice of paths. I could maybe have worked it out after a while but it would have taken me a long time to be honest'.

I smiled.

'The only real difficulty I had was with the drain hole cover once I had climbed down into the main tunnel under the prison', he said.

'That was entirely my fault', I said. Happy to concede one minor point. 'I made it sit too flush inside its housing in the main exit pipe. I was usually pushing it up from the other side when I came to inspect or put in the finishing touches, and left it off for my return. I should have made a folding handle or something to make it easier to access from above'.

'In the end I tore strips from the bottom of my trousers and fed them through the little hole. It took ages, but there was no other way I could get a grip. Once I had a make-shift cotton handle I lifted the lid. It wasn't heavy, just awkward, then I slipped down into the other tunnel'.

'Did you pull it shut after you?' I asked, holding my breath.

'Of course', he laughed. 'I also made sure there was nothing left either inside the walkways or by the lid, no bits of rope or saliva. No piss, no hair as far as I'm aware. There was a dot of the same blue paint on the lid but I don't think anyone not looking for it would have noticed', he said. 'I tried to rub it out with the heel of my shoes anyway', he said.

'Good man', I said. Once more relieved that chance and intelligence had chosen the right man for the job. Both of our jobs.

'Then I got to the exit, with the knife, the money, the instructions. And the whisky of course'.

'Was everything dry?' I asked.

'The papers were a bit damp at the edges but not torn or anything', Frank smiled and shrugged his shoulders.

'I spent a little extra getting the thicker polythene sleeves, so I'm glad they stood up to the test', I said, thinking back on the full day I had spent going to various stationary shops before settling on a suitable sleeve from Winston's in Yoker. It was an old-fashioned place which seemed to have everything. If I had asked for a Daguerreotype copper plate, I'm sure the owner would've shuffled off to the stockroom to get a pack.

'It was a long walk to the bus station', Frank said, 'but since it was still quite dark people were driving with their headlights on. It was easy to see oncoming traffic and cars catching up with me, so most of the time I just sat down in the ditch or hid behind a tree whenever anyone passed.

On the bus I slept with my jacket over my head. I must have looked almost the same as when I came out of court'.

We could now see the world outside the tunnel. Mostly it was just a bright semicircle, but beyond it were the green pastures of England. Probably private cricket fields and pharmaceutical labs covered by sculpture parks and bridleways.

It's not pleasant to look back at one's younger self and shudder. I took a deep breath, then said, 'You've lived, you've seen things. You can probably tell, I used to drink. Then I had to stop, and I needed the distraction. Especially in the small hours of the night'.

'So you replaced the drinking with the Cromlix project. Then you replaced Cromlix with planning the trip, and now you're replacing the planning of the trip with actually doing the trip?' he said.

I didn't reply. But I felt that this silence was me conceding a point.

'What will you do once this is over?' he asked just as we exited the tunnel. I stepped on the gas a little, leaving behind us a purple cloud of used up petrol. An apparition of spent, finite resources at the mouth of the tunnel.

'I don't know'. It was a precipice I didn't want to approach. Luckily this train of thought was interrupted by a crack of lightning on the horizon. The forked streams of light burned on my retina for a second and then it was gone. A huge amount of wasted energy, nature's way of release. God showing off.

'I don't know', I said again, quieter. A Mercedes Marco Polo sailed past without indicting.

If Frank hadn't used the tunnel, and no one else had, I would still be in Glasgow, eating breakfast and lunch at Morrisons, going about my business. Not buying my sister a coat. Instead I was playing piano on the steering wheel of her car, coming back out into the light, leaving the hole through the mountain behind us.

Chapter 22

11.08 Monday

I was soon lost in thought about overpopulation and wondering if artificial sunlight could be achieved. If so it could be released at appropriate intervals, and we would be freed from the notions of night and day. If we could build skyscrapers going down the way we'd be fine for centuries. A series of inverted ziggurats, or in the case of a prison, a tower of Babel, a quiet shaft of anti-Babel, could solve a lot of our problems with us running out of surface area and climate changes. Also there would be natural heating from the core of the earth. That way a correctional institution could be housed underneath a motorway, a town hall, a school or a hospital. Under the ocean in fact. Once we knew it was safe, we could rehouse large swathes of the Earth's population into luxury caves, illuminated as well as powered by sunlight. My thoughts were interrupted by a bang.

'What was that?' Frank asked.

'It sounded like a gunshot'. I said looking out of the car in case there was a deer hunt on or something.

'I wouldn't know. I've never heard one', Frank said and it surprised me a little. A second or two later he said, 'The car is leaning over to your side. Seems like you've got a puncture'.

'*We* have a puncture', I said, eager to point out we were still in the same boat, whether the boat was my sister's or not.

'Front left', he concluded, like some kind of mechanic's Poirot.

'We can't stop here, there's not even a hard shoulder', I said.

'Have you got a spare?' he asked.

'In the boot, underneath all the stuff', I said, 'but I don't really know how to change the tyre. I mean I've done it before but it's been a long time since I have had to get my hands dirty'.

I made no effort to pull over and Frank turned to me,

'You can't drive on the rim. If the tyre comes off we're screwed', he said, and I was happy to take his word for it. After all he had been around vehicles needing repairs a lot more than I had.

'How much do you weigh?' I asked, still not taking my foot off the accelerator.

'Close to sixteen stone. Why?' he asked and looked down at his stomach.

'So if you sit behind me and we both lean over as much as we can, that should help'.

'Or you could just pull over', he said.

'Again, there's no hard shoulder and I don't want anyone to come and help us. I especially don't want the police to stop by', I said. We had slowed down a little, as if we were suddenly driving through golden syrup. I knew I was pressing the pedal the same as before but I was getting less back from the Twingo, and this got me worried.

'I saw a sign for York a while back. It can't be far', I said. 'We should be able to sort it out properly there'.

Franks said, 'Come on. Stop here and change the tyre'.

'And how do you suggest we do that? Remember you threw the jack into a field?' I said, not a little annoyed.

He went quiet and looked at his hands.

'Get behind me Frank', I said. 'Now'.

After a lot of huffing he was sitting in the back. I wasn't entirely comfortable having him behind me, but it was better than a long stop on the side of the road and a phone call to Green Flag, if we could find a phone, as neither of us had a mobile.

I couldn't see him very clearly, apart from a glimpse of his arm on the side of the car in the right wing mirror, the main rearview mirror was still missing. The already pretty mediocre ride quality of the car was now completely shot, as we made very lumpy progress, rubber periodically squealing against the wheel arch.

We drove like this for a while. Both windows open. Both of us leaning out as much as we could as if we were the crew of a small sail boat trying to gain purchase on the elements. Eventually there were lamp posts and clusters of houses. I pulled into a petrol station and sat back, sweat pouring from my brow. I had held on to the wheel so hard that my hands were seizing up.

There was a big parking space further on where lorries sat immobile, and with a great effort I put the Twingo in gear and manoeuvred us over to a quiet corner. Then I sat back and listened to my own raspy breathing.

Eventually I got out of the car and walked on foal's legs to the little shop. I put a six pack of Coca Cola and a small jack on the counter, made a little joke about Jack and Coke to the attendant but she can't have heard me properly because all she did was to hand me my change. I repeated it to Frank who appreciated it a bit more. I quickly drank one of the colas but I was still shaking. Frank must have seen the state of me because he got out and walked around to the boot in search of the spare wheel.

'What's all this stuff Cecil? Are you going on holiday after this?' he asked from the back.

'It's just all the different kits I've prepared for the journey'. I said wearily.

'How many do you need?'

'Covering all eventualities, that's all'.

Frank placed a beautifully clinking case gently on the ground.

'Never leave home without a case of Eminasin Verdejo', I said. 'The best alcohol-free wine money can buy'.

'Where's this wheel?' he asked.

'I think it's underneath the carpet of the boot. It's probably one of those space saver wheels you can only use for a restricted time and not drive too fast on. We'll have to go to a garage for a real wheel'.

'Do you know how to do this Cecil?'

'I thought you'd be an expert'.

'Why?' he asked.

'Not sure. You're big', I said.

'And working class?' he said, and crossed his arms over his chest.

'You told me you rented out diggers for a living', I said, flicking open another can.

'That involves Excel and good banter with contractors, not oil sumps and wheel bearings'.

'Sorry', I said, mouth full of Coke, the bubbles rising to my nose.

'Let's just get this wheel on'.

We hunched over the wheel arch and the tools like Burke and Hare, but incompetent. Eventually, after more dirty words than I have used in many years, we managed to resurrect the Twingo, and the hiss of the jack coming back down and the car resting on four wheels again was a beautiful testament to our working partnership.

As it was too difficult to put the real tyre back into the space where the spare had been, and since it was hopefully getting repaired soon, I put the punctured wheel in the back seat, strapping it in like a toddler.

The traffic and the houses were getting denser as we got closer to York. Careful not to stray over the newly imposed, even lower speed limit due to the skinny spare wheel, we drove on in silence, my eyes temporarily straying up above the city, attempting to locate the spire of the famed Minster.

As it was coming up to lunchtime my stomach was grumbling. The fizzy drink exacerbating the issue. The weather was neither here nor there, as if the season couldn't make up its mind. The day had started with lightning, then turned clear, but now the sky had a flat, aluminium texture, difficult to interpret or divine.

Once we crested the hill I could spot the Minster and my heart soared a little.

As this was the beginning of the end of our time together, we would be heading for the south coast after this stop, I plunged in and asked a question. One I knew the answer to, one that had been on my mind since we set out together.

'Why were you in prison Frank?' I said quickly, before I had time to change my mind. I knew full well of course, but I wanted to know his position on the matter. I was still convinced that operation Griffin had to take precedent, but I wasn't heartless. I still thought about Jennie and Janice.

He turned and looked at me and then looked out of the window. 'I'd rather you didn't ask. I won't ask about your private affairs', he said, palms up.

'I've told you most of them', I said and put the car in third for a slow descent.

'And I appreciate it. But that's your choice'. That's all he said. I couldn't tell whether he was absolving me from telling him more, or if he wasn't interested in my reasons.

A minute passed, then another.

'We need to go to a proper garage to get this tyre looked at', I said, once it was clear there was nothing more coming from Frank.

We entered the city and soon I pulled over and asked a man leaning against his fence if he knew of a garage. He gave me directions to a Kwik Fit further up the road, not far off the A1036, which we were on.

The man walked back into his house and closed the door quickly. I couldn't tell if he was desperate for a cup of tea or afraid of us. His front garden was full of sizeable statues. I wondered if his little plot of land was used to advertise and sell these monstrosities or if was just some kind of enthusiast. There were gargoyle fountainheads and horses with feathered hooves. A mad array of pubescent nymphs embracing each other, dogs tripping on their own ears, and unlikely flower arrangements coming out of broken barrels. All rendered in concrete plaster cast, all frozen in time. I leaned out to get a better look and was scared by a cross-eyed, predatory badger peeking out from under a Creeping Jenny. Both concrete. A miniature Brutalist nightmare. I shuddered and we took off, heading for living civilisation.

There were roadworks all the way to the garage and Frank asked me why I had had been so hell-bent on building a prison instead of a normal house.

'Before Cromlix I knew all the technical aspects, the economies and the ways to cut corners. I knew how to construct both safe and palpable joists and rafters, about material stress and vanity height. The era of the spectacle was upon us, imported from the States. For Cromlix I was more interested in the unspectacular, dull and safe. The good'.

I had sat through hour long meetings over socket points and knew the frustrations of dealing with narrow-minded clients and how difficult it was to get my vision of a building across. I was tired of the same procedures, which in the end was a maddening carousel of bureaucracy and legislation. There was no soul left, there was no compassion. This project was different.

'For me, Cromlix was from the heart. A little from the hip. Initially at least. I hadn't stopped to consider any wider questions with any of my other projects. Not thought about the wider social implications'.

'Or personal implications', Frank said in his dry voice.

'I used to think that a room is a room is a room. As long as it conformed to building regulations and I got a cut of the contractor's final bill'.

Frank stretched his neck this way and that. Like a boxer warming up.

Unlike Euan, I wasn't wet behind the ears. I knew about the human scale and the Bauhaus thing of having no central viewpoint. That the building would only work as a whole, made up from well-designed portions. I was aiming for Corbusier's *machine for living*, the tired refrain everybody kept singing, despite the old master's inability to do proper quality control. Just ask the owners of his villa

Savoy. It's easy to have ideas, harder to make them last. My building would have been different. Was different.

There were hundreds of measurements some anal stickler with a tape measure would come out and check once the building was completed. And if the numbers were a bit off, a bottle of whisky could make them right. During the design of my Cromlix I realised these measurements had real value. That was another of the reasons why I felt superior to Euan. I felt that he was still at the box, box, box stage, and that I had evolved, graduated somehow, into philosophy. It wasn't about the building; it was about the idea of the building.

He was encouraged to build an evil sugar cube. By the powers that be, or were, and by the sheer economies of it. Ninety degree angles are much cheaper than eighty-four ones followed eleven feet later by a ninety-six and so on. And that's not even talking about any kind of organic, free-flowing form. Anything that can't be constructed in pre-existing moulds costs money. Or to the stakeholders it looks like it will cost more money, which isn't necessarily true. But more to the point, Euan *wanted* to build a box. I didn't. And that's what had brought me to a standstill in a Twingo with this Frank.

We rolled through one set of lights, just to come to a complete stop at the next. At least I could see the sign for the garage on the horizon beyond another crew of roadworkers. The dance routine performed by the asphalters in front of us was quite moving. Like parts of a clock, all full of purpose. There's nothing quite as entertaining and relaxing as watching other people work, and the crew surrounding us were as precise as the Bolshoi.

'I believed that a building could be more than the sum of its parts. More than a series of hypotenuses. I was hoping a prison could be more than a corridor with cells off it'.

Judging by the speed of the work crew around us I was wondering if it was maybe the end of their working day, despite it being quite early still. They seemed too keen to be in the middle of their shift.

'I think I could have built some really interesting structures if I had had these kinds of thoughts in my thirties, rather than now in my very, very early sixties. Back then I was only interested in drinking, and chasing skirts, and cocaine in moderate doses'.

Frank nodded.

'Then Cromlix came along, and I think that's maybe why it hurt so much when I was stabbed in the back'. I sniffed a little. 'I wished I had stopped to think about what I was doing earlier in life', I said.

'No one has time to sit and think about what they do', Frank said. 'You make money and then you spend it. Then for two weeks a year you go somewhere and spend twice as much as you planned and spend the rest of the year paying that off'.

'Where do – did, sorry – you go on holiday?' I asked, the car still idling.

'Depends. We usually did year about because of my ex-wife's family and the kids and that. Also depends on what my ex-wife has in mind. That's very hard to predict'.

'Ayr, Loch Lomond, Butlins that sort of thing? Or just Glasgow Green with a football?' I asked.

'Either Haiti or the Highlands', he said casually, 'we rent a house in Aberfeldy sometimes'.

'What?' The light turned green but I was so surprised I forgot which pedal was which at my feet and the car stalled. The angry honks from behind me sounded like a herd of murderous geese as I struggled to untangle my feet.

'My wife's from Haiti, from Port-au-Prince', he said, proudly, pronouncing the words with a certain flourish.

'What is she doing here?' I asked and wrestled with the key in the ignition to start the car.

'Excuse me?' He turned at me, quickly. 'I'm sick of this attitude'.

'Oh, you mean... No, I realise that came out sounding racist. I'm not like that. What I mean is that Haiti sounds great and warm and dry. The sort of paradise people go on holiday to'.

Frank shrugged his shoulders, and I wasn't sure whether he thought I was against foreigners coming here, which I wasn't, or if he thought it was merely a slip of the tongue. He said, 'Not a lot of jobs. Always hurricanes, poverty, a broken system. She was down in Sharpness, like I said before, for a while and then came up here, and we met and now she's here permanently'.

'Does she work?' I asked. Out of interest, not from some sort of racist pre-conception.

'Of course she does. I told you we are hard-working, tax-paying people'.

'I didn't mean...'. I said, feeling that it was all coming out wrong.

'She has one of those salons in town that specialises in black hair'.

'Is it different from white? Or ginger?' I asked, realising I had never really thought about hair other than when I went to the barbers for a short back and sides.

We swerved into the huge car park in front of the Kwik Fit.

'Have you been in contact with her? Or the kids?' I asked anxiously.

'Not since coming out. They were up last week, but it's hard to see them. Too hard sometimes. Especially the kids. They grow so much between visits that it hurts to look at'.

We circled the car park a little. I was trying to gauge how to best approach the garage. I didn't want them to spot me letting Frank out.

He continued, 'I was only in for a very short time compared to some of the other guys. They will have teenagers they have never seen out in the open. Kids who are as old as they were when they were jailed. Some guys in Cromlix will never walk out. The only way they'll be coming out is in a coffin', he said.

'Your wife – does she speak English?' I asked, still looking for the perfect spot.

'Yes, but her mum came and stayed with us for a while and she had very little English, and she kept saying that people in Glasgow weren't speaking English anyway', he laughed. 'I spoke English to the kids and my wife would swap between French and English, but she had been here for years before we met so the kids speak mostly English. It's the most useful language for them right now with school and all that. But I guess I've picked up some of the language from her'.

We got stuck behind a huge Range Rover trying to find the perfect parking space. It was an impossible arithmetic.

'Don't get me started on living with your mother-in-law', I said, thinking back on the final months with Maud.

'Did you live in a two-bedroom flat on the 11th floor with a broken lift and five kids?'

'Is that where you lived?' I asked.

'No, I'm being ironic, but you get my point. Where did you stay?' he asked.

'In a six-bedroom house in Bearsden. With no kids. But it was still enough to drive me insane'.

'I didn't mind it', Frank said. 'My wife's mum was great with the kids. Really helpful when we were both working a lot'.

Eventually the driver of the Range Rover pulled into the disabled corridor of the car park and stalled his war-winning jeep across two spaces. Probably expecting a knighthood or a medal.

'Where do you live now?' Frank asked.

'In a tenement, just off Dunbarton Road', I said vaguely.

'I thought you'd live in some sort of glass and concrete spaceship'.

'No, I can't stand those things. They're maybe fine for others but I like the ceiling height, plaster work, the soul of an old place. And if the central heating is unreliable, rent can be quite cheap'.

I found a spot to the left of the garage, closer to a row of shops and slowly reversed in. To be able to take off faster if we needed to.

'Is your mother-in-law still here?' I asked, anxious that there would be more and more people who missed Frank and would want to hear from him soon.

'She couldn't hack the weather, and getting permanent residency is almost impossible anyway. She comes over to visit as often as she can, but she's getting on in years'.

I turned off the car. We decided it would probably be better if I dealt with the mechanics on my own. Turning away from Frank and unzipping my bum bag I got out six twenties. I felt bad about him having to live with his mother-in-law, and for presuming he fished the Clyde for his holidays.

'Why don't you go and buy yourself something nicer to wear? Something that fits?' I said and slipped him the money.

Frank had nodded, the same way he had when we first met at Buchanan bus station. Keen to be on his way.

'Wait, Frank', I said. Like the bag expectant mothers pack in preparation for rushing to hospital and deliver a new life, I had kept a sports bag packed and ready. I was delivering a new life too.

On the day we left I had packed and re-packed this bag. Like an idiot I must have forgotten to put in pants for me. There was a question I had hoped to be able to avoid, but as it was I couldn't.

'Could you buy me some underwear?' I asked him quickly. It was one of the most embarrassing things I have ever done.

It is unusual for one man to buy underwear for another. On the surface it is quite an easy purchase, if you put aside your qualms, as long as you get the right size. Easier than any other garment in terms of fit and taste, bar socks. The choice comes down to briefs, generous boxers or tight boxers. Colour, pattern and superfluous buttons is not a thing one has to take into consideration really. Unless it's a first date or something but it had been a long time since I went on a date. If I slept with someone she was either as lonely as I was or expected some kind of remuneration and didn't mind whether my pants had a paisley pattern or the outline of the Burj Khalifa on them.

'Sure. Medium? Large?' he asked.

'Medium', I said and peeled off another 10 pounds for him. It felt like I was sending a teenager out for his first solo trip down the high street. The nervous wait, the inevitability of money wasted. We decided to meet in the cobbled square in front of the Minster in 2 hours' time and Frank walked off towards the warren of medieval streets. Whistling and cocking the Cape Canaveral hat I had made him put on. I could see he wasn't used to wearing sunglasses, and it looked a bit funny as it was overcast but he had agreed that it was for the best.

'Nothing silky or frilly. I'm a cotton man', I shouted as he wandered off, putting aside my secretive nature for a second. I hoped he would come back. Going commando gets uncomfortable after a while.

Chapter 23

12.15 Monday

'Let's take the tour Frank. While we're here we might as well'. I pointed over to where a petite woman with a bob and thick spectacles was standing holding a stick, not unlike a bishop's crosier, displaying a proud tricolour. He just smiled and nodded. The big clock above us chimed musically.

We joined a substantial throng of retirees. The first stop was the Five Sisters stained glass window, and while we waited for some of the slower members I chatted to my neighbour. If I understood him correctly they were a busload up from Bordeaux, but he might have been talking about something else. We shuffled around the inside of the cathedral, going from station to station, from magnificent chapter house to John Thornton's quirky details, only really appreciated up close. It was lovely to hear French again, and the guide's voice reminded me a little of Madame Morvan's. Having the language echo around the walls must have been a little like it had been many generations ago, when it was still spoken by queens and monks.

I was only listening with one ear. I had a lot of prior knowledge of construction in general and the Minster in particular as I had always wanted to visit and had read lots on the subject. Strangely I had never found the time. York is neither London, abroad, or home. Not a destination in itself I had thought, but I was slowly changing my mind.

Frank seemed happy to learn about buttressed walls and the difficulties of octagonal construction. I wasn't sure how much he understood. I couldn't tell whether he was pretending or actually following what the guide was saying. Either way he was smiling left and right, probably sure that none of these foreign and retired people had heard of his crime or cared what happened in the UK beyond their coach trip. One of the oldest women, bent double and brandishing a walking stick like a conductor's baton, had latched on to his arm. He seemed happy to help her up and down the inevitable half-steps. I soon found myself lagging behind the group, but it was nice to be on my own in a sacred space for a moment or two, and Frank was never out of my sight.

We had been walking around in the petrified forest of stone, pillars towering above us like red firs, for over an hour when the tour came to an end. The bus load clapped their hands, and were led to the souvenir shop by their tour operator. It was undoubtedly part of some complicated percentage scheme between the travel agent and the Minster. I thanked the guide using her language and shook her hand, concealing a folded-up 10 pound note. She seemed surprised but it was a small price to pay for the peace of mind I was feeling. I had ticked another box. It was a box I hadn't been aware of until the stress of the sex forest incident threw up York Minster as a bucket list top 10. I could do nothing but obey my heart's wish, but now we had to move on.

Time had passed quickly in the gentle light of the cathedral with the French woman pointing to the same things as her English-speaking counterparts a few steps behind us, a herd of his own at his heels. In comparison our guide had been more poignant in her gestures, more entertaining also.

'Fancy getting some real food, something not coffee and sandwiches?' Frank asked once we were outside in the little square again.

'What do you want? Pie?' I asked. I felt relatively safe milling with the throngs of tourists. With our hats I thought we blended in quite well There was a large group of people following a man holding a bright orange umbrella high up in the air, presumably towards either food or something else worthwhile to see. 'Did you get the thing I asked you to get for me?' I asked.

'Oh, yes', he said.

He went on to tell me that after getting himself clothes and a pair of shoes, here he pointed to his smart, new Australian half-boots, there wasn't much money left, so he got me pants from Matalan.

He handed me the sealed pack. 'Three pairs for £9.99, not bad', I said, then I fell silent. The pants were all variations on the theme of Cupid's arrows piercing a heart. I wasn't too thrilled, but they would see me through the trip down to Bournemouth and back, barring accidents. Then I would dispose of them. I would treat them as NHS pants, one-offs. The top pair of pants in the pack was mostly black. If Frank had picked up the pack in a hurry there was a chance he hadn't seen the rest of the motifs.

I saw a sign pointing towards 'Betty's Café' which sounded homely and cheap, and we walked to it. I had Frank stand outside at a bus stop, the best place to loiter. Once I got inside I realised this was no place to get bacon rolls or black pudding. Instead I got us a huge bag of meringues, cream puffs and assorted sweets. We had a long way to go still and these perks, apparently handmade by one of the very pretty girls behind the counter, would keep us right long into the night.

I did, however, realise that Frank was maybe after something more substantial as he was the one who had asked for real food. I asked the cashier girl for directions to KFC, as I thought it was probably better if we could eat and travel at the same time. She happily drew me a map. It looked quite far to walk and seemed to be on the way out of town, heading south anyway. When I came back outside I gave Frank a Yorkshire curd tart, and told him we had better get back to the car.

'Did they tell you a time when the tyre would be ready?' Frank asked.

I swallowed some of my ganache macaroon and told him, 'The car's been ready for ages. I just thought since we were here that we might as well go on the tour, and see some of the town. It used to be the capital of the Viking world', I told him.

'You mean we could have been on our way ages ago? The car's just sitting there in the car park?'

'It was important that we concluded this phase of the trip. Now I can move on', I told him in my calmest voice. I wanted him to understand the difference between the whims of navigation and the soul's desire. He didn't say anything, so I think he got it. Or maybe he was just hungry.

'Cheer up. We're driving south through the Peak District. It's a stunning part of the world. Unfortunately, we'll miss the Snake Pass, but there are lots of gorgeous roads'.

'You should be a tour guide too Cecil', Frank said and finished off his sweet snack.

'Maybe one day, when all this is over, I'll be able to lead reconstructions, following in my own footsteps', I joked. 'All the way back to your cell'. Frank didn't laugh.

'In the coming few hours you're going to have to be pretty sharp with the map', I said. 'Some of the national park bits we are going through are quite remote. There's no deadline really to this, but we mustn't fall too far behind the schedule, even though the itinerary is flexible'.

We walked back to the car in silence, and I got it back from its custodians at Kwick Fit. At KFC I chose the drive-thru option and made sure Frank had his hat pulled down low as we came up to the cashier to pay for our steaming trough of chicken pieces. I also popped inside to put on my new pants in a toilet stall.

Once we were underway we propped the Family Feast bucket between us and made good time out of York, joining the A64 without much trouble. Two white vans from the same kitchen fitting company passed us. Three burly men squashed together in the front of both vans. All six of them looked down on us and I felt decidedly uncomfortable. I tried to hold up the bucket of chicken for them to spot, but I wasn't sure it worked.

'We have to be careful Frank', I said. 'Two men in a car carries with it whiffs of homosexuality. That's not my opinion per se but that's what a lot of people will think. You don't have to worry, I'm a ladies man all the way and by all accounts you're married, so that's that. I'm just saying', I told him. 'This car doesn't help'.

'Because it's small and purple?' Frank said.

'It's a car for interior designers down on their luck', I said, pointing out the obvious.

'And what would be a masculine car?' he asked.

'As in heterosexual?' I asked.

'I suppose. I've never given the difference much thought', he said.

'A masculine car is either something really rusty and old. Maybe an Alfa. Something only an enthusiast would drive. A labour of love more than a car'.

'Something useless?' he said. I had to remind myself that he used to rent out things that worked, that was their only real function. In his world I presumed machines were meant to have very little aesthetical value.

I thought for a moment, then I said, 'Or it is something more *nouveau riche*. Something only a footballer's kind of money would buy. A gold leaf Bentley Continental GT or a matte black Overfinch with bright yellow brake calipers'.

'Cecil, you're mad. People don't reason like this. A car is a box that transports you from A to B. Maybe you want a faster, bigger, flashier one but most people just have a car'.

'Maybe. But to me it sounds like you never took time to reflect on it'.

'That's true. I was busy working for a living', he said a little testily.

'Yet you rent out these big, powerful, brightly painted machines to manly men all day. Men who might or might not have all kinds of complexes tied into their educational and sexual history. Or failings to compensate for'.

'I used to rent out vehicles', he said. 'Nothing more'.

I let his comment hang in the air.

We were barrelling along the A630, passing through a slew of villages with impossibly English names. Conisborough, Hooton Roberts, Dalton Magna.

'Me, for example, I'm a SAAB man. They are clearly the thinking man's choice. Solid, clever, luxurious but not flashy'.

'Didn't they go bankrupt a few years back?' Frank asked.

'That's a glitch', I said, 'I'm convinced they will go down in history as one of the greatest car manufacturers'.

We drove south on the A61 for a while, to enter the National Park further down than most people. The journey's internal compass was still aimed South, but as far as confusing the authorities I think we were doing a fine job. And it was enjoyable too, just looking out at the peaks and valleys of the park.

'Tell me what you drive and I'll tell you who you are', I said. 'Did you never play that at conferences or trade fairs?'

He frowned and said, 'Sounds more like some sort of weird horoscope'.

'Some people believe in the stars', I said, raising a hand off the steering wheel to a man that had allowed us to pass his wide trailer, 'others in cars', I laughed.

I was sad to miss the Ladybower Reservoir, where I could have pointed out the ghost of the Derwent church tower to Frank. It was drowned by the drinking water meant for the East Midlands, a beautiful picture really. But that was the architect in me thinking, not the logistics officer who was in charge after all, and it would have to wait for another time.

To save on petrol I tried to coast down big hills in neutral. I tried to work out which was better, to let the engine rest while we rolled down and to then pop it into gear, or keep it in fifth as much as possible.

After some experimenting where the rev counter would drop to about 1,000 while coasting downhill to then shoot up to about 4,000 when I engaged fifth gear, I managed to get the second number down by a 1,000 revolutions per minute if I engaged the gear gently, like stroking the wings of a butterfly.

For no reason Frank turned to me and looked kind of expectant. As if I was his guide. Maybe he was bored of the trip already? I didn't have anything more than cold, breaded chicken to offer.

I dragged a finger along the top of the grey fascia in front of me. It came away a little grimy and I wiped it on my trousers, leaving a stain there instead, adding to the tang of vinegar from before.

I sighed and thought of my sister and how different we were. Through my otherwise messy periods I always kept my car clean and tidy. Sometimes I would hoover and buff it but not drive it because I knew I was too drunk to find the right controls with my feet. It was enough for me to restore it to a shadow of its former showroom glory. Sometimes driving it was secondary.

'I could do with a pick-me-up now'. I said. 'In another life I would have had a line about now'.

'I never did any drugs', Frank said.

'Really?' I said.

'Or sold any. I don't even smoke cigarettes'.

'Why?'

'I guess I was never into it. I was always into football, I did a couple of trial matches for the under 16s, and I didn't want to risk that by being hung over for a game. I've always liked being in shape'.

We skirted Sheffield and managed not to stop for tiffin, cut-price cutlery or any other local attractions. The road took a turn for the better after that. The heavy pockets of the tourist board had made sure the entry to the Peak District was well looked after. It was a joy to be re-united with nature again after the journey to York.

'Alcohol was my big downfall', I said. I'm happy to admit it. I've trained myself to be happy to admit it. I could never say no to a glass of wine. Or a bottle for that matter'.

'Are you drunk now?'

'I'm driving'.

'And?'

'I'm not, but I'll forever be a drunk. You know, sober alcoholic and all that. I've not touched the stuff for 1,413 days. And for 695 before that'.

'What happened?'

'My mum died', I said quickly before I choked up, as I always did when I thought about her.

'That's a hard one', Frank said. I could tell his mother was no longer alive either.

We passed through the English heartland in a blur of sports fields in disuse and tractors driven by survivors in tweed caps.

'Whatever else happens, please don't tempt me with a drink', I said.

He nodded. I nodded. That's as profound as it gets between men.

We were moving along, part of the conveyor belt of traffic and apart from it at the same time. Doncaster looming on the horizon. The people around us were mostly commuters, delivery men, tradespeople, maybe one or two holiday makers. We were pioneers. A sliver of mixed class intelligentsia, blazing a trail south. Or South-East at least.

Despite the decorations of the boxers Frank had gotten me I was getting used to the shape and the cut of them. I was surprisingly happy with them and made a mental note to thank him for introducing me to the polyester/cotton mix, I had always stuck to 100% cotton. This trip was proving to be quite the eye-opener for both of us.

Chapter 24

14.30 Monday

Coming out of the Peak District we hit the town of Leek and pulled over at a service station. It was a sad goodbye to the hills and waters as we now had almost no national parks between us and the next natural distraction, the sea. Not counting the Malvern Hills which I didn't think we would have time, let alone energy for.

While I was waiting in line to pay for a host of nibbles I picked up a postcard. It had a steam train on it and the black beast was letting out a huge white cloud, as if the passengers on-board had just voted unanimously for a pope. It was crossing some gorge, on a bridge full of rivets. Iron crafted by Victorians high on laudanum and empire. I paid for my bits and pieces and walked over to the palm-sized table with its attached pen where people try to find the right numbers for the lottery.

Dear Genevre,

Hope you're well. I'm traveling and enjoying myself. I would like to say that I saw this and thought of you, which is true, but not in relation to the train, the bridge or the Vatican (Have you ever been, would you like to go one day?) We have seen York Minster and now I think I would like to see the Sistine Chapel too. Hope to see you soon!

Cecil

I went back to the cashier and asked for a stamp, with my heart beating a little extra. The service station kiosk didn't carry them, I was informed, so I wrote out the address to her bakery, which I had memorised, and put the postcard in my personal valise in the boot of the car.

Not long after entering the outskirts of Stoke-on-Trent I was coasting down a long hill on the A520, doing my bit for the environment, traveling for free. A long row of articulated lorries, *Anderson Haulage, Luton*, overtook us, black smoke from struggling diesels enveloping the Twingo. The drivers were staring straight ahead, fueled no doubt by amphetamines and sucrose. In their wake, a Seat. The young couple inside were cardboard cutouts modeled on the pictures you get in frames at IKEA. They appeared so normal I could smell their matching perfume and aftershave set. After them a Chrysler Voyager full of women who looked like they were on their way to a hen night at a discount brewery in Blackpool. I shuddered and took my foot off the gas. Silently coasting past to give them some space.

'See that Frank?' I said, 'It's fine for them, but a group of men traveling together is only inconspicuous in certain circumstances. Two women traveling together is not automatically thought of as dodgy. Two men are'.

'You mean we'd be less likely to arouse interest if we were a man and a woman?'

I nodded and continued, 'Of course we are. For a while I thought about packing a big dress and a bra full of newsprint for the escapee to wear, but I realised that although escaping might be ultimate goal there were certain discussions I didn't want to have. Certain rules I didn't want to impose'.

'I'll wear a dress if it makes you happy Cecil', Frank said, his face straight.

'That's really not what I mean. Don't be absurd'.

'I was joking', Frank said and smirked like a boy with a frog in his pocket.

'Good. I just mean that a man and even an ugly woman, like you would make, still wouldn't attract as much attention as we do – by default'.

'If I'm so ugly, maybe you should wear the dress?' he said.

'No one is wearing a dress', I said sternly, annoyed that he had already derailed a very valid argument. 'I'm just saying that we need to provide onlookers with an easy answer to their inner query about us. About the nature of our relationship'.

'You spend a lot of time on your own don't you?'

'Always did', I said, not without pride.

Now that I couldn't see the people carrier full of drinking women I put us back at the speed limit.

'So what's your big idea?' Frank asked. I wasn't sure if he wanted to know or if he just wanted to kill time.

'I have three strands that I think can work in our favour', I said. 'The first one is *Sports*. If we wore the same team colours we would be on the way to or from a game. I'd wear a scarf and you a team replica shirt, preferably of either a really well-known team like Manchester or Chelsea, or a tiny regional team that no one outside the area would know. Partick Thistle, Mountsorrel FC or even a much smaller club, and it doesn't have to be football. Shinty, rugby, net ball, women's underwater hockey, something like that'.

'Hate to admit it but it kind of sounds like a good idea', Frank said after chewing a little on his lower lip.

'But this means I would have to read up on sports, which I couldn't hack. And some people, like yourself maybe, are funny about wearing a shirt of a team they've hated their whole life. I get that. Even if the team was small there would still be the risk of running into other dedicated supporters and there is no way we would be able to cover up our lack of knowledge. Things like the finer points of badminton, the latest league standings of tractor pulling, the difference between a woman's golf club and a man's'.

Frank giggled. I couldn't tell if he was laughing at me or my ideas. Or at the image of me in a Premiership getup.

'On the theme of sports there is another alternative. If we are active ourselves it's not strange to be traveling two men in a car. We could be mountain bikers, all dressed up in pads and with scars from falling into bushes, or curlers or even tennis coaches going to gain a further certificate. If I had thought that these were viable alternatives I would have filled the car with props', I said.

'Rackets and stones and stuff?' he asked. I wasn't sure if he was goading me on or if he was interested. I didn't care either way. My blood was up and this was important. Camouflage is no joke.

'Two full suspension bikes on a rack or an Albion racing dinghy strapped to the roof, more like it', I said.

'Why such expensive sports?' he asked, clearly not anywhere near as visionary as me.

'Hillwalking and bird-watching are cheap. But two men in woolly socks and binoculars sipping tea from a flask seems a bit fishy to most. There are whiffs of suppressed sexuality about a lot of outdoor pursuits, but the more technical ones full of equipment and accessories circumvent a lot of uncomfortable introspection. You can talk about stuff instead of feelings'.

'Which men are good at. How are you feeling by the way Cecil?'

'A bit bloated. Thanks for asking. Chicken wings have never really agreed with me', I said.

'Shame'. Again this giggle from Frank.

I continued. I was convinced there was a pretty important life lesson in it for him.

'I'd still dread being found out', I said. 'The casual question in a car park by a real expert, or the seemingly innocent advice on where to go sailing, the best route for cycling, something like that would be too much for me in my already heightened state of nerves'.

'So sports are out?' he asked, amused if not altogether in rapture.

'Yes, but there are alternatives. I called one of the other scenarios *Master and Apprentice*. You're a bit on the old side so I'm glad I didn't go down that route'.

'Too old?' he asked, sitting forward in his seat.

'If we were traveling in a panel van and wore matching fleece jackets, I would have a clipboard and you a toolbox, which could be quite good. I would be the boss plumber or surveyor or something and you would be the apprentice. It's a hierarchy that's easy to understand for the passing eye. You get the teas, I drive. You smoke, I have given up on my doctor's orders. I am married but have a roving eye, you are single and might even wolf-whistle – something I must publicly disapprove of but actually don't mind'.

'Is this in real life now?' he said.

'No. Still acting. The world is a stage for people like us. I used to design sets, buildings if you will, and now I am supplying us with roles. Plausible roles for this play. For this act in the performance at least'.

'So why are we not wearing matching jackets?' he asked, and it looked like he was almost missing the chance to zip up a grubby fleece with a company logo on.

I sighed and said, 'We did initially, but with me being retired and you a bit on the old side to be starting out in a profession I think it was good idea to be more incognito'.

There was a wall of light and a screech like from a hundred fog horns 10 inches from the back of the car. A huge lorry had sneaked up on me and the entire rearview mirror was filled with the chromed, and roaring, lion of the MAN lorry manufacturer. I pulled over as quickly as I could but received neither wave nor wink of his hazards as the letters, *Anderson Haulage, Luton*, sped past us.

We settled back into our dreary rhythm, the Twingo shuddering.

'Any other scenarios?' Frank asked, barely hiding the irony in his voice.

'*The family connection*'.

'Like you're my dad?' he asked, his voice not far from incredulous.

'Along those lines. But I am not old enough to be your father'.

'How so? I was too old to be the apprentice', he asked.

'I look young for my age, you less so. I might, however, be your uncle or a cousin. We could be traveling to a wedding or a baptism somewhere'.

'How would people know?' he asked.

'We would make sure we looked a little like each other and walked a lot like each other'.

'We don't look alike in any way'.

'But we could quickly learn to move in similar patterns. Have a look at dads and sons, they almost always walk like each other. And sometimes daughters and mums, and daughters and dads too, but only if the girl is tall for her age or a tomboy'.

'Cecil, you crack me up', he said, gently punching the dash in front of him with a balled fist.

'If we were family we would either be silent, because we knew too much about each other, or bicker and argue', I continued with impeccable logic.

'Is that the mark of a successful family bond?'

'To some extent. If you show someone your worst side for years and years and they still stick by you, something must be right'.

'Why can't we be just two guys going somewhere?'

'We are', I said. 'That's the beauty'.

'And what about your scenarios?'

'I thought it would be best if we either invented one together, that way it would be a lot easier to keep our web of lies together. Or we could just not have one and the sheer incredibility of this trip, the first one of its kind in the history of man I should think, would be our mantle'.

'But if someone asks?'

'Who would that be?'

'I don't know. Someone at a petrol station or in a queue'.

'Tell them the truth Frank. The truth will set you free'.

'Are you mad?' he asked. For the first time since we broached the subject of disguise, it looked like he was listening.

'Then wink', I said. 'They'll think you're joking. If I pointed at you and said, *He's a prisoner and I'm giving him a lift to Dorset*, people will presume you're my nephew and that I am being made to drive you somewhere by my wife'.

'Is that your idea of a cover?' Frank asked.

'Hiding in plain sight has been my grand plan for many years'.

'Like you did with the prison?' he said. Closer to my wavelength now that he could see the connection.

'I suppose you could say that', I said. 'And with the drinking. I was drunk most of the time back then, but very few people knew. Partly because I was so rarely sober that few people would have known the real me. Partly because of menthol cigarettes'.

On the hard shoulder, at the end of four long skid marks was the Chrysler, sliding doors fully open. Lined up like gaudy ducks at a fairground, a row of women being sick. I looked at Frank and he nodded.

* * *

Before I knew it the panel showed 16:04 and I realised we had been on the road a long while, zooming south on the A34/A449 all the way past Kidderminster. Over the fallow fields and neglected pastures, a soft rain, lending the world a sense of Vaselined lens. I wasn't tired but my thoughts, and the quiet realisation that it was still the same day as the Lauriston B&B, waking up with Frank staring down at me, made me tired.

Like a warped self-fulfilling prophecy my eyelids were suddenly lead heavy. The continuous ebb and flow of adrenaline – self-inflicted or brought on by external events – was starting to take its toll too.

'Talk to me Frank, I'm falling asleep here. This road is too monochrome; it's sending me over the edge'.

'Monotone?' he asked.

'That too', I said.

The rain had increased and a Jeep Cherokee in front of us kept changing lanes, sending up spray. I had to turn the wipers to their fastest setting. The lulling motion of the wipers slushing back and forward right in front of my eyes didn't help with the onset of sleepiness either.

'Frank, look at that row of silos. Like sentinels watching over a Somme trench'.

'Quite scary-looking things', he said, shuddering.

'Spoken like a true victim of the style', I said, offering consolation.

'Spoken like a person who doesn't like buildings to be huge, concrete blocks', he said.

'To me they're not beautiful either but that was never the aim of them. The silos were storing grain, that was their only aim. You can't say a hammer is ugly or an earwig is scary. They are just tools, just function, and nothing extra. It's the same with these silos. It's just the scale that's different. If you imagined a hammer or an insect that size, they'd look scary too'.

He nodded as if spellbound. I realised I could have made a career as a lecturer at the Open University. The Cherokee was still driving erratically ahead of us and if it hadn't been for my precarious situation I would have phoned the police to get them out to breathalyse the driver.

'But more than scale, it's all about intent', I said. 'I mean if the same building had been housing Katyusha rockets or American warheads, they would have scared me to death, but the actual buildings wouldn't necessarily have looked any different'.

Frank shrugged and we lapsed into silence as the silos disappeared behind us, my lecturing dreams submerged again.

The conversation left me thinking about intent and concrete. The purpose of a building had many things in common with crime I thought. The difference between accident and being evil is intent. But in principle, and with the benefit of hindsight, brutalism is odd more than scary. Oversized more than useful.

There's a whole generation of badly poured concrete buildings, designed as if for an asymmetric race of giants. Un-usable for people. Looking like they were constructed for a breed of long-limbed, colour blind aliens that failed to descend to Earth.

Their war-time heritage is always too obvious to disregard. A brutalist block of flats for young families will look like anti-tank structures. Czech hedgehogs for living in. A community theatre will look like a dictator's last bunker. Brutalism, neo, or post-neo isn't suitable for civilians. But then again, there will probably never, ever not be conflict in some part of the world, so maybe these structures are a perpetually timely reminder.

Regardless of lofty ideas, on a grassroots level who wants to live inside a remnant of the Atlantic Wall, but in Croydon? And it wouldn't even have a sea view? Homes in the style of, the Central Post Office in Skopje should have gone out of fashion as soon as they were conceived. It's a set of ideas that's been too stubborn. A rude guest who's overstayed his welcome. But then again, look at Montreal 76.

To me the silos and newer universities were just remnants of total war. Untimely reminders of what our grandparents fought so hard inside, and what I'm sure they hated to see on home soil. Bunkers and coastal battery structures, but on a massive scale. Out of the fire of D-Day and into the cauldron of Birmingham Central Library.

These defensive structures, useless in times of relative peace, are now the height of fashion again. The wheel of time and trends getting smaller and smaller. In the wake of the war these fortifications, watchtowers, and turrets which were originally designed to house anti-tank guns and grim-faced soldiers were soon housing lovers and hopeful professionals. These prefabricated monstrosities became homes, out of sync, designed for a future that never happened. The intentions of the builders were put highest on the list of priorities rather than the reality which surrounded them. This was a kind of hopeful socialism. Pleasant in its intent and terrifying in its execution. Towers like monoliths. Celebrating Bloc pharaohs.

Despite my best intentions Cromlix had ended up yet another useless contribution to the plethora of badly thought-out brutalist building blocks. A seemingly insolvable Rubik's cube. Over the years I had transformed it into a concrete apple with an unknown worm living inside it. The worm, who peeked out of a water pipe not 3 days ago, was now sitting next to me.

If there was something positive to take away from the building it was the fact that I had broken the spell a little. By digging under the foundations of brutalism, I had undermined a widely accepted set of ideas. I, the sapper of my own fortress, had also been the liberator of its brutal spirit, which had been caged up for so long.

The marks left from the timber which had held the concrete as it coagulated and hardened was the only natural impression and remnant in these buildings. And it was nothing more than a by-product. Those planks were soon rotten or burnt, quickly forgotten despite the many years it would have taken for a tree to grow to a size where a suitable plank could be harvested from it. On this concrete, the most constructed surface, an organic fingerprint had been left, and then quickly overlooked.

My eyelids were still heavy. I have never been one for energy drinks but if some young person had offered me one of those fluorescent cans full of riboflavin and dopamine I would have chugged it down no questions asked. Coffee – I could have had a pint.

We passed the Cherokee sitting on the side of the road, steam coming out of the open bonnet, its driver kicking the front bumper over and over again. Either Frank didn't see it or he didn't care. The Jeep had faux wood covering the sides, some kind of homage to the early pioneers, I guessed. In a different life I would have stopped to help, and we could have talked about casting concrete in wooden frames.

But we had our own agenda, and our needs for anonymity. Sometimes Samaritan acts have to be postponed until a more suitable moment. And maybe it would also teach the driver to not travel so inconsistently. A little time-out, the adult equivalent of the naughty step, brought on by mechanical failure, which in turn was brought on by incompetence, was maybe just the right medicine for that particular driver. Making sure I kept the needle at a steady 58 miles per hour I drove on, affecting a difference in space by using up time.

Chapter 25

16.30 Monday

Frank was quiet, sitting still. I coughed loudly a couple of times to see if he would react but he didn't move a muscle. I thought he had died, and wasn't sure if that was a relief or a worst case scenario. I reasoned I could drive back to the Ladybower Reservoir, weigh him down with some of the suitcases from the boot and bury him in a watery grave. Then he sneezed and turned to the window, as if he had overheard my thoughts and was disgusted with the way I would treat his corpse.

We lumbered on. The A449 merged with the M5 just north of Worcester, so I found the quieter A4538/A44. I was really sleepy now.

Frank grunted and started to slowly peel off his shoes. One toe at the other heel, pushing against the expensive, but admittedly handsome, Australian boots he had bought in York. It was a sure sign he was planning to sleep. I realised that aside from my father brushing his teeth, a sure sign he was going to bed, Frank was the only other man whose nocturnal habits I knew intimately. I had always been a quick learner. I decided to be charitable and let him sleep if that was his desire. This left me to my own thoughts as the tyres moaned over the tarmac.

He sneezed again, a violent rupturing of the calm atmosphere, startling me out of my calculations of buoyancy and sink hole suction, and I decided to open my window a fraction more to wake me up.

Soon he was snoring again and I was alone in the world. Memories, unbidden, resurfaced. Not unlike the hypothetical scenario of the bloated body I had tried to hide in the inky waters of the reservoir.

In the plans I submitted to Stewart and the others I had considered the corridors and the cells. Every measurable surface obeying the Golden Rule, two fingers to the normative. I made sure to have as few ninety-degree corners as possible, as few straight lines as possible, as little obvious surveillance as possible. A caravanserai more than an institution.

I had imagined a lot of natural light and positive images of nature and messages of freedom. Wide open meeting spaces, *Agoras*. As much as possible my prison would resemble a home, or at least student halls. There was space for a gymnasium and a theatre, a music room with a slightly raised stage. I took a lot of inspiration from the Greeks, or what I thought was the Greeks at least. Sound mind and body and all that. There was also a series of religious rooms, decorated to match the five world religions, as well as chambers for atheists. A computer lab and an educational unit. A mini campus for prospective high-achieving students. I remember thinking I would hopefully be invited back a few years after completion, to give a master class on the art of architecture, geometry, arithmetic and the inspiration behind the design of the prison itself. That would be my community payback. A great way to top up my architect's fee.

I made sure the spaces were unruly and more complex than mere boxes connected by corridors. If nothing else than to remind the prison population that they were not alone in thinking that *being* means *being confused*. The way we were traveling now was an extension of that idea. The kernel of that confusion had blossomed into this haphazard-looking journey South.

Thinking back on it I realised I a different person back then, but even in my most inspired and liberal moments I wasn't totally ignorant. I was deluded maybe, but not a bad architect. My main fault was that I was too invested. My prison wasn't dangerous, but not as clinically safe as Euan's either, but that sense of trust was also part of my design, which was something that no one seemed to pick up on at the time. His idea was a *padlock* in bricks and mortar. Mine was a Berlin Key in sweeping roughcast.

A coughing attack overcame Frank. He woke himself up hacking and a swig of cold tea from a cup in the centre console. Stretched his legs as much as was possible.

'There was one thing I always wondered about', Frank said, rubbing his eyes. 'The boys inside were always petitioning to be allowed to play more football, but the answer was always that the yard was too small. Which it wasn't'.

'In my defence, as part of the initial design, I had put in enough space for general sports usage'.

'Did you have goals though?' he asked, and I remembered that he had told me something about a football-related injury and presumed he was probably still keen on sports. Everyone has vested interests.

I said, 'Well, no goalposts, the netting would have been a health and safety nightmare. But, within the main complex, my plan, which admittedly was never realised, made allowances for a wide, undulating lawn. Borders full of flowers, seasonal and evergreens in a considerate mix. There was a sunny corner with a greenhouse full of herbs and edible produce. A cluster of beehives and a set of compost containers'.

I didn't tell him about the acoustic baffles and the rubberised bricks in the isolation cells. Or the proposed astrolabe crowning the emergency cistern – an onion dome for keeping eternal time.

'It sounds really nice. Too nice. More like a summer camp', Frank said.

'Well I was trying to balance pain and rehabilitation. Being locked up, denied freedom of movement is enough punishment for some. I was sketching out the ideal prison – if in hindsight not a perfectly working one'.

'I think you were designing one for the ideal prisoner'.

'Maybe'.

'Who also doesn't exist', he said, his voice dead flat.

'In the end I lost creative control to Euan, so if anything the lack of a proper pitch is his fault'.

I was quite proud of my proposed castellated façade. I knew I was guilty of some Disneyfication, we all are. My aim was to placate the general public. It's not a Potemkin village if you know it is one, someone once said. The prison, however progressive, had to look like a prison.

About a week before I was due to unveil the plans to the committee, I realised I wasn't sure which way the view out of the prison would be best. I had Jeanette, one of the girls in the office, nip out for an Ordnance Survey map while Lise opened the Friday bottle of wine. It was only 1 o'clock but I always practiced a little leniency with my employees; it was good for their morale too.

Once Jeanette came back to the office we opened a second bottle and I enlisted the girls' help working out the best way to superimpose my structure on the landscape. Then the girls had to leave. I think Lise had a little one at home but she never mentioned it. Maybe she thought I would have fired her if I knew. I stayed on and worked out which way the sun would wander across the sky. All I had waiting for me was Maud and she preferred the TV.

The building brief had been quite vague. Not much more than a site just outside the little town of Cromlix and the number of folk needing to be locked up. I had decided to think of them as residents or even guests, and to work backwards from there. I thought of my uncle, who had served his time so stoically, more than anything. And I knew that they were after something quick, something modern. A building which they could say had the power to save. At least on the surface.

Despite getting quite involved I interpreted my job to be quite simple. Throw together something, a formality more than anything, to release the funds. Get the photo of Stewart and some of the other old boys breaking the first soil at the site. I'd produce a couple of stunning watercolour-effect sketches, more a mood board than a final product. A handful of A2 foam boards populated by humanoids to show scale. A light crew of smiling clip art characters engaged in rehabilitation.

I drew an outside walkway that would connect two wings of the building. This would have no roof, and prisoners and guards alike would be united in their hatred of the elements. For the smokers, a small concession, a translucent half-roof offering some, but on purpose not enough, shelter. In the middle of the complex an empty champagne lawn. An aspirational reminder of the outside.

Nothing I didn't think would help them help themselves. My only concession, the crawl space, was added later, once I had been betrayed. If anything I would try to create a series of honest Nissen huts. An architecture that would balkanise people enough to dissuade riots, yet be so inclusive that conversations on life's big questions could emerge. Enabling men to act in unaware concert, controlled and free at the same time. After a bottle of wine that felt quite achievable.

It was quite a different business climate back then. People knew people, who knew people, and that's how contracts happened. I presumed that Stewart knew what he was doing. Didn't think he'd stab me in the back. I had fed him biscuits all through school.

Either way I hadn't been building HMP Heatherville entirely for my own benefit. It was far from the type of *luftschloss* some of my colleagues were designing, fueled by the Dubai economy. I was also doing it for them. For the criminals, like my uncle, who could use every bit of compassion, understanding and help. I was convinced my prison would go a long way towards building a brighter future for them. I think the one I presented would have made a bit of difference.

The prison they ended up building did exactly what it was meant to do. It kept people in, nothing more, nothing less. Only it didn't. Ha! I was very tempted to let Euan know about the success of my plans. Very tempted. But I knew I couldn't make myself known. If it one day turned out that I was terminally ill and only had a month to go, he'd be the first person I'd call. By now Frank had qualified for a phone call too if I knew where he was then. Maud would have to wait for the *Times* Obituary.

Tired of my own company, I cleared my throat loudly. I must have made a wrong turn somewhere just after Evesham because now the road was much smaller than it should have been and quite deserted. The last place of dwellings I remembered going through was Aston-sub-Edge. 'You still awake?' I asked the phantom next to me.

'Sure'. Frank said evenly.

'See that?' I asked and he just nodded. His face granite. I shifted down, and came to a complete stop. It had been ages since we were still.

There was a traffic light in the middle of a long stretch of road, showing red. There was no junction, no single lane bridge or tunnel, no ramp, roadworks or diversion. There was no overturned lorry spilling toxic waste over the road. This wasn't a temporary stop weighted down by sandbags, tethered to the ground by the local authorities as a short-term measure. This was a permanent red light, completely incongruous. It stood in splendid isolation, surrounded by flat fields and mist, yet powered, yet powerful. A reminder of right, wrong and consequences. The council had supplied the wiring for the light, and the state had provided the legislation which kept it relevant.

For a long while nothing happened, and I realised I had been waiting for a reason where there was maybe none. I had always been quite law-abiding, and now with Frank in the car I was even keener to stick to the rules. Whether the consequences of me breaking the law were immediately visible, as they are in the city, or slightly more lax, as they can sometimes be in the countryside, I wasn't sure. So I waited, firm in my resolve.

After 5 minutes when the light still hadn't changed I turned off the engine and put on the hazards. After another 5 minutes, and this time I had paid even closer attention to the little digital clock on the dash, I got out of the car and tried to see if there was something I could do to influence the light. If there was some kind of trip wire, a switch or even a battery or a lead I could unplug. Nothing. There was no phone number or any other kind of information to be gleaned either. The lights were clearly broken, but the law was still the law.

Around us there was nothing but a flat field. No ditch, no pavement, no camber to the road. I looked along the horizon, but I could see no school, factory, train station or any other structure that would have a large and temporary influx of people, followed some hours later by an exodus. There was nothing that would have short bursts of pedestrian or even animal traffic, milk cows returning from pasture, some kind of heritage duck species. Nothing to justify the light.

I got back in the car and looked at Frank,

'I don't know what to do', I said. 'We can't sit here'.

'Just go', Frank said.

'I can't', I said, almost surprised at his gall.

'Why not?'

'We're not above the law, Frank'.

He snorted. I could see the irony, but I knew I was right. In the car we were not criminals. Before and after the Twingo maybe, but in transit we were complete gentlemen.

I turned off the hazards. No point in calling attention to us. There had been no traffic in either direction during the whole time we had been sitting by the light, and if a car came up from behind I reasoned they would stop at the light too.

In a past life I had no patience and didn't care much for the rules. That had led to excess and to bankruptcy and to drink. Possibly divorce, but that might have happened anyway. After the visit to Weston-super-Mare and a couple of very dark months in the flat off Dumbarton Road I realised I had to apply some stringent commandments to my life if I was to survive. I wrote down my own Highway Code and told myself I would never, ever break my own rules. I had to make some solid promises to myself, and like many before me I found the 12 steps quite helpful. Luckily I found nonalcoholic wine at the same time, and since I was formally retired I was also able to spend more time on Cromlix. Though the prison was built, inaugurated and fully functioning, there were still some things to deal with in the aftermath. The provisions for a potential escapee's safety if nothing else.

There was ample time for overt and covert inspections and soon I was clocking up the miles going up and down the country in the SAAB. Though I was often tempted to speed up, I made myself drive carefully. It was part of my quiver of self-regulations. Paying regular visits to the concrete structure that had brought the village of Cromlix plenty of job opportunities and certain fame, but lowered the property prices, kept me sane. If I was to lose my licence, I would be lost again. My car was a safety valve as much as a car.

Despite this, after another carefully measured 5 minutes, I had enough.

I edged off the road onto the field and drove as closely as possible to the red light, yet outside it. I opened my window and folded in the rearview mirror. With the rear wheel catching on something we bumped back onto the road, innocent and unscathed. The ocular stelae fooled. I flipped the rearview mirror back out and exhaled.

Frank looked like he wanted to give me a high five, so I asked him to find us the right road on the map which had fallen onto the floor.

'Straight on', he said, after consulting the road atlas, and we rumbled along into the dark. Frank got us off the B4035/B4632 which I had strayed onto and back on to the much busier A44/A429 heading for Cirencester, my mind plunging back in time again. Down into the cheerless waters of an age I had sworn never to return to. I was a victim of my mind and simultaneously happy for its push towards catharsis.

When I realised that I had lost creative control of the prison I locked myself in my office and screamed until the girls had to ask the police to break down the door. As the burly ambulance men carried me out I fired Lise and probably said lots of horrible things, but I can't quite recall. It was a bad spell.

Afterwards I went away to a quiet place. I knew it was either that or an early grave. In the hotel-like dry house in Weston-super-Mare I took a long, hard look at my life, and it wasn't pretty.

Returning sober, I knew I would spend the rest of my days undermining, both figuratively and literally, Euan's prison. Like a magnifying glass pointed to the glare of my earlier failures I needed to focus, and direct the beam of my inert gifts onto a project where my efforts would pay off.

Once back in the office, Lise re-hired at a nominally increased wage, I kept myself busy sketching out more concrete realisations of this rebellious, righteous concept. My Trojan horse, invisible to the naked eye.

I was well aware that the tunnel was in many ways a life vest for me. That I had to come up with more and more ideas to keep my mind occupied and my head away from the drink. The final sign-off of the escape tunnel, and whatever optional extras I could conjure up a need for, would be a small funeral for me.

The whole escape plan was a non sequitur. I was willingly undercutting the use of logic, which for an architect can be quite the exercise in self-denial. Euan's building looked, and still looks, like a logical fortress but the conclusions I, and now Frank, had been able to draw from it didn't follow from the prison's premises. To me that was a very funny lie. To me it was a necessary truth.

Back when I was designing the passage I often woke up both crying and laughing, and all I could do was to get up, shave and get on with designing, and re-designing the plans, sometimes long before dawn. Asking myself every day, the architect's eternal question: Is it flush?

I was keeping the drink at bay, one joist, two girders at a time. Until it became a habit.

Chapter 26

17.30 Monday

Leaving the angry red cyclops behind us made my spirit soar. The crimson optics supplied by the State had been staring us down, but we had won. By circumnavigating its ray, we had blinded it, and it would be shouting our names out into the darkness until the next victim, or a repairman, came along. We had encountered an obstacle and overcome it – that's all you can ask for in life really.

As the broader vistas of the A429 slowly became dark, I whistled a kind of sea shanty I must have picked up from the radio or a Pathé reel, digitised and re-broadcast on the telly. No sirens tried to sing us into sin at Cirencester, but it made for a good tongue twister which amused us both for almost 20 minutes.

The road opened up a little, intermittently using two lanes in each direction to enable overtaking of slower traffic. All of a sudden there appeared next to us a new, ivory white Fiat 500 with a stubby roof box. The box was shuddering in the wind, keen to be pried open by the force of the speed and the poorly calculated aerodynamics. Thule, or whoever had made the box, should have forked out the extra for wind tunnel testing.

I noticed that Frank was trying to adjust himself in the seat a lot but thought he was just bored or maybe had sore legs.

'You ok there?' I asked.

'My arse has fallen asleep', he said.

'You know what they call pins and needles in Japan?' I asked. He shook his head. 'Pins and noodles'.

'Good one Cecil', he said, not quite condescendingly, but very close.

He was still wriggling in his seat a while later when we passed through a series of roundabouts by Milbourne. Then he sighed and brought out a long sheath.

'Is that the knife from the exit?' I asked as he put the knife in the inside pocket of his jacket. Was this a show of strength or just an oversight on his part? Why was he showing me the weapon now?

'Have you had it in your pocket all this time?' I asked and he nodded. 'Could you throw it out the window please?' I tried to sound convincing and like a buddy, not an easy balancing act. 'As soon as the Fiat is out of sight'.

He shook his head and said, 'I'd much rather keep it. Who knows when it will come in handy?'

'You're safe now. You're in a car with me. For God's sake, Frank. Get rid of it'.

'But you're dropping me off somewhere in a couple of hours'.

'You don't need that where you're going. There's a full tool kit in the house in Saint-Nazaire and everything you need for the boat journey is either in Kit #3 or stowed in the dinghy already'.

'I found it. I'm keeping it'.

'Well, technically I put it there for you to find', I said as tartly as I dared.

The Fiat pulled away a little and that's when I noticed the string and the four tin cans attached to it hanging from the back bumper. A sign saying *Just Married* had been put on the back window with the painter-decorator's thick beige tape. I accelerated a little to pull up next to the couple and peered in to see whether the man's hands were stained with Dulux, but they looked clean. The bride was texting and looking radiant at the same time. The couple were dressed up but not decked out like some people are, so I guessed it had been either a civil service or a small gathering. Maybe they had been together a long time? After all they had chosen to tie the knot on a Monday.

They were in their chosen ceremonial regalia and would probably appreciate some time away from prying eyes. I presumed they were on their way from a church or Registrar's Office to a rented hall and a party. Probably hungry, elated and confused at the same time.

Tearing my eyes off the happy couple I said, 'It makes me pretty uncomfortable. Could you at least put it somewhere in the back?' He just shook his head and made no attempt at bargaining. I would have hated renting heavy machinery from him if these were the kind of tactics he employed.

'What if we are searched and they find a knife in your pocket?' I asked. 'In the back with the other stuff it's a tool; in your pocket it's a weapon'.

'It's not been a problem so far. It'll be fine', he said, as stubborn as a child.

I should have asked earlier.

Ten miles on, the ignis fatuus made from sharp, polished metal still preyed on my mind. The feeling that Frank had death in his pocket made me break out in a cold sweat. He was big enough to strangle me if he wanted to so maybe he always had death close, but a weapon is a weapon. My only defence would be to quickly unbuckle his seatbelt and crash into the concrete foundations of a bridge or flyover.

I shouldn't have taped the knife to the exit wall in the tunnel in the first place, but it had seemed like a logical idea at the time. It was a tool more than anything, a deterrent and, I suppose, for a desperate prisoner, maybe a road to seppuku.

I should have searched his clothes while he was sleeping at the Lauriston B&B, but when he was sleeping so was I and he wore most of his clothes to bed.

Rummaging around under the covers searching his pockets would have pushed the already weird situation over the edge.

Once we parted company the knife would be his sole responsibility. Until then the idea of it was a wasp buzzing around in a small, hot tent.

'Slow down Cecil', Frank said. I looked down on the instrument panel and saw I was doing 85. A wish to get where we were going must have subconsciously set in. I would have to try and put the knife in perspective. He'd been polite so far, not aggressive in the least, and if we were stopped long enough to be searched then we might be in a different kind of trouble anyway. Hopefully Frank was seasoned enough to make the knife disappear if it looked like we were about to be grabbed by the long arm of the law.

I had in mind to alert the newlyweds to the wobbly roof box but thought the better of it. Instead I slowed down a little and let them pull away. This might be their first moments alone as newly minted Mr and Mrs Something and having an old man shouting and pointing while there was a big man fiddling with a sharp blade in the seat next to him, might be a fun memory on an anniversary in 10 years' time, but I didn't want to shatter the bubble of marital bliss which had presumably formed inside their car. Who knew how long it would last?

I wished the young couple the best of luck and settled into a slower pace behind a horse trailer, empty by the looks of it, pulled by a dirty Toyota Land Cruiser. I seemed to recall it was the same model the militarised arm of the UN uses. This made me feel safer somehow.

The knife was now my Damocles sword. It was maybe time to reel in the amount of sidestepping and time spent away from going to Bournemouth.

'I think we should cancel our outing to Sharpness', I said by way of reproach and punishment.

'That's fine', he said, unaffected. On the surface at least.

'But I'm sure we can get fish and chips somewhere else', I said. I didn't want to be too hard on him.

'We've had a good run so far. Let's not push our luck anymore', he said. 'Let's just get to where we're going'.

Whether it had to do with the knife or not we were in agreement, so I pulled out to overtake the Toyota, leaving the safe wake of the trailer, and took up the chase for the Fiat, to put us on the coast faster.

I was concentrating on the road and tried my best not to think about the knife but it was proving impossible. I knew the handle, the anti-slip silicone in a herringbone pattern, the stainless blade, so sharp that I had very easily shaved off a big patch of arm hair back in the tunnel, what now seemed an eternity ago. Most of it I gathered and put in my jacket pocket. I couldn't afford to treat DNA lightly.

I had trouble getting enough air into my lungs and decided to focus on my breaths. They were gathering like a cotton wool cloud in my left, or right, lung. Do they alternate origin or is it half from left, half from right?

On the horizon the white blob of the Fiat. I focused on that, on my hands holding the steering wheel and trying to breathe and calculate the miles remaining to Bournemouth. It was quite difficult, as I wasn't entirely sure where we were and I didn't want to ask Frank either. The A429 turned into the A430, one of the few logical progressions over the course of the entire trip, and we drove past Chippenham.

Luckily, as my knuckles were going white on the wheel, Bournemouth started to appear on signs. I mouthed the remaining miles.

To lead us into more secure ground I decided to talk about buildings and dreams. These were the two things that I had tried to connect in Cromlix and the two things that connected me and Frank.

'What's your favourite building Frank?'

'Why do you ask?'

'Because I'm interested. I'm also tired and some chat might do me good'.

There was a lashing of rain on the windshield and Frank said, 'I've never really thought of a single building as a thing. I liked my house growing up I suppose. I loved going to my grandpa's messy garage. He let me play with sharp things and dirty bits of machinery which my mum wouldn't. The only other one that has really blown me away is Grand Central Station, which we passed through on our last family holiday. The only ones I can't get on with are prisons', he said and laughed. I joined in, but not too loudly.

The windshield wipers squealed back and forward in front of me on their second fastest setting. 'I've not been to America', I said. '"Would have liked to, just never happened'.

'It's great. I'd like to go back one day. See the Empire State building again. But to be fair I'm not sure how likely it is I'll ever be able to travel anywhere again. What about you?'

'Don't know if I have one to be honest. Apart from the Minster maybe, but that's different. I've always been interested in spaces, and non-spaces. You know the little unknown, unbidden, unplanned bits in-between, like we talked about when we just set out on this trip. The margins and leftovers. I think some exist in real life, and some exist in our minds'.

Frank merely nodded, so I continued. I wanted him to know what I meant.

'The prison is a perfect example of this kind of liminal space. Where free and imprisoned people move side by side along invisible borders. Where floor space takes on different meaning depending on who walks on it. The prison is the law made real. The only other equivalent I can think of is the zebra crossing. This curious mix of absolute rule and uncertainty is what got me interested in the project in the first place'.

'So you're a philosopher who thinks in bricks and mortar?' he said, half-mockingly.

'Nothing as grand as that'.

'I think your in-between spaces are great', he said.

'You're the exception that confirms the rule', I said.

I was tired and my mind was misfiring more and more. We were nearing the end and I wanted Frank to know everything. Almost everything.

'When I was in high school my uncle was sent to prison for tax fraud or something', I said. 'We were quite a small family and about a year or so in, about Christmas time I think, we went and saw him in Barlinnie. I think the experience affected me more than I thought it did at the time. It was drab and uncomfortable. I remember there was no sugar for the tea. I knew my uncle. He wasn't a criminal, I mean, no offence, but he wasn't a dangerous man. He was an old accountant who had made some stupid mistakes, who had tried to make his pension last a little longer I suppose, but he didn't belong in prison'.

'Who does?'

'Bad people. But he wasn't bad', I said.

'*Bad people*. You're funny Cecil'.

We sped past a lorry full of frozen foods going to Morrisons. From the side of the truck an oversized, jocular man smiled down at us. He was wearing a fish-monger's white hat with a yellow and black insignia, brandishing a stick of celery and a prime cut of salmon like it was an ancestral sword and shield.

I continued, 'About three years later when my dad passed away I went and saw my uncle on my own. I was missing my dad, and my uncle was the last bit of family we had left on that side. I was now the only man left to carry the name. I remember him looking even more drawn and ill than the last time and he, who used to be quite funny, used to always magic a coin from behind my ear, was now barely able to string together two sentences. I came away feeling dirty somehow. Like I never wanted to be poor. That I wanted to always have fresh clothes and new things. That I never wanted to do anything that would put me in prison. And look at me now'.

'So you had been to visit twice? When you were a boy?'

'Maybe three times. Look, I'm not saying I was right about my Cromlix, it was just, I don't know. Back then, there was a culture of winging it, just going for it. Facts were one thing, connections and the will to succeed something else. More important'.

'Did you succeed?'

'That's up for debate', I said.

At that point we ran out of words and I resumed counting miles. I was hungry and I thought about asking Frank to root around behind the seats to see if there was a Mars bar or something but I didn't want to disturb him. I didn't want him to reach behind me. In a bout of wishful thinking I thought I could taste the salty sea air, that I could hear the waves pounding the coast, but as I swallowed I realised I had a nosebleed. The vital fluid was pouring down into my throat, trickling down into my stomach. It was a macabre circle of life.

My ears were pounding and all I could do was to lean my head backwards. Looking down my nose, like a haughty member of a Habsburg princeling's entourage, I tried to breathe in only through my mouth while roaring down the A350. I pinched the bridge of my nose, gently moving the cartilage. I knew that eventually the blood would clot. This wasn't the first time my nose gave me away. The 1980s had been quite hard on my nasal cavities. And the air in the car was dry.

There were no bright fairy lights, like those strung up between the masts of visiting cruise ships, in sight yet. My body was shutting down and some of my psyche was crumbling with it. I needed to restore my routines, I needed to eat when I wanted, sleep when it suited me and not strap myself into the rolling torture chamber of fetid air and insufficient stereo wattage any more. I was still convinced I had done the right thing, and that my planning had been impeccable, but the mode of execution was starting to wear thin.

It was too cold and noisy to always have the windows open, but I felt that the oxygen-starved air inside the cocoon of hierarchies and personal histories was a fecund breeding ground for nightmares and doubts. I would not let my life's greatest achievement be undermined by the flatulence of another man and the meteorological events of southern England.

Shaftesbury, Compton Abbas, Fontmell Magna, Sutton Waldron, Iwerne Minster, Stourpaine, leading us to, or rather conveniently around, Blandford Forum. Along the A350, a glittering row of towns and hamlets spilled out like fake pearls. I pressed my foot down a smidge harder on the accelerator, watched the needle tremble past 60. The coast was looming, calling me. Soon I would be rid of my charge and my responsibility.

First it felt like there was nothing. No progress, just an endless industrialised, abandoned wasteland. Then, with no fanfares or streamers, no popping corks or medals, we reached our destination. As we navigated the streets of Poole, with the sea lapping on our right hand side, I felt unbearably sad. Afraid that my sniffling would set off the nosebleed again, I decided not to case the ferry port first for a possible police presence, like I had planned to, but to just drive straight there, no fuss. The ferry port was neither quiet nor busy. It was perfect, just like I had imagined it would be.

Chapter 27

20.50 Monday

Turning the key in the ignition to let the weary Twingo rest, one last time as a couple in the car, felt both momentous and mundane. In front of us was a lit up sign, supplied by the Poole Harbour Commissioners, beyond it a dismal waiting hall, designed more like a cattle abattoir than an airport lounge. There was a line of people queuing up to walk to the ferry gangplank, past the hard plastic chairs. A man bent over his phone in a glassed-in cubicle was nodding permission to step aboard, hardly looking up. Fortune favours the brave, even more so if the brave ones plan correctly.

I got out of the car and opened the boot. I selected suitcase #11 and #2B for Frank which would cover all eventualities. Some he couldn't even fathom but which I had planned for, and some which would hopefully not happen. Putting the suitcases on the ground I reached out to shake his hand.

'That's you Frank. Safe travels. Send me a postcard to say that you made it. If you want to'.

'Where?' he asked.

'C/o Frazer & Frazer, on Lynedoch Place'.

'Is that where you live?' he asked quite innocently.

'No, it's where I used to have an office. I don't anymore, but I know the people below. They would keep a postcard for me I'm sure'.

'After all this you don't even trust me enough to tell me where you live?' he asked, as disappointed as a child forgotten by the school gates.

'I've told you exactly where my house in France is. Isn't that enough?' I asked, but he made no reply.

I turned away from him. Looked out over the sound. There was a damp wind coming from the sea, carrying the smell of diesel and the sounds of angry sea gulls. It was a frightening scent and one of real excitement. Apart from the diesel it was the exact fragrance that would have spurred Christopher Columbus on to find a new world and everlasting fame.

Somewhere out there in the darkness Jersey loomed, Frank's promised land; Part One. Once I let go of him it would be impossible to find him again, unless he wanted to be found. He turned in the direction I was looking, but it was pitch black. I had provided a Part Two, but I wasn't sure he would see enough sense to use my outstretched hand. The friendly arm extending across the Channel, across the arbitrary lines of nation states.

'Well', he said, and went to grab the suitcases, about to head off into the milking shed that was masquerading as the departures hall.

I felt a lump in my throat and I realised I was about to lose him forever. I had to ask, had to. 'You don't recognise me do you?'

'Not really. I mean, when I met you the first time I thought you had a vaguely familiar face, but I've seen a lot of new people in the last year or so', he said, scratching his chin, by now a familiar gesture.

'You really don't know who I am?' I asked, and took a step back so that he could see all of me. And to be out of his immediate reach.

'Did we go to school together?' he asked, and I could see him trying to calculate the years between us.

'You would have known', I said. 'I was always handing out broken biscuits. It made me pretty popular'.

'Are you famous? I don't watch a lot of telly'.

'This whole episode might make me famous', I laughed.

'Sorry, I don't know. Or I thought I knew. I thought you were Cecil, architect and all that'.

I took a deep breath, and said, 'I am'.

I wanted to tell the absolute truth for once, but I was becoming less and less sure about my reasons. I had kept my conscience at bay for most of the journey, but here at land's end my resolve was beginning to crack.

'Jennie, the girl who died, was my niece. I loved her very much', I said, my back as straight as a rod.

'Fuck', Frank said reeling. He put a hand on the bonnet of the Twingo to stay upright.

'I loved her', I said again and it looked like my words hit him like nails hammered into a plank. They tasted sharp in my mouth, like a molar had come lose. It was the first time I had said *love* out loud since high school, and even then it was for the wrong reasons, and not true. I had hoped to lose my virginity but failed.

Frank looked me straight in the eyes and said, 'I'm sorry. You don't know how sorry I am'.

'When I saw you come off the bus and realised I had freed *you*, I was almost sick', I sad. 'Instead I focused on the principles I had made so important for myself'.

'It was a mistake. She just stepped out...' he said, his voice cloudy.

'The fact that you have earned your way out means a lot to me. Despite what you have done I think you have deserved this'.

'I don't know what to say', he mumbled.

'Say nothing. Just be grateful. And careful. Most people don't get a second chance. No one gets a third'.

'Is this all some kind of revenge then?' he asked. 'Will the police turn up any minute?'

'No. You're free to go', I said.

Frank took a step nearer and at first I became quite afraid, but then I saw that he wanted to shake my hand. Instead I pointed out into the darkness. There were now flickering lights. Blue and green and red and white. A whole host of strobes and sounds. The ferry was coming to life below us, men in overalls scurrying with huge mooring lines over their shoulders. The wind was picking up and I was dying for a cup of tea. For a big fry-up somewhere. Some kind of return of normality. And with that came the realisation that the project I had kept myself occupied with for the last 10 years was about to fold in on itself. HMP Cromlix, my fateful *fait accompli*, killed my career and my marriage, and it saved me and lent me thousands of hours. Planning and building. Subterfuge and a childish protest rolled into one. As the grand finale – a road trip with a manslaughterer.

'One more thing Frank', I said.

I got a set of keys on a length of elasticated string out of my pocket.

'These are for my house', I said and went to hang them around Franks neck. He bowed, like a humbled Olympian, and when he straightened up I could feel his moist eyes search for mine.

'Keys on a string. Just like your mum and dad did for you, Cecil', he said.

'That's right', I said, again relieved he was an intelligent person and not a thug. If nothing else the escape hatch had selected the right person to release, at least based on IQ.

He picked up the case with the life jacket, the key to the dinghy's padlock and the other bits and pieces. He nodded and walked off, heading for the drawbridge with the sign *Foot passengers only*.

I was finding it hard to breathe. Holding onto a cold railing and counting slowly to a 70 made me feel better. By the time I had reached 100 I knew he wasn't coming back. I didn't know whether he would board the ferry or not, but in any case he was no longer my responsibility. My lungs expanded a little and I realised how much I missed my own bed. And how hungry I was. Leaving the car, I went off on a search for a café open at this time of day. *There's nothing a cup of tea can't put right*, my mother always used to say, and this time I was keen to agree with her.

Chapter 28

22.00 Monday

It was lonely and dull in the car on the way back. The game of chance was over, so I stuck to the motorway. I was relieved to have completed the journey, my para-religious venture to a shrine of my own making. I realised I would always feel the echo of the anonymous spot by the ferry port where I had delivered my Moses into the safe hands of France. I hoped he would soon be watched over by the gentle eye of Madame Morvan, my keyholder.

As I progressed North a crevasse was slowly opening inside me. All kinds of unhelpful thoughts and memories bubbled up despite my best efforts.

I tried listening to the radio, I tried eating sugar but I was hollow. The gentle purr of Katie Williamson suddenly seemed contrived, and Radio 3 had embarked on a festival of Hungarian dances.

Clocking up the miles, looking at the numbers slowly changing on the instrument panel became my main distraction. With no one in the car to amuse me my thoughts soon whirled. I hadn't even reached Dursley before my mind was reminiscing without permission.

Maybe I should have followed Frank across the sound? I could have disappeared into the unchartered bits of the European mainland too. Not sure if anyone would have missed me. I never thought that I would have a hankering for Frank's quiet company, but I did. I realised I would find it difficult to go on long car journeys on my own again.

I drove as far as I could and when my eyes went too blurry to see I opened the window and stuck my head out. When that stopped working I pulled into lay-bys for 20-minute naps or service stations for coffees and muffins. At a Wolverhampton service station, next to the Costa, there was an honesty box with a pile of books next to it. The novels were all glossy stories of horrible murders that I couldn't have stomached, but at the bottom was a box containing a set of Learn French cassettes. I got a relatively clean fiver out of my bum bag and crammed it into the money box.

In the car I discovered that the last of the four tapes were missing, and at first I felt jipped, but then I reasoned that if I ever got so advanced that I could follow the fourth tape I could probably manage without it. Thinking vaguely of *pain riche* and *chocolat chaud* and Madame, or widow, Morvan I pushed the first tape in and set off. With the semi-stern voices of the two tutors, a male and a female alternating between exercises and taking on the different roles in the conversations – usually transactions – burbling away in the stereo, I made good time north in the plucky car. I was keen to return it to Janice and rid myself of the evidence of any rebellion against the state. I also longed for the seven proper speakers of my SAAB.

Being alone wasn't good for me. Passing site after site of substandard suburbia was hard. Architects – are we glorified engineers or undervalued artists? Or simply salarymen in black and grey? Slowly but undeniably pushing up house prices, gentrifying zone by zone. Walking hand in hand with regeneration officers and infrastructuralists. Waltzing on newly laid tarmac. On roads not yet leading anywhere, streets which'll lay dormant until the public realm has been overtaken by private investors. Streets that might never see proper use, if the political wind changes, and the agenda starts to smatter in a different area. Same, same, but a radically different cladding.

While I was digesting the full English in the café just after leaving Frank, I had composed another card for my French friend. This time a freebie I had picked up at the terminal.

Dear Genevre,

Hope you're well. I'm doing a grand, or rather, petit tour of Britain. The weather, and the food, is appalling. Spoken/written like a true weary traveler. I am now on my way home, North. Looking at the bulwark of the ferry, and its gleaming white colour, has put me in a mind for a long warm trip. Maybe I will investigate what cruises originate from around Saint-Nazaire, and start saving up. You know what they recommend: Port Out Starboard Home.

Hope to see you soon! Cecil

Ps. Would you please look after my "TOM CAT" if he comes by? Merci. Ds.

And since I still hadn't found neither stamps nor red pillar boxes, I had added this postcard to the other one, in my personal valise in the boot of the car.

At one point I came off the M6 to stretch my legs and to pee. I had been driving for 5 hours and knew I had another three or four to go. While driving around a little, looking for a quiet spot, I found a deserted bit of wasteland. In one corner of the field, at a jaunty angle, was a half-filled container, and in it the debris of a playground. It was topped by a layer of junk thrown in by local opportunists, an apocalyptic giant's confetti.

Looking around while I drained my bladder I felt secure that no one would spot me dumping the evidence, the carefully labeled suitcases from the boot, into the container. They fitted in perfectly. It was a little bit odd to see years of planning being chucked but maybe that's what life is. A lot of worrying, planning, saving up and buying, which'll quickly end up as landfill as soon as you die. Giving my former dreams a casual military salute I set off. There was nothing else I could do.

In the end it took me almost 12 hours to get home. I entered Glasgow proper at about 10 and the streets were busy with deliveries and people dashing off to meetings. I had just started on the B-side of tape 3 when I pulled into the same multi-storey as where I picked up the Twingo. For a while I just sat there, eager to finish the lesson. Once the tape stopped I walked to Central Station where you can have a shower for £4.10. Feeling much better afterwards I placed my wash kit on top of one of the pay phones by platform 2 and arranged with Janice to go straight to hers, then went to M&S to pick up a box of chocolate for her. On the phone she had seemed so happy that I had remembered the anniversary, a year to the day when Jennie passed away. I didn't have the heart to tell her it was just a coincidence. Out of guilt rather than anything else I happily agreed to help her move some things and even said I would happily stay over if it got late. All I wanted was to go home to my bed, but I realised this was the price I was paying for using her car, whether she knew that or not.

It was almost two by the time I drove out towards my sister's house. With any luck Frank had located the dinghy by now and was either resting on the beach or cresting the waves with the French coast in sight, depending on the tides.

Chapter 29

14.00 Tuesday

On the way to my sister I had the Twingo valeted and waxed by two separate companies. I filled it up and changed one of the windscreen wipers that had started to squeak. I checked the oil and the pressure in the tyres. I was pretty sure she wouldn't have noticed the odometer setting before lending it to me, but I hoped she would appreciate the full tank.

Janice stood in the doorway to meet me. She was dressed in a gabardine skirt and polyester cardigan, both cream. She looked like she had aged 10 years in the last year. Coming back from my trial by fire, it was even more obvious. Her hair might or might not have been going grey at the temples before but at least she kept it dyed. Now it was put up in a sloppy ponytail which looked slept on. I remember her spending ages and a fortune on her hair as we grew up. That was one of the things that made her alien and female to me. Before that she was just a sister, a constant in the house rather than a person in her own right. It also showed the age gap to me. I was still into Meccano when she passed her driving test and started to be away from home more and more.

She walked around the house listlessly, holding the chocolate box as if it was a pan and brush. I could tell from stale air and her reddened eyes that she had not been out of the house in a while. She told me she had been crying for hours, quite matter-of-factly, as if she was talking about repotting an azalea or something. The tour of the house apparently over, she took me through to the lounge where she had laid out the saddest feast I have ever seen. Sausage rolls and vol-au-vents on little tinfoil trays – straight from ASDA to my mouth. To one side a selection of Italian style cold cuts and for some reason a family-sized jar of raspberry jam. She must have read something in a food magazine about sweet and sour but got it all wrong.

My sister, bless her, had even bought a two litre bottle of Fanta. I could see her in the aisles trying to work out what this morose anniversary would require drinks-wise. For her, easy, the same rosé as always. For me it was a little more complex. I couldn't have coffee or tea with my food.

'Milk is weird and water is for peasants', she always used to say when she was a teenager, on the rare occasion when she came back to eat with the rest of the family. Now she had bought the pee-coloured beverage of children's parties for her little brother. As usual I was amused and touched in equal shares by my sister's strange choices.

'Thanks for letting me use the car. I couldn't have done it without it', I said.

'Don't mention it', she said, one finger pushing plates around to form for her a more coherent picture on the table. 'That's what family is for'.

I couldn't talk after that. Luckily she seemed too hungry to notice and we took turns reaching for the golden parcels on the table. The only thing which remained untouched was the jam, but I hoped Janice had planned a pudding.

As if it was a real party we stood up and ate. Even chinked glasses at one point. There was no one to mingle with, and the kitchen lights were very bright. The radio was on, but so low that I couldn't hear music or talk. It was more as if someone had left the tap on in the upstairs loo. Once we had had a few things each she quickly cleared the table, and there was no evidence of either a cold cake or a warm pie. Janice was spraying the wax cloth and wiping it clean, veins standing out on her arms. Before I had even finished chewing, she had whipped off her apron and put the bleach spray away. I could see more tears well up and she excused herself, talking a couple of quick half-steps out of the kitchen.

I had no mission and no one to guide. I was suddenly feeling empty and in the face of that I was defenceless. Quite suddenly, as is the norm with gastrointestinal cramps, I felt sick to the stomach and had to spit out a big bit of quiche Lorraine in the bin. With the lid open I couldn't stop myself. Retching as quietly as I could I emitted a long string of bile and some of the finger foods.

Once I was done I felt bad. I didn't want my sister, who had obviously put in a lot of work preparing the dishes, to think that I hadn't appreciated her efforts. I scouted around for some kitchen roll to cover the sorry mess in the bin. After rooting around like a burglar I found some in a cupboard above the sink and leaning in to get it I caught a whiff of my own breath. It was grim, and another thing my sister would probably be able to smell. Behind the kitchen roll was a small bottle of Grant's. Not full, not empty, just convenient.

My stomach gurgled again and I knew that Janice would be back soon, so without stopping to think I poured myself just a pinch of whisky in a mug from the washing up rack. I've never liked the taste of whisky, or even the smell, so to me that was always an inbuilt safety mechanism. This was just to clear my breath. Still, the first alcohol I'd had in 1,414 days.

'It's an anniversary. It's not every day you have to deal with something like this', I said out loud as if Frank was still with me. I drained the mug in his honour, then felt terrible again. I decided to think of the whisky as cough drops, my own rightly deserved Night Nurse, rather than alcohol, and went to pour another finger or two into the mug.

Before I could work out why Janice had a bottle of Grant's in the cupboard I heard her flush the toilet. Grant's is neither a showing-off whisky for guests nor pleasant enough to warrant buying for private consumption. 'Is there such a thing as cooking whiskey?' I wondered and thought that maybe it was part of the hopefully forthcoming pudding.

My breath was still stinking of sick and before I noticed it I had poured whisky almost up to the rim of the cup. I heard her unlocking the toilet door and some kind of practical, economical impulse took over. I couldn't make myself waste the drink by pouring it out, so against my better judgement I finished the cup.

The taste of the drink was awful on my untrained tongue. I was always a white wine man, and even when I smoked I always had sensitive taste buds. I suddenly found it amazing that people paid good money to drink whisky. It tasted like window cleaner. In the close proximity of my older sister I had regressed into the child I once was, a fussy eater and a younger man – a drinker not able to deal with life. My thoughts were unhelpful and unruly; a drove of suckling pigs drenched in Fairy liquid, slipping through the arms of sense.

With the whisky burning my throat I grabbed a Bic biro and scribbled a train line, sleepers and all, on my left hand. A graphic promise not to drink anymore, and to not let myself fall off the tracks. Not again. This time I knew it would kill me. The first time I was younger and I still had some work to do, somewhere to go. Not like now, when I had just finished my biggest project ever and didn't even have an office to go to. With all the time in the world and no one to check up on me I would quickly descend down into drink and not be able to resurface. I grabbed the ballpoint again, this time gouging, drawing blood from the top of my left hand. The fear of the void I had glimpsed again, behind the curtain of my promise, scaring me to the core. Then I felt the familiar warmth in my stomach and I smiled like a fool.

I rinsed out the teacup and gulped down a brimful mug of water to wash away the taste. What was left, as my head started to whirl pleasantly, was the vile taste of betrayal. Like a soup made out of mothballs and dog feces. Like a rotten tooth had come loose in my mouth. I was almost sick but had another cup of water holding on to the sink, my knees bent.

I looked up and saw a photo collage of Janice and Jennie arranged with meticulous care, pinned in place by magnets on the fridge door. It was unbearably sad. The house which had been perfect for the mother and child, the woman and the girl about to become a woman herself, was now a black fortress of grief. All Jennie's hopes had been Janice's too. The older woman had attached the future to the younger. Unhelpfully and exactly the way it should be.

I realised I would have to spend the rest of my life making up lies and excuses to protect my thought experiment and my sister from the sordid truth. The rest of my life, or Janice's, depending on who went first, would be a taut network of deceit, held in place by pegs of my making.

I couldn't go back on my actions. There was no way I could explain the revenge that had fueled me for years. The project drawers which had slowly filled up with ideas and sketches of prisons. Of kennels, recycling centres, solar panels, all within the walls of my imagined Cromlix. The garden plots, the natural light, the projector rooms, the telescopes directed at the Pleiades, the music rooms, and so much more. Reams of more or less realistic ideas filling my office hours, spilling out into my life. The care and attention I had paid to colours and lines, to shapes and angles, luxuries we take for granted outside. My work in trying to translate the irregular and arrhythmical soul of normal buildings into the carceral.

I had tried to reintroduce to the institutional and the correctional a gentle chaos. The natural, which on some level keeps us sane outside the walls of a prison, where nothing is straight and regulated. Inside, benign irregularities are measured out in mean portions. The hard facts and hard angles act as absolutes, made for impact or punishment. The shapes and structures, textures and colours found in the organic chaos of nature, in grimy cityscapes, in weather and seren-dipitous coincidences are removed from prison. Left is a void, impossible to fill. I had tried to put some of these elements back. That was all. I wasn't a bad man.

I felt sick.

I closed my eyes, but it didn't help.

I always avoid eye contact with the man who lives inside me.

I could not explain to my sister about the horrible coincidence that had brought Frank of all people to my car door. I could not convince her that my response had been in any way defensible. The surreal chain of events that made me open the door for him and drive him to the end of the land and the salvation beyond. Why I had turned the other cheek.

Unscrewing the bulb to have a look confirmed my suspicions.

How he came to sit in the passenger seat of my sister's Twingo was beyond me, so to convey this to her would have required either telepathy or divine intervention. I had wanted to be a different me, I had wanted to make a difference, and I wanted to see my project through to its logical conclusion. The fact that it was Frank who was the lucky winner of the freedom ticket was almost inconsequential. That would have been impossible to tell Janice.

Frank was fiddling with the controls of the radio. He nodded and walked off, heading for the drawbridge with the sign Foot passengers only. *Mine was mounted upside down, like Hitler's dick.*

I was feeling more and more sick. My mind reeling. Also, my stomach wasn't settling. If anything, these new thoughts accelerated my bowel motions. I struggled to keep my oesophagus in check, but I was finding it hard.

Eyesight blurry. Thoughts encroaching on language. Half-ideas difficult to explain. I was struggling to work out what I could say and what I couldn't say. Both in terms of what I had just returned from and what would be insensitive to say to my sister in her present situation, the black anniversary hanging in the air.

Excusing myself to the girl at the till I jogged back to the car, stationary between pumps 7 and 9. Once outside I was shaking a little but the cold wine helped and by the time I walked down the hill I was whistling happily. It struck me that I didn't know how my niece's killer took his tea.

Now I knew.

Janice came back, sniffling but brave again. Rouge or something in a dark smear across her chin, applied no doubt with a shaking hand. I took as many deep breaths as I could, tried to corral my thoughts into order.

'Should we get on with it?' she asked and all I could do is nod. Janice was asking me to help with the excavation. I was in no shape to go through with it, but it was impossible to explain why. I shouldn't have driven Frank to the coast. I shouldn't have chugged down Grant's in the kitchen. I shouldn't have crawled around the innards of an institution for a hobby. I shouldn't have been sick in the bin. Instead of telling her anything of substance I nodded and we walked upstairs, her first, me holding on to the balustrade with white knuckles.

I knew Janice had kept Jennie's room intact but the effect of it in real life was horrible. Looking over the threshold at the shrine of sudden grief which set in a year ago, I felt a shiver down my back. The room was a temple to her daughter's dreams and hopes, now derailed. Interrupted by crumbled metal and shattered glass. By broken ribs and a last breath, the body of the young girl held in place by the front left wheel of the red Golf. By Frank. By the monster who had sped off right after the impact as if nothing had happened.

I had never been inside Jennie's room in this house before. I had stood on the threshold telling her tea was ready or that a friend of hers was at door, but never been more than a foot further into the room. Before Janice's divorce they had lived in a different, nicer house, and I had been in to play a lot in Jennie's room whenever I was over. Set up the dolls and horses, the cakes and the teddies, helped with Hama beads and played incomprehensible trump-like card games which she would win. Since then Jennie had become a teenager, and the house she had lived in with her mother right up until the end was not conducive to play.

Jennie had never asked me not to go into this room, but she had not invited me in either. I was her childless uncle, unfamiliar with the whims and wishes of a teenage girl, so I had left it at that.

Maud liked her things in order and didn't really like children or my sister so even though we had space in Bearsden, Janice and Jennie hadn't been over more than a handful of times, and even then Maud made sure that they didn't fit in. I could have asked them to come to my office, but I was usually busy. I had never had Janice or Jennie over to my flat off Dunbarton Road, as it was usually not very inviting, even after I fixed the hole I had kicked in the wall.

Pinned to the walls of Jennie's room were posters of sultry boys and A4 sheets of stark timetables. Jennie herself had exited time, sidestepping both further adolescence and the future, set in such regular boxes by the Scottish Credit and Qualifications Framework Committee or some-such. On a shelf by the head of the bed a trophy from a school athletics day, *High Jump under 16s*. The bedspread, taut and untouched, a scene from a tropical island, the carpet fluffy and perfectly circular, the shape only interrupted by a purple stain of what looked like nail polish. On the sideboard by the bed a lamp with a glass hood covered in stickers, a collection stretching from My Little Pony to rude four letter words in a punky style at odds with the rest of the room. The room smelled both stale and of strawberry hairspray at the same time.

The suburb where Janice lived was confusingly uniform. Unless internal structural work had been done, all houses would have a space in the same location and of the same dimensions as the room we were about to clear out.

I looked at Janice, who was in the room, and she invited me to cross the threshold. Just as Frank had had his cell, so Jennie had had her room. Their small but closely guarded kingdoms. From what Frank had told me and from what I had seen from other cells, the inmates had done as much as they could, and as much as they were allowed, to change the look and feel of their abodes.

I hadn't seen Frank's cell, but presumed he had acted the same way as Jennie. Gone to great lengths to stamp their personality onto the blueprint commanded by regulations and economy. By a parent or the state. Both Frank and Jennie straining to reach out beyond their physical boundaries. Via pictures and by subtly re-arranging the furniture, they had ached to make their minds fly. Frank and Jennie, linked in so many ways, had tried to alter the make-up of their personal environments. It was painful to admit that I had been involved in terminating their scenography mid-process.

I entered the room carefully. It was just as if she had stepped out for a pint of milk or cut-price mascara. I looked at notes she had left behind on the desk. A forest of post-its with cats on, stacks of papers relating to school and revolting against school at the same time, judging by the angular scribbles. I didn't understand much despite it being in English. Criminals and teenagers use slang. To hide behind. To mark them out as separate from society. They deface surfaces, to make them their own – a nightmare for an architect. They use graffiti, the bad kind, not the one commissioned by the council, to hide secrets in plain sight. They pee with pens to mark their territory and here within Jennie's boundaries I felt achingly aware that I was an intruder. An unwanted foreigner without even the most basic of language skills. A quisling in the guise of an uncle.

Carting down box after box of Jennie's stuff, which Janice had somehow found the strength to divide into three piles, *Keep, Give away, Throw away*, my back was aching and my mind was slowly breaking apart. All that would be left once we were done was the bare essentials, the furniture, nothing more. The room was to be ready for a lodger, a student about the same age as Jennie presumably, who Janice hoped would surface in the next couple of weeks.

Looking at my sister, her face contorted, with tears and snot running down her cheeks, I felt subhuman. We were taking turns going up and down so I would meet her on the stairs time after time as we made our way out to the trailer she had borrowed from a neighbour. The contents destined for the Salvation Army. Whenever she was out I tried to rest and to draw deep breaths but I was finding it hard.

Once we had been up and down the stairs a handful of times I couldn't stand meeting Janice's gaze anymore. I told her to sit down while I finished putting the boxes in the trailer.

'Cecil, when this is over, do you think I could go and stay at your house in France?' she asked. 'It wouldn't be for long. Just a couple of days'.

Pretending to be out of puff due to the box I paused.

'Of course, whenever. I'm just getting some work done at the moment, but I'll tell you as soon as they're done. Can't really trust French roofers to keep to any kind of schedule'.

'Thanks', she said and took a deep, double-swallow kind of drink of wine.

Once I had stashed the last few things and padlocked the trailer I found her in the kitchen. I drank as much Fanta as I could stomach, in the hope of diluting the now regretted Grant's, while she nursed glass after glass of wine. As the wall clock slowly ticked above our head we talked about nothing. She never challenged the story about my car being in for an MOT and that I had used her car to pick up a chest of drawers from Homebase, and to be fair there was no reason for her to. I presumed she had heard the message I had left on her answering machine. I wasn't sure if the clean car would surprise her or if she would even notice.

After a while she said something about a takeout and went to find her phone, stumbling on the way to her handbag, steadying herself on a wall.

Twenty minutes later a young man with glazed eyes and a steaming carrier bag turned up at the door, hand already outstretched for the bills and a tip I had prepared.

'We usually get Chinese on a Friday', Janice said while tearing her chopsticks apart.

'That's nice', I said.

There was no present continuum as far as Jennie was concerned but I couldn't tell my sister this. To correct her grammar would be to shatter the temporarily undisturbed surface of her mind.

'Then on Saturdays we take turns to make breakfast', Janice said, nodding to a shelf with a toaster. 'I need to remember to pick up more blueberry jam for her. It's her favourite'.

As we ate my sister mixed her tenses in a heart-wrenching way. It was as if her mind still could not compute that she had to change the grammar of her life to before and after.

'Jennie goes out on a Friday night, then comes in late, glued to her phone, but I always know where she is'.

I felt full to the brim of ready-to-go food bought from service stations up and down the country. I poked around in the containers with my chopsticks but made little headway. Janice didn't notice. She was eating for two.

'She was everything I had', my sister said in a dead voice. Then she stood up and went to the fridge for the next bottle. I put the fortune cookies in my pocket. Whatever they were going to say wouldn't apply to my sister.

Chapter 30

22.30 Tuesday

After the meal I put my sister to bed and tucked her in. By this stage she was blubbering and incoherent, propelled by rosé.

'Remember dad used to eat the whole thing? And mum would always make a face'.

'What are you talking about Janice?' I said, immediately sorry I had asked. She needed sleep, not more nostalgia, and I needed my peace and quiet.

'He would shine them against his trouser leg. Always Granny Smiths'.

'Sure', I said, pushing a pillow in under her floppy neck.

'She beat the school record and all she got was that trophy. 5′ 9″ ½, but she just flew straight up in the air', Janice was saying, her eyes closed. Tears and mascara slowly gumming up her eyelids.

She turned on her side and fell into a shallow snore, quick as a rabbit's breathing. I sat down on the floor, fearing she would swallow her tongue. After a few minutes I deduced she was fine.

'Cecil', she said and my heart skipped a beat. 'Do you believe in heaven? Do you think I'll meet her there?'

I stood up and the room was kaleidoscopic for minute. While trying to bat away the stars in my head's cosmos I tried to formulate an answer, but with no moral or theological foot to stand on I faltered. It didn't matter, as Janice turned over and was fast asleep within the minute. I stopped flinging my arms around like a human windmill and sat back down.

I had thought the quiet would make me feel better but I felt worse. My stomach wouldn't settle and she looked so lonely and vulnerable in the big bed she slept in. A relic from the divorce many years ago.

I put an empty saucepan and a big glass of water by the side of the bed. Once Janice was breathing evenly I went downstairs to watch TV but I couldn't make her digital box work. I fell sick and the cold, and by now coagulated, Chinese staring at me from the counter didn't help.

I put on my jacket to go outside to check that I had put on the padlock properly on the trailer with all the stuff we had cleared out of Jennie's room. Of course I had. I couldn't remember the last time I forgot something.

Janice liked her windows closed and the boiler roaring. I felt strange from carrying all my niece's possessions, untouched for a year. I felt dirty from the friction between Janice's reality and grief and my convictions. The outside air was crisp, and it was nice to breathe deeply. Away from the car, away from the house.

Across the road near the gutter was a stuffed mallard from the RSPB, just like the one Jenny used to have sitting on her bed. I walked over to it, thinking that it must have escaped the trailer somehow. Maybe been carried off by a cat or a fox. I stumbled a little, put a hand on the kerb for leverage. My knee was creaking, its ligaments sacrificed to squash, and the alcohol wasn't helping my inner ear. Sitting there I suddenly caught up with myself. While listening to my own ragged breaths the truth of what I had actually achieved started to be less and less coherent.

By taking that long sip of whisky I had broken a sacred promise to myself as well as to my family. I had let my sister down. My mind was spiraling and with a lightning flash, like a fist in my solar plexus, as I realised I had been a dick my whole life. That I was only now understanding the magnitude of my delusions.

Rescuing the mallard would save me. Urged on, no doubt by Grant's and Frank, and my sister's salty tears, I became convinced that restoring this piece of Jennie's childhood was the only remaining ticket to redemption. The square edge of the kerb glinted with mica and fool's gold. The stone agreed with me. It nodded when I nodded. It roared when I roared.

I heard a sound, distant at first, soon near. My ears prickled and I felt my hackles rise, instantly imagined myself as a hyena. The noise was moving closer. Fuel injectors, the hiss of a turbo, a deep bass drum. The mating call of a certain species of boy, pent up with underused testosterone. The same kind of boy who thinks that a handbrake turn is the surest ticket to someone's pants. I was never like that, but if I had been able to afford a quick car I might have entertained the thought.

The screech of rubber wasted on asphalt preceded a streak of metal lightning. A souped-up, lowered hatchback, driven by a youth in a backwards cap, came shooting out of one of the suburban side streets. He didn't see me, or if he did he ignored me, an old drunk sitting blubbering on the side of the pavement. The car skidded a little on the fresh surface and the little bastard behind the wheel made a beeline for the soft toy. The music in his car sounded like a warship sinking into the waves. By the time he closed in on the bird he was doing at least 50 miles an hour and his low-profile tyres shredded it.

Once the car disappeared around the corner I tried to gather the mallard in my hands but the stuffing was so light it flew off in the wind and I couldn't seem to find the head anywhere. It made my blood boil. Irresponsible people in cars, ruining the lives of others. Cars killing people, running over loved ones, leaving nothing but a mess for others to sort out.

I found the bottle of Grant's in my jacket pocket but couldn't work out how it got there. For a split second I suspected that my sister had planted it on me, then I let that thought go. If anyone was innocent in all of this, it was Janice.

After another sweetener from the palm-shaped bottle I decided I had been too lenient, too stuck in my rut. I had been soft and an idiot. Frank couldn't get away with this. Groaning and cursing, holding the headless body of the bird in one hand. I howled like a wolf, but silently, as it was a semi-respectable neighbourhood. I started walking and couldn't stop.

After leaning the bird effigy against a substation, the triangular sticker warning us all about the Danger of Death, I set off to do something about the situation. The bubble I had constructed for myself had imploded, and though I didn't want Janice to find out what I had done, I now felt I had been too kind to Frank. Timing has never been my forte.

I put one foot in front of the other, stopping every now and then to wash out my mouth. The bottle was small and I soon ran out, which was probably what saved me.

I couldn't implicate myself. I couldn't use the landline at my sister's. I considered a letter but with fingerprints and handwriting experts I ruled that out. Even if I composed a confession on a computer, on my behalf, or on Frank's behalf, and printed it, sending it in the post, I was sure there was traceable ink or secret watermarks on the paper put there by the printer. I was savvy enough about IP numbers to not even consider an email or a text message. There was no need to make anything of my person. I felt that would be a silly and obvious way to highlight my role. I convinced myself that I was nothing really in this whole mess. All that remained was a pay phone. I was sure there were all kinds of numbers that handled tip-offs or clues but I didn't want to try to find any of those. I didn't want that showing up on my electronic footprint. I would just have to phone 999, it was the logical option.

At first it seemed impossible to find a phone box. I sympathised with the ghost of Frank walking around Stirling in search for one, a lifetime ago. After rambling around the quiet neighbourhood for almost an hour, eyes straining for the Queen's signal red, I went through my pockets realising I had no cash and that I had no idea how much a phone call would cost these days. Or what kind of coins the machine would take. If they were operated only by debit or credit card these days, I would be traceable. I didn't have time to find out from some kind of anorak website which coin-operated phone boxes were still in use in the wider Glasgow area. I plodded on.

At the end of a block, on a dismal corner, a newsagent, incongruously open this late on a Tuesday night, and just beyond it a dismal phone box. I calculated the risk of getting money out at the bank machine outside the newsagent, which annoyingly would charge me £1.75 for the pleasure, to then make a call half a block away, but concluded I should be ok. It was a slim chance someone would look at ATM records to match them up with anonymous callers. I was sure it would show up on some kind of record somewhere, and I was sure I was being filmed by CCTV or drones too, but it was dark and I was wearing a hat. The police would be able to pinpoint the exact location of the telephone as soon as my call came in, not like in the movies where the cops have to keep the baddie on the line for 3 minutes while computer spools turn around calculating. I hoped that I would be shielded by the Seal of the Confessional that surely doctors, police people and priests are forced to adhere to, and that the question of my identity would fade against the backdrop of the bombshell I was about to drop.

I got cash out, relieved to see the notes were old and well used, and bought three Lion bars from the newsagent. I made sure the man gave me as many different coins as possible for my change and walked over to the phone box. I took a deep breath, poured in a fistful of coins and pushed the bottom right button three times – only to realise the call was free.

While the dial tone was ringing out I unscrewed the empty bottle of whisky and stuck my tongue down into the opening, hoping for a drop of courage.

When the operator answered I panicked and looking out the already steamed-up window of my cubicle I noticed an Indian restaurant, and decided to try to replicate the accent. Again I failed. I sounded like I was from Cardiff and that something was wrong with my larynx, but I couldn't change my voice one I had started.

'Do you need fire, police or ambulance?' the operator asked me. She sounded like a nice, middle-aged lady.

'I have information regarding Frank'. I said, a tremble in my voice.

'Where are you sir? she asked and I felt like I could have asked her the same. If I couldn't meet up with Katie Williamson, maybe this woman wanted to go for a drink. Goodness knows her job must be stressful.

'He just shredded the mallard, low profile tyres should be outlawed', I said.

'Are you sure this is an emergency? Where are you calling from?' Her voice now sterner, like a schoolmarm. I didn't mind though. It brought out her dialect. I was trying to pinpoint it. North of the Yorkshire Dales, but south of the border. I returned to the matter at hand.

'I have information regarding Frank', I said, breathing hard, holding on with both hands to the mouthpiece. I imagined this was like traversing crevasses on Mont Blanc. One wrong step meant certain death. 'He has escaped from prison'.

'Sir, this is not a joke'.

'I'm perfectly aware of that', I said. 'Can I speak to the Chief of Police please? This goes all the way up. Would it be possible to arrange a conference call with the head of the SPS, is it still Roger, Roger what's his name? Something with a G, I think. Do you know?'

'Does this escaped individual have a last name?'

'Yes he does. But he uses his wife's. Not his first one, the second. Though the kids use their mum's. Not the second one's last name. There's also another kid. I'm not sure what his name is. One of them is from Haiti'.

'Are you in any immediate danger sir?'

'No, no not really.'

'That's fine. I will patch you through to somewhere more helpful'.

'To where?'

Before I got an answer I heard the calm voice of a male Samaritan, asking if I was ok, if I wanted to talk about things, or not. It was entirely up to me.

It was a dismal walk back to Janice's house. She had forgotten to make up a bed for me, but after some rooting in the boiler cupboard I had a motley assortment of blankets.

'I'll just camp out on the floor. It's supposed to be good for your back', I told myself. An echo of an episode which happened in a different life, just off the A614.

Chapter 31

07.30 Wednesday

In the morning Janice looked puffy and disheveled. I thought, or at least hoped, that it was the alcohol more than the grief that had bruised her. I couldn't wait to get home to my own bed. I felt terrible, but despite my Grant's lapse I hadn't turned feral so it was maybe lack of sleep, rather than alcohol, which made my tongue feel like it was made out of asbestos. I made a vague promise to myself to drink one small glass of whisky a year – on Jennie's anniversary.

Janice told me she would go to work, but I could see she was trying to convince both herself and me. She told me, probably not for the first time, that she volunteers somewhere a day a week and does a day or two of locum nurse work at a vet's practice. Either way she was in a small way part of the workforce despite being quite a few years older than me. I was able to retire early with a bit of capital a while ago; she was working late in life – a single-person mortgage and a divorce doesn't come for free. I wondered also if Jennie's expenses had been part of the reason my sister still worked.

Janice gave me a lift into town. It was very strange sitting in the passenger seat. The same seat that Frank had occupied. I had a different worldview in the left seat. When Janice crunched a gear, trying to get the car into reverse, I winced so loud she turned and looked at me, and I had to pretend to sneeze. After what the Twingo and I had shared I was feeling very protective about it and for a fleeting moment I was about to offer to buy it off her, but then I didn't.

I told her I would walk to the MOT place that had been looking after my car, and that I had been busy putting together the chest of drawers I had carted home from Homebase in her car. Lies, lies, lies, I was now deep in them. Janice just nodded.

She didn't look ready for work so I presumed she had lied to me too, but then again maybe for volunteering you can look a bit so-so. She dropped me off outside Gregg's by George Square and I reached in through her half-open window for an awkward hug before a lorry honked her away.

My car was parked on Glenfarg Street, in a quiet neighbourhood not far from the motorway or town. Not by my flat, and not near anyone I know. I walked there with a milky coffee in a paper cup. The coffee got cold quite quickly but I could neither drink nor pour it out. Instead I carried the white cup through town, like an altar boy approaching the priest.

Getting into the SAAB and grasping the walnut steering wheel I felt both home and completely lost. I sat in the car for ages before starting it. A whole host of new hobbies I could take up flew through my mind, but I wasn't good at anything but architecture – and even that was up for debate.

In the end I turned the key in the ignition and switched on the radio. It was only when I drove off with a satisfying squeal of the front wheels, that I remembered that I had placed my coffee on the roof of the car. I could hear the cup fall over and pictured the white foam, the brown streaks and the sticky hazelnut syrup the girl in the café had convinced me to try, create a giant bird mess on the roof. For once it wasn't raining. For once the sun was out and would probably bake the concoction into a disgusting concrete cake forever attached to the roof of my car. I set out for a car wash but couldn't remember where any were.

On the radio *Also sprach Zarathustra*. I had never got the hang of German but music is music, I don't feel I have to understand the story behind something to appreciate the sounds. I couldn't face my flat so I drove around aimlessly for a while, hoping to come to a red light next to a friendly taxi driver I could ask about a car wash but it didn't happen.

As it was nearing lunchtime I set my sights on something more positive. I turned left whenever I could in the hope that a lunch opportunity would materialise. Quite soon I was lost in the industrial maze of individual units and big warehouses in Bridgeton. I kept my eye out for a greasy spoon or a trailer serving food. The whisky was sitting uncomfortably in my stomach and I felt I had to bind it with fat. Strangely I felt no desire, psychological or chemical, to drink again. This had been my greatest motivation for not drinking – the fear that one sip would instantly re-transform me into an alcoholic. That it would render me broke, homeless, spat at by society, in one fell swoop. If that wasn't the case, I was either safe or in a lot of trouble. If I was fine, the five terms of AA meetings had been a monumental waste of time, and not drinking for a few years had been a total waste of enjoyment.

At one point I pulled over to ask a man, who was walking along with a brown sandwich bag and a cup of something steaming, for gastronomical advice but when he came closer I noticed he was on the phone and I didn't want to disturb him. I drove another block, then put the car in neutral and rolled gently to the kerb, like an admiral in his frigate, the double harps of Zarathustra applauding me. I applied the handbrake and it closed on the disc somewhere below me with a satisfying click, an experience so unlike the one in the Twingo and I was relieved I had held my tongue instead of buying my sister's French folly.

When the music came to an end I turned off the radio and looked up. Four men in overalls were wrangling ropes and pulleys, lowering a sign from one of the units to the ground. It was an end of an era for someone and I decided to celebrate that. I sat in the car, my stomach growling and watched the men load the sign into a container full of scrap metal. When they were almost done a truck came and picked up the container and drove off. And that was that.

I had lost my appetite. Before I could stop I wanted to corroborate some of the things Frank had told me. I drove into town and tried to locate a hairdresser specialising in black hair. There might have been one in the Savoy Centre but it was hard to stop for a proper look. There was something boarded up that could have been catering to people's hair but whether it was for black hair or not I couldn't tell. I have no black friends to ask. Not by design or any kind of racism, just by growing up in the west of Scotland. And stopping a person in the street based on their colour of skin to ask about a specialist service, I obviously had no need for, felt too strange.

I came home more confused than when I left. I had taken Frank's life story with a pinch of salt. Him being married to Haitian hairdresser, for example, which to me had sounded like the beginning of a lewd limerick. His history, his children, his claims – to me not more or less real than a serialised radio drama based on real-life events. I hadn't wanted to confront him and say I thought he was lying because he was my guest stowaway, but also because he was quite big. And he could have been telling the truth. I had felt those questions were beyond my jurisdiction. I was in charge of logistics, not morals. I had one simple mission which did not include pastoral care.

I got two old bedsheets out of the bedroom wardrobe and hung one over the mirror in the hallway and one over the mirror in the bathroom. Feeling a little like Queen Victoria, I was at least safe from my own stares. I even contemplated growing a beard to do away with shaving altogether.

Part of the sadness was loss. All this work goes into make a building perfect. And it is immaculate, for a very brief moment in time between sign-off and population. Before people soil and spoil it. Cromlix had been perfect, now it wasn't.

I had a long hot bath and tried to think about nothing, which is almost impossible. I tried to not want anything and succeeded better at that, making use of Frank's neat little trick from the carpark after the night at the B&B.

For a little while I was content. Then I got up and retrieved a long extension lead from the tool cupboard. I was tired of myself and slipped back into the bath with the radio playing. Despite feeling a bit down and out I didn't balance the radio on the side of the bath, but on the floor well away from any splashes. Soon the gentle swell of Brahms echoed in the room. Soon I wasn't sure who had won. Maybe HMP Cromlix was the only clear winner in all of this.

Chapter 32

12.30 Friday

For 2 days I had kept my eyes on the news, but I didn't see anything worth noting. That's not to say nothing was happening behind the scenes. I bought both *The Digger* and *The Times* to triangulate the information, but to my relief there was nothing alluding to a manhunt for Frank. I didn't want to go on the Internet to search for him as that would surely trigger a red flag somewhere. 'Damn you Swindon', I thought.

On the Friday I woke up in a panic. I couldn't work out if I was hungry or if it was withdrawal symptoms from my two big addictions. Standing in my flat, quickly spiraling downwards, soon shivering with fear, I wondered if I should hand myself in. I managed to keep quiet, apart from a shrill giggle when the thought hit me that if I was caught I might exchange places with Frank. I still had the spare keys for the padlock covering the last grill of the pipe. I would just swallow it. Once inside I would carefully rake through my excrements with a plastic fork, and then I would be as good as free. My mind was racing and I placed a hand over my mouth, fearful of myself.

I stopped breathing. First my eyes welled up, then I started thinking about the easiest way to end my life. Was it possible to pry the little row of razor blades in my Gillette apart, or would I have to go out and buy separate razor blades from somewhere before drawing a last bath? If I was under surveillance there was no way I would be able to retrace my steps yet another time, all the way to Saint-Nazaire. I should write a testament leaving my belongings to Janice, on the condition that the truth about my trip was forever kept secret.

Before I let myself do anything rash, I put on clothes and went to Morrison's for brunch. For the remainder of the day I put myself outside, like I was my own pet. Walking and walking to keep the dread at bay.

On the morning of the third day I woke up so worried that I had to buy all the newspapers, ranging from deep red top to broadest highbrow. I decided not to buy a whole bouquet of them in the same shop as I didn't want anyone to think I was looking for something, so I got one each in separate newsagents. It took me all morning, trundling around to 13 places. After half a day leafing through them over a series of fried eggs, all I found was a couple of lines in the *Scottish Daily Express* informing the public of Frank's escape and urging anyone to call the police or Crime Stoppers if they had any information.

That was it, no picture, no real information. And judging by the article, no real clues to his mode of escape and his current whereabouts. I broke out in a sweat, and then promised myself to buy the *Express* for the rest of the month to see if they had any follow-ups on the story. It was such a relief to see that Frank's liberation hadn't caused more of a stir that I went out and bought coq au vin for my lunch. From Sainsbury's Taste the Difference range no less. It would obviously be nothing resembling a proper drink, but at least it would taste a bit like wine.

Once I had eaten I cast around my flat for something to do, but there was nothing to sort out anymore and I was soon faced with my thoughts. Without Janice's tears, or the whisky, I was no longer keen to lay bare the facts. Cromlix had worked, so I had my own private glory to bask in. There would be no confessional calls to or attempts at memoirs baring all.

I went out and stood in the street. It was raining and it helped a little. At least surrounded by people I was distracted into peaceful submission. I shuffled back to my flat, clothes soaked and shivering with the cold. I turned on the gas fire and sat myself down on the sofa, as carefully as if I was an egg.

I heard the services buzzer and then the slam of my storm doors thrown open by the postie. On the welcome mat a postcard, a dog in a party hat, chewing on a streamer. It had no message apart from a hastily drawn smiling face, no more than two dots and a single horizontal parenthesis. It had been forwarded by Frazer & Frazer, but the original post mark read *St Malo, République française*.

I sat down on the floor, a plaster statue in the shape of me, rendered useless. I remained in one position, and one position only, until I saw the night buses turn out of Partick station for their rounds. The sequelae of my trauma was a predatory animal yet to surface. I hoped it would stay submerged.

I went through to my bachelor's bedroom, austere and messy at the same time. Set the alarm for six in the morning, to avoid some of the morning rush. I put on clean pyjamas and duffed my pillow so many times my fists hurt.

I couldn't sleep. I tried warm milk and everything; but it had me going to the bathroom more times than I usually have to. By 4 o'clock in the morning I gave up and got dressed. I put on dark trousers, a thick sweater with polyester elbow patches and shoulder straps, similar to the costume I had worn at the bus station. I shrugged into a hi-viz waterproof jacket with a high collar, lanyard in the inner pocket. On the back of both Frank's jacket and mine I had glued a panel with a made-up company name. I stood in the kitchen and had Weetabix with the remnants of the milk I had heated up in the night. After brushing my teeth and flossing I fetched a white hard hat from the shelf in the bedroom wardrobe.

Armed with an armload of padlocks I set out for the culvert leading out into a marsh 2 miles south of HMP Cromlix. Once at the gate to the tunnel I secured the door to the fence covering the hole he had emerged from. Standing back, regaining my breath, I realised I had turned our gateway into something resembling the fence over the Seine. Love locks and thrown-away keys, a myriad of human fates, a picture of human complications. Our passage now sealed by nine padlocks from B&Q's value range.

Back in the car, a couple of miles down the road in a lay-by, with a flask of tea perched where Frank had sat, I opened the glove compartment. I kept an A6 pad, pilfered from a Sheraton a long time ago, there in case of sudden inspiration. Now I started to compose a message to my own house in France, in case Frank was there. Even if I could never tell Janice, and never talk to Frank again, I felt that I would have to realign my convictions and doubts. I had to reconcile myself to feeling like it was ok to want the best for Janice *and* for Frank, and that the two wishes weren't mutually exclusive.

I started writing with my left hand, as that would disguise me a little, but then realised that would also tie me to the notes I had left inside Cromlix, so I changed and wrote the remainder of the note with my right hand. Then I tore it up and put it in the ashtray. I put the nine keys into an envelope to be dropped into the Clyde, then decided it was time for elevenses.

Once the tea and sandwich was finished I searched the airwaves for Katie's gentle voice, but couldn't find anything classical. All I got was some daytime DJ who played a pretty aggressive song by The Clash. When the line 'I fought the law and the law won', rang out in the seven pine-scented speakers of my old SAAB, I found myself convulsed with laughter. Laughing so hard that I cried and cried.

Bibliography

Sources for *A Circular Argument* by chapter. All web material accessed 06/06/2018, unless otherwise stated

Adey, P. (2008). Airports, mobility and the calculative architecture of affective control. *Geoforum*, *39*, 438–451.

Armstrong, S. (2018). The cell and the corridor: Imprisonment as waiting, and waiting as mobile. *Time & Society*, *27*(2), 133–154.

Augé, M. (1992). *Non-places*. London: Verso Books.

Bentham, J. (1791). *Panopticon*, (Preface) Volume 1 of 3 (*Panopticon, or the inspection-house: Containing the idea of a new principle of construction applicable to any sort of establishment, in which persons of any description are to be kept under inspection; and in particular to penitentiary-houses, prisons, houses of industry, work-houses, poor-houses, lazarettos, manufactories, hospitals, mad-houses, and schools: With a plan of management adapted to the principle: In a series of letters, written in the year 1787, from Crecheff in White Russia. To a friend in England by Jeremy Bentham, of Lincoln's Inn, Esquire.*) Reprinted; and sold by T. Payne, Mews Gate, London.

Burnyeat, M. F. (May 1998). Art and mimesis in Plato's republic. *London Review of Books*. Retrieved from https://www.lrb.co.uk/v20/n10/mf-burnyeat/art-and-mimesis-in-platos-republic

Campbell, J. (1968). *The hero with a thousand faces*. Princeton, NJ: Princeton University Press.

Che, D. (December 2005). Constructing a prison in the forest: Conflicts over nature, paradise, and identity. *Annals of the Association of American Geographers*, *95*(4), 809–831.

Dickens, C. (2001). *David Copperfield*. Peterborough, ON: Broadview Press.

Dostoyevsky, F. (2004). *The house of the dead (1862)*. New York, NY: Dover Thrift Editions.

Eggebeen, J. (2007). *Airport age: Architecture and modernity in America*. Ph.D. thesis, City University of New York.

Fontana-Giusti, G. (2013). *Foucault for architects (thinkers for architects)*. New York, NY: Routledge.

Ford, J., & Plimmer, G. (2018, February 12). Momentum stalls on UK's private prisons. Retrieved from www.ft.com/content/3c356914-0d9c-11e8-839d-41ca06376bf2. Accessed on October 01, 2018.

Foucault, M. (1977). *Discipline and punish: The birth of the prison*. London: Allen Lane.

Goffman, E. (1990). *The presentation of self in everyday life*. London: Penguin.

Goffman, E. (1991). *Asylums: Essays on the social situation of mental patients and other inmates*. London: Penguin.

Hanley, L. (2007). *Estates: An intimate history*. London: Granta Books.

Hart, H. L. A. (1959). The presidential address: Prolegomenon to the principles of punishment. *Proceedings of the Aristotelian Society, 60*. (pp. 1–26).

Hillier, B., & Hanson, J. (1984). *The social logic of space*. Cambridge: Cambridge University Press.

Holliss, F. (2015). *Beyond live/work: The architecture of home-based work*. London: Routledge.

Horace. (2008). *Odes, 2, 14*. Oxford: Oxford University Press.

House of Commons Library. (2018). *The prison estate*, Briefing paper, Number 05646. Retrieved from researchbriefings.files.parliament.uk/documents/SN05646/SN05646.pdf

Irwin, J. (2016). *Derrida and the writing of the body*. London: Routledge.

Jacobs, J. (1957). *Downtown is for people*. In The Exploding Metropolis (Ed.), *The editors of fortune*. New York, NY: Doubleday.

Jacobs, J. (1993). *The death and life of great American cities*. New York, NY: Vintage Books.

Jacobs, J. (2011). Jane Jacobs on neighborhoods, placemaking, and active living [VIDEO]. Retrieved from https://grist.org/urbanism/2011-07-21-jane-jacobs-on-neighborhoods-placemaking-and-active-living-video/

Khoolhas, R. (2006). *Junkspace*. Rome: Quodlibet.

Lawler, S. (2011). Symbolic violence. In *Encyclopedia of consumer culture*. Thousand Oaks, CA: SAGE.

Liebling, A., & Stanko, B. (2001). Allegiance and ambivalence: Some dilemmas in researching disorder and violence. *British Journal of Criminology, 41*(3), 421–430.

Matthews, R. (2009). *Doing time, an introduction to the sociology of imprisonment*. New York, NY: Palgrave Macmillan.

Medlicott, D. (1999). Surviving in the time machine. *Time & Society, 8*(2–3), 211–230.

Moran, D. (April 2013a). Between outside and inside? Prison visiting rooms as liminal carceral spaces. *GeoJournal, 78*(2), 339–351.

Moran, D. (2013b). Carceral geography and the spatialities of prison visiting: Visitation, recidivism and hyperincarceration. *Environment and Planning D: Society and Space, 31*(1), 174–190.

Owens, F. (2012). *The little book of prisons*. Hook: Waterside Press.

Reveley, W. (2004). *Oxford Dictionary of National Biography*. Oxford: Oxford University Press. doi:10.1093/ref:odnb/23393

Shakespeare, W. (1992). *Hamlet, Act 1, Scene 5*. Hertfordshire: Wordsworth.

Shakespeare, W. (2015). *Henry V, Act 1, Scene 1*. London: Penguin.

Scheer, D., & Lorne, C. (2017). Chapter 5 introduction. In D. Moran, & A. K. Schliehe (Eds.), *Carceral spatiality: Dialogues between geography and criminology. Palgrave Studies in Prisons and Penology*. London: Palgrave Macmillan.

Silvestri, A. (2013). *Prison conditions in the United Kingdom*. Rome: European Prison Observatory, Antigone Edizioni.

Smith, C. L., & Ballantyne, A. (Eds.). (2012). *Architecture in the space of flows*. Abingdon: Routledge.

Sparberg Alexiou, A. (2006). *Jane Jacobs: Urban visionary*. New Brunswick: Rutgers University Press.

Sterritt, D. (2008). *The films of Jean-Luc Godard: Seeing the invisible*. Cambridge: Cambridge Film Classics.

Sutherland, E. H. (1949). *White collar crime*. New York, NY: Dryden Press.

Wilkinson, P. (2017). *Phantom architecture*. New York, NY: Simon & Schuster.

Williams, T. (2009). *The Glass Menagerie, Scene 7*. London: Penguin.

Wilson, A. (2000). There's no escape from the Third-Space Theory. In D. Barton, M. Hamilton, & R. Ivanic (Eds.), *Situated literacies: Theorising reading and writing in context* (p. 66). London: Routledge.

Yanow, D. (1998). Space stories: Studying museum buildings as organizational spaces while reflecting on interpretive methods and their narration. *Journal of Management Inquiry, 7*, 215–239.

Index